I0636071

Operation Cover-up: Rise of the Black Mamba

By P D Baldwin

Copyright © 2013 **P D Baldwin**

All rights reserved.

ISBN: 0615996205

ISBN 13: 9780615996202

Dark Half Productions, LLC

Acknowledgements

Operation Cover-up is the culmination of nearly twenty years of hopes, wishes, and prayers. The original story came about after having a nightmare. I dismissed it at first, but I kept having the same nightmare over and over. After consulting a friend, I started writing down the details of my nightmares and before long, a story started developing. It took years to develop because I had no idea what direction I wanted to go in. I considered writing a comic, but found it difficult to get traction in that industry. I tried going through a few publishers, but didn't have any luck their either. To make a long story short, I spent nearly two decades writing, studying, and researching this book until at last I decided to self publish it. At long last, here it is.

Operation Cover-up started off as a simple title, but has developed into its own series; my series. As such, it has all of my favorite story elements; suspense, drama, action, and eroticism. I took elements from all my favorite movie characters and stories and created my own world. Best of all, my characters are realistic and have depth. Their stories are so intense that you can't help but be emotionally involved. You'll either love or hate them. In fact, this story promises to shock and amaze you.

As with anything in life, *Operation Cover-up: Rise of the Black Mamba* is not intended for all audiences. This story contains ideas and accounts that some will regard it as vulgar, sexist, tasteless, perverted, and sacrilegious. It touches on subjects ranging from erotica and murder to faith and redemption. It will grab onto your senses and shake them to their core, just like a good story should. Fasten your seatbelts and prepare for an erotic thrill ride that will leave you breathless and wanting more, while keeping you guessing about what is going to happen next. Enjoy the ride.

Finally, no list of acknowledgements is complete without actually acknowledging someone. First and foremost, I'd like to thank the Most High God for the talent, the courage, and for surrounding me with a circle or supporters and well-wishers who have pushed and motivated me. It's people like you that make this fun. And last, but certainly not least, I'd like to thank the doubters, and non-believers because whether you believe it or not, you have inspired me too.

Sincerely

P. D. Baldwin

P.S. Check me out at
www.darkhalfproductions.com for a list of
upcoming projects and their release dates.

* Check out *Erotic Verses: A Collection of Erotic Poems and Short Stories* available on Kindle and through Amazon.com.

* Be on the lookout for Operation *Cover-up Presents: Crimson Storm and Erotic Verses II: Bedside Chronicles* coming soon

Gusting, gale force winds swirled outside the penthouse, pelting its windows with tiny hail stones and hard, driving rains. The relentless crash of icy waters on the patio was reminiscent of drums beating off in the distance. Though the storm outside was intense, it was nothing compared to the one raging inside the master suite. Atop the California King, they lay making passionate love that generated enough heat to create fog on the smoked glass windows. With candles burning brightly on each nightstand and flashes of lightening outside, he saw glimpses of her beauty. He wasn't sure if it was the sexy way she bit her lip after calling his name, the tears of ecstasy that rolled down her Hershey-colored cheeks, or the sensual way she cupped her breasts while arching her back. Whatever it was, it was fueling his desire to keep thrusting deep inside her while devouring her hardened nipples.

"Alex!" she gasped when another climax erupted from deep within her abdomen.

His name escaped her mouth two more times while she sat perched on his lap with her creamy walls pulsating and milking him with each up and down glide of her soft, round hips.

"Tell me you love me," she pleaded while pinning his hands to the bed and thrusting her pelvis to his.

She needed to hear him say it. She needed to hear his words. She needed to know that this moment was real. Nothing else mattered, not even the buzzing that was vibrating the nightstand to their right.

"I love you, Tisha," he whispered while staring into her eyes.

His words triggered an orgasm that sent rapid-fire shudders up and down her spine. She collapsed onto his chest and when her lips met his, Alex's tongue began probing the depths of her mouth. He repeatedly inhaled her passionate moans, while gripping her ass and thrusting upwards harder and faster inside her.

"Shit baby, *shit!*" Tisha cried when another orgasm erupted, sending her G-spot into a pulsating frenzy of sheer delight.

Was this her fifth or ninth climax? Tisha was so engulfed in Alex's pleasure that she'd lost count of them. It didn't matter though because her body was his to command. His every touch, kiss, and caress sent chills coursing through her body all the way to her soul. No man, not even her husband, had ever made her feel this way. She belonged to Alex; mind, body, and soul. As she bounced up and down on his thrusting dick, her soft green eyes rained tears of ecstasy onto her soft cheeks and fell to her glistening breasts. Her ivory and gold manicured nails raked his arms and chest when she sat back up, causing tiny, crimson streaks to appear on his flesh.

When her back hit the black satin sheets, Tisha knew that her pleasure ride wasn't quite over. The look on Alex's face was *so* intense, *so* sexy. His deep, purposeful thrusts were honing in on her G spot like guided missiles. Harder, deeper, and faster he went, plunging into creamy depths while staring into her shimmering eyes. Not content to just lie there and take it, Tisha tried

7

matching his thrusts with her own. Each rise and fall of her hips sent streams of her juices spilling down the crack of her ass. The intense euphoria of their love making had her ready to faint, but she didn't. With her legs high atop his shoulders, Tisha delighted in each passionate stroke. Seconds turned into minutes and minutes became hours as he pleasured her over and over in every position imaginable.

"You love this pussy, don't you, Alex?" Tisha gasped when she felt him swelling and pressing hard against her sugar walls. "Show me, Alex! FUCK ME!" she demanded while grabbing his hips and thrusting her pussy hard against his dick.

The sensation of his sack banging the crack of her ass while his tongue circled her nipples almost made her head. As his relentless pounding continued, more creamy juices rained down from her flower and pooled beneath her quivering ass. She wanted Alex in every way possible, even if it meant surrendering her tender, virgin asshole which only his thumbs had probed thus far. Whatever he wanted, Tisha didn't mind because this was her man, and she was willing to do whatever it took to please him.

Now Alex was behind her and with his hands locked onto her waist, he was feeding Tisha more than she could handle. The ripples across her chocolate-colored ass intensified his desire to leave his mark on this sexy vixen. His touch, his power, and his passion were perfection. He cupped her left breast and gently massaged her nipple while leaning down and kissing her tattooed shoulder. Her back arched when his hot, wet tongue touched her spine. As another orgasm hit, her body felt weak and Tisha thought about tapping out. For whatever the reason, Alex seemed more vigorous than normal. No matter what she tried, he couldn't seem to get enough. There was pleasure in the pain that she was feeling, and because of that, Tisha was not about to throw in the towel. She prayed silently that it wouldn't end; that he would continue taking her body to new heights of ecstasy while ignoring the intrusions from the nightstand.

"Damn, Alex, *shit!*" she cried when she heard his primal cries.

The gush of cum from his thrusting dick caused her dam to rupture simultaneously. Flashes of lightening brightened the bedroom once again as Alex's head snapped back and he howled toward the heavens like a wolf atop a mountain's peak. His long, ebony hair rested on his chiseled, caramel-colored shoulders while cum erupted from him like an orgasmic volcano. He repeatedly smacked her ass as she thrust against him, her pulsating sugar walls milking him of every ounce he had to offer. After one last thrust of his dick, Tisha collapsed onto the bed and buried her face in a pillow. As she lay there quivering, Alex was positive he heard the sheets ripping.

"Again? Damn," he sighed silently.

Alex lay down beside Tisha and watched her body's reactions, pleased with his performance, especially when her tiny fists released the shredded fibers intertwined between her fingers. As she laid face-down on her pillow still trembling and shivering, his tongue traced the length of her spine from her neck to the crack of her round ass. After a few trips up and down her back, Alex

9

lay beside her and allowed his fingers trace the same journey. He continued beyond the base of her spine, through the valley of her ass where they gently teased her puckered hole. After moaning and writhing in an orgasmic frenzy, Tisha grabbed his wrist before his middle finger descended too deep. Seconds later, his wayward fingers settled between on swollen clitoris, touching and teasing as it pulsated. Her thighs quivered frantically before finally locking on his hand.

"Why...are...you...teasing...me...like...that?"

"Because you like it so much," he replied in a voice that made her body cry out for his tender kiss.

He leaned down and repeatedly obliged her shoulder with his lips while making small wet circles with the tip of his tongue.

"You better quit that shit, Alex. You know that's my spot," she cooed while willing her body to relax.

"One of many," he whispered before lying down on his pillow.

After making sure he was comfortable, Tisha laid her head on his chest and began running her fingers over his tattooed abs. Chills coursed through her body when she closed her eyes and allowed her fingertips to read his body like a Braille board. Her hand continued its descent until she reached his dripping, semi-erect manhood. She caressed and stroked it slowly, feeling it expand in her hand while circling his cum-soaked head with her thumb. While continuing to stroke his shaft, she placed soft, wet kisses on him, beginning at his shoulder and moving down his chest to his stomach, and finally to his waistline. Alex shuddered when he felt Tisha's soft lips and wet tongue gently kissing and swirling his head. Her strokes became shorter and slower while taking inch-after-inch into her hot, wet mouth. His whole body shook with delight when she began repeatedly deep-throating his dick before looking into his glassy eyes.

"You like that, don't you, daddy?" she asked before allowing her pink tongue continue its dance.

She knew head was his weakness and without a doubt, Tisha was a "head master." His moans and the way he called her name were like music to her ears. Her pumping fist and flicking tongue made it impossible for Alex to speak. Much to her delight, he gently palmed the back of her head while thrusting slowly in and out of her tightly puckered mouth. The sensation of him gently banging the back of her throat and swelling between her jaws had juices running down the insides of Tisha's thighs. Alex's pleasure was her weakness.

"Damn, Tisha damn! *Shit!*"

Her hand and mouth glided up and down his shaft like a piston, building speed and intensity with each stroke. Alex tried to hold it back, but couldn't and before Tisha knew it, he was coating the back of her throat with blasts of sweet pre-cum. Though she hated the taste, she felt some vindication from making him writhe in passionate agony. After all, Tisha was so accustomed to his sexual dominance that she was determined to turn the tables on him whenever she could. She took Alex even deeper into her mouth, repressing her gag reflex but being careful to exhale which sent shudders across his head. Sensing his eminent explosion, Tisha pulled him out of her mouth and watched the fireworks.

"Hello!" she laughed when a thick, white blast arced from his head and landed on her pumping fist.

"Why'd you move?" Alex gasped with hints of both satisfaction and disappointment in his voice.

"You know I don't like the taste of that shit, Alex. And besides, you're not my husband, remember? And why didn't you use the flavored condoms I brought? You know I hate the taste of latex and that lubricant makes my mouth numb."

"Sorry Tish, but given the circumstances, I couldn't find that specific condom. And correct me if I'm wrong, but weren't you just in control of this?"

"But..."

"That's what I thought," he interrupted sarcastically. "Now wash your hands and go to sleep."

"Fuck you, Alex."

Later that morning, Tisha woke up and found herself alone in his bed. She struggled to get her bearings while looking for the source of that incessant buzzing. Her Blackberry lay on the nightstand just beyond an empty bottle of Paul Masson and two overturned glasses. She picked it up and cringed when she saw the ugly face on its screen. After quickly looking around the room, she pressed the *send* button.

"Hello?"

"Weh a yu?" barked an angry, thick West Indian accent. "Mi a call all night!"
"I got tired and had to…"
"Cha? Naa badda mi wit dat shit!" he fired back angrily. "I an da clock and yu fuckin' it up for mi. Move yu backside! Undastan, Tisha girl?"
"Yes honey. I'm…"
"Click."

The phone went dead before she could say *"sorry."* After taking a deep breath, she stepped out of the bed and on to the plush beige carpet. Though logs were still burning in the fireplace, the room seemed much cooler than before. She picked Alex's shirt up off the floor and draped it over her shoulders, becoming instantly intoxicated by the scent of his Burberry cologne. She walked through the bedroom's French doors and through a short corridor leading to his massive living room. Even though it was the middle of the day, the penthouse was still rather dark because thanks to the custom blinds mounted over the smoked glass windows and the patio doors. Tisha smiled to herself when she saw their clothes and shoes strewn carelessly about the living and dining rooms. With her legs still wobbly from the night before, she looked around to see if he was lurking in the shadows.

"Alex? Alex? Asshole," Tisha sighed finally before picking her black lace thong up off the smoked glass and brass coffee table.

She walked through the living room and passed the nook that lead into the kitchen. She was instantly frozen by the scene inside the wall's built in aquarium. The

13

blue light cast an eerie haze over the rapid movements behind its smoked glass. *Yuck,* she thought while watching their scaly, leathery bodies coil and contract. Tisha regained her composure and continued into the kitchen, which like the most of the penthouse was decorated in black, marble, and polished chrome. She grabbed a rocks glass off the counter and walked to the massive, double-doors on the refrigerator. The bright light illuminated the darkness and bathed her shapely silhouette as she stood looking for nothing in particular. The cool air hardened her dark, round nipples which were poking through his shirt like daggers. After pouring some orange juice, she closed the doors.

"Got-dammit, Alex!" she cried after dropping the glass and clutching her heart.

Meanwhile, he stood there silently watching her through the strands of hair that were matted to his head and face. For a split-second, her eyes feasted on the masterpiece in front her; a sexy, chiseled, and tattooed, body glistening as he gripped the white towel that was draped around his broad shoulders.

"Why-the-fuck-are you always sneaking up on me? You're worse than..."
"Simon?" he interrupted sarcastically.
"No, Alex, a fucking cop."
"Don't start with the cop shit again," he warned before squatting to retrieve the glass and wipe up the spill.
"Kiss my toes while you're down there," she said before lifting her juice splashed foot towards his mouth.

He glanced lustfully at her rose and vine tattoo that that began at her ankle and wrapped around her leg and thigh before disappearing under his shirt.

"Oh you'd like that," he replied in a low, raspy voice while gazing down into her green eyes.

His piercing glare and smooth voice were Tisha's weakness and it was beginning to show. Even though she was on borrowed time, looking into Alex's hazel eyes, smelling his cologne, and seeing the sweat on his half-naked body made hers ache for his touch. She was silently begging to be taken right there on the floor. The electricity Alex was emitting had Tisha filling her panties with her creamy juices. Her knees almost buckled when he leaned in closer, the heat from his body damn near melting hers.

"I have to go," she whispered with his lips hovering ever so close to hers.
"I know."
"It won't always be like this," she whispered, her voice cracking as tears formed in the corners of her eyes.

Meanwhile, Alex stood motionless. Even when Tisha buried her face in his chest and began to sob out loud, he never made a move. His first impulse was to push her away, but he knew he couldn't; not yet anyway.

"Please don't ever leave me, Alex," she pleaded while clutching his body tight to hers.
"I won't," he surrendered before wrapping his arms around her shoulders.

Tokyo, Japan

In the luxurious penthouse suite of the Kadoyu Hotel, a petite but shapely young woman was pacing nervously near the balcony door. Through his scope he watched as

15

the wind gently kissed her blonde-streaked hair which was lying on her caramel-colored shoulders. Her shear, spaghetti-strapped nightgown, red bra, and matching sheer panties clung to her curvaceous frame like gloves.

"Relax, Lexi," interrupted the voice from her hidden earpiece, "You're gonna be fine."
"Easy for you to say, Ko," she replied nervously. "A Yakuza boss isn't planning on drugging and raping you."
"And he won't be doing that to you either. Follow the plan to the letter and you'll be out of there before anyone knows it. Besides, I'm right here to bail you out if you get jammed up."

Meanwhile outside the lobby, a stretched Maybach limousine crept to a stop underneath the hotel's burgundy and gold canopy. Two men, one tall and young and the other shorter and older, exited the rear before the nervous driver could open the door. Both men were dressed in black, Armani suits, matching patent-leather Cole Haans, and dark glasses. The shorter of the two had gray, tapered haired that was well oiled and brushed to the back. When they entered the hotel lobby, his young counterpart quickly concluded a conversation on his cell phone.

"The Jamaican has guaranteed both the security and delivery of our shipments. He has also proven able to expedite them when necessary while maintaining an exceptional level of purity. I suggest we..."
"Quiet, Ryugi," demanded the older man with a wave of his hand. "Is she here?"
"Yes she is, sir," Ryugi responded half-heartedly.
"Show me!"

Although annoyed by the request, Ryugi complied. After scrolling through his messages, he held his cell phone out for the old man to see. On the screen was a picture of the same young woman who was pacing upstairs. He scrolled through several more pictures and much to the old man's delight, each one showed her in different outfits and sensual poses.

"She is exquisite. Does she have a nice booty?" he asked while pulling a pill bottle from his inner blazer pocket. "
"Mr. Nakamura, this is hardly the time to be..."
"Silence, Ryugi!" he demanded again. "A man such as myself is entitled to an occasional indulgence and this just happens to be one of them. Any other affairs can wait until morning. Now, bring me to her and hold all my calls."

During the elevator ride to the top floor, Boss Nakamura quickly downed two blue pills before taking a sip from the silver flask in his other pocket.

Meanwhile in the suite, Lexi continued pacing nervously while waiting for her suitor to arrive.

"Relax Lexi. I'm with you every step of the way so listen to me carefully. His routine is always the same. Avoid the cognac because it's laced. If he offers you a drink, request bottled water. I switched it out earlier. He's very quick with syringes. He keeps them in his pocket and they're full of a sedative. He drugs his victim then rapes her before tossing her to his bodyguards."
"You witnessed this, Ko?" she asked nervously.
"I've been watching this sick fuck for the past six months, Lexi. This is his routine. He has a number of strange fetishes and one of them is rap video vixens.

17

He's gonna ask you to do something to take your mind off him like dancing, stripping, or making a drink. That's where I come in. I'll be watching his every move. If you slip, I'll put one in his eye. You got all that?"

"Sorry, Ko but I can't help being nervous. I'm not used to being this close to a target, and Alex would go ballistic if he knew I was this close to Boss Nakamura."

"I know but Alex is handling the N.Y. job, and Karma wasn't available, remember? So relax 'cause I got your back. And um...by the way."

"Yes, Ko?" she asked while rubbing her hands together.

"I love that um...uniform."

"Ko Hinomura, are you flirting with me when you're supposed to be watching my back?"

"Trust me, Lexi. I'm watching your back and your front," he mused while admiring her through the scope of his high-powered, Mk-11 sniper rifle.

"Alex would whup that ass if he heard you talking to me like that."

"Well, he's not here now, is he?"

"I guess not," she replied while standing in front of the door and winking at him.

At that moment, the door of the suite swung open and in the doorway were Boss Nakamura and Ryugi. Lexi watched in silent disgust as the two men ogled her while whispering and smiling. After a vigorous hand shake, Boss Nakamura nodded to Ryugi before patting him on the back and closing the door behind him.

Showtime, she thought before casually stepping away from the balcony door.

"He just promised you to the head bodyguard. It's time to go into Jinx mode."

"That shit ain't happening, Ko," she whispered as Boss Nakamura stood there salivating.

Even though she had every reason to be afraid, Lexi was as cool as a cucumber. With a smile on her face and the wind at her back, she silently recited everything Ko had told her. Tonight she was going to be a video vixen for Boss Nakamura and tonight, if only for a brief moment, she was going to fulfill his erotic fantasies. By the time he stopped staring and began his approach, Lexi had already settled into character.

His handsome appearance and charm aside, Boss Nakamura was the lowest form of life imaginable. In addition to being a one of the most powerful gangsters in all of Asia, he was a sadist and a rapist. During his tenure with the Yakuza, he had either ordered or participated in the murder of over 200 men, women, and children. His greatest pleasure however, was sexually degrading women. Rape and torture were among his favorite tools. In his wildest dreams, Boss Nakamura never imagined that this beautiful woman was on a mission to assassinate him.

"You look *so* beautiful. How many videos have you danced in?"
"More than I care to count," she said softly while teasing her fingertip with her tongue.
Damn, Ko thought while eyeing her body the way a lion stalks a gazelle.

Lexi's breasts were round and firm. Her flat stomach flowed smoothly into her round hips. Her ass was exquisite: round, smooth, and very enticing. A perfectly-timed breeze came thru the balcony door, blowing her gown against her skin and hardening her nipples.

19

"Would you like a drink?" Boss Nakamura asked after becoming noticeably aroused.

"How about you relax while I fix you a drink instead, you sexy hunk-of-a man?"

"Vodka and tonic with a twist of lime, please," he replied giddily.

"Make yourself comfortable, Mr. Nakamura," she cooed with her hips swaying side-to-side on the way to the bar. "This is your chance, Lexi."

Her every movement was exaggerated, sexually hypnotizing and mesmerizing Boss Nakamura the longer he watched and she made sure to keep him in her line of sight. Both Ko and Boss Nakamura secretly fantasized about the things that they would love to do to and with her. Even though his mission was to protect her, Lexi's seductive demeanor were making Ko lose his focus. The longer Boss Nakamura ogled her, the more jealous he became. At one point, Ko had his head in the crosshairs of his scope and his finger on the trigger.

After a brief session of dancing and teasing, Lexi selected a rocks glass from the bar and filled it with ice. She looked over her right shoulder to see what Boss Nakamura was doing, and not surprisingly, he was undressing. For a man in his sixties, he was in pretty good physical shape and his body was tattooed with an exquisite green, yellow, and black dragon.

"Your tattoo is beautiful. Does it mean something?" Lexi asked while secretly wishing she could kill his bodyguard as well.

"It means I am a very powerful man," Nakamura replied with a sinister grin.

With a smile on her face and a not-so-subtle sway in her hips, Lexi continued teasing her target by gently squeezing and massaging her right breast. Nakamura's lust-filled hypnosis caused him to miss her stealthy removal of a vial from her bra. After she turned around, Lexi quickly opened it and dumped it into his drink. When she faced him again, she had the drink in one hand and the lime in the other. While slowly strolling towards him, she dropped lime twist in the glass and licked its juice from her fingers. She was amazed at how quickly he snatched the glass and, gulped it down; lime twist and all.

"I love American rap music. Will you shake your booty for me?"
"Anything you like," she replied with a smile.

She watched carefully as he reached into the nightstand, pulled out a remote, and activated the stereo across the room. The thumping base and suggestive lyrics made her role even more seductive. Without any provocation, her body began swaying to the rhythmic beat. Lexi cupped her breasts while gyrated slowly; her hands instantly becoming her lover's hands as they caressed her body. Sweat began pouring from Nakamura's brow when she dipped it low and brought it back up nice and slow. It was when she smacked her own ass that his heart started racing. With his hands shaking and his vision blurring, Boss Nakamura reached into his blazer pocket and pulled out a small platinum case.

"He's going for the syringes."

Even though his senses and motor functions were rapidly deteriorating, Boss Nakamura still managed to insert the syringe into a small bottle and fill it with clear liquid. He thumped the needle a few times while watching Lexi swing to the beat and found himself becoming more intoxicated by the second. He stood on his weary legs and began a slow stagger towards his dancing vixen.

"He's on the move. The serum is taking effect."

With the needle poised between the fingers of his left hand, Boss Nakamura reached for Lexi with his shaky right.

"Now, Jinx!"

Moving in rhythm with the beat, Lexi whipped around and grabbed his left hand with her right. After twisting his at the wrist, she used her free hand to snatch the syringe from his fingers, spun it in her palm then plunged it into his chest. The sensation of warm liquid filling his heart dropped Boss Nakamura to his knees.

"You still wanna fuck me?" she asked after cupping his chin in her right hand, slowly lifting his head, and looking into his eyes.
"Who are you?"
"My friends call me Jinx," she whispered before gripping the crown of his head with her left hand and violently snapping his neck. "Ko, I felt his neck snap in my hands. Does that mean...?"
"Oh yeah, he's dead," Ko replied after Nakamura's lifeless body slumped to the floor. "Clear the room and make it to the balcony. Your ride will be waiting."

Once she disappeared from sight, Ko pulled a grappling gun with a three-pronged hook from his duffle bag. After attaching a cable to the hook, he aimed and fired. Seconds later, the high-speed projectile was embedded in the wall next to the balcony door. He then fastened a motorized pulley with a harness attached and sent across the cable. Meanwhile, Lexi had donned a gray overcoat before walking out onto the balcony, grabbing the harness, and buckling it around her waist. She stepped over the rail and waited for Ko to release his end of the cable.

"Okay, ride it down to the ninetieth floor. The pickup crew is waiting for you."

After taking a deep breath, Lexi stepped off the ledge and began her rapid decent towards the street below. When she reached the other balcony, two black-clad men, caught her, lifted her over the rail and helped her out of the harness. Ko breathed a sigh of relief while watching her wig and one of her heels sail off into the darkness.

"Loved the wig," he said while looking over the side of the building.
"I wish I could have kept it," she replied while breathing her own sigh of relief. "Were you nervous?"
"What do you think?" he asked while watching the activities across the street. "I guess you really are bad luck to men."
"Not to you, baby," she whispered while slipping into a slinky, black cocktail dress.

Meanwhile in the penthouse, eight men including a half-naked Ryugi were standing over Boss Nakamura's body. Frustrated and frantic, they searched the room for signs of the mysterious woman who had seemingly disappeared into thin air.

"We'd better pack it up, folks. The natives just became very restless."

Back in Denver, Alex was sitting at a quaint sidewalk café dressed in black Dolce & Gabbana slacks, matching square-toed Fratelli Rossetti gators, and a cream-colored Hugo Boss shirt. With his legs crossed and his head slightly tilted, he pretended to read the menu. In actuality, he was studying a pair of olive-skinned gentlemen seated a few tables from him. Using his x-ray equipped glasses, he studied the Walther P99s holstered under each man's left arm while his facial recognition software scrolled their vital statistics before his eyes. Within seconds, Alex had their names, height, weight, aliases, places and dates of birth, and a list of crimes committed. Last and certainly most interesting, a bounty for each of them appeared. The turban-wearing man on the left was only worth two hundred-fifty thousand dollars.

Hardly worth the effort, Alex thought while shaking his head.

The balding Armenian on the right in the navy-blue, Perry Ellis three-piece and matching Bacco Bucci leather boots however, commanded a much higher bounty.

One-million-two-hundred-fifty thousand, he thought while grinning. *That's more like it.*
"Excuse me, sir? Is this seat taken?"

Alex lowered his blue-tinted glasses to the tip of his nose and found himself instantly mesmerized by the stunning, bronze-colored goddess standing at the opposite side of his table. Her softly scented perfume was so intoxicating that he was at a loss for words.

"I don't mean to bother you, but there's nowhere else to sit. Do you mind if I join you?" she asked nervously.

"By all means have a seat," he replied while standing and motioning to the padded wrought iron chair opposite him. "This place does get crowded from time to time."

His warm smile and gentlemanly charm quickly calmed her nerves. This tall, statuesque beauty appeared to be moving in slow motion when she sat down and crossed her long, bare, curvaceous legs. Auburn-streaked curls hung just below her shoulders while her navy-blue, Michael Kors business-suit fit closely to and accentuated her slender, yet well-rounded figure. Her white, low-cut silk blouse gave way to a butterfly pendant that lay nestled between her bronze melons. Sensing his stares, she playfully brushed her hair behind her ear with her right hand.

Damn! Alex thought to himself while trying not to stare at the lace bra and panties underneath her suit.

"I'm Lynn," she said, answering the question he'd forgotten to ask. "Do you have a name?"

"I'm sure I do, but it escapes me at the moment."

She looked up from her menu at Alex and quickly noticed his wandering eyes. Though he was maintaining a visual on his marks, Alex found himself becoming more and more distracted by the moment. With her manicured eyebrows slightly raised and a smile on her glossy lips, Lynn quickly appraised the handsome gentleman across the table from her. She could smell his cologne on the breeze. His hair was pulled back in a ponytail, and was the smoothest and blackest she had ever seen, especially on a man. His dark-caramel skin was immaculate, his beard perfectly trimmed. His baritone voice was as smooth as melted chocolate.

This brotha is fine! she thought to herself.

"So," Lynn began after gathering her wayward thoughts, "you don't remember your own name?"
"It's Alexis," he replied after a brief pause. "Alexis Stratton, but you can call me Alex."
"Pleased to meet you, Alex," she replied as her extended hand made its way across the table.
"The pleasure is all mine," he replied after taking it and kissing it softly. "Please excuse me if I seem forward, but you are truly breathtaking. I mean…I've seen beautiful women before, but none of them compare to you. Are you a model? Are you in town for a photo shoot or something?"
"Thank you, but no," she replied after being caught off guard by the familiar yet silky delivery.

The look in his bedroom eyes made her cheeks red and her skin hot. Their mutual gaze continued until she slowly withdrew her hand from his.

"How long have you been in Denver?"
"What makes you think I'm not from here?" she asked curiously.
"I know this city like the back of my hand, so trust me when I say that I'd remember someone as stunning as you."
"You've got me," Lynn replied, trying not to melt before his eyes. *Damn this brotha is good,* she thought while holding her glass and watching him fill it with water.

She hoped he hadn't noticed that her breasts had swollen, or that her hardened nipples were poking against her blazer.

"I'm here from Cincinnati, Ohio, on business."
"How long are you planning on staying? I mean, I was hoping that I could see you again before you left."
"I'd like that, Alex. So, what do you recommend?"
"You mean off the menu?"
"If I didn't know better, Alex, I'd think you were flirting with me."
"Is it that obvious?" he inquired while watching the activities over her shoulder.
"Yes, and I think it's *so* sweet," she replied before the tingling sensation at the base of her spine crept between her tightly clinched thighs.

Sweet didn't describe what Alex was doing. His demeanor was downright seductive. His flirtatious banter continued over grilled chicken salads and warm-buttered bread. Though an hour had passed and his attention was firmly fixed on Lynn, Alex never lost sight of the two men who had originally caught his eye.

"What do you do in Cincinnati?"
"I'm in nursing school," she replied after dabbing the corners of her mouth. "I hope to become a doctor which is part of the reason I'm in Denver."
"You're here to study medicine?"
"No, I'm here to settle my father's estate. I'm hoping to use the money he left my sister and me to pay for my education."
"Sorry to hear about your father's passing."
"Me too, but he's in a better place. His suffering is over," she sighed very somberly.

27

"Touché," Alex replied after searching for something else to say. "If I ever get sick in Cincinnati, I'll be sure to look you up, Dr. Turner."

"You'd better," she replied, her radiant smile returning as quickly as it left. "Do you have the time, Alex?"

"It's two-forty five," he replied after looking at his Diamond encrusted Bulgari.

"Oh shit! I'm supposed to be at Weltman, Reid, and Myers by three o'clock. There's no way I'll make it in time."

"Relax," he replied calmly while reaching for his phone. "Dave Weltman is a personal friend of mine. I'll tell him you're with me. You'll be fine."

"You really are a knight in shining armor, Alexis Stratton," she declared after breathing a sigh of relief. "Allow me to treat you to lunch at least."

"Some other time," he replied with a smile while motioning for the maître de.

Lynn watched as they entered into a brief, but quiet exchange. She stared curiously when he leaned in close so that Alex could whisper in his ear. After quickly glancing at Lynn, the maître de nodded to Alex and left the table.

"I told him to charge it to the house," he said after lifting his glass and sipping, answering the question she was silently asking.

"The house?"

"Yes, I own this café," he replied nonchalantly.

"I have to go to the bathroom," she said after shaking her head and smiling.

"I'll be here waiting," he smiled before standing and watching her leave.

Once Lynn was out of sight, Alex picked his cell phone up off the table and began scrolling through its phonebook. After making a selection, he pressed *send*.

"Dave Weltman's office, this is Pam speaking."
"Hello, Pam, this is Alexis Stratton. Please inform Mr. Weltman that I am en route with his 3PM appointment."
"Will do, Mr. Stratton."
"Thank you Pam."

After disconnecting the call, Alex immediately began pecking at the phone's virtual keyboard.

"File number 46723942 acquired. BM."
"Where? Delilah."
"Denver. BM"
"When? Delilah"
"Now. BM."

After placing the phone back in its case, Alex got up from the table, and walked over to the serving stand where he was greeted by the same maître de. After draping a towel over Alex's left forearm and handing him a pitcher of ice water, the maître de watched him walk over to the table where the two targets were seated.

"More water, sir?" Alex inquired to the balding Armenian who arrogantly held his out glass. "And for you sir?"

Not to Alex's surprise, he was completely ignored by his turban-clad table mate. After the balding man took a healthy drink of water, Alex returned to the stand and dumped the pitcher into a nearby drain. A busboy casually strolled up to Alex and placed it in his tub of dirty dishes. When Lynn emerged from the café, Alex took her by the hand and escorted her to the curbside where his charcoal-gray, Aston Martin DBS was waiting. Holding the door open as she climbed in, Alex peered over his shoulder to check on his target. Much to his delight his mark was clutching his heart and quickly turning blue. When the coupe pulled away, the man collapsed to the ground taking the entire table with him. Minutes later, the DBS's V-12 purred to a stop in front of a brick high-rise with Weltman, Reid, and Meyers on the marquee.

"So, I'll pick you up at your hotel at seven, right?"
"Yes," Lynn replied with her beautiful smile beaming like the sun. "Thank you for lunch, the ride, everything, Alex."
"It was my pleasure."
"See you later, Alex," she cooed.

He fought the urge to pucker his lips when she leaned over and caressed his stubble-covered cheek while staring deeply into his eyes. The sound of her voice and the touch of her hand created a twitching sensation in Alex's slacks. He was completely oblivious to the fact that he had just killed a man.

He watched her every movement as she exited the coupe. Feeling his stares on her hips and ass, Lynn put a sensual swing in them before disappearing through the building's smoked glass entry. Just as the door closed, Alex felt a buzz on his hip. He pulled out his cell phone and read the message.

"Kill confirmed. Delilah."

North of Denver in the city of Boulder Colorado sits an exclusive community called *Whitman Estates*. This gated subdivision with its quiet streets and walking trails was far removed from the hustle and bustle of Denver and is home to some Colorado's most elite citizens. Situated on these sprawling landscapes and their carefully manicured lawns are homes priced from five hundred-thousand to five-million dollars.

On a street aptly named Aspiration Lane and in its cul-de-sac sits the largest and most expansive plot in the community. On this ten-acre, tree-lined property sits a massive ivory manor-house that was modeled after a Civil War-era Victorian mansion. It featured a pair wrap around porches; one on the first level and one on the second. A large Jamaican flag hung from the second floor balcony flapping proudly in the cool spring breeze. In front of the house is an ivory birdbath that sits in the center of a plush green island. Surrounding it is a circular, cobblestone driveway with four vehicles parked on it: two white Range Rover Sports, a white S 550 Mercedes sedan, and a candy-apple red Porsche 911, all of which were adorned with Jamaican flag-styled vanity plates. In the rear of the house was a miniature soccer field, a basketball court-sized patio with two wet bars, a pair of hibachi grills, and an Olympic-sized swimming pool that was flanked by a pair of Jacuzzis. In the grass just off the patio were four tables with large white umbrellas, and beyond the tree-lined rear, was a helipad. Patrolling these lavish grounds was a team of armed sentries and Cane Corso Mastiffs on leashes.

On the mansion's second floor overlooking the patio was the master suite, and inside atop the covers of a massive California king, Tisha Norman was pinned beneath a humping, grunting. With her legs spread wide and her mind wandering, she lay there in total disgust at the thought of this dark-skinned, half-a-man heaving on top of her. But there he was perched between her thighs sweating and panting like dog in heat. When he buried his bald head in the pillow near her neck, Tisha gazed out of the patio doors to her right and prayed silently that he would cum and bring an end to this madness. To escape this sexual degradation, she tried to imagine he was Alex, but it was no use. He was nowhere near the suave, sexy, and sensual lover she had left just hours ago.

"Mi a cum now, gal!" he proclaimed when he raised his sweat-covered head.
About damn time, she thought while scowling at him.
"Oh, *shit!*" he cried repeatedly with his body quivering and shaking until he went limp inside her.

Tisha tried desperately not to dry heave when she felt his bursts, which in her mind were akin to being pissed on, or in this case pissed in. Grinning like a mad-man and proud of his performance and, he rolled off of her and to the opposite side of the bed. Now free of his bondage, Tisha clutched the sheets to her neck and quickly turned her back to him. Lying there in disgust but pretending to fall asleep, she was suddenly gagged by the pungent odor of marijuana. When she opened her eyes there was a thick cloud of smoke hovering over the bed. When he began coughing and hacking, she secretly hoped he would choke to death from the smoke he was blowing so liberally into the air.

"Wan some ganja, gal?"
"No thank you, honey."
"Wa mek?" he asked, clearly insulted by her refusal.
"I'm just not in the mood now, daddy. That's all."

"Mi a know, gal," he replied before taking a long hit. "Mi a true grindsman!"
"Yes baby, you certainly are," she replied while choking back tears. "Your dick is always too good for me, daddy."

Though his hacking and coughing were sickening by themselves, it was his sadistic laughter that hurt the most. Moments later, silence fell on his side of the bed. Tisha rolled over and saw that he had fallen asleep with his hand on his chest and the smoking cigar still between his fingers. She carefully removed it and took a long hit. With smoke in her cheeks and tears in her eyes, she contemplated putting it out on his pitted face. Sadness coursed through her when she stared at him then looked around the bedroom. After taking another hit, Tisha snuffed the cigar out in the ashtray on the black-marble nightstand. Attempting not to disturb the snoring "sex machine," she gently stepped out of the bed, put on her robe, and grabbed her cell.

She walked out the French doors onto the porch and looked out on the trappings of her lifestyle: money, cars, clothes, jewelry, servants, and of course the armed guards. She was a modern day celebrity and had everything a twenty-four year old sista could ever want. She turned around and looked at him once again. Her sobs became so loud that the guards below stopped and began staring up at her. When they began whispering amongst themselves, Tisha backed slowly away from the rail. Her legs gave way when her back found the wall, and she slid down it until she was sitting on the floor with her knees drawn to her chest. After pulling herself together, she retrieved the phone from her pocket and began to dial.

"Hello. Tisha? Is that you?"

"Yes, Dawn, it's me," she sobbed.

"Girl, why are you crying?"

"You know why, Dawn. I hate him."

"Who girl... Simon?"

"Yes, Dawn. Simon."

"Girl, don't trip. You got a good man. So what the dick ain't no good? Every marriage has a flaw, right? Some men don't work. Some men are drunks and some are even junkies. Your man can't fuck. So what?"

"So what? Are you serious, Dawn? You think it's just the sex?"

"My bad girl...damn. Does he still hit you?"

"Yes," Tisha replied while trying valiantly to maintain her composure.

"Oh. Well girl, you know some men have a problem expressing how they feel and sometimes a nigga might put his hands on you."

"I don't believe you, Dawn. That *nigga* put me in the hospital three months ago. Has Roger ever hit you?"

"Hell no 'cause he knows I'd kill his ass," she snapped before realizing how insensitive she'd been. "Okay, so the nigga got a little physical with you. You know how them Jamaicans are, and what did you expect anyway? You got fly with him in front of his peeps, right?"

"Alex has never hit me, not once. He treats me like a queen all the time and makes love to me like I'm something sent from Heaven."

"You ain't thinking of leaving Simon for Alex again, are you? I mean don't get me wrong. That is a fine, car'mel-colored nigga with a body! Oh my gawd he has a body! And yeah, he owns a few businesses, some cars, and has some dough, but girl, please. Simon is rich! He could buy Alex and ten more niggas just like him. Are you insane?"

"You're right, Dawn. Guys like Simon don't come along very often."
"Tisha, gal, weh yu?"
"Your brother-in-law is beckoning so I have to go."
"Make the best of it, Tish. Call me later."
"Bye, Dawn."

Tisha quickly disconnected the call and proceeded to fix her face as best she could. When she returned to the room, Simon was lying there in bed with the covers turned back. To her disgust, he was stroking his dick while puffing on his cigar.

"Come now, mi hose need some lovin."

Recalling her pep talk, Tisha crawled back into the bed by his side and closed her eyes before moving in to kiss his cheek. The pain of her hair being yanked and her neck being snapped back made her eyes shoot open with fright.

"Mi nuh wan no kiss, woman!" he barked while shoving her head towards his lower extremities.

There was nothing sensual about the way he gripped her hair. Clearly, he wasn't the tender lover that Alex was. He taunted her and grunted while aggressively thrusting his dick in and out of her mouth. Tisha contemplated biting him, but flashed back to the severe beating she took the last time she did and decided against it. With tears in her eyes, she endured it like she had countless times in the past. A primal roar escaped his thin, blackened body before releasing his load into her mouth and held her head in place while his thick white paste coated her throat. Tisha dry-heaved several times on the way to the master bath before puking into the cold porcelain toilet.

"Yu hab da hang of dat one day, chile," he declared with a laugh while she sat crying and vomiting into the bowl.

Chapter 2

Denver, Colorado

Alex reluctantly entered the dimly lit conference room and sat down at a long, mahogany conference table where six other men were seated. Like him, each one of them was handsome, well-dressed, and meticulously groomed. Also like him, each one of them was a trained assassin. Two seats to his left was Gary Anders, a tall well-tanned ex-Navy Seal with a buzz cut, a rigid jaw line, and a hulking athletic build. Two seats to his left, at the end of the table, was Terrance Michael Wayne, aka Big Mike. He was a burly, dark-skinned brother with a broad chest, a shiny bald head, and a neatly-trimmed goatee. Though it was dim at his end of the table, the six-carat stud in his left ear was flickering like a beacon. Three seats to his left was Warren Jeffries, a fresh-faced young man with boyish good looks, tapered blonde hair, and ocean blue eyes. In the two seats to his left were the twins, Richard and Nicholas Chang. Both were short, medium-built Asians with spiky, gelled hair. The only distinguishing mark between these identical twins was a small, permanent scar on Richard's right cheek. At the other end of the table opposite Big Mike was Gregory Austin McCallister, aka Doc. He was a very distinguished looking, older gentleman with tapered, salt and pepper hair. His square, gold-rimmed glasses sat half the distance of his fairly long and pointed nose. His skin was tight and tan, a stark contrast to the white Hugo Boss shirt he was wearing. In front of him was a newspaper with a headline that read "Mobster Killed by Doorman."

37

"Welcome home gentlemen," Doc began after folding the paper and laying it neatly to the side. "As you can see, we're short a few members short today. Business however, will continue as normal."

"Where are Lexi and Ko?" Alex asked after looking past the same newspaper article and picking up the brief sitting next to it.

"They're en route from Tokyo. They should land later tonight."

"Something on your mind Rick?" Alex growled seconds after hearing whispering and snickering from the other side of the table.

"Not at all, boss?" he replied while sinking into his seat and praying Alex didn't cross the table.

"What about you Nick?"

"Not at all, big man," he replied before gazing nervously off into space.

"So, Black Mamba," Mike began after observing the tension, "I hear you had Italian takeout last night. My bad, I mean you took out an Italian last night."

"Yes, Alex, tell us all about New York," Doc interjected giddily while leaning on the table with his hands clasped.

Alex, on the other hand, wasn't interested in recounting his evening. In fact, as he settled into the high-backed leather chair and closed his eyes his mind was else where.

Manhattan, N.Y., six o'clock PM, yesterday.

Shortly after the sudden death of one of New York's most prominent crime bosses, a selection process began to crown a new 'Don.' Several 'made men' within the ruling families rose to the challenge and attempted to usurp the throne, but after the "mysterious" deaths of four would-be 'Dons', and the successful intimidation of three more, Tony 'The Pick' Castiglione took up the mantle. As the new 'Don', he would also be the head of a five-family council that controlled organized crime from New Jersey all the way to Southern California. Prior to assuming the throne, this square jawed, rough-looking, Italian brute was carving out a sizable business for himself and his many associates. His modest career began thirty years earlier when he was a pick up man turned enforcer for many of the mafia's 'insurance' rackets. His foul temper, lack of mercy, and taste for excessive violence made him a favored hit man. He earned his nickname, 'The Pick', because he always carried around a pearl handled ice pick that was trimmed in gold. Rumor had it that he'd murdered at least fifty nine men with it.

After being 'made', he continued his rise through the ranks until at last he was crowned the 'king-of-the-hill.' To mark the occasion, he threw himself a lavish party in *The Gallery of the Carlyle Hotel* and partied like royalty. In attendance, were members of the other families who had come out to witness his coronation. Also present were some of New York's elite citizens including some high ranking police officers, attorneys, judges, and other political figures. In true mobster fashion, there was live music, drinking, eating, dancing, and of course, half-naked women.

Throughout most of the evening, heavy rains pounded the city and afterwards, a dense fog settled over the streets making it nearly impossible to see more than a few feet in any direction. Around midnight, a pair of Armani-clad bodyguards walked through the lobby and towards the front doors. When the doorman ushered them out, they walked to the curbside where they looked up and down the street several times before waving to an entourage of men waiting in the lobby. 'The Don' exited *The Carlyle* and was met by the doorman who quickly opened a massive golf-umbrella. To his right was a short, homely looking man carrying a black, leather attaché case, and a few feet behind them, were three additional men who were also dressed in dark Armani suits. As 'Don' Castiglione waited on the sidewalk, he decided to humor himself at the doorman's expense.

"Where's the regular guy, Frank?" asked the drunken 'Don.'
"He took ill, sir," replied the doorman while watching the men standing curbside.
"Guess that affirmative action thing extends to doormen too, huh bro?" Castiglione asked before he and his associates burst into fit of a loud, obnoxious laughter.
"I guess it does, sir."
"Don't be so uptight, bro. I'm just busting your balls. Between you and me, I personally love colored...um...nig...um black people. You guys are superb athletes and the ones I deal with are very loyal. They remind me of, ya know, dogs."

Again, the Don's banter caused his associates to burst into a hysterical fit of laughter. The doorman, however, remained unmoved. Seconds later, a pair of headlights appeared through the dense fog to their left. 'The Don' took a cigar out of his jacket pocket and lit it while his men continued their laughter and taunting.

"I mean, the fact that you're not out robbing, raping, or rapping makes me feel good. This good, honest work you're doing makes you a credit to your race."
"Thank you sir," the door man replied calmly.

The rumble of thunder in the skies above nearly drowned out their annoying laughter. As lightning flashed, the doorman's left hand flew from his side with blazing speed and grabbed the umbrella handle in his right. With a twist of his wrist, he pulled a narrow, three foot dagger from the handle and slashed Castiglione's throat. In the same motion, he flipped the blade in his palm and plunged it into his sidekick's chest. Before the bodyguards behind 'The Don' could react, the doorman tossed the umbrella aside and thrust his right hand into his coat. After yanking a nickel plated .40 cal from the small of his back, he fired three bullets; one into the forehead of each henchman standing behind the fallen mobster. Turning his attention to the men who were curbside by the limousine, the doorman thrust his left hand into his long red coat and pulled out an identical .40 cal. Before they could open fire, the shiny barrel had dispatched two shots; head shots like the others. As the men lay on the ground in pools of blood mixed with rain, the doorman turned hit-man stepped over their bodies and into the street. Lightning flashed again, briefly illuminating the night sky above the ominous assassin. With a smoking gun in each hand, he stared briefly at the petrified driver who was standing by his limousine door. The sight of the dark, menacing figure staring back at him caused the driver to slip and fall while trying to seek refuge inside the limousine. He watched and prayed as the doorman walked calmly across the street, climbed into a cab, and disappeared into the foggy night.

Now back in Denver, the news of the murders was on the front page of every paper.

"Nice touch posing as the doorman, Alex," Mike said in his deep, thundering voice. "I bet he almost shit when you jacked him for his uniform."

"Yeah Alex, it was a nice touch. I hope you realize that if one of them had gotten the drop on you, your ass would be dead. You broke protocol by going in there alone. It was supposed to be a drive-by, not a point-blank hit. Ko wasn't there watching your ass like he normally does."

"I modified the mission to account for the weather and to protect any innocents wandering in the area. Besides, no one's complaining but you."

"What's the matter, Gary?" Mike asked with a chuckle. "Are your pockets beginning to feel light? I mean after all, Alex bagged Castiglione and one of the Middle East's most notorious arms dealers in less than 48 hours. What does that come to? It sounds like three-point-five mil by my count."

"It's not about the money, Mike," Gary snapped before turning to his right. "Alex is careless as hell. His tactics are flashy, brash, and obnoxious. The hit was on Castiglione, not his whole crew. That's time wasted! What happens next time when nobody's there to bail his ass out?"

"Relax old man. Nobody's fast enough to get the drop on me. Remember Baghdad? Besides, given their proximity it would've been stupid for me to just kill Castiglione and hope they missed me. Besides, it now looks like he was killed by a rival faction inside the mob. His death will insure division and confusion for a long time to come."

"The sun shines on every dog's ass occasionally, Alex," Gary growled with his fists clinching the arms of his chair as if he was poised to pounce.

Alex meanwhile was cool as a cucumber. With his elbows resting on his chair's arms and his fingertips joined like a pyramid, he was waiting for his nemesis to make a move. This nonchalant behavior fueled Gary's anger so much that sweat began forming on his reddened forehead.

"Now getting back to my original question, where are Lexi and Ko?" Alex growled without breaking eye contact.

"Like I said before, they're en route from Tokyo and they should land later tonight."

"Why were they in Tokyo?" Alex demanded after turning his attention to the man on his right.

"Ko was sent to Tokyo to watch Lexi's back during the Nakamura hit."

"Nakamura, as in Peter Nakamura, the Yakuza Boss?"

"Yes Alex, the same Peter Nakamura."

"The Nakamura hit was mine! It was already decided that Karma and I would…"

"That decision was changed, Alex," Doc interrupted.

"When?" he growled through his clinched teeth.

"We decided to act when we discovered that a more opportune moment had arisen. You were in New York and we couldn't wait."

"You son-of-a bitch!" Alex growled when he bolted up. "You're telling me that you sent Lexi into the den with that sick fuck? Who else was in on this decision?"

"You would have been if you weren't so busy fucking your mark's wife," Gary interrupted.

Alex spun around when Gary Anders, who towered six inches over him and outweighed him by at least eighty pounds, sprang to his feet. Alex however, wasn't intimidated. In fact, he stood toe-to-toe with the smirking behemoth and stared furiously into his eyes. The room went silent once they became locked in a stare down like two gladiators preparing for battle.

43

"I'm not the same kid you thought you could push around ten years ago. This time, I'll break both your arms."

"Enough!" shouted while standing and pounding on the table. "Meeting's over! Everybody out except you, Alex!"

The vicious stare down continued until the other men escorted Gary from the room. When the door closed, Alex turned his attention to Doc who was visibly shaken, but determined to not to show it.

"Sit down, Alex!"

"I'd rather stand."

"I said sit down, got-dammit! What the hell's gotten into to you, son? This isn't like you. You've gone from having ice water in your veins to being a hot-headed pain in the ass. What's the problem?"

"Nothing," Alex replied while slumping back in the chair.

"Nothing my ass. Why isn't Simon dead... or at least in custody?"

"Because you mutha-fuckas keep pulling the plug on me, that's why! Three times in the past five years I've had this mutha-fucka in my sights and three times your connects have called me off him. Why is that?"

"That's irrelevant. The point is now..."

"The point is he's out lived his usefulness; again. He's stopped ratting out his own connections to save his ass; again. The CIA wants him dead because they can't use him; again. You're as full-of-shit as they are!"

"Do I need to sit you down? Is that it?" Doc threatened angrily.

"Sit me down?" Alex asked half-laughing. "You can't sit me down, asshole. I'm the best hitter you've got."

"I don't care. You need time to sort out whatever demons you have swimming in that thick skull of yours. No one here is attacking you, yet you're constantly on the defensive."

"Whatever. Why did you send Lexi on this mission?"

"Based on Nakamura's habits and fetishes, using her talents gave us the perfect opportunity to get close to him. With Karma in the field and no other female operatives available, it just made sense."

Alex sat back in his chair and began massaging his temples. He wasn't ready for what he was hearing and was getting sick to his stomach thinking about Lexi being anywhere near an animal like Peter Nakamura. Though he cringed at the thought, Alex had to know what happened.

"Did he...? Did she...?"

"He never laid a finger on her, Alex. She killed him before anything happened."

"She's not built for this lifestyle, Doc. I've been telling you that for years, but as usual, you refused to listen. Lexi is a kid, not a killer. This was Karma's job. Lexi belongs in school, not flying all over the world playing assassin."

"Playing assassin? Alex, Lexi is one of the best female assassins on the market right now."

"But she's not the best; Karma is."

"Well, the jury is still out on that one, but Lexi is better than half the guys in the world. To be perfectly honest, I think you're afraid she's is going to steal your thunder. Besides, what's the difference between you watching her back versus Ko?"

"For me, it's personal. For him, it's just another assignment."

"That's bullshit and you know it, Alex. Ko is your best friend. Hell, he's your only friend! He'd be pissed if he heard you saying that."

Although Alex hated to admit it, Doc was telling the truth. Even though Ko was his best friend and their skills were almost identical, he wasn't good enough to watch over Lexi in Alex's eyes. Nobody was. As far as Alex was concerned, it was his right and duty to question anyone who put her in harm's way. While he believed in holding his ground until the very end, Alex wasn't naïve. His behavior had created a rift within the team and as a result, was costing him their trust. That cost, however didn't matter because he was the best in the business and had the track record to prove it. The rest of the team knew this as well, and it often added to the tension and division. Though part of him could justify his feelings, Alex felt isolated deep within.

"Are we done here? I have a date."
"A date? I hardly call what you do with Tish..."
"It's not with Tisha. It's with a young lady I met earlier today."
"That's all well and good Alex, but you still have to deal with this Simon issue. Do whatever you're going to do with this girl and send her on her way. Then get back to work. And I need you to go see Constance."
"Constance?" Alex demanded after sitting up in his chair. "Why?"
"Because you need someone to talk you down off that ledge, that's why. You're a ticking time bomb. You're no good to me or anyone else when you're like this."
"I'll get around to it."
"Make sure you get around to it quickly."

With that, Alex exited the room leaving Doc alone to stare at the newspaper and its ominous headline.

Hours later, Alex's black Cadillac ATS-V rumbled into the parking lot of the Ramada Inn. After stepping out of it and adjusting his single-breasted Versace blazer and matching royal blue slacks, he grabbed the bouquet of white roses and bottle of wine from the ebony back seat. He also grabbed the attention of several female employees and some of the hotel's guests as well. On the eighth floor, he quickly looked for the signs that pointed to Lynn's room. Within seconds, he was standing outside room 819 with a smile on his face, gifts in hand, and condoms in his pocket just in case.

"Just a minute," he heard after knocking three times.

When the door opened and saw Lynn's face, Alex knew his evening was over before it started. The radiant beauty he'd met earlier was gone. Lynn's soft brown eyes were bloodshot and had bags underneath them and when she saw the roses, tears began streaming down her swollen cheeks. Though it was just past seven, she was dressed in her hotel robe and slippers. Seeing her like this left Alex at a loss for words. He couldn't imagine what happened at Dave Weltman's office, but whatever it was, it couldn't have been good.

"These are for you," Alex managed, unsure of what else to say.
"Thank you," she replied with her voice cracking. "Come in and have a seat. As you can see I'm clearly in no condition to go anywhere with anyone."
"Yeah…um, I noticed," he replied after closing the door and following her into the suite. "What happened?"

Lynn laid the flowers on the bar before opening the chilled bottle of Beviamo Moscato D'asti and helping herself to a large glass. Moments later she was sitting on the end of the couch opposite from where Alex was standing. After curling her long legs up under her body, she patted the cushion and motioned for Alex to sit down. After unbuttoning his blazer, he sat down and tried to imagine what could possibly have happened between lunch and now. After several long sips, Lynn began her painful story.

"He wiped me out, Alex?"

"Who?"

"My no good brother, Desmond, that's who."

"I don't understand."

"My brother got to the accountant before I did and had the money wired from Denver to his account in Cincinnati this morning. He left us with nothing, Alex. My sister and I have nothing our father intended for us. I needed that money to go to medical school. My sister and I were planning on buying a new home. Now, all that's gone."

"How much did he take?"

"He took everything my dad left us... just over a million dollars."

Damn! Alex thought to himself. "How?"

"I don't know. What am I going to do?" she sobbed.

"Maybe you could reason with your brother."

"Reason with Desmond, that jackal? His life revolves around how much money he can get and who he can get it from. He wiped out all of my dad's accounts, sold his house, and now he's robbed us blind."

"Maybe there's something David can do. I mean... "

"The money's been withdrawn and wired, Alex. It's gone."

"I'm sorry, Lynn," he said after pulling her into his arms where she continued to cry.

After about twenty minutes of silence, Alex noticed that she'd cried herself to sleep. After waiting awhile longer, he picked her up and carried her to the bed. Before leaving, he scribbled out a note and laid it on the pillow next to her. He kissed her forehead gently then let himself out. Back in the lobby, Alex made a quick stop at the customer service desk.

"May I help you, sir?" asked the bubbly blonde behind the counter.
"Yes, my name is Alexis Stratton," he began while reaching into his blazer, "and a friend of mine is staying in room 819. Charge all expenses to my account for the next week, two if necessary. Be sure to include all meals, phone calls, and anything else she needs."
"Wow! That is very generous of you, Mr. Stratton," she said while swiping his card and notating the account.
"Will there be anything else, sir?"
"Yes, have your florist send up a dozen pink roses tomorrow."
"Will do, Mr. Stratton."
"Thank you."

Moments later, the Cadillac left the lot. Alex cruised around the city for a few hours before finally heading home. Later that night as winds howled outside his windows, Alex tossed and turned in his bed. The images in his mind were so crystal clear that his body thought they were real. He could see the little boy and girl lying asleep in their beds, when suddenly the boy was awakened by the sounds of yelling and gunfire. He sprang from his bed, locked the door, and grabbed his baby sister just like he'd been trained. He wrapped her body in a sleeping blanket then opened the window. Just as he climbed out on the window sill, the door flew open. Without looking back, he leapt a few feet onto the narrow platform that his father had built. It was attached to a tree house that that had been designed not only as a place to play, but a place of refuge in times of danger. Though he could hear the monsters closing in on him, the little boy refused to stop moving. He had to protect his baby sister. That was his mission. With the sleeping infant in his arms, the brave little soldier climbed out of the tree and onto the cold ground below. As he fled across the yard, he heard more gunfire. Gravel and wood chips flew up, stinging his legs and feet as they churned across the dewy grass. Bullets barely missed him as he darted through the adjacent yards with the sounds of huffing, puffing, and men yelling in a language he couldn't understand at his back. Suddenly, out of breath and with tears streaming down his face, the boy crashed hard into someone's arms.

"Get behind me son," was all he heard while trembling behind his protector and listening to the gunshots erupting around them. While listening to his sister's cries, the little boy made a silent vow. *I'll never be afraid again.*

After gasping for air, Alex sprang up in the bed and looked around. His arm muscles were coiled like cobras waiting to strike at whatever was in his path. His tensed body was covered in sweat and his hair was matted to face. When his breathing slowed down, he looked at the digital clock next to the bed.

"5A.M. She's not here. Fuck!" he exclaimed before throwing back the covers and bolting for the bathroom.

A while later at a secluded airport east of the city, a custom G-6 taxied to a stop in the dense fog that had settled. A small group of technicians quickly filed out of a brightly lit hangar and rushed to the jet's door and when it opened, a ramp was quickly pushed up to it. Ko and Lexi, who were dressed in evening attire, were the first descend it. They were followed by the pilot and three other men who were dressed in tactical gear similar to what Ko had been wearing in Tokyo. As they gathered outside the hangar, the plane was attached to a cart and dragged inside. Holding hands and laughing, Ko and Lexi began their walk away from the rest of the group and across the field towards a group of parked cars.

"Listen beautiful," he began as he broke stride, "you did great out there."
"You really think so, Ko?" she asked, nervously seeking his approval.
"Absolutely," he replied after lifting her chin with his curled index finger. "The bad guy is dead and you're still in one piece. That's the name of the game."

She looked lovingly into his almond shaped eyes before their bodies instinctively moved in closer together.

"I only hope Alex thinks so," she said softly with her face hovering inches from his and their lips tingling with anticipation.
"You hope Alex thinks what?"

Like a pair of busted teenagers, they quickly separated and looked for the source of the alarming, yet familiar voice. Approaching them through the fog was a dark, ominous figure and even in the moonlight, they could see the agitation etched on his face. They glanced at each other nervously before returning their sights to him.

51

"Alex," Ko began while searching for words, "how was New York?"

"Wet," he replied dryly. "How was Tokyo?"

"Tokyo? Tokyo was okay. Everything went without a hitch. And Alexandria...she was awesome man. You should have seen her."

"Is that so?" Alex quizzed while staring at the petite young woman who was staring at the ground near her feet. "I'm sure you'll tell me all about it, right?"

"Yep," she replied abruptly.

"Thank you for watching out for her, Ko."

"Anytime, Alex."

"Incidentally, Ko, if you weren't my best friend, I might take your life for this."

"I know, Alex."

The two men stared each other down briefly as cool winds and fog whipped around them. Sensing the mounting tension, Lexi took Alex's hand and dragged him towards his Aston Martin.

"Thanks for dinner, Ko. See you at the office."

Ko watched helplessly while Alex held the door of the DBS open. The two men made eye contact once more when Alex walked around the car and climbed into the driver's seat. Seconds later as their speed rose, so did the tension inside the cabin. Lexi could tell by the way Alex jammed the clutch to the floor and threw the shifter between its gates that he was beyond upset. He was pissed. After all, this DBS was his baby and it was taking a beating in his hands.

"Dinner?" he demanded through his clinched teeth while whipping the steering wheel, causing the car's rear to drift from the gravel onto the two lane road leading from the airfield.

"Yes, Alex. We had a late dinner in Tokyo. That's what took us so long to get back here."

Alexandria watched calmly as the DBS's speedometer rose rapidly towards triple digits. She didn't even flinch when they passed and dodged slow moving and sometimes, oncoming traffic.

"Dinner, huh?" Alex asked after briefly gazing at the black Elie Saab evening gown she was wearing. "Is there anything else I should know about your time in Tokyo?"

"Why don't you ask me if I fucked him, Alex?" she barked defiantly.

"Did you?"

Her slow response only fueled his anger. Feeling the heat from his glare, she looked out of the passenger side window and began staring into the distance.

"I asked you a question, Alexandria."

"That's none of your fucking business, Alex!"

When his foot hit the brake, she quickly braced herself against the dashboard and held on tight as the DBS fishtailed before coming to a stop across multiple lanes.

"Have you lost your fucking mind?"

"What do you mean it's none of my fucking business? You're five minutes past grown and don't have a clue about what you're involved in! It's clear that you're the one who's lost their mind 'cause you sure as hell aren't using it right now."

"No, Alex, I didn't fuck him. Is that what you wanted to hear? And you'd better watch the highway before you kill somebody."

"You shouldn't even be here. You should have your narrow ass on campus where it belongs, instead of traipsing all over Japan."

"First of all, Alexis Stratton, you are not my father," she growled with her arms folded across her chest. "And how dare you tell me where I should be and what I should be doing. I'm a grown assed woman who's capable of making her own decisions."

"Really?" he quipped half-smiling. "Well, after you're debriefed I want your grown ass on the first plane out of Denver. Playtime is over."

"What?!! Why? My vacation isn't over. I still have 4 days."

"Wrong. You need to concentrate on being a student, not being..."

"Not being what?" she demanded with tears forming in her eyes.

"Me," he replied coldly.

A brief stare down ensued before she resumed looking out the passenger side window. After a brief spin, the coupe's rear tires connected to the road and hurled it forward down the expressway. Except for the roar of the V-12, the rest of the ride to the penthouse was relatively quiet. No words were exchanged between them in the elevator either. Lexi stood in the far corner still with her arms folded and her head down while Alex leaned against the back wall with his eyes closed. When they finally arrived at the penthouse, she stormed out of the elevator and through the great room. She made a sharp right around the corner and into her bedroom where she abruptly slammed the door. Alex trailed her slowly but said nothing. While standing outside her door, he heard her pitiful cries. He thought about knocking, but changed his mind and retired to his own bedroom.

A few restless hours later, he reemerged and saw Lexi standing in the kitchen dressed in white satin pajamas, and rapidly chopping vegetables on a cutting board. After observing her body language and taking a deep breath, Alex walked up to the counter.

"Hey. I just wanted to say…"
"You know what your problem is, Alex?" she snapped while waving a paring knife at him.
"No, tell me."
"You try to mask your fears by dominating and intimidating others. It's not right. You have no respect for people or their feelings. You're lonely, depressed, and make a habit of dragging people into your pit of despair. If you keep this lifestyle up, you're going to self-destruct."
"That may be the case, but my way has worked thus far therefore, I see no reason to change it."
"No reason to change? Are you listening to yourself? Alex, you've been carrying around the same guilt for years. When are you going to forgive yourself?"
"Let it go," he said in a tone that was more advice than request.
"Their deaths were not your fault."
"Let it go," he demanded with anger building in his tone.
"Why? Because you don't want to hear the truth or are you too stubborn to face it?"
"Because you are treading on thin ice little girl," he advised again while standing with the refrigerator doors open but looking for nothing in particular.

"You don't scare me, Alexis Stratton. I see right through you."

"And what is it you see?" he demanded after slamming the doors and turning towards her.

"I see a man who instead of facing the truth, lashes out with deception and violence. You're not the villain you make yourself out to be. At your core, you're afraid to let go of the past and live. You're afraid that if you let your guard down, someone else is going to get hurt."

"Not a villain, huh? Ask the former 'Don' of New York whether or not I'm a villain."

"I'm not impressed, Alex," she grinned while rubbing his stubble covered cheek. "I killed a man with my bare hands, babe."

"The Nakamura hit was Karma's and mine, not yours. You had no business being alone with him. Too many things could have gone wrong."

"But they didn't, Alex. I had it under control and Ko was with me every step of the way."

"Ko," he murmured quietly before looking away.

"Yes Alex, Ko," she replied while turning his face back to hers. "He's your best friend, and he wasn't about to let anything happen to me."

"I don't want this life for you."

Alex took her by the hand and gently removed it from his face before turning and walking towards the patio. Not willing to let the conversation end there, Lexi followed him as he walked towards the fence surrounding the patio but stood silently at his side while he looked out over the city.

"Why don't you want this life for me?"

"Because you're not some random hitter out there on a job. You're my sister and besides, mom and dad wouldn't want it for you either."

"That's the first time you mentioned them in ages, Alex. Why?"

"Because when I look at you, I see her. I see mom. You may be too young to remember, but I'm not. I remember how she used to cry when dad went away, and I remember how happy they were when you were born."

"Granted," Lexi said while grinning, "I'm sure they wouldn't want me repelling down buildings and killing crime bosses, but I think they'd be proud none the less."

"They'd be proud if you stop being so stubborn and do what I tell you to do. What I mean is finishing school and leading a normal life."

"What about you, Alex? You could lead a normal life too. What makes you any different than me?"

"You still have a choice," he replied in a near whisper.

"But Alex, it's my choice to make, not yours."

Meanwhile, across town at *Tango's Tattoos, Bikes, Auto Detailing & Repairs*, Ko, Richard and Nicholas, Gary, and Big Mike were gathered in a run-down garage that looked more like an exotic car showcase. Much to Ko's chagrin, they were discussing the details of his last mission. More specifically, they were interested in what took them so long to return to the states and how Alex reacted when he saw them.

"I bet you almost shit when you saw Alex coming through the fog," Big Mike laughed in his thunderous bellow.

"I admit I was a tad startled. The dude is just...I don't know. Tense."

"Tense?" Gary quipped while adjusting the headers on his blacked out Shelby GT 500. "The guy is wound tighter than Dick's hat band. Young Mister Stratton needs to be brought down a peg."

57

"I thought you let that go, G."

"Let it go hell. Man fuck that shit, Mike! I don't care how many fighting styles he thinks he's mastered. He needs to be taught a lesson in manners and one day real soon I'm gonna do it!"

"Just let it go, Gary."

"Oh look, the golden boy can speak after all," Gary joked after pointing at Warren who was usually quiet.

"Don't start with me," Warren snapped while ratcheting sparkplugs into the massive engine. "Alex has every right to be uptight. Jinx is his kid sister and she's all he has in this world."

"Damn that," Richard interrupted. "Tell us about that outfit she was wearing."

"Hell yeah!" Nick demanded while rubbing his hands together in eager anticipation.

"You guys are pigs," Ko growled when he opened the door of his burgundy Bentley GT Coupe.

"Call us what you want, Ko, but if Alex finds out you're tapping his sister, he's gonna forget your lifelong friendship. He might even come for your head."

"Shut up, Rick!" Warren snapped viciously.

"What's eatin' you man?" Nicholas fired back as Warren rounded the hood of the Mustang.

"Just the fact that you are talking about Alexandria like she's a piece of meat and not the girl you two grew up with."

"In their own way, the twins are right, Ko," Big Mike said while approaching the Bentley's passenger door. "Alex is your best friend and despite his ways, he deserves to know how you feel about his sister, especially if you plan on marrying her."

"I know, Mike. We're just waiting for the right time to tell him, and now isn't that time."

"If not now, when?" Big Mike asked before the engine roared to life.

"I know man, I know," Ko replied before speeding out of the garage.

Back at the penthouse, Alex and Lexi were at the table enjoying her gourmet veggie and cheese omelets, toast, and assorted beverages. Much to Alex's dismay, his sister's analysis of him continued.

"Since the subject of mine and Ko's relationship came into question, I have to ask you. Are you still sleeping with Tisha?"
"Why do you *have* to ask?" he huffed while sipping water and pretending to read the paper.
"Why do I have to ask? Because you are playing a very dangerous game with very dangerous people, that's why. Most husbands don't take too kindly to infidelity."
"I know. That's why I am doing it," he smirked.
"That's sick," she barked before dropping her fork on her plate. "What's the price of revenge, Alex?"
"The price of revenge is a life for a life," he replied while gazing through narrowed eyes.
"A life for a life? Alex, do you really think that you can live out the rest of your life seeking vengeance? What we do isn't about revenge; it's a job. You didn't do a job five years ago and now you've let it become personal. You live, eat, and breathe this madness and you and I both know that isn't healthy."
"Now you know why I don't want this life for you," he replied while looking calmly onto her eyes.
"I don't want this life for you either, Alex. Why can't you just let it go?"
"Let it go?" he growled. "Are you serious? You said it yourself. I had a job to do and I didn't get it done. Now, I'm going to right that wrong."
"You're in a fight you can't win, Alex."

"Why not? I've never lost a fight or walked away from one. Why should I start worrying now?"

"You can't win *this* fight, Alex. You can't win it because you've lost sight of the real enemy. It's not Simon or Tisha. It's the guilt you're carrying around inside of you and as long as you carry it, you'll never be free."

"Are you done?" he asked, frustrated more by her logic than her voice.

"No. I have one more question."

"What is it now?" he groaned.

"Do you love her?"

"Who?"

"Tisha, Alex; do you love her?"

"No," he replied in a tone that was as cold as it was emotionless.

"And what do you think that revelation is going to do to her when you do finally resolve this issue with Simon?"

"I don't care."

"C'mon, Alex. Nobody's that cold, not even you. You don't love her plus you're going to kill her husband? What's that going to leave her with?"

"Her freedom."

"One more question and I'll let it go."

"What is it?" he asked as his frustration slowly began subsiding.

"What happens at the end when Simon is dead? Will you finally forgive yourself and move on?"

"I don't know."

Lexi shook her head while staring at this stranger she once knew as her brother. *How could he have no emotional attachment at all? This isn't the same man who taught me how to ride a bike or protected me at the turn of every corner,* she thought while watching him pick over the rest of his food. His silence spoke volumes. Though she wanted to, Lexi said nothing when he wiped his mouth, got up from the table, and disappeared into his bedroom. When he reemerged, he was dressed in black jeans, a tan thermal shirt, and matching tan boots. She remained silent when he walked through the living room and towards the door. It was the moment that when it closed that she broke down.

"GOD, please protect my brother. He's *all* I have."

Chapter 3

FBI Regional Headquarters, Denver, Colorado.

Gathered in a conference room at the rear of the fifth floor were ten of the bureau's top field agents. Sitting at the far end of the cherry table was their leader, Agent Stanley Burroughs, a seasoned veteran with a spotted, balding head and a cleanly shaved face. The sleeves of his white tailored shirt were rolled up tightly around his stubby arms. He and the eight other agents seated at the table were anxiously sifting through stacks of folders, photographs, and briefs. The lead investigator, Jason Blackhawk, a tall Native American with an athletic build and a close buzz cut, was standing at the end of the table near a projector screen. On it were a series of pictures stacked in a pyramid-shape, and at the top of them was a man they knew all too well. Using his laser pointer, he highlighted the pictures in the pyramid one-by-one.

"Okay Jason," Agent Burroughs began, "what do we have so far?"
"Thank you, Agent Burroughs. As a result of years of investigations, intelligence gathering, and several lucky breaks, we have successfully compiled a list of the major players in Simon Felix's Kingston cartel. This handsome gentleman with the bald head, pitted skin, and facial scars is Simon Peter Felix as you all know. He's the head of the U.S. wing of the Kingston Cartel, a notorious Jamaican posse that controls seventy-percent of the drug traffic coming in and out of Jamaica. Five years ago, they only controlled thirty percent of the trade which indicates they're always looking to expand. We estimate that if unchecked, they will dominate over ninety

percent of that market by the end of the decade. He has connections in the U.S, Asia, Europe, and South America. This is his wife Tisha Norman," he began after clicking on the slide below Simon's. "She acts as a mule for her sister in Ohio and others in the Midwest."

The next slide contained five pictures; an elderly black woman, a young black woman, a young Caucasian male, and two beautiful, mocha-colored little girls.

"This is Dawn Tyler, her husband, Roger, and her mother Evelyn Norman. These are her two daughters Lexus and Mercedes. Dawn is an LPN at the University of Cincinnati Medical Center. Roger is a foreman for Pierce Construction. According to last year's jointly filed tax return, their combined income was about seventy nine-thousand dollars. Strangely enough, they live in a six-hundred-fifty-thousand dollar home in West Chester, an upscale suburb north of Cincinnati. They both drive Mercedes Benz SUVs and the girls attend a private academy where tuition is roughly twenty five-hundred dollars each per month. Lastly, is her mother who lives in an exclusive retirement community that costs considerably more than her SSI and her husband's pension can afford."

"Are we absolutely sure that Tisha is supplying the family through Simon's enterprise?" asked agent Carver, a clean cut ex-marine who was taking notes on a legal pad.

"Yes we are, Agent Carver. Based on what we've been able to discover, she's both supplying and supporting them. We have surveillance photographs of Tisha in Dallas, Philadelphia, Shreveport, Chicago, Des Moines, and Seattle. Their combined efforts allow them to distribute cocaine, heroin, and marijuana throughout the country. A majority of the transactions take place in remote locations, though some have taken place on Roger's job sites."

"Who are the guys below the family?" asked another agent who was also taking notes.

"These five men form the Inner Circle of the operation. Like Simon, they're Rasta but only Simon shaves his head. They're also bound by blood, meaning that they're blood relatives and they're straight from the island."

"Who is that long haired fucker next to Ms. Norman?" asked Agent Burroughs, which brought attention to a picture which seemed out of place among the rest.

"This guy is Alexis Stratton, a local entrepreneur. He works for a multi-national real estate investment firm that specializes in buying, rehabbing, and reselling high dollar properties globally. His firm also owns a few restaurants and nightclubs in the area."

"What's his link to our girl?" asked an agent at the far end of the table.

"He's sleeping with her," Agent Blackhawk replied flatly.

"Well, he's either the bravest or stupidest son-of-a bitch walking the planet," Agent Burroughs replied while looking at the picture which was blown up on the screen.

"Actually, I believe his involvement with Tisha is more of a front for her operations as well as his own business ventures."

"Please elaborate, Jason."

"Everyone who works for Simon is a disposable tool, and Tisha's no different. She's a commodity. This Stratton guy travels the world, is clearly well connected, and just the type guy who can move drugs and cash in and out of the country undetected. His company is an excellent front."

"A front, huh?" asked a young female agent who seemed unconvinced.

"Yes, a front. What makes this guy unique is that he's a ghost. He has no credit cards or personal bank accounts to speak of which probably means his money is either off shore or in someone else's name. His personal tax returns don't jive with his assets. All his possessions are in the name of an LLC which owns at least eight vehicles, including a two-hundred-ninety-thousand dollar Aston Martin, four restaurants, two nightclubs, and a couple other smaller businesses. There's also a penthouse in downtown Denver valued at over two-million dollars."

"Great work, Jason," Agent Burroughs declared after standing up and walking towards the projector. "Step up the surveillance on Mr. Stratton. He may be the weak link we need to crack this case."

"Agent Carver, how are the wiretaps going?"

"Not well, sir," he replied while shuffling through papers and looking for phone transcripts.

"Why the hell not?"

"So far none of the phones we have taps on have given us anything valid. Simon uses numerous phone lines, never talks very long, and changes carriers frequently. It's as if he knows what we're planning before we can execute."

"Agent Burroughs, it may be necessary to revisit the notion that Simon has compromised someone within the bureau."

"That's utter nonsense, Jason. Look son," he began while leaning in close to Agent Blackhawk, "I know you feel that you have a personal stake in this case. Given your history on it and what happened with your former partner, I can understand your concern. In the past four years I've taken every possible measure to make sure that only a few choice hands touch this case. There is

65

absolutely no chance that we've been compromised again."

"But sir, what's the status of our agents who have actually infiltrated his cartel?" Jason asked, not willing to dismiss his assertion.

"No one but me knows who they are and I get frequent reports. That's the basis of most of your information, remember?"

"Yes sir," Jason replied with hesitation still lingering in his voice.

"Let it go, son. This op is airtight. Do you understand me?"

"Yes sir."

"Now that that issue is behind us, you said Simon controls seventy-percent of the trade. Fill us in."

"Well," Jason began after switching screens, "we're still sorting that out. Simon's organization has managed to unite over seventy percent of the drug posses in the U.S. and fifty-percent of those operating in Europe and Canada. Currently, he's able to bypass Mexico and move his shipments directly through the Caribbean from Columbia. This helps maintain purity and speeds up delivery, but he's also clipping the Mexican cartels' wings, which hasn't gone unnoticed. In fact, the cartels have recently begun conspiring against his organization and even attacked some of his supply boats."

After a click of the pointer, a list of the numerous posses and the regions of the United States, the U.K., and Canada under their control appeared on the screen. The posses under Simon's control were highlighted in yellow, and next to them were the various cities they dominated. After hovering above the United States, all the active posses were listed. Of the thirty shown, all but seven were highlighted in yellow.

"Shutting him down will cripple trade in the Caribbean and across the globe."

While listening to his words, Jason's fellow agents gazed at the lengthy list of posse names and cities. After clicking the laser pointer, Agent Blackhawk advanced to the next screen which had a newspaper article whose subject was the late 'Don' Tony Castiglione.

"Simon's primary U.S. connection was Tony Castiglione whose ties to organized crime stretched from New York to L.A., and as far away as Sicily. Surveillance cameras outside *The Carlyle* in Manhattan picked up this video of his recent assassination. NYPD is analyzing it now."
"I can only imagine how that investigation is going to turn out," Burroughs quipped sarcastically.

The room went silent when the grainy video began. They carefully studied the assassin's movements, rewinding it several times and even watching it at various speeds.

"The newspaper reports he was possibly taken out by a rival family or a jealous member of his own family. Even the Mexican cartels were mentioned because of his affiliation with Simon. Whoever this killer is, he's quick with a blade and damned dangerous with a gun."
"What kind of firearm did the shooter use?" Agent Carver asked while watching the video.
"Ballistics reports the slugs fired were from a modified .40 cal. They were clean too; no prints and no identifiable markings on them or the casings."
"This guy's a pro," Burroughs began with his hairy arms folded and half-resting on his hard, round belly. "Look at him; fast, precise, and not a single wasted move. I'll

bet the blade was clean too. Look there. He could've smoked the driver but didn't. Freeze it right there! See that? He pauses and looks at the driver but doesn't fire. Get a team to New York and interview that guy. He may be able to ID the shooter. Also, see if NYPD recovered any prints from the scene."

"I understand Simon has connections in Asia as well," interrupted Agent Carver. "What do we have on that, Agent Blackhawk?"

"His primary Asian connection was Yakuza Boss, Peter Nakamura. He was found dead a few days ago. The report out of Tokyo is that he had a heart attack. During the attack, he apparently fell and broke his neck. We have reason to believe, however, that he was the victim of an assassination as well."

"Look alive, boys," Burroughs declared when a surveillance photo of Boss Peter Nakamura and an accompanying newspaper article appeared on the screen. "This case is about to bust wide open."

"Yes sir," replied Agent Carver.

Moments later at Simon's compound, he and Tisha were on the patio seated at opposite ends of a long glass table. It was decorated with fine china and expensive crystal which sat atop a white satin table cloth. Fruits, pastries, other foods, and beverages lined it from end to end. Buxom and shapely dark-skinned servants stood watch at each end of the table tending to their masters' needs. While Tisha ate in silence, Simon was yelling and cursing into one of the eight phones which were spread out in front of him.

"Wa da fuck yu mean him dead? Dis naa hap'ning! Deh's too much on da line for dis shit! Wit da Jap dead, I an haffi strike another deal wit Yakuza to move dis product! Nakamura mi best customer! Ooo dead da damn Italian?"

"At the present time, we don't know," the voice on the phone replied.

"Den fine out! Dat's why I an pay you, undastan?" Simon barked while looking at the surveillance video of 'Don' Castiglione's execution on the laptop in front of him.

After another profanity laced tirade, he threw the phone towards the pool. He pounded his fists on the table repeatedly until at last Tisha couldn't tolerate his disturbances any longer.

"Is there something wrong?" she demanded in a tone that was dripping with sarcasm.

"Yea, deh si'ting wrong! Yu still ere!"

"Excuse me?" she demanded while rolling her eyes at him.

"Pack yu shit! Yu outta ere on da next ting smokin'!"

"What? Why? I just got here!"

"Well, now yu lef!" he shouted before standing up and slapping the dishes off the table. "Lang time mi a wait an yu sista naa deliver! Move yu backside to Cincinnati and check mi loot. Mek haste!"

"Fine," she groaned before throwing her napkin across the table.

Once his wife was out of sight, Simon summoned the servant who had been standing nearest to him. He slid his chair back and spread his legs as the smiling woman strutted slowly over to him. After stepping over the clutter on the ground, she squatted and unzipped his pants. After pulling his dick out, she began slowly licking and sucking on its head while stroking the shaft. Simon caressed the back of her bobbing head while watching as her thick, pink tongue teased each and every contour. He panted and grunted as she repeatedly deep-throated him before humming and spitting on his swollen head.

"An wa yu gwaan dun by sendin' har away? Dat nuh righted."

When Simon's eyes opened, he saw Gabriel, a tall, slim, dark-skinned brother with long dreadlocks and a thin goatee sitting in Tisha's seat. Though he was agitated by the intrusion, the lively servant kept his anger at bay.

"Yu craven bwoy!"
"Naa now, Gabriel. Yu nuh see mi busy?" Simon gasped while she stroked and teased his shaft and head.
"Yes, Simon, now. She can keep doin' what she doin', but yu need to listen ere. Yu losin' control of ya so call empire and pissin' people off to boot. "
"Wa...yu...mean?" Simon gasped and groaned as she licked and sucked on his balls.
"Yu need to be tinkin' bout how wi gwaan move da next shipment coming from Columbia; and da one after dat and after dat. I an hab obligations or we lose credibility, undastan?"
"Mi tink pon it," Simon groaned.
"Really now?" Gabriel asked while leaning back in his chair and placing his clasped hands on his knee. "Look to mi like da only ting yu tink pon is fixin' yu wood."

Simon continued gasping and groaning until at last he released his load. His head draped over the back of the chair as she spread his cream on her lips while milking him dry with her hands, mouth, and tongue.

"Enough!" he cried, out of breath and with sweat dripping from his brow.

Gabriel shook his head as the smiling woman stood up and adjusted her clothing before disappearing into the kitchen. After adjusting his linens, Simon returned his attention to the intruder with the angry glare.

"Coo yu, Gabriel. Mi a know wah at stake an' before da DEA, feds, or anybody come in ere, we be long gone. Da FBI tell pon deh every move."

"Ooo said anyting bout leaving and what bout da sista in Cincinnati? Da FBI watchin' her too. Wa'ppun dey decide to buss har?" Gabriel barked while leaning forward in his chair.

"Den har dead," Simon replied nonchalantly. "I an dead da pussyclot whore before dem play card pon mi!"

"In da meantime, yu need to link up wit da Africans."

"Da Africans? Naa bumboclot way! Dey too likky-likky!"

"Dem a guarantee fass payment. And unlike da payments from da Yakuza, it won't be short."

"Mi naa waan fi do it!" Simon protested.

"Ooo yu radda deal wit, da Mexicans perhaps? Dem a hot right now an' dey know yu chop dem head!"

"Mi dun know, but I naa wan deal wit no Africans!"

"Dey nu odda way," Gabriel snapped sarcastically with his eyes narrowed at Simon.

Meanwhile at Alex's penthouse, Lexi and Ko were happily taking advantage of his absence. Using her caramel-colored legs which she'd wrapped around the small of his tattooed back, she guided her lover's thrusts in and out of her creamy walls. As they lay atop her bed engulfed by flames of passion, her red nails traced the length of his spine while tasting his tongue deep in her mouth. One deep thrust after another had her back arched and her thighs quivering. His intensity and the ways he was touching her body made Lexi forget that Alex could walk in at any moment. When Ko hit her G spot and another climax erupted, she stopped caring. She missed and wanted this man and no one, not even her possessive, over-bearing brother could keep her from him. She looked deep into Ko's eyes while running her fingers through his tapered hair and held him close as another orgasm hit. Emboldened by Lexi's sensual moans and requests to *"go deeper"*, Ko reached down underneath her thighs and placed her legs high on his chiseled shoulders.

Her wish was his command. Lexi found herself gasping as his dick beat against her G-spot like a drummer in a rock band. The sheets beneath her back and ass were drenched in cum and sweat, and the room was so hot that the windows were beginning to fog up. They were determined to release every pinned up emotion they'd concealed from Tokyo to Denver. Their dance continued when Ko turned her around and took her from behind. Beads of sweat ran down the red, black, and gold dragon tattoo on his back. Tears formed in Lexi's eyes as she gripped the sheets one hand while stroking her clit with the other. Her breaths quickened when her face hit the pillow and his name escaped her lips over and over again.

"I love you, Ko!" she moaned when her walls began to pulsate around his thrusting dick.
"Lexi!" he screamed when he erupted and began filling her cup with his hot, bubbling lava.

Exhales of pure ecstasy escaped their mouths before they collapsed onto the bed shuddered and panting. After several passionate kisses, Ko laid down behind her and wrapped her body in his arms.

"Damn baby, that was incredible," she cooed while nestling into his arms and chest.

"Yeah, I just wish we weren't sneaking around in your brother's house to be together."

"You have to admit, it's kinda fun, babe. I mean here we are like two horny teenagers all because my brother has such a massive ego. Besides," Lexi began after turning and looking into his eyes, "the last thing 'Alexis the Great' needs to see is my car at your place."

"Yeah, I know" Ko replied while gazing into her eyes and chuckling. "We do need to sit him down and tell him though, honey."

"I know, baby, and when the time is right we will. We made each other a promise, remember?"

"Yes, I do remember, beautiful," Ko said before leaning down and kissing her soft, puckered lips.

Their kiss lasted for several moments before she lay back down and resumed her position in his arms.

"Ko?"

"Yes love?"

"Tell me what happened in Miami," she said after some hesitation.

"I'd rather Alex told you what happened."

"But that's the problem, Ko. Alex won't open up to me and he barely even mentions Simone or our parents anymore. He walks around with a massive chip on his shoulder and dares anyone to touch it. I know his depression is related to the guilt he carries with him. I just wish he'd let it go. It's like someone tore pages out of a book and now, no one can read those parts of the story."

"I know, baby. I love Alex like a brother and I know he's hurting, even though he denies it. He cheated death in

73

South Beach but it came at a price. Simone's death combined with the deaths of your parents sent him over the edge and that's the reasons he fled to Japan. When he came back though, he was changed. He was even darker. The Alex we knew was gone for good."

"But Ko, you were there and you're his best friend in the world. Why won't he open up to you of all people?" she begged with tears in her eyes.

"Like I said earlier, baby, Alex has to tell you that. But if you search your heart, you'll find the answers you're seeking."

After a few moments of silent contemplation, Ko decided it was time to give his lover a little more insight into her brother's past.

"You know that Alex blames himself for Simone's death. The fact that he could do little to prevent it means nothing. Alex carries the weight of the world on his shoulders, right next to that chip you mentioned. I've seen Alex dissect a room full of men, some of them twice his size without breaking a sweat. The harder they hit, the more he likes it. He doesn't fear death. That's why he lives so close to the edge."

"Ko, is my brother suicidal?"

"I don't know," he responded in a near whisper. "I do know this. Since we were kids, we've been trained to do what we do, mastering all manner of fighting styles and weaponry. Your brother took it one step further. While we spent years mastering weapons, Alex spent them becoming one."

Ko's words sent chills up Lexi's spine. The thought of her brother's torments made tears flow from her eyes. She couldn't imagine how someone could keep so much pain bottled up inside. She wanted so much for the men in her life to open up and let her in, but they were both holding her at bay. Though she was a grown woman, they were still treating her like a little girl and she didn't know if it was for her own protection or if it was because they felt she wasn't ready for the truth. While part of Lexi was angry, it was only a small part. More than anything, she was afraid that Alex was going to self-destruct and like Miami, she wouldn't be there when he did.

"Do you ever think about your parents, Ko?"
"Every day since they died," he replied before pulling her even closer to him.
"I don't remember much about my mom and dad. Alex stopped talking about them years ago and Doc says the assassins tried to burn the house down. There weren't many pictures left after the fire was put out."
"I know what you mean, babe," he said before kissing her shoulder again. "It seems that everything we knew was stripped from us in a hail of bullets and gunfire, yet look at us now... all trained assassins. How ironic..."
"Yes it is, baby," she replied before closing her eyes and drifting off to sleep.

Later that afternoon in Aspen, Alex reluctantly entered the office of Dr. Constance R. Willows, resident psychologist. She was a voluptuous and shapely, fair-skinned woman who was a blend of French-Canadian, American Indian, and some African American sprinkled in for flavor. Her career began as Doc's protégé, a role which she happily accepted, even though at times she found herself afraid for her life. Though she'd grown accustomed to Alex's behavior, Constance hated the way he stood silently by the window staring off into space. It wasn't very therapeutic and it gave her mind too much time to wander. She was a professional first and foremost, but she was also a woman who couldn't ignore her attraction to him. The tailor-made suits were one thing, but she was surprised at how much sexier this new rugged look was. He didn't bother pulling his hair back and his beard was thicker than normal. Seeing Alex this relaxed made her wish he would sit down so that she could straddle him and help him release all his pinned up frustration.

Her attraction, however, was marred by the fact that over time she had grown to fear his darker side. Constance kept reminding herself that beneath the glossy veneer of money, designer clothes, and sports cars beat the heart of a trained killer. His ability to hide behind his façade made Alex her most enigmatic client. His mind was like a maze; full of twists, turns, and dead ends. In the years that she had been treating him, Constance had watched him develop an unhealthy detachment from his emotions. In fact, he made it his business to show almost no emotion at all. The only exceptions were his love for his sister and his hatred of Doc. He managed to block his feelings for Constance, even though she knew what was in his heart. She was afraid that his suppression was slowly causing him to lose touch with reality. The silence was unbearable.

"It's been quite a while since the last time we met, Alex," she said while studying his body language.
"I've been busy," he replied while leaning against the window frame.
"Is that so? What have you been up to?"
"The usual."
"You know Alex," she began while wiping her rose tinted glasses with a soft cloth, "these sessions would go much smoother if you actually talked to me instead of talking at me."

"I've never been a big talker, Constance. You should know that by now."

"I know that you talk when you want to. I also know that if you don't start to open up about what's inside you, it's going to consume you."

"How do you know it hasn't?"

"I don't know if you won't tell me."

"Guess we're at a stalemate then, huh?" he asked in his usual nonchalant tone.

"We don't have to be."

Alex turned around and leaned against the wall next to the window with his legs crossed at the ankle and his arms folded across his chest. Though he was looking in Constance's direction, he wasn't looking directly at her which irritated her even more. Plus, she could that he was already on the defensive. This meant modifying her approach in order to reach him.

"Your avoidant personality isn't going to get us anywhere."

"What do you want to know?" he asked in a voice that was barely above a whisper.

"I want to know what you're thinking right now at this very moment."

"I think my little sister is fucking my best friend."

"Okay...I wasn't ready for that," she replied, clearly caught off guard. "That thought seems to bother you. Why?"

"Because she's my sister and Ko is too much like me."

"You mean he's a playboy?"

"No...not exactly, and I'm not a playboy," Alex replied abruptly, this time looking directly at her. "He and I are in the same line of work. It's not the life I want for my sister. She deserves better."

"Maybe I am a little naïve, but I'd think that based on your personality, you'd want a man like yourself to marry your sister. Am I wrong?"

"That's flattering for fathers, not older brothers."

"You said Ko was a lot like you. Are you afraid he'll break her heart?"

"I'm afraid that one day I'm gonna to have to tell her that he isn't coming home. I can't protect her from that pain if she insists on defying my wishes."

"Why do you still think that it's your job to protect her even though she's a grown woman?" she pressed, sensing a break-through in their communication.

"It always has been."

Constance was taken aback by his conviction. She couldn't remember the last time Alex showed this much emotion or attention during their sessions. She was so used to him being elusive that she had to think fast on her feet to avoid another shut down.

"Have you communicated this to Lexi? Does she know your true feelings about her dating your best friend?"

"No and she doesn't need to. It'll just make her more persistent in trying to convince me that she knows what she is doing and push them closer together. I really don't have time for that now."

"Why not, Alex? Isn't she here with you on Spring Break?"

"Not for long. She'll be leaving soon."

"Is it by her choice or by your demand?" she pressed sensing that real progress was near.

"Does it matter?"

"Yes it does. It's been you and Alexandria for a very long time, Alex. You've done your job. She's a grown woman on the verge of an exciting new career. Why are you so unwilling to let go?"

Without answering, Alex stood up, turned around, and started looking out the window again. Instinctively, she could feel him putting up another wall in his ever expanding maze. Her mind raced while trying to find a way to keep the door open before he managed to shut it again.

"Tell me about your nightmares, Alex. Alex?"

"Do you know what it's like to live in fear?" he began in a tone that sent shivers up her spine. "Do you know what it's like to have everything stripped from you in the blink of an eye?"

"No, I can't say that I do."

"Well I do. I spent the first half of my life afraid that one day the boogey man would come back for me and my sister."

"You said you spent the first half of your life in fear. What have you done with the second half of your life?"

"I became the boogey man," he replied in a tone so icy she thought the temperature in the office had dropped.

"How has that worked for you?"

"Read the newspaper."

"I have. How does it feel, Alex?"

"How does what feel?" he asked, growing more irritated by her intrusive questioning.

"How does it feel to take a person's life? I mean for a moment, you hold them in the balance between life and death. Do you like playing God?"

"I don't play God," he uttered rather callously.

"Then what do you call it?"

"I like to think of what I do as balancing the scales between justice and vengeance."

"Don't you mean retribution, Alex?"

"No. Retribution is enacted by due process of the law. What I do is administer a form of justice to those who think they're untouchable."

"Why vengeance, Alex?"

"There comes a time," he began after turning around, "when men are so far above the law that they can become shielded by it. My job is to go behind the shield and do what the law can't. I don't make the rules. I simply pull the trigger."

"How does it make you feel when you exact vengeance?"

"I get back a piece of what I've lost."

At that moment, a timer sounded signaling the end of what Constance believed to be a successful session, the first quite a while. For the first time in years, she was able to peel back some of the layers and begin to see Alex for what he really was; an angry but scared little boy whose innocence was stolen. There were so many more questions that she needed to ask in order to break down the walls and finally begin his healing process. However, there were other questions she had which were not a part of his healing process. They were a part of her own. Though Constance battled valiantly against the urge to ask, she had to know the truth.

"Can I ask you a question off the record?"

"Sure."

"Do you ever think about us?"

Alex's first impulse was to say "no," but he hesitated. Like a movie trailer, scene-after-scene began playing in his mind. The first was of him sitting on the office sofa with Constance on his lap. His hands gripped her thick thighs and voluptuous ass as she fed him her round tits and chocolate colored nipples. With her walls clamped onto his shaft like a vice, he guided her up and down while fighting the urge to explode deep inside her. The next flashback was of Constance lying on the hood of his Aston Martin. With her skirt around her waist and her creamy thighs spread wide, Alex pounded her pussy while squeezing her soft, bouncing tits. The heat from the hood warmed her back and ass while his thrusting dick sent chills up her spine. His final flashback almost sent a shudder up his spine. Alex was lying on his bed with Constance perched between his legs. Her soft, pink tongue and tender lips sucked and kissed his swollen head her while her hand pumped his shaft like the pistons in his coupe. Before he could catch his breath, her hand and head were moving up and down his shaft in unison making torrents of his thick, creamy cum splash into the back of her throat.

"No," he managed finally.
"You're lying!"
"No, I'm not."
"Yes, you are!" she fired back defiantly.
"How do you know?"
"It took you too long to answer, Alex. When you're certain of your answer, you fire it off as quickly as you do your gun. But when you hide something, there's an instant of hesitation. I know you're trained to hide your emotions and that includes lying to me. But no one, not even the best actor can fake what we shared."
"You're right," he began after conceding defeat. "What we shared was real, but it was forbidden and you know it."
"Why, Alex? Why is it forbidden? Why do you deny what you know your heart truly desires?"
"I've told you, Constance. Being with me is dangerous on so many levels. The agency is monitoring you and if they sense that you're compromised..."

"Do you think they would send someone like you to kill me?" she pleaded from the depths of her soul.

"They might."

"If they ordered me to be killed, would you pull the trigger?" she asked, nervously awaiting his response.

When he didn't answer, icy chills began racing up and down her spine. They were so intense that Constance had to rub her arms to stop the shivering. She wanted to believe in her heart that there was no way that the same man who had made such passionate love to her could be capable of killing her too. But as she looked at Alex, Constance remembered that this was the same man who was sleeping with a woman just to punish her husband. He had no emotional attachment to Tisha at all. Constance had no way to knowing if Alex would really take her life or not. She also began questioning whether or not he'd been brainwashed into losing his emotional attachment to her as well. The air in the office suddenly became cold and thin. The walls all around her began closing in. She was trapped with a killer. *Who would hear her or even know she was gone before it was too late?* Constance stumbled while back-pedaling and before she knew it, she crash landed on the sofa. This was it; the moment she'd feared the most. Alex had seduced her and now he was going to kill her. Before she knew it, sweat was pouring beneath her blouse.

"Calm down before you stroke out!" Alex shouted when he noticed her hyper-ventilating.

"Calm down? Calm down?!! Did you hear what you said?"

"Yes, I heard what I said and what I didn't say. Do you honestly think I'd let anything happen to you?" he asked in disbelief.

"Would you, Alex? What would you do if they said I was compromised? Would you pull the trigger?"

"I promise you that nobody, especially me would ever harm you. And if they tried, they'd have to come through me first."

"You promise?" Constance asked, searching for assurance in his eyes.

"I'll never let anyone hurt you. I promise."

"You told the truth that time," she replied with tears in her eyes and a smile on her face. "Is love totally forbidden for you, Alex?"

"It's not advisable."

Constance knew from past experience that it didn't take long for Alex to shut down and for the walls to go back up. It was his nature to keep building them stronger and taller than before. She searched for words as he leaned on the windowsill looking outside into the bright blue sky. She wanted desperately to go to him, hold him, and chase whatever fears he had away. In her heart of hearts though, Constance knew he wouldn't allow it. Alex seemed bound and determined to shoulder his guilt and pain alone.

"When will I see you again?"

"I'll call to schedule," he replied.

"I hope you do."

"One more thing before you go, Alex and depending on how you respond, I'll know what I should do next."

"Ok, shoot."

"Tell me that you don't love me. Tell me that I imagined everything we had and that none of it was real. Tell me it was a lie. Tell me that you don't want me and I'll walk away forever."

"I can't," he replied after a long silence that had Constance on the edge of her sanity.

She needed to hear the truth, his truth. She needed to know that somewhere in the dark caverns of his soul was a light that shined for her and her alone. She didn't have to question whether or not he lied, because she knew the answer. Alex was telling the truth. The look in his eyes and the pounding of his heart had betrayed him. He was still deeply in love with her, but his fear and uncertainty was keeping them apart.

"Do you remember the poem you wrote for me?"
"Of course I do."
"Forbidden yet hidden, yes my love is true. How can my life go on when I'm still in love with you? Do you remember that?"
"Of course I remember," Alex replied with a grin. "I still have the original in my bedroom."
"Just checking," she replied with a loving, tender smile.

Alex turned and stared into her eyes briefly before exiting her office. She stood in the window with her palm pressed firmly to the smoked glass as his Triple Black, Dodge Challenger roared out of her driveway. That night as he lay in bed, his sleep was once again haunted by horrific images of her face flashing in his mind. "Simone," he murmured while tossing and turning; so much that his body was becoming entangled in the covers.

Panic set in when he and Ko rounded the corner and he looked into her face.

What the hell are you doing here?

Suddenly, everything around him went silent except the sounds of a wailing engine and screeching tires. By the time he reached her, it was already too late. Three of the shots had struck Simone in her chest. Ko returned fire killing two of the Explorer's passengers and wounding the driver. Meanwhile, Alex's salty tears rained down on her mocha-colored face as she lay cradled in his trembling arms.

"No! No! *NO!*" he cried when he sat up in the bed and ripped the red satin sheet in half.

Still in a deep trance with his eyes half opened, Alex panned the empty room. It wasn't empty though, and he wasn't in his home. He was sitting on a sidewalk in Miami with his dead lover in his arms. Tears streamed down his face as he struggled for air.

"Alex, are you okay?" Lexi whispered when she opened the door and saw him.

She cringed when she saw his horrific display. His sweat-drenched hair was matted to face with only the whites of his eyes and gritted teeth showing. He was trapped somewhere between sleep and consciousness, totally unable to discern his surroundings.

"I'm sorry I didn't protect you, baby," he repeated between shallow breaths.
"Snap out of it, Alex," Lexi begged in a soft voice. "It wasn't your fault. You didn't know what was going to happen."
"I didn't protect you, baby...I'm so sorry," he repeated while clinching the covers in his fists.

With her hands covering her mouth and tears streaming down her face, Lexi watched and listened in dismay when he began to cry her name out over-and-over again.

"Simone! Simone! Simone!"

For the next few minutes, Lexi cowered on the floor near the door watching Alex be engulfed by this mental and emotional torture.

"SIMON! You bastard, I'm gonna fucking kill you!" he cried before snapping his head back and releasing an ear-splitting cry.

Suddenly, his arms went limp and his body slumped back onto the bed. Minutes later, Alex sat up, brushed the hair out of his eyes, and looked around the room. When he saw the shreds that used to be his covers, he looked up at his sobbing sister.

"I can't shake it, Lexi. She's dead because of me."
"You didn't kill her, Alex. Simon did."
"If I had just…"
"There was nothing you could do, Alex," she interrupted, trying to console his tormented heart.

For the next few hours, they cried silently at opposite ends of the massive California King. Four days later, at Lynn's request, Alex returned to the hotel. With disappointment on his face and at a loss for words, he sat on the couch watching while she scrambled about the suite packing her belongings. She barely said a word as she stuffed clothes into her bags, pausing only long enough to put her hair up in a ponytail. Her body language and silence said it all. Even though she was smiling on the outside, Lynn was crushed on the inside.

"I don't see why you have to leave. I mean… what are you going back to?"
"As much as I'd like to stay Alex, we both know I can't. I have no money, no job, or friends here. At least back

home I can stay with my sister and continue on my old job until I can get into med school. I have faith that things will work out," she announced proudly, even though she was holding back tears.

"I could help you. I have connections locally. You'd be working in no time. Besides that..."

"And where would I live, Alex, here at the hotel?"

"Sure, why not?" he asked stopping short of offering his own home.

"Honey, I don't know if you've noticed, but I can't afford all this. I rented this room for a couple nights just to get away until I tied up my dad's loose ends. When I called the front desk and was told I owed nothing, my heart dropped because I felt like God was really smiling on me."

"Maybe He is. That being said, why not stay? You may find that you like it here."

"I'd like that Alex, but I don't wanna wear out my welcome. And between you and me, I know it was you that paid for all this, and I promise I'll get every penny back to you."

"I didn't do it to obligate you to repay me, Lynn," he said after gently taking her hand in his.

"Then why did you do it?" she asked, frozen in time by the softness of his touch.

His touch. I was so pure, natural, and peaceful that she found herself both relaxed and afraid at the same time.

"I did it because... because... because I care."

"You care? Alex, you don't even know me. How can you care so much for a complete stranger?"

"I'd like the time to find out."

A single tear ran down her face when she looked into his eyes. The sincerity of his words and the warmth of his hand had her floating on air. Before either of them realized it happened, they were locked in a passionate kiss. For those seemingly endless moments as their lips touched, tongues danced, and hands explored, all their cares disappeared. The world that had initially stood still suddenly ceased to exist. The only sounds they could hear were the rhythmic beats of their hearts. With her eyes still closed, Lynn exhaled from deep within her soul. Stepping back, she looked at Alex and took him in once again. *Why now?* she herself over and over again. She searched his eyes for the answer but found a loving, tender gaze instead. She wondered what was going through his mind but dared not ask. Lynn found herself drawn to him like a moth to a flame. *This is dangerous,* she tried to tell herself, even though her body was calling him.

"That felt so natural," Alex whispered while staring into Lynn's eyes.

It had been ages since he'd felt such peace. Although he knew he couldn't force her to stay, Alex wasn't content to just let her go either. He continued watching Lynn while she seemingly floated throughout the room. He was so caught up in the moment that he could barely make out what she was doing, even though she was only a few feet from him.

"My address in Cincinnati is on this slip of paper," she said before shoving it in the front pocket of his jeans. "Send me a copy of the bill and I promise to get you your money."
"I told you, that wasn't necessary. Sometimes our faith is tested and at the end of our struggles, that faith is rewarded."

"Thank you, Alex. I'll remember that."
"Since I have your address, can I visit you some time?"
he asked before gently taking her hand in his.
"You'd better. And when you do dinner is on me."

Minutes later, after carrying her bags to the lobby, Alex
stood on the curb and watched Lynn's taxi disappear.
The miles ticked slowly away on his odometer as his
Jaguar XKR-S sped up Interstate 10 outside Denver.
With his head resting against the black Ricaro seat, Alex
listened to Phil Collins and tried to drown out the voices
in his head. He was thinking and feeling things that his
mind and body had forgotten. He was so accustomed to
being alone that he'd stopped desiring a woman's
intimate touch. Sex was just a passing fancy to occupy
his time. His relationship with Tisha proved that. Lynn
was different, though. For the second time since Simone
died, his heart was crying out for a woman; this woman
he barely knew. That night as he lay in bed, Alex was
glad to be alone, even though Tisha was blowing his
phone up. *What's wrong with you Alex? Her perfume is
lingering in the air and she's never even been here,* he
thought to himself while staring at the ceiling.

Chapter 4

One week later, Port au Prince, Haiti

Jean Paul La duc was once one of Port au Prince's most prominent business owners. Not only was he well known and highly respected in that province, he was also a trusted friend to the citizens of the surrounding boroughs. Speaking perfect English peppered with a French accent made him the ideal salesman. Trading in fine fabrics, electronics, and exotic foods, La duc was able to accumulate a great deal of wealth, which helped him establish numerous international business ties. In turn, these ties opened Haiti's shores and majestic beauty to the rest of the world.

In the years since the great earthquake however, much of Haiti's majesty had all but vanished. Despite the efforts of numerous humanitarian agencies, much of the island country still lay in ruins. Sickness, disease, and death had stripped away most of the life that once existed there. Widespread looting and theft became the norm. Rich or well-off Haitians abandoned what was left of the island, taking with them what they could and leaving the rest; mostly memories of the past. For the less fortunate, the outlook was far grimmer. They were left behind and forced to live amid the chaos and destruction. Their desperation made them prey to various forms of exploitation by foreigners and even their countrymen alike.

Seeking to reestablish his own prominence and wealth in the disaster's wake, La Duc once again used his international ties to establish a new business: human trafficking. Using his good looks, charm, and influence,

La Duc convinced desperate parents and 'eligible' orphans, mostly young girls, that he could find temporary or even permanent homes for them away from Haiti. Their new families would care for them until order was reestablished and afterwards, they could return home. Believing that a better life awaited, innocent youth were entrusted into La Duc's care. But instead of being sent to loving homes as he promised, many were sold into slavery. Rich clients from around the world paid him thousands for healthy boys and girls to become indentured servants. The majority, however, were sold into prostitution rings and ultimately became sex slaves. Though outraged, the world at large could do very little to stop such operations and as a result, La Duc and men like him became very wealthy.

At 4:00AM in a deserted borough outside Port au Prince, La Duc was preparing to strike a deal with four new clients; a pair of Asians and two Americans, one black and one white. Amidst the chaos and destruction, La Duc and his eager clients stood dressed in tailored suits and expensive leather footwear. There were also six other men in army fatigues guarding a white container truck.

"You've seen the merchandise, Mr. Smith," La Duc began while lighting a Cohiba, "now it's time to deal."
"My Asian friends want to purchase the older girls. My friend and I will sort through the rest. Whatever we don't want, we'll dispose of."
"Let me assure you and your clients that they're purchasing the finest that Haiti has to offer. Having sampled a few of them myself, I can certainly attest to their quality."

Behind the gold-capped teeth, two-carat diamond earrings, and a cloud of cigar smoke was a heartless jackal; a pedophile who sold his own people for profit. Mr. Smith and his counterparts looked on as La Duc and his guards exchanged smiles and laughs. Along with their fatigues, they carried Russian AK-47 assault rifles and wore red berets. Meanwhile inside the truck were fifty frightened boys and girls who had no idea what awaited them on the other side of those locked doors.

"What's with all the hardware?" Mr. Smith asked in his deep, thundering voice while studying the entourage.
"Some people don't approve of my business," La Duc replied after looking and smiling at the rugged-looking sentries behind him.
"Fair enough," Mr. Smith replied before snapping his fingers which summoned his three briefcase carrying associates.

Smith's Caucasian associate held his briefcase flat in his massive palm so that he could easily access it.

"You know what I hate most, La Duc?"
"What's that my burly American friend?" he asked while staring at Mr. Smith's broad back and shoulders.
"I hate animals who exploit their own people, especially kids."

Smith reached inside the briefcase and pulled out a chrome-plated Bulldog .44 magnum. When he turned back around, he quickly emptied all six chambers into La Duc's chest. As his limp body slumped to the ground, Smith's America partner pulled a sawed-off, pump-action Ruger from his blazer and fired two shots, blasting the chests of two men nearest the rear of the truck. Moving with synchronized precision, the Asians dropped their suitcases, thrust their hands into their

blazers, and pulled identical pairs of .45 caliber
Berrettas. With gunfire erupting all around them, fifty
children clung to each other while crying out in fright.
Within seconds, every sentry had fallen, not one of them
having fired a single shot.

"What do we do with these kids, Mike?" asked the
Caucasian brute as he emptied smoking shells from the
shotgun's barrels.
"Nothing. They're safer in the truck. We leave'em inside
until we get to the embassy. Relief workers can find their
families or put them in real homes."
"What about these guys?" asked one of the Asians while
motioning towards the bullet riddled corpses.
"We leave the trash with the trash. It's poetic justice.
Rick, you drive the truck. Nick, you ride shotgun. Gary
and I will follow in the Hummer. Don't stop 'til you
reach the embassy. This monster may have dudes on
point watching his back. Let's move."

Within seconds, the container truck and the Hummer
were rumbling across the cracked and cratered Haitian
roads. The thirty mile trip to the embassy seemed to take
forever as four armed, tense, and weary men kept
watchful eyes on the roads ahead of and behind them.
Meanwhile in the back of the truck, fifty frightened
children ages five to sixteen sat huddled in silence while
being bounced up and down over the rugged terrain.
Their ride, like that of their drivers, seemed to last an
eternity. Overcome with fear, the younger children
continued crying which made the older children even
more restless. With the little light that was available,
they sought comfort in each other's faces but found
none. Suddenly, the truck stopped. Doors opened and
closed. Hearts stopped pounding and tears dried up.

Horror set in. After a few tense moments, laughter could be heard all around them, and without warning, the rear doors flung open. There waiting for the children were open arms and smiling faces. Relief workers and embassy officials rushed them out of the truck and into shelters where they were fed, clothed, and given medical attention. The four men and the Hummer disappeared and were never seen or heard from again.

Two days later. Cincinnati, Ohio.

On a warm spring afternoon inside *Mitchell's Salon and Day Spa*, Lynn and her sister Ni'Chelle were lounging in a pair of large massage chairs. Dressed in white robes with matching towels wrapped around their heads, they sipped Pinot Grigio and laughed while soaking their feet in whirlpool baths. Though Ni'Chelle had a lighter skin tone and was slightly heavier through the hips, both women were strikingly gorgeous. They relished in the fact that some of the patrons and even the staff wondered how they could afford the pampering that they were receiving.

"Lynn, stop yo lyin," Ni'Chelle demanded while staring at her sister. "You mean to tell me that this man, Alex, paid your hotel bill, prepaid for you to have twenty spa treatments, and you barely even know him? You lyin!"
"I'm not lying," Lynn replied while laughing at the insinuation.
"And I bet you want me to believe you didn't give up no ass, right?"
"Nope, I sure didn't," replied Lynn with a smile while the mechanical fingers massaged her back and buttocks.
"And you didn't suck his dick either, huh?"
"Girl, hell no! I told you, I barely know him. He let me cry myself to sleep in his arms. Afterwards, he laid me down on the bed and left a note on my pillow."

"Then that nigga's in love!" Ni'Chelle declared after looking around the spa and settling back in her massage chair.

"What did you say?"

"You heard me, Lynn. He's in love with you."

"No he's not," she replied in shock while sipping her wine. "Besides, he doesn't even know me and I don't know him. He's just being nice."

"Nice? Honey, nice is opening doors and complimenting your hair when it's tight. This man is feeling you, Lynn. Haven't you heard of love at first sight?"

"Oh, you mean like you and Kris?" Lynn asked jokingly.

"Girl, that wasn't love. That was lust," Ni'Chelle replied while holding her glass out to be refilled. "Oh, I ain't trippin 'cause Kris could put it down in the bedroom," she replied with clinched thighs and puckered lips. "But love wasn't on that nigga's mind, not even after five years and two kids. But I ain't bitter, girl 'cause when we had fun, we had fun! Whew!"

They shared another heart-felt laugh as Lynn's mind continued contemplating Ni'Chelle's revelations. She was convinced that she was living out some sort of fantasy. This handsome, suave, well-dressed stranger in the *007 coupe* was sweeping her off her feet. Lynn replayed their kiss over-and-over while Ni'Chelle was busy making her case.

"Lynn, when was the last time Terrence sent you flowers?"

"Terrence who?" she asked sarcastically.

"Exactly. Alex has sent you flowers four times since you got home. You got a damned botanical garden growing in your bedroom. If it was me, I'd have stayed my ass in Denver, shot you the deuces, and been like peace!"

95

"Chelle, you're a fool!" Lynn declared as her sister sat there with her lips poked out and holding up the peace sign.

"I'm for real, girl. I'd be riding in his Aston Martin by day and riding his dick at night. You think he'd like my fat ass?"

"Girl, you ain't hardly fat, but you could give me some of them hips through," Lynn said while poking Ni'Chelle's thick, light-chocolate thigh.

"And you could give me some of them titties," Ni'Chelle replied before pinching Lynn's nipple through her robe.

The happy siblings continued their banter until Ni'Chelle glanced outside the door and became enraged. Standing next to a brand new burgundy, S-Class Mercedes on 22" Giovanni rims was their sister-in-law. Phyllis was a gorgeous, short, mulatto sister with a gorgeous figure and long auburn hair. Though Ni'Chelle constantly warned him against it, their brother Desmond was determined to give Phyllis all the things she wanted and in her case, that was everything! Over the past six years, he'd amassed a small fortune hustling coke and heroin on the streets of Cincinnati, Dayton, Covington, and Indianapolis. Now, in the wake of him receiving over a million dollars from his dead father's estate, Phyllis was living the life of a celebrity. With her head held high and a swing in her hips, she strutted across the lot towards the door dressed in her white DKNY two-piece suit, matching stilettos, and a white Versace purse under her arm.

"Your brother's high priced ho is on the way in," Ni'Chelle scoffed while leaning towards Lynn with her drink in hand.

"Let it go, Chelle. We're here to relax, not fight."

"Oh, I'ma let it go. But if that bitch starts with me, I'ma let her fake Mariah Carey-lookin' ass have it."

"Lynn and Ni'Chelle?" Phyllis gasped while standing at the counter signing in, "I didn't know they took food stamp cards here."
"I thought they took the trash out on Saturdays. But here you are, so I guess not," Ni'Chelle fired back.

Lynn immediately sat up in her chair and stared nervously at Ni'Chelle who was standing up in the whirlpool with her fist around the neck of the wine bottle. To maintain some level of decorum and to prevent a scene, Lynn quickly deescalated the situation.

"Phyllis," she began while gently tugging at Ni'Chelle's robe, "girl, you're rocking that outfit and those shoes are definitely on point."
"Thank you, girl. Dez took me shopping when he settled big daddy's accounts."
"You mean cleaned 'em out, bitch," Ni'Chelle mumbled before sitting back down.
"He even bought me a new Mercedes. What did y'all get?"

Lynn thought about her trip to Denver and found herself fighting back the urge to tackle Phyllis and beat her head against every tub and basin in the room. Determined to remain dignified however, she took Ni'Chelle by the hand and squeezed.

"We have each other."
"That's so sweet, Lynn. I knew you had all the class in the family, girl. Well I have to go ladies. We're flying out to Vegas later and it takes work to maintain this beauty."
"You should have let me beat that bitch's ass," Ni'Chelle growled when Phyllis walked away.

"She ain't worth it, Chelle. Besides, how much fighting were you gonna to do in a bath robe?"

"Sheeeiiit! I'm a hood bitch. All I need is some Vaseline on my face and it's on and poppin' up in here!"

Lynn shook her head and smiled when her sister grabbed another bottle of wine from the ice bucket and refilled their glasses. Her mind continued to race while thinking about what she'd heard earlier. *Is Alex in love with me?* she asked herself when the attendant turned the whirlpools off and escorted them to the rear of the salon for body massages and mud baths.

In West Chester, which is north of Cincinnati, two other sisters were engaged in a conversation that wasn't quite as jovial. Tisha and Dawn were at the kitchen table counting and arguing over numerous stacks of money. In addition to the cash, there were four kilos of cocaine wrapped in cellophane on the counter next to a digital scale.

"Simon is pissed at you and Roger," Tisha declared while rifling through a stack of one-hundred-dollar bills.

"Pissed at us? Why?" Dawn asked, seemingly in shock.

"You're taking too long to move this shit and your money keeps coming up short. I'm getting tired of covering for you, Dawn. What the fuck is your problem?"

"We ain't hardly comin' up short. And as far as the time it's taking, tell your husband that we have to watch our asses down here too. We don't have the kind of protection he has in Colorado. The cops ain't on our side."

"There's the phone," Tisha replied while nodding towards the phone. "I'm sure he's up and would like nothing more than to hear that bullshit."

"It's okay, girl...I'm good," Dawn stuttered while trying to maintain count. "Once we unload these four keys tonight, I'll have all the money and you can get back to Denver."

"Yeah, great. I get to leave here and drive back to Denver with over four million dollars in my trunk. I have to make pickups in Chicago, Kansas City, Omaha, and Little Rock on the way back. Did I mention that I'm driving alone?"

"Yeah, Tish, I know. But it's all good, right?"

"All good? Are you serious, Dawn? I've got a good mind to take all this money and disappear."

"You can't do that! Simon would kill us all! Don't even think that crazy shit!" she pleaded with her skin crawling.

Dawn stared across the table at Tisha who seemed poised to sign all their death warrants. She'd already lost count and her hands were sweating. She desperately needed to regain her composure and that only way to do that was to change the subject.

"What's Simon going to do since his two primary connects are dead?"

"I don't know, girl. He flipped when he saw that surveillance video from the New York hit. Can you imagine a doorman flipping out and killing seven people like that?"

"Doorman?" Dawn quipped, as if surprised by Tisha's ignorance. "That was a hit-man!"

"And how do you know that, Ms. CSI?"

"Girl, that shit is all over the news. How'd he get the video anyway?"

"Don't worry about that. But if you keep fucking this money up, your video will be all over the news next."

"Stop talking like that, Tisha! We ain't fuckin' up no money! Do you think we wanna have Simon all up in here trippin'? FUCK NO! We ain't crazy."

Again, Dawn cringed at the thought of what might happen to her and the family if Simon really was mad at them. He'd made it clear years ago that he wouldn't hesitate to kill them if the money wasn't right or they sold him out. Simon's words, "Mi kill yu dead, yu ere me, chile?" resonated so loudly inside Dawn's head that she lost her concentration. She began questioning her reasons for being involved in this madness in the first place. She desperately wanted to believe that she started dealing for the right reasons. All she wanted was a better life for her family and moving a little dope now and then was easy enough. It was a simple arrangement. Move a little here and there, make a little extra money on the side, and live the good life.

Sure... this is the good life, she thought while looking around her new, custom-built home.

Dawn and Roger were the envy of all their friends. They had the big house, the nice cars, and bragging rights to the family vacations they took every couple of months. Unlike most of their contemporaries, they had money in a few different banks and because their brother-in-law was footing the bills, very little debt. The Tyler family wasn't struggling like many others she knew. On the surface, it was all perfect. No one had to know that they lived in constant fear of arrest, embarrassment, and most of all Simon. That fear made it *so* difficult for Dawn to relax, let alone sleep. She'd secretly begun taking Xanax and other medications in an attempt to get some peace.

There's enough loot for me and the family to run away, she thought to herself while staring at all the money spread out on the kitchen table.

"Got-dammit Dawn, are you listening to me? You're mixing the bills again! That's why your counts are so fucked up! Pay attention!"
"Sorry, Tish...I need a minute," she gasped before getting up from the table and running upstairs to the master bathroom.

There in the medicine cabinet was her saving grace. She quickly downed two pills and chased them with a glass of water. *You can do this,* she thought, a pep talk she'd given herself hundreds of times in the past. Her buckling knees and gurgling stomach forced her to seek refuge atop the toilet lid where she sat massaging her throbbing temples.

Denver, Colorado

It was midmorning and Dr. Willows was welcoming another client, Warren Jeffries, to her Aspen office. As was the norm with members of '*The Agency*', she was methodical in her approach to dealing with them. She kept track of the time while silently observing his movements and mannerisms. What stuck out the most on this particular day was that Warren looked *so* drained. His ocean blue eyes were bloodshot and had dark circles underneath them. His normally cleanly-shaved face was covered by a scraggly beard and random stubble. To Constance's, he looked 10 to 15 years older than he actually was and smelled of alcohol. Her patience turned into deep concern while watching him rub his thighs from time to time and even fiddle with his watch. After a few more moments of observation, she decided to break the silence.

"So Mr. Jeffries, per your message, your nightmares have returned. You also reported that you had some recent panic attacks while in the field and as a result, you were almost killed."
"Yes," replied softly.
"I understand that you've resorted to drinking again. Is that correct?"
"Yes, it's all true," he began while staring blankly at his tan Timberland boots, "and please, call me Warren."
"Ok, Warren. First and foremost, are you alright? Were you hurt in any way?"
"No, I wasn't. Crossha... I mean Gary saved my ass."
"Tell me what happened, if you don't mind."
"The one thing that should never happen in the field; I froze up. I got the drop on a target and couldn't pull the trigger. My slip almost got the entire unit killed. I don't think I can stomach this anymore."
"How does your team feel about your latest episode?" she asked while scribbling on her notepad.
"Gary thinks I'm a fruitcake. He didn't want me anywhere near Haiti, and frankly, I didn't wanna go."
"What about the rest of the team?"
"Ballistic...I mean Big Mike thinks I need some time off and even offered to counsel me. And the twins...they don't take much of anything seriously. They suggested I go to Vegas and get laid. That's pretty typical of them, though. Alex is the only person who seems to understand."
"Alex...really?" she asked, barely able to hide her curiosity.
"Yes. He's been cool about helping me cope with it, especially since I almost got him killed eight months ago in Sao Paolo. In his own way, Alex really isn't a bad guy. He's just misguided."

"I see," Constance replied, attempting to disguise her interest in his assessment of Alex.

To date, Constance had never heard anyone speak this highly of her enigmatic ex-lover. As much as she wanted to delve into those details, she knew it was inappropriate. She needed to help Warren come to grips with his issues before he got himself or someone else killed.

"In your own words, tell me how this makes you feel, Warren."

"I feel like a liability," he replied after a long deep breath. "Guys who used to depend on me don't trust me. I haven't fired a gun in months. I can barely eat or sleep. And when I do, the nightmares get worse and worse."

"Do you still see images of your own funeral?"

"Yes. From time to time, we all do."

"I see," she replied before making more notes. "Tell me about your last nightmare."

"It wasn't a nightmare. It was more like a flashback."

"Ok then, tell me about your last flashback."

Warren took a long deep breath before closing his eyes. Three years ago, after serving four year tour as as a Navy SEAL, he was honorably discharged and from there, joined the Boston Police Department. The following year he was promoted to S.W.A.T. With his help and expertise, Boston's S.W.A.T. division quickly became the standard by which teams across the nation were measured. Then on one fateful night, Warren's team was deployed on a mission that left him scarred forever.

"I remember it like it was yesterday," he murmured while leaning forward on the sofa and becoming edgier with each passing moment.

A probation officer and two sheriff's deputies had gone to an address at an inner city tenement to perform a routine check on a recently freed felon. Unfortunately, they didn't know that this young man had resumed his illegal drug activity and had no plans on returning to prison because of it. What began as a mundane assignment quickly escalated into a blood-bath.

"Officer down with another taking fire!" was the frantic call that came over the wire. "Suspects are heavily armed! Requesting backup at..."

Additional shots rang out right before the transmission went dead. 911 dispatches became flooded with calls about two dead deputies and another taking fire. Within minutes, the streets at either end of the block were sealed off. Repeated attempts to negotiate with the shooters had failed. An unknown number of gunmen had seized control of the four story building, made hostages of the unlucky tenants, and were firing on officers and other first responders as they arrived on the scene. News crews from all over the city broadcasted the horrific events until dusk when the police forced them to vacate the area. A while later the order was given to cut power to the entire block. Just after midnight, police and S.W.A.T. units moved in and secured the two adjacent buildings and the one directly across the street. After the tenants were cleared out, trained snipers packing Remington 700 SPS night-vision equipped tactical rifles took positions on the opposite roof. Warren's strike team was positioned atop target building preparing to repel down and enter through four of the windows on the top floor. The snipers using kept watch while ground units with shields moved up the block from either side. Just after 2A.M., flash-bang grenades were shot into the building followed by the six man unit crashing through the windows, surprising the weary, unsuspecting gunmen.

Room-by-room, the team cleared the top floor while another team cleared the first. They took their lead from the snipers who were busy neutralizing any armed suspects careless enough to get too close to the windows. With the top floor cleared, Warren and his team moved slowly down the stairwell to the third floor. With the aid of his goggles and a carefully 'tilted mirror, he saw movement inside the unit down the hall to his left. Using hand signals and other non-verbal commands, he directed them to follow him and in seconds, they stormed the apartment.

"Police, throw down your weapons!" I yelled when we busted in.

Three gunmen were quickly neutralized by suppression fire before the four remaining threw down their guns and dropped to their knees. Two stray shots rang out from down the hall when a dark figure darted from one room, and locked himself in another.

"I got him!" Warren declared after raising the butt of his MP5N submachine gun to his shoulder and stalking down the hall.
"On you, partner!" a voice yelled from behind him.

Suddenly, a door flew open.

"'Get down!' I screamed when I heard that shotgun being cocked. The guy got off two shots and killed Matt instantly."

Slugs from the pump-action Mossberg obliterated Matt's vest and flung his lifeless body backwards down the hall. Stunned and filled with rage, Warren sprang to his feet, kicked the door in, and emptied his clip into the dark figure crouching in the tub. Moments later after the building was cleared and the power restored, they found the shooter. Lying dead in the shower was the bullet riddled body of a young black boy. Reports later revealed that he was only twelve-years old.

"'It was him or us,' they told me over and over again. After a lengthy Internal Affairs investigation, and months of bad P.R., I left the force. Shortly after that, I was recruited into 'The Agency'. Since that day, I've had to live with a murdered kid's blood on my hands."

Oh my God, Constance thought while sitting silently and listening to Warren relive those horrific events. Though he'd been her patient for years, Constance couldn't begin to imagine the magnitude of pain that he was living with, or the torment he was feeling until now. Sitting motionless with tears streaming down his face, Warren stared straight ahead at nothing in particular.

"I've seen combat in the Middle East, Asia, and even Russia. It took a night in Boston to screw my life up forever. In the past few months, I've had more panic attacks than I can remember, both in the field and at home. The first one was in Brazil with Alex. We'd be dead now if he hadn't shot the lights out in the room. I stood there frozen and watched while he disarmed and dismantled seven guys. Even though I almost got him killed, the only thing he said when he was done was, 'Keep your head in the game.'"

"That was it?" she asked in amazement.

"That was it. He's never even mentioned it again. Like I said, in his own way, he's been very supportive."

"Interesting."

"You seem shocked, doctor. Alex isn't the asshole he makes himself out to be. It's just the façade he hides behind."

I know, she thought to herself. "I appreciate your assessment of Alex, but this is your time, Warren. I think your panic attacks are directly related to PTSD beginning with your episode in Boston. You're going to have to come to grips with what happened and let it go. You have to forgive yourself and move on. You didn't wake up that morning with the intention of killing a 12 year-old boy or anyone else for that matter. Matt's death wasn't your fault either. It happened in the line of duty."

"You weren't there, Doc. You didn't look into his cold, dead eyes, but I did. I'll never forget what I saw. There was fear in those glassy eyes. He was somebody's son, somebody's brother, somebody's grandson, and I took him from them in a fit of rage. I snuffed out a kid's life. And as for Matt, he left behind an infant daughter and a grieving fiancé. He was my partner and it was my duty to watch his back. I failed."

"No Warren. He made a choice, and Matt responded to it. You all did."

At that moment, the buzzer sounded ending the session. Though he was relieved that he had a chance to speak candidly with Constance, Warren still had no resolution to his issues. In fact, the more he thought about it, the worse he felt. *How do I forgive myself for killing a child?* he asked himself over and over again while driving from

Aspen to Denver. That night while tossing and turning in his bed, an empty bottle of Jack Daniels fell from it and crashed to the floor. In his mind, faces began appearing in rapid succession. His dead partner, the young boy, the crying faces at both funerals, and finally the faces of fellow officers and numerous investigators kept swirling around in his head. Warren could hear their accusations followed by their cries of misery.

"It wasn't my fault," he groaned while kicking at the covers.

In a teary eyed rage, he sat up in the bed, pulled a revolver from the nightstand, and cocked it.

"Get out of my head!" he cried while holding the gun to his sweaty temple.

3:00 A.M., Lawrenceburg Indiana

Not long ago, the city of Lawrenceburg was a quiet and peaceful Midwestern town without much going for it except for Middle American charm and a wholesome rural atmosphere. That all changed when casino gambling was introduced to the city. Suddenly, the little town of Lawrenceburg became the new Mecca for Midwestern gambling. Located just over fifty miles west of Cincinnati, and even closer to the Kentucky border, Lawrenceburg welcomed would-be gamblers from as far away as Illinois and Pennsylvania. With numerous attractions along the casino strip, some began to calling it 'The Vegas of the Midwest.'

The latest attraction was the 'The Tiberius' resort and casino. With fifteen floors of luxury suites, fitness centers, pools, and spas, this resort was all about providing an experience unlike any other in the region.

The casino's gaming floor had several tables, rows of slots, a buffet-style restaurant, and live shows. It had all the makings of a Vegas-type atmosphere mixed with a lot of Midwestern charm. Conspicuous by their after five attire and the speed at which they were losing money, Tisha and Dawn sat at the Blackjack table downing *sex on the beach.'* Combined, they had lost well over seven thousand dollars in less than three hours.

"This is bullshit, Dawn. We've been here for hours and there's no sign of your marks."
"They'll be here, Tish," Dawn replied while trying to read the faces of the other players and study her cards.

Feeling confident about the jack and nine of diamonds in her hand, she threw another two hundred dollars onto the table.

"Twenty-one, house wins again," she heard before the smiling dealer scooped up her two-hundred dollars and the rest of the money she'd bet.
"Bitch, stop before you lose everything you have! If your friends aren't here in the next five minutes, I'm calling it a night."
"Relax, Tish," Dawn began before gulping the remainder of her of her fruity concoction. "Here they come now."

I don't believe this shit, Tisha thought when she turned around and looked at them. Sauntering towards her and Dawn was an entourage of young brothas dressed in sagging jeans, boots, throw back jerseys, and ball caps turned in various directions. Gold teeth lined their mouths while gaudy gold and fake diamonds hung from their ears, necks, and wrists.

"Whassup, Dee?" asked the short one in the front with the nappy beard. "Whuz had'nen shawtay?" he asked with a smirk while undressing Tisha with his glassy, lust-filled eyes.

"These are your buyers? Please tell me you're joking," she scoffed while shaking her head with her palm pressed against it.

"Whassup wit yo girl, Dee? Don't she know I'm Loco, the Midwest's finest?"

"It's cool, Loco," Dawn smiled, relieved that they'd finally arrived. "This is my sister, Simon's wife."

"Oh shit...my bad, shawtay," he replied, visibly shaken by the revelation.

There was a brief period of murmuring and whispering as the men studied the pair.

"Look, Loco, or whatever your name is. I need to apologize to you but there won't be any deals tonight. We're leaving."

"What-the-fuck?" he barked after quickly looking around at his confused entourage. "We got the loot and came all the way to Lawrenceburg and you tellin' me we ain't dealin'? Oh dat's straight bullshit!"

"Like it or not, Loco, we aren't dealing with you," Tisha replied calmly but sharply.

"Oh dat's some bullshit! Clearly you don't know who you fuckin' wit!" barked the tall light-skinned brother in the white, number 23 Chicago Bulls jersey and matching hat.

"It's you who doesn't know who you're fucking with. My husband could have you clowns killed by simply snapping his fingers. Judging by your appearance, I'm sure he'd agree that dealing with you is too risky."

"Risky? What-the-fuck is this bitch on, Loco?" demanded the short brother wearing the green, Boston Celtics number 33 throwback.

"Call me another bitch and I'll have you, your mother, and your grandmother killed. That's what I'm on *BITCH!* Where do a bunch of clowns like you come up with enough money to buy keys? Nobody in their right mind would deal with you. *Niggas* like you are just too hot and our business can't afford the liability. Just look at you."

"Dee! You gonna let this bitch roll on us like that?" Loco demanded with fire in his glassy eyes.

"She's the boss," Dawn responded, both disgusted and defeated.

"That's fucked up, Dee, but it's cool. We'll get our shit elsewhere. She just fucked it up for all of us. We were doubling up next trip."

"Doubling up?" Tisha asked half-laughing. "Nobody in their right mind would sell you clowns eight keys! You're hotter than firecrackers on the 4th of July! The cops and feds are probably watching you as we speak. You're too loud and too flashy. Your clothes are ridiculous and your jewelry is a joke. You're guys stick out like sore thumbs."

Dawn stood there in shock and ready to cry. She couldn't believe how easily her own sister had stepped in and undermined her in front of her customers. This business was all about respect, and Tisha had just snatched it away right in front of their eyes. Not only was this deal dead, the prospect of future dealings with Loco might be dead as well. *Eight keys,* she thought while Tisha continued insulting them. Dawn could barely raise her head, but knew she had to save face in order to retain what little respect she still had with both Loco and her sister.

"Look fellas, we girls are having a misunderstanding and need some time to talk. Give me a few days, and I'll make this right. We've done too much business to fall out like this."

"Look, Dee, I like you but yo girl is trippin! We came here to deal and she's spazzin, the-fuck-out!"

"I personally don't give a fuck what you came here to do, Loco!" Tisha barked with her hands on her hips and her neck rolling. "I said the deal is off!"

"I ain't talkin' to you, bitch! Stay in yo' place when grown folks is talkin'!"

"Loco! Tish! Chill-the-fuck out!" Dawn demanded when Tisha reached inside her purse. "I'ma handle this shit."

"You got a day, Dee," Loco barked before he and his entourage turned and walked away.

Dawn watched helplessly as her money and her freedom slipped right through her fingers. She turned around to confront Tisha who had already walked away. Minutes later, the pair was standing in the parking lot at the rear of Dawn's Cranberry Mercedes where they continued arguing while patrons and security looked on.

"Dawn, if you weren't my sister, I swear I'd blow your fucking brains out all over this parking lot! How could you be so careless?"

"What the fuck are you talking about, Tisha?"

"Look at them!" Tisha demanded while pointing at a pair of Chevy Suburbans riding on twenty six inch chrome wheels with paint jobs resembling one-hundred-dollar bills. "What person in their right mind intentionally brings that much attention to themselves?"

"They're a rap group, Tisha!"

"A rap group? Are you fucking serious? They're not even legitimate dealers? They're rappers pretending to be dope dealers so they can have street credibility! Niggas like that are dumb enough to think that they can live the lives they rap about. They're too damned obnoxious to be taken seriously. The cops are probably watching them 24/7 and you just tried to sell them four keys. If Simon knew, he'd have your head and as your sister, I wouldn't protest one damned bit!"

"How could you say something like that to me, Tisha?" Dawn asked with tears forming in her eyes. "Simon has never questioned me, and I know for a fact that Roger and I have made him millions while he's paid us nickels!"

"It doesn't matter how much you've made him. His main concern is what you'll end up costing him in the long run."

"That's bullshit and you know it. I can't believe you'd come at me like that, especially since my hard work keeps you driving Porsches and living in a mansion."

"I didn't pull you in Dawn; you volunteered," Tisha snapped viciously. "And last time I checked, if it wasn't for me, you'd be still living in the hood struggling to put your daughters through school. You couldn't afford to live like this without me."

"Since you're so high on the hog, what about our mother?" Dawn snapped back desperately.

"What about her? Thanks to me, she is a much better community than that rat trap you had her in."

"Tisha, what happened to you? Before you met Simon, you were a humble dental assistant who barely had a GED. Now you're all about the money; the queen of Colorado cocaine."

"And what about you Dawn? You're a fake ass nurse who got knocked up on a one night stand, found a sucker, and made him believe he got you pregnant. Does Roger even know the twins aren't his?"

"Does Simon know you aborted his child?" Dawn fired back abruptly.

"It wasn't Simon's," Tisha replied meekly as if shattered by what Dawn had thrown up in her face.

In her own pain, Tisha selfishly refused to acknowledge the pain she had just inflicted on her own sister. They sat in complete silence during the almost 80 mile journey from Lawrenceburg to West Chester. Upon arriving at Dawn's house, they exited the Benz and took separate entrances. Dawn listened tearfully while Tisha stormed through the house before slamming her bedroom door. After downing three shots of Vodka and two Valiums, Dawn sat sobbing in the bay window of the great room. Life as she knew it was spiraling out of control. There was nowhere to run and no one else to turn to. Her sister, her own flesh and blood was treating her like a stranger on the streets. Dawn had known for years that she needed to get out of this life before it was too late but had no clue how to do it.

Denver, Colorado

Later that morning, the city's local parks were teaming with happy children who were merrily running about playing with their parents, pets, and other kids. One pink jogging suit-clad little girl seemed to be having more fun than the rest. Her little legs churned as fast as they could while peddling her *Dora the Explorer* big wheel throughout the park. Her long, brown ponytail swung back and forth while close behind her was a golden-brown Pomeranian she called Ginger. With her chubby cheeks aglow with excitement, she peddled up to a happy couple who was cuddled up on a bench and grinned while leaping into the man's arms. After grabbing the sides of his head, she gleefully planted kisses on his cheeks. The couple took turns holding the happy toddler while the other tickled her pale, round belly.

Even with the windows of his black Yukon barely cracked, the burly driver could hear her laughter loud and clear. Sitting behind the tinted glass, he watched as the couple walked hand in hand behind the little girl, her big wheel, and Ginger. He tried to ignore the buzzing from the seat next to him, but as they faded out of view, it grew even louder.

"Report to the office. Delilah," was the message he read when he picked it up the I-Phone and read the text.

He started the engine and after looking for them again, sped off. A while later, the Yukon pulled into the underground garage of a high-rise office building in downtown Denver. It screeched to a halt next to a Chrysler 300C SRT8. At the rear of the silver sedan was Big Mike leaning against its trunk with his arms folded. The driver, who was both angry and intoxicated, exited the truck and walked around to its rear.

"Gabby took that T.P.O out for a reason, Gary. If you keep violating it, the court is gonna keep denying your visitation."
"Fuck that shit, Mike!" he barked while pacing back and forth behind their cars. "She has no right to keep me away from my baby!"
"And do you think stalking her is gonna make her give you visitation rights? Do you think the court is gonna let you to see Claire if you keep pulling stunts like this?"

"You don't fucking get it, Mike!" Gary yelled before punching out the Yukon's back window. "She has some jerk in my baby's life! That's my child, not his!"

"It's you that doesn't get it, bro. Look at you. You're a mess. Gabby has every right to be afraid of you. You're a ticking time bomb that's waiting to explode."

"Bullshit! She even told the judge that I was so dangerous at times she was afraid for her life. I'd never hurt Gabby or Claire. She knows that!"

"Does she? Gary, you busted up the furniture and punched holes in the walls throughout the house. What did you expect?"

"You know how hard it is to cope with this bullshit, man! Nightmares, dead bodies, suicide missions...anyway, whose side are you on, Mike?" Gary demanded while squaring up and facing Big Mike, who despite the threat, remained calm and collected.

"Look bro, I've had your back when nobody else did. You and me? Get real. We've bled in jungles, deserts, all around the world. I've always had your back and always will. I love Gabby and Claire like my own blood and I'm telling you that you need get some help if you're ever going to have a relationship with Claire."

"What about Gabby?" Gary asked, almost but not quite surrendering.

"That's not my call."

"I just want my family back, Mike," he said in a lower, much calmer tone.

"I know you do bro. But don't just say it. Start living it, breathing it, and praying for it."

"Praying? When did you get to be so holy Mike?" Gary asked while surveying the damage to his rear window.

"Man, my daddy is a preacher and one thing he made sure we could do was pray. And brotha, in this line of work, we need to stay covered in prayer."

"Does your dad know what you do?"

"Are you serious?" Big Mike asked before bursting into a fit of laughter. "He thinks I work for an international real estate company."

The two hulks shared a heartfelt laugh followed by a man-hug and a fist pound. They continued to laugh and chat while heading towards the elevator in the corner. Meanwhile in the top-floor conference room, Alex, Ko, Richard, and Nicholas sat at the mahogany table reading through dossiers filled with photographs, maps, and documents labeled "Official", "Top Secret", and "Shred after reading." At the head of the table in his usual seat sat Doc who was impatiently tapping his fingers on the table. Behind him, was a 3-D color coded map of Mexico which had been divided into three, unequal sections. Pictured in the photographs were military officials, police officers, stacks of cash, palettes of drugs, and several container trucks. No heads rose when the doors at the far end of the room suddenly opened and closed.

"Glad you gentlemen could finally make it. Please take some time to familiarize yourselves with the dossiers in front of you."
"What's this about, Doc?" Alex asked while thumbing through his folder. "We already know what's going on in Mexico, and we've never been told to intervene. The closest we got was the hit in Brazil. What's with the new interest?"
"Well Alex, to date we've never had the authorization necessary to go into Mexico and technically, we still don't. We have however, been given some 'privileged' information that requires our specialized attention."
"Privileged information and specialized attention?" Mike asked after looking across the table at Doc.
"Yes. Our involvement is strictly off the books."

117

"It always is," Alex murmured sarcastically.

"Contained in your files is all the information that various investigative agencies around the world have compiled on the Mexican cartels. Included are numerous entries about their leaders and their operations in Mexico, South America, Europe, and Asia."

"So what's the job?" Ko asked while studying the images on the overhead projector.

"Our job is to eliminate the heads of each of the three major cartels before they can unite and overrun what's left of the Mexican government."

"Eliminate them as in one at a time or all together?" Alex asked after looking around the room at all the stunned faces. "Tactically, that's impossible and at best, this is a suicide mission. The cartels control the military and the police. The numbers are overwhelmingly in their favor, so how do we contend with that?"

"I understand your concerns, but please allow me a few moments to explain. As you can see from the information in front of you and on the screen behind me, we've been able to successfully identify the heads of each cartel. Juan Carlos Pedilla is the current head of the Lobo Brothers. Pablo 'Blanco' Mendoza is the head of the Mexacali Border cartel. And last but not least, is the youngest and most powerful of the three, Pedro Luis Ruiz aka 'Diablo por el hombre', or devil made man. He is the head of the Nuevo Orden Mundial, or New World Order. Ruiz is the most powerful of the three leaders because he controls the largest territory as well as factions of the state police and military in Mexico."

"So in addition to fighting the cartels, the police and military are fighting amongst themselves? No wonder there's so much chaos and confusion. Are you sure a pair of nukes isn't a better option, Doc?"

"I understand your concern Gary and I'm getting to that. As you know, the cartels have battled for control of Mexico for the past thirty years while the Columbians have reaped the benefits of almost uncontested trade in the region. Unfortunately, these battles have pushed north and presently, they're nearing the border. Ruiz has called a cease fire in order to negotiate this new unification his 'new world order'. If these three cartels unify, they're going to come across the border backed by rogue cops and the Mexican army."

"Have the other two agreed to this partnership?"

"Not yet, Nick, but it's going to be hard for them to refuse. Like I said before, Ruiz is the most powerful and the smartest of the three. Rather than continuing to fight the other two, he plans to use their resources in combination with his. Even if he only gets one to agree, they can easily crush the other and absorb that territory. Local police, border patrol, and the guard won't be enough to stop these guys if they enter Texas and using the military on domestic soil is a last resort due to the number of civilians in the line of fire."

"So when do we go in?" Richard asked while scratching his head in disbelief.

"We have reason to believe that three weeks from now these guys will meet. The location has yet to be disclosed, but we believe it'll be in neutral territory. The mission is target acquisition and elimination."

"This is a cluster-fuck. What kind of backup do we have?" Gary asked while slumping back in his seat and massaging his temples.

"I agree with Gary," Alex began while looking over at his distressed teammate, "what kind of backup do we have, Doc? With Jinx in school, Warren out of action, Tango semi-retired and other assets scattered around the world, we're quite a few guns short."

"For now, there are no extra guns Alex; we're it. Because of the nature of the mission, we won't be getting personnel from the FBI, DEA, or the military either. The CIA gave us all the intel they could provide, but no personnel. And we sure as hell can't take the guard in."

"I know," replied Alex with a sinister, almost demonic grin on his face.

"Whatever you're thinking in that hell you call a mind, the answer is no!"

"No? No my ass, Doc! We don't have a choice. The six of us will be target practice if we roll up in there trying to face an entire country. With these three in the same place at the same time, there's going to be security on post everywhere. The area will be locked down tighter than Fort Knox. You know damned well we don't roll under circumstances like that. There's too much damned risk involved."

"I'll call Washington as there is another vested interest in this situation as well," Doc replied while looking around the room into the faces of the men who had clearly united against him.

"What interest is that?" Ko asked curiously.

"Simon's activities in the region have all but cut the Mexicans out of trade in the Caribbean. According to our data, they're not happy about it and are preparing to go the war with the Jamaicans. We can't allow the Caribbean to erupt in a bloody drug war. Our intervention is very necessary to prevent that from happening."

"So in addition to eliminating the cartel bosses, we're protecting Simon's interests as well? This just keeps getting better."

"Look, Mike, we..."

"We're once again being forced to turn our backs on Simon while he operates uncontested, isn't that right, Doc?" Alex interrupted sarcastically. "I mean, let's face it. Right now, he's more useful than the Mexicans, so they have to go. That's the old 'sleight of hand' at work again. Are we repaying a favor of some sort by eliminating his rivals?"

"That's not entirely the case Alex, although there is some merit to your assertion. Like, I said, I'll call Washington."

"Yeah, you do that. Meanwhile, I'll be in 'the dungeon'," Alex concluded before standing and exiting the conference room with his comrades in tow.

A short while later Alex entered an underground target range where Warren was sweeping empty shell casings up off the floor. Although he felt uneasy discussing mission details without him present, Alex knew in his heart that his deeply disturbed friend wasn't mission ready. Forcing him into the field now would likely result in unwanted casualties, including his own. At the same time, Alex was happy that neither Warren nor Lexi were anywhere near 'the office.' He didn't want his overly eager kid sister trying to prove herself on a mission that none of them wanted to undertake in the first place.

"Whassup, Flashpoint?"

"Alex," he replied while smiling and dumping the shells into a canister in the nearby corner.

"We missed you at the office. We could really use you in Mexico."

"Don't blow smoke up my ass, Alex. We both know I was purposely omitted from that meeting and frankly, I'm glad I was."

"So what's next for you, Warren?" Alex asked while stepping into one of the stalls and donning a set of headphones and yellow tinted goggles.

"I don't know," he replied while donning similar equipment. "Maybe I'll do some tech work and gun maintenance; just not interested in field work right now."

Alex clamped a target onto the pulley and sent it to the far end of the range. After selecting an AR-15, he set the gun to full automatic and aimed the laser sight at the center of the target. Within seconds of squeezing the trigger, the clip was empty. After taking a deep breath, Alex laid the gun on the shelf and admired his handiwork.

"Are you okay, Alex? You didn't nail the head or torso once," Warren said after retrieving the target and staring at the holes in it.
"It's not me; it's the gun. The sights are off."
"That's bullshit, Alex," Warren replied while looking through the scope, and aiming down the range. "I tuned these guns myself, and I'm telling you, you screwed up."
"I fucked up? That's not possible. I'm telling you the sights are off on that gun."
"Fine," Warren said before selecting a fresh target and clamping it to the pulley.

He sent it to the end of the range where Alex's had been. After loading the rifle, he stepped into the adjacent stall, assumed the position, and opened fire. Upon retrieval of the sheet, they counted 30 shots; 6 in the head, 19 in the torso, and 5 in the crotch.

"How'd it feel?" Alex asked with a grin.
"Cute," Warren replied after angrily slamming the rifle down on the counter. "I appreciate what you are trying to do, but I'll say it again. I don't want any parts of the field anymore."
"How long are you gonna hideaway in this basement? Look, I know you're a hell-of-a weapons tech, but you

belong in the field with the rest of us. We need you in Mexico."

"C'mon, Alex, even if I thought I was ready, there's a group of guys that would seriously disagree. You and I both know this. Thanks, but no thanks."

Warren patted Alex on the shoulder as he walked past him and exited the target range. Awhile later, Alex and Ko were speeding down the interstate in Ko's Bentley. While they talked about their next mission, Ko was busy texting on his cell phone.

"Look Ko, I know you're a super secret agent and all, but texting at over 90 mph just isn't smart, bro."

"Don't tell me the man with ice water in his veins is scared of a little speed," he replied sarcastically while passing slower moving vehicles like a burgundy blur.

"Not at all bub. As far as I know, speed never killed anyone. It was always those abrupt, unexpected collisions," Alex replied before his own phone began ringing.

After seeing the face on the screen, he turned down the stereo and pressed *talk*.

"Whassup lil girl?"

"How is the world's best big brother on this fabulous day?" Lexi asked gleefully.

"Ok, what do you want and how much is it going to cost me?"

"Wow, Alex that really hurt. Can't a grateful little sister show her handsome, awesome, big brother some appreciation every once in a while?"

"I could have gone along with it if you didn't start this call off by blowing smoke up my ass. So again, I'll ask you. What do you want and how much is it going to cost me?"

"Fine, Alex, it costs one-hundred-forty-seven-thousand-three-hundred-fifty-two dollars."

"And what exactly does one-hundred-forty-seven-thousand-three-hundred-fifty-two dollars buy?"

"It'll buy your ever so grateful little sister a black, drop-top Maserati GT."

"You're kidding, right?" Alex asked, half-laughing and half wanting to hang up the phone.

"Don't hang up the phone, Alex. Just hear me out."

"Trust me sis, I am all ears," he replied before putting the phone on speaker so that Ko could hear her as well.

"I was just thinking that since I did earn some extra money over spring break, I could use some of it to buy a new car."

"What's wrong with your current car?"

"Alex, are you serious? It's a Chevy Equinox."

"Yeah, and it's a top of the line Equinox that gets great gas mileage too."

"C'mon, Alex, don't be like that. I come home and get teased with Bentleys, Bimmers, Benzes, and Aston Martins and go back to a Chevy? What's wrong with that picture?"

"Nothing as far as I can see," he replied sarcastically.

"It's not just a sports car, Alex. It's a GT."

"You don't need a sports car or a GT either. You need to be concentrating on brain power, not horse power."

"Alex, please. I'm begging you!"

"Look, I'll make a deal with you. Finish this term and if your grades are where I think they should be, I'll consider letting you buy a car."

"Why do you have to consider it?" she demanded defiantly. "It's my money. Why can't you just let me spend it on what I want to?"

"I don't have a problem with you spending your money, Lexi. My issue is what you want to spend it on."

"I don't get it, Alex. Why can't I have the car I want?"

'First of all honey, you don't have a job. Do you have any idea how much attention you'd draw walking into a dealership with that kind of cash? Aside from that, a Maserati is going to draw a lot of attention to you and then back to me. *The Agency* can't afford that and neither can I."

"Then order it through the dealer network you use."

"No," he replied flatly

"Why are you always trying to tell me what to do, what I need and don't need? When are you going to stop treating me like a kid?"

"I'll stop treating you like a kid when you stop acting like one. Look, I'll think about a car, but forget the Maserati."

"Fine dad, what can I get?" she groaned angrily.

"I'm not your father, but I probably love you just as much, and your cap is fifty."

"Fifty thousand?" she asked, offended by his counteroffer. "What can I get for that?"

"You're in school. Research it."

"Fine, Alex you win. Can you at least kiss Ko for me?"

"Yeah, right," he replied before quickly disconnecting the call. "What?"

"Where's my kiss?"

"How about you kiss my ass?" Alex fired back, making Ko laugh uncontrollably.

"Seriously, bro," Ko began while looking back and forth between Alex and the road ahead, "I hear you complain that Lexi acts like a kid. Has it occurred to you that she might act more like an adult if you treated her more like one?"

"When did you get to be so fucking wise?" Alex inquired while adjusting the stereo.

"I'm just saying, Alex. If you loosen up a little bit and try being her brother instead of her father, Lexi might begin to open up and confide in you more."

"Is that what she does; confides in you?" Alex asked while gazing suspiciously at his best friend.

"You're missing my point, Alex. Lexi is a grown woman. Believe it or not, she is capable for making rational decisions."

"Rational decisions, like choosing boyfriends and assassinating Yakuza bosses? Yeah, right. Ko, you and I chose this life. Your parents worked for 'The Agency' and were murdered just like mine. Fate brought us to where we are. I don't want the same for Lexi. I want her to have a normal life instead of turning out like us."

"Is that what you really want?"

"Yes, Ko it is."

"Then let her be normal. Let her grow up and make her own decisions like a normal person."

"So you think I should let her buy a new Maserati convertible?"

"No. She earned her money and you need to let her decide how to spend it. Trust her enough to let her make a rational decision."

"And if she doesn't, then what?" Alex asked while peering out the passenger side window.

"It's her choice, Alex. Good, bad, or indifferent, she's earned the right to make it. In the long run, she'll appreciate you more for letting her make it, even if it's a mistake."

"I don't know, man. Let me think about it. Who the fuck are you texting now?" Alex barked when he noticed Ko's busy fingers.

"Nobody in particular," he replied nonchalantly. "By the way, what's wrong with Lexi's choice in boyfriends?"

"She chooses assholes, Ko. She has a bad habit of choosing guys who see her as cute, naïve, and gullible. Then when they realize she's not and break her heart, she runs to me and I end up nearly beating the shit out of one of them."

"That's an unfair assessment, even for you. She's grown up since Marcus. Give her chance, Alex. The next guy may surprise you."

"Unfair, really? Ted, Pete, and then Marcus... need I say more? The only thing that'll surprise me about the next one will be if I don't whup his ass up front and save myself the trouble later. Why do you care who she dates anyway?"

"She's my family too, Alex," Ko replied, attempting to ease the tension he was feeling. "How'd it go with Warren?"

"He doesn't want any part of Mexico. Sierra Leone really fucked him up."

"Well bro, if we don't get some extra guns quick, Mexico is gonna fuck us up."

"I know," Alex replied before cranking the stereo.

Chapter 5

Cuidad Juarez, Mexico

Like many towns along the U.S.-Mexico border, Cuidad
Juarez was once a bustling metropolis. Like its sister
cities, it was used not only as a link between border
towns, but the two countries as well. Millions of dollars
in merchandise, supplies, and other goods passed
between these towns each year. In the early 1980's, these
towns also became the main hubs for drug trafficking
between U.S. and Mexico. During the 1990's, Columbia's
Pablo Escobar was the main exporter of cocaine and
dealt with criminal organizations throughout the world.
When the 'War on Drugs' intensified in South Florida, the
Columbian cartels formed partnerships with Mexico
based traffickers to move drugs into the U.S. At the time,
it was estimated that 90% of the cocaine that enters the
U.S. came thru Mexico via Columbia.

Since the 1980's, power has steadily shifted back and
forth between warring cartels. Following the demise of
Columbia's Cali and Medellin Cartel, Mexican cartels
have seized control of the U.S.-Mexican drug trade.
Presently, three cartels are at war for control of Mexico.
Bribery, murder, and kidnapping, have allowed the
cartels to manipulate, intimidate, and eliminate officials
on every level of the Mexican government, including the
police and the military; both of which are often used as
bodyguards and security for dealers and shipments.

In an effort to curb the amount of drugs trafficked
between the two nations, the U.S. has fortified the
border with additional patrols and posts. Unmanned
aerial drones have been used to scan the desert for
coyotes or smugglers on foot. The U.S. has even

considered using the National Guard to secure the border at key points, a measure which has proven to be very expensive.

Today, cities like Cuidad Juarez are nothing more than lawless, boarded up ghost towns. The few remaining residents refuse to go out after dark for fear that they'll become casualties of the bloody drug wars being waged on the streets. The cartels have become so powerful that the police department of Guadalupe Distrito Bravas has been completely shut down.

To prevent the cartels from uniting and bringing the war across the border, the U.S. government approved a covert operation to assassinate all three cartel leaders during their secret unification meeting.

Denver, Colorado

That evening around midnight, a road weary Tisha Norman pulled into the driveway of Simon's compound. When the red Porsche stopped in front of the manor house, an armed sentry opened its driver's side door and ushered her out. Before exiting, she grabbed the pink duffle bag from the passenger seat, while the sentry grabbed suitcases from the trunk. She dragged herself into the foyer and began the long climb up the winding staircase. All she could think about was taking a long, hot shower and climbing into bed. She prayed that Simon wouldn't be on his usual bullshit and would simply let her be. Having sex after days of arguing with dealers, dodging cops, and driving with her nerves on edge was the furthest thing from her mind, unless it was with Alex. That trumped everything. Her hopes for a peaceful evening went up in smoke when she opened the ivory, double pocket doors to the master suite.

There in the center of her bed was Simon, her husband, deeply engulfed in the throes of passion with two of the house maids. In fact, they were in so deep that no one noticed her standing in the doorway. Rage filled Tisha as she watched her husband tenderly sucking the maid's nipples while thrusting between her quivering, chocolate thighs. When he wasn't sucking her tits, he was kissing the other maid who was kneeling beside them stroking her clit. Tisha's jaw dropped while watching Simon displaying a level of passion that she as his wife had never experienced. Sighs of ecstasy escaped one of the women after he laid down and she climbed onto his lap. *I must be dreaming,* Tisha thought while Simon and the first maid took turns licking and sucking the rider's hardened nipples.

Nasty Jamaican bitches!

Before Tisha's very eyes were her servants fucking her husband and each other in the middle of her bed! The sound of the duffle bag crashing to the floor startled the women who quickly began fighting over the sheet which barely shielded their robust, naked bodies.

"Tisha gal...wa mek yu come fass?" he stuttered in disbelief while struggling to focus his drunken eyes.
"Is this the shit you do when I am gone; fuck the help?"
"Sum da time," he laughed before snatching back the sheet and licking on the hardened nipple of the woman nearest him. "Yu wan join us?"
"Your dope is in the bag," she replied with a scowl before storming out of the bedroom.
"Tisha, gal come back!" he yelled as she ran down the hall to the parlor.

"Wa a dis? Why yu bring back mi dope?" Simon asked when he entered the parlor several minutes later.

"Cause Dawn was being careless, and jeopardizing our operations! She was dealing to a group of wanna-be-rappers in a fucking casino. But why do you care?" she barked with Simon standing a few feet from her in a white bath robe and slippers.

"Getcha finga out mi face!" he demanded through his clinched teeth.

"You send me travelling all over the place looking after your affairs, and while I am gone, you're fucking the help? Of all the women in the world, why the maids?" she demanded with her index finger still inches from his nose.

"Yu best be mindin' yu tongue, ooman!"

"And to think, you show your ass the minute a man looks at me. And for all the times you accused me of fucking somebody else, I wish I had been! That way I wouldn't have to stand here pissed at you...you fucking bastard!"

The force of her finger pushing against his forehead was nothing compared with the thunderous crash in Tisha's ears. The back of his hand collided with her jaw and sent her crashing to the floor where she lay in a daze as he walked over to her, grabbed her by the collar, and proceeded to punch her repeatedly before letting her slump back to the floor.

"Na badda mi wit disrespect again, yu rass claat haad American bitch! Yu do whacha do because yu paid to! Yu, yu sista, yu mudda, an' yu fambly nuttin wit out me! I an own yu! Memba dat! Yu naa help me build shit!" he growled before kicking her in the stomach.

131

His blows were so dizzying that she barely felt it when he began tearing her clothes off. Tisha lay there in a daze while he brutally raped her before leaving her naked, battered body on the parlor room floor. Hours passed before anyone came to her aid and after they did, she spent the rest of the morning curled up in the fetal position in the corner of the tub while the resident nurse attended to her wounds.

"Yu took a nasty fall chile," the nurse chided while tenderly dabbing the wounds on Tisha's swollen head, nose, and lip.

Later as she lay in bed, the sound of barking dogs resonated in her throbbing head. She could hear Simon yelling various commands to them in his thick, West Indian accent. Her mind flashed back to when he first began training them as puppies and the vicious beatings he gave them to enforce their obedience and establish his dominance. Today, like many other days, she too was beaten like those dogs. The scraps Simon fed them from the dinner table were like the scraps he was feeding her family as rewards for their obedience and loyalty.

I an own yu! kept ringing Tisha's ears as tears began forming in her swollen eyes. She came to the realization that she and her family were nothing more than disposable possessions to be used and abused at his every whim.

Tisha, Dawn, and the rest of their family were Simon's slaves; his dogs. Once he got tired of them, he'd simply replace them. Judging by what she'd seen in her bedroom and the beating that she'd taken, Tisha figured she was about to be replaced soon too. She cringed while wondering how long it would be and how they'd be disposed of. While she lay there silently staring off into space, Tisha was a wreck on the inside. Right now more than anything, she longed to be with Alex and feel the assurance that being in his arms brought her. When she ran her fingers across her swollen face, Tisha knew she couldn't face her lover like this. How would she explain that in a coke filled rage, her own husband had beaten and raped her again? *Besides, what could Alex do about it anyway?* she thought while watching the nurse exit the room. When the door closed, Tisha grabbed her phone and quickly dialed Alex's phone number. Her heart sank when his voicemail picked up.

Meanwhile back in the conference room, the team had reassembled and was seated back at the long mahogany table listening intently while Doc completed a call via the intercom.

"Well, you heard it," he began after slamming his pen down on the table, "we're on our own."
"That's bullshit, McCallister!" Gary barked from the far end of the table.
"I'm afraid it gets even better. Our sources in Mexico have informed me that the meeting has been moved up at least a week leaving us with an even shorter time frame than we originally anticipated."
"I agree with Gary," Big Mike said after lifting his head. "This op has way too many variables. We're outmanned, outgunned, and lack sufficient intel to proceed. Like Alex said this is a suicide mission, and I've been on too damned many of those already."
"Black Mamba?" Doc asked nervously.
"When's the meeting, old man?" Alex asked while texting.

"It's three weeks from tomorrow in Mexico City, which is considered neutral territory because of its international ties and tourism. Their thinking is that no one would believe them to be foolish enough to meet in the middle of all that heat. Besides, international police and military would be tripping over each other trying to make that large scale of an arrest."

"Your sources are wrong, Doc. They won't be anywhere near Mexico City. They're going to move further in-land and keep changing the date to cover their asses. They know they're being watched and are trying to confuse everyone until the last minute. They're not going to risk an attempt by a unit like ours."

"So what are you saying, Alex?" asked Doc with heightened frustration

"I'm saying we're fucked. Scrub the mission. It's not worth the risk."

"Scrub the mission? Are you insane?" Doc asked in shock. "Not only might we never get another opportunity to cripple the drug trade in Mexico, but do you realize how much money you all stand to lose?"

"We'd never live to spend it," Alex replied before standing up and walking towards the door. "Besides, I'm perfectly content with letting the Jamaicans shoot it out with the Mexicans. Fuck'em all. Let the devil sort'em out."

"Where are you going? We're not done yet," Doc growled while leaning forward in his chair.

"We are, if we take this mission," Alex snapped. "Thanks, but no thanks. I may not see eye-to-eye with every man at this table, but I refuse to watch them be sent to slaughter. No offense, but I'm going back to bed. Washington is playing chess and using us as pawns. I won't have any part of that."

"Then what would you have me do, Alex?"

"We call in our own backup. We call in 'The Renegades,'" Alex replied while leaning against the door frame with his arms folded across his chest.

"Oh no, hell no!" Ko yelled while staring at Alex with his almond shaped eyes stretched wide.

"Are you sure you wanna go down that road again, lil brotha?" Big Mike asked after turning around in his chair and staring into the shadows of the door way.

"Think about this mission and ask yourselves what choice do we have?"

"There has to be another alternative, Alex."

"You tell me, Gary. What's the alternative?"

Cincinnati, Ohio

In the town of Hamilton which sits north of Cincinnati, Lynn had just laid her elderly client down for her afternoon nap. After deciding to take a short breather, she quietly entered the old woman's kitchen and poured herself a cup of tea. While sitting and sipping, Lynn decided to call Ni'Chelle who was also taking a short break from work.

"Hello."

"Whassup, Chelle?"

"Damn Lynn, you sound happy as hell. What are you up to?"

"I've been talking to or rather texting with Alex. He said he's been busy finalizing deals in Denver and Mexico and when he's done, he wants to come visit us."

"That's cool, girl. Just don't get your hopes up too high with this man, ok?"

"What do you mean, Chelle?"

"I mean, you still don't him that well, honey. I love you, Lynn, and I got your back. But as your sister, I'll put a

135

nigga in his grave over you. Just know that. You're all I got."

"Thank you, Chelle, but I got a good feeling about Alex," Lynn replied with a smile. "Even though I barely know him, when I'm with him it's like I've known him a lifetime. When I'm with Alex, I don't feel like anything can hurt me."

"Damn girl, slow down! Don't put it on him too good when he comes, okay? Take it easy on him," she laughed.

"Quit it, Chelle. It ain't goin' down like that. He's coming for a visit."

"Honey, the man is coming all the way from Denver to see you. Give my brother-in-law something to go home with."

"Brother-in-law?" Lynn gasped before almost choking on her raspberry concoction. "Don't you think you're being a little presumptuous?"

"You obviously didn't hear yourself when you called me. You're probably feeling moist right now, ain't cha?"

"Bye, Chelle!" Lynn laughed before hanging up the phone and leaning back in her chair.

Though she tried to hide it, Lynn really missed Alex. Everything about him was etched on her mind's landscape. She wasn't sure if it was the tea or the thought of him being close to her, but an alluring, tingling sensation began at the base of her spine and crept between her tightly clinched thighs.

Meanwhile, the team's heated debate continued. Though the arguments were mounting against him, Alex sat in his chair calmly refusing to budge. In fact, his calm demeanor and reasoning had everyone in the room on edge.

"I can't agree with your logic at all, Alex," Doc protested while massaging his temples. "Their tactics are too unpredictable and too difficult to contain."

"How so?" Alex quipped sarcastically.

"How so? Have you forgotten what they did in Taiwan?"

"Of course, I haven't. They successfully neutralized a pair of snipers who'd been terrorizing a village for weeks."

"Alex, they burned the whole damned village to the ground just to catch two snipers!"

"So, what? The threat was neutralized and the Red Cross rebuilt the entire village, even going so far as to modernize it with actual plumbing and electricity."

"Let's not forget about that stunt off the coast of Somalia," Gary interjected while shaking his head.

"What are you talking about? They rescued a civilian vessel and its crew which was being ransomed. Its cargo was also recovered intact. As far as I'm concerned, that was another successful mission."

"Yeah, until that news crew showed footage of sixteen pirates hanging by nooses from their own boat."

"The British used to hang pirates as form of punishment, so I don't see why you're making such a big deal of this," Alex replied with a grin.

"What about the inferno in Afghanistan?" Ko asked, still in disbelief.

"What do you mean? They destroyed a one-hundred-sixty-thousand acre poppy field that was being used to fund Al-Qaeda forces."

"Alex, Big Mike lost all his hair in that fire!"

"Ok, Ko, first of all there was no way to predict that the winds would suddenly change directions while we were in that valley. Second, Big Mike was admittedly going bald anyway. Third, he wasn't hurt and his eyebrows finally grew back."

All eyes suddenly turned to the end of the table where Big Mike sat silently rubbing his shiny, bald-head.

"Are you sure there isn't another way, Alex?" Mike asked while stroking his goatee. "I mean, there has to be better alternative. 'The Renegades' are a walking demolition crew."
"There isn't any and given the circumstances, they're just what the doctor ordered."
"Yeah, if the doctor's last name were Kevorkian," Ko snapped under his breath.
"Or Frankenstein," Richard quipped.
"Okay, Alex, if we call them in, how many do we call?" Doc asked in disbelief.
"We call whoever's available."
"Whoever's available?" Gary snapped after leaning forward in his chair. "Alex, the possibilities for wanton destruction are endless. The problem with 'The Renegades' is you never know who or what you're getting. They're a network of mercenaries, hit-men, and assassins from all over the globe."
"So are we."
"Unlike us, Alex, they operate with no structure and no parameters. They shoot first and never ask questions."
"So, what?" Alex growled. "The cartels aren't playing fair, so why should we? Why not introduce some anarchy? Look, we can sit here and debate their tactics for the rest of the day, but the fact of the matter is they get the job done."

Later that afternoon at his café, Alex was sitting at his usual table reading the paper. Four of the patrons immediately caught his eye. At one of the tables in front of him and another behind him were two pairs of men in dark suits.

Feds? I wonder who they're watching, he thought while studying their bios, clean cuts, cheap suits, and the badges inside their blazers. He concluded their presence must be related to the death of the Armenian arms dealer and quickly dismissed it.

Later that afternoon, Tisha was still lying in bed when she was suddenly startled by the closing of the bedroom door. Using a remote on the nightstand, she turned on the lights and to her surprise the bed was surrounded with dozens of shopping bags. Beside her pillow was a black, satin-finished box with silver writing on it. When she opened it, her swollen jaw dropped. Inside it was a Platinum V-shaped, herringbone necklace with a blue, four-carat teardrop diamond dangling from it. Flanking the necklace, were a pair of matching three-carat teardrop earrings, also in Platinum settings. Warmth flooded her chest when she sat up and removed them from the box.

She snatched off the jewelry she was wearing and replaced it with the new trinkets. Though she tried to admire them, she couldn't avoid looking at her mangled face. Seeing herself all battered and bruised brought weakness to her knees. Her nose was black and blue. One of her eyes was swollen shut and her lips were swollen and filled with deep lacerations. Turning her back to the mess in the mirror, Tisha leaned against the dresser and began to sob into her open palms. Suddenly, the she heard the door open again, and through her tear-blurred vision, she saw Simon walking slowly and shamefully towards her. She couldn't imagine why such a 'devil' insisted on dressing himself in all white. In his hands was a shiny black envelope with silver lettering on it. Though her initial impulse was to turn and hide her face, Tisha defiantly stood her ground so that Simon could see the damage that he'd done. Like he did many times in the past, Simon barely made eye contact with her, instead opting to look at the floor in front of him.

"I an sorry, Tisha gal," he managed pathetically. "It's da drug...mi naa wan bring harm to me queen. Mi lub yu kyuan done. Please forgive mi."

"Forgive you? Look at my face, Simon. Look me in the eye. Look at what you did to me and tell me again that you *love* me," Tisha demanded while staring at him with salty tears stinging at her cuts and bruises. His head, however, never rose from the floor. "You beat me, raped me, and left me for dead...again."

"It's da drug, gal...not me. Neva do mi wan no harm to come to yu."

"What's that in your hand?" she asked, shifting her focus but refusing to hide her disgust.

"Jus si'ting for you," he replied before laying the envelope on the bed and retreating from the room.

When he closed the door, Tisha picked the envelope up off the bed and quickly noticed the all too familiar, three pointed star with the circle around it.

A Benz? she thought when she dumped the contents onto the bed.

Tisha gasped at the sight of a new key fob and the brochure for a bright red Mercedes Benz 550SL AMG. Best of all, it was a convertible! A flood of emotions filled her when she looked around the room and thought, *How could a man this evil be this loving at the same time?* Joy, depression, and sadness battled inside Tisha as her life flashed before her eyes, because she was happier before she met him. She didn't have all the expensive trappings she had now; exotic cars, expensive vacations, custom jewelry, nice clothes, servants, or money at her disposal, but she was safe. Her family was safe.

As a dental assistant, Tisha dreamed that one day a handsome man would come along and take her away from what she thought was a life of boredom and misery. She longed for a man who would shower her with love, affection, and the finer things in life. Then she met Simon. His clothes were nice and his game was tight. He was far from the fine brotha she had dreamed about, but he was rich and he spoiled her. Not only did Simon spoil her, but he spoiled her family as well.

He insisted that Tisha's mother be moved to an exclusive retirement community, bought her sister and her family a new home and cars, and kept money in their pockets. Little did they know he was grooming them. Not long after they married, Simon put Tisha's family on his payroll. Because of her hustler mentality and street sense, he put her in charge of many of his financial operations, which included supervising his dealings in the Midwest. Dawn and Roger were his distribution networks with Tisha as their supplier. She turned a blind eye to his short comings; the infidelity, the drugs, their issues in bed, and the beatings, for what she thought was the greater good.

Then Alex came along, the one she dreamed about. He was every bit the man that Simon could never be. He was passionate, romantic, and damn he was fine! To top it all off, he could put it down in the bedroom and his pockets were loaded! He made up everywhere Simon failed, but she wasn't quite ready to give up on him just yet. Beneath it all, Tisha believed he could be a good husband, and she was determined to be a good wife.

Her determination however, had many consequences. To Tisha, the greatest consequence was that one day it would all come to an end and she would be left with nothing. If Simon didn't kill her, going back to being a 'regular woman' would. In a sad and twisted way, Tisha had made up her mind that it was worth it, at least until she could get out for good. In the meantime, everything else was just another small sacrifice. She looked at herself in the mirror across the room. *"You can do it."*

Later that night, after a long day of arguing his case, Alex tried to relax in his shower. Purple steam surrounded him while recessed, florescent lights shined down onto the black marble. Three chrome jets sprayed his body as he stood with hands pressed against the wall in front of him. Out of nowhere, he felt a rush of icy air around him, and seconds later, Alex felt a pair of soft breasts pressed against his back. He closed his eyes and leaned his head back when she began planting soft, wet kisses on his shoulders while caressing his chest. His knees almost buckled when her hands moved across his abs, down his thighs, and toward his crotch. His body began to tingle as her tongue swirled up and down his spine. Suddenly, he came to his senses and broke the hypnotic spell.

Alex spun around and stood face-to-face with his tormentor. Like the Black Mamba he was named after, his body was poised and ready to strike. With his back to the wall, and his fists clinched, he bared his fangs and prepared to fight.

"Ola, chico," she said in a low, sultry tone peppered by her thick Dominican accent.

His eyes traced her curvaceous, honey-colored body from head-to-toe; her tiny manicured feet, her smooth legs, her deliciously round thighs, slim waist, and her round tattooed breasts. Alex stood frozen and watched while she washed her long black and blond-streaked hair. When their eyes met, his body almost went limp.

"Simone? Am I dreaming? This can't be real."
"No, papi, you're not dreaming."
"Then this is a nightmare."
"Why would you say that, papi?" she asked before stepping towards him.
"Back away from me, demon," he demanded angrily.

Taking his hand in hers, she pressed it against her breast right over her beating heart.

"This isn't possible," he declared after feeling the passionate thump against his palm.
"Love makes anything possible, baby."
"Not this...not cheating death," he replied while struggling to make sense of what was happening to him.

She looked lovingly into his eyes before reaching to stroke his cheek. Though he wanted to believe she was real, Alex knew better. He turned his head just as her hand approached his face.

143

"Papi?" she pleaded.

"What is it you want me to know, Simone?"

"What do you mean? Alex, why are you being so cold to me? You cry for me in your dreams, long for my touch in your sleep, and whisper my name on the wind. Papi, I want you to know that I've heard you, and I'm here for you."

"That's not possible."

"Why isn't it possible, Alex?"

"Because you took your last breath in my arms. Simone, I was at the morgue with Ko and the coroner. I identified your body."

Alex stood there watching as she searched the swirling water at their feet for answers. She released his hand and stepped back, and before Alex realized it, tears were running down his face. Simone folded her arms over her breasts and began rubbing them with her hands.

"What is it you want to tell me, Simone?" he asked again when he noticed her shivering.

"I love you, Alex, and my death wasn't your fault."

"But..."

"No, Alexis; hear me out. You didn't kill me. You tried to protect me. It was me... I didn't listen. I love you papi, and I miss you."

Before Alex could reach out to her, she disappeared leaving him standing in the middle of the shower alone and confused. He wanted to believe he was having another nightmare, but he wasn't. In fact, Alex was wide wake. He tried to lie down in bed and force himself to sleep, but he couldn't stop thinking and reminiscing.

Five years ago, Alex fell in love with an up and coming model named Simone Santiago. The first time he saw the Puerto Rican beauty, Alex fell madly in love with her.

Though she was seated at a table with eight other equally attractive women, something about her was infinitely more captivating than the rest. The sound of her voice sent chills up and down his spine. Her sexy accent made each word she spoke sound like poetry. When she walked, her round hips and ass seemed to move to a rhythm all their own. He sat alone in a dimly lit corner of the restaurant watching and undressing her with his eyes while she laughed and danced. Suddenly, all the lights seemed to be on her as she stood alone on the dance floor amid all the couples. Just as Sade began to serenade the crowd, Alex grabbed a rose from his table's vase and slowly walked up behind her. He watched quietly as she moved in rhythm with the music, slowly tracing her curves her own tiny hands. His hazel eyes appraised every inch of her body from her face and breasts, to her hips and thighs. From head to toe she was absolutely perfect!

"May I have this dance?" he asked, interrupting her seductive solo.

Though she was slightly startled, the Puerto-Rican goddess turned around and greeted him with a smile. The model in her gave his style an instant appraisal. His tapered hair was cut close while his beard and goatee were trimmed to perfection. When Alex removed his blue tinted glasses, she was instantly mesmerized by his bedroom eyes and smooth caramel skin. Gold and diamonds shimmered in his left ear while the bright red rose he was holding stood out against his black, Versace suit, which lay on him like a tailored skin. Though it was dark and his shoes black, she could tell he hadn't skimped on them either.

"I'm Alexis, Alexis Stratton."

"I'm Simone Santiago," she replied while continuing to take him in and inhale the hypnotic smell of his cologne.

"I know," he replied in a low, seductive tone.

"Really?" she asked while gazing into his eyes.

"I've seen your work. You make even the ugliest dresses look gorgeous."

"Thank you," she cooed, with her face reddening under his lustful gaze.

Each word that rolled off her tongue was like the notes of the sexiest song never written.

"For me?" she asked before gently taking his hand and guiding the flower to her nose.

"Yes."

Before Simone could formulate another thought, she was in his arms with her body moving rhythmically against his. While holding the rose in her hand, her arms found their way atop his broad shoulders, and for the next couple of hours, they danced and talked about everything and nothing simultaneously. After the restaurant closed, they spent a few hours walking hand-in-hand around downtown Denver. By dawn, they were standing in the lobby of Simone's hotel, which unbeknownst to her, Alex owned. The uncharacteristic kiss goodbye sent chills up and down both their spines. Her soft hands caressed the back of his head and neck while he traced up and down her back before cupping and squeezing her soft, round ass. Six months later, they were engaged.

Now, while the city of Denver slept under another blanket of falling rain, Alex was sitting at a multi-screened computer console looking at pictures of him and Simone while reading newspaper headlines.

"Violent Jamaican drug gangs battle in Miami." "City streets continue to run with blood." "Mayor considers curfew." "Puerto Rican model becomes the latest victim of violence." "Model gunned down in midday drive-by." "Three suspected gang members gunned down, two thrown off a roof." "Cathedral destroyed during gunfight." "Reputed Jamaican drug kingpin eludes capture again."

"Why couldn't you just listen to me?" he asked out loud to no one in particular.

Chapter 6

Four years ago, Denver.

In the early hours of a quiet Saturday morning, Alex and Simone lay atop the covers of his bed. With her legs wrapped around his back, she commanded his powerful thrusts into her silky wetness while engaging him in a rhythmic exchange of intense, erotic kisses. The tips of her manicured nails teased his back while hers arched, and she cried out his name. His hard, thrusting dick felt *so* good massaging and teasing her tightly-clinched sugar walls. Though he had erupted twice, Alex's desire wouldn't allow him to stop feeding her stoke-after-passionate stroke. Their hot, sticky juices pooled on the sheets below her soft round ass before Simone flipped him onto his back and proceeded to slide up and down on his pole. Alex gasped with delight each time her cum drenched flower pounded down onto his lap.

"Aye papi!" Simone exclaimed when she reached another climax, more intense and hypnotic than the last. "Mas! Mas!" she demanded as he lay on his back, thrusting upwards faster, harder, and deeper while gripping her soft cheeks in his powerful hands.

She cradled her tits and teased her nipples with the tip of her tongue while bouncing up and down on his dick. Simone knew Alex loved the sight of her pink tongue on her dark, chocolate nipples and was determined to give him a show this morning. She could feel him swelling and pressing against her quivering walls, a sensation that sent chills up and down her spine. She couldn't wait to feel her *papi* erupt inside her again. The thought of it has her spilling her hot, creamy juices all over her lover.

"Ooh papi!" she gasped with delight before collapsing onto his chest.

"Si, mami!" Alex moaned before squeezing her tender breasts and licking her hardened nipples.

As Simone continued her ride, slowing her pace and using her walls to milk him, Alex fought hard against the building pressure. With his volcano threatening to erupt, Alex grabbed Simone's hips and squeezed her ass while thrusting upward harder and faster than before. Each stroke left her G-spot engulfed in flames of passion! With one hand planted on his chest and the other squeezing and massaging her tits, her pussy milked him with each rise and fall of her hips. Suddenly, their juices clashed with orgasmic fury. They repeatedly cried out each other's names while their bodies writhed in ecstasy. With each kiss, they inhaled each other's passionate moans. Once their spasms subsided, she laid her head on his chest and held him close while being serenaded by sounds of his beating heart.

"I love you, Mrs. Stratton," Alex whispered while holding caressing her hair and listening to her soft, purr-like snore.

Hours later, they were seated on the penthouse's patio enjoying a breakfast of omelets, fruits, croissants, and numerous icy beverages. As usual, the table was decorated with a white table cloth and fine crystal. They sat at a ninety degree angle at the end of the table, feeding each other while teasing and playing lustfully.

"You better stop looking at me like that or this apple wedge won't be the only thing in my mouth, Mr. Stratton."

"Don't threaten me with a good time," he replied while spreading his legs beneath the table.

"Ooh papi…you so nasty," Simone cooed while fanning her face and sipping her water.

"I don't know if I like the idea of your agency sending you to Miami for a shoot," Alex said, shifting the conversation and interrupting their playful mood. "Don't they know what's going on down there?"

"Papi, please don't go down that road again. I know you don't like or trust Marty, but he's assured us that we're safe this time. We'll be on the beach, miles away from the city."

"He told the same lie about Rio and three of you almost died. Marty is getting rich while putting you all in danger. It's not worth it."

"Alex, please!" she protested.

"I'm serious, Simone. I don't want you in Miami. It's too dangerous. It's not like you need the money. Look around…we're set!"

"I know, papi," Simone conceded while staring at her four-carat engagement ring, "but I need this exposure. This could be the biggest shoot of my career and if I nail this one, I can write my own ticket."

"No," he replied flatly.

"NO?" she cried after standing up and staring down at him.

"Simone, last time I scared Marty," Alex said as his mind flashed back to the sight of the scrawny, cheap-suit wearing man dangling by his ankles from the roof his own building. "If something happens to you, I'm going to kill him."

"Do you really feel that strongly about it, papi?"

"Yes, I do," Alex replied while hugging her around her waist with his head against her stomach.

"Then I guess I'll be right here when you return from your trip."
"I promise I'll make this up to Simone. I just don't know what I'd do if I lost you."

Four days later, she died in his arms on a Miami sidewalk. Tears streamed from his eyes when he went back to the headline *"Reputed Jamaican drug kingpin eludes capture again."* In the center of the screen was Simon's black and white photograph. He was grinning while standing there dressed in white and flanked by two, smiling Caucasian attorneys. That was four years ago. Though, it was believed that he had fled to his native Jamaica, Simon was actually living a life of luxury in Boulder, Colorado. Much had changed in the past four years. Simon's operation had grown much larger than before and he was even more untouchable. Having layered himself behind armed security, fake businesses, and high profile attorneys, he was running most of the drug trade from the Midwest and the Southwest.

Much had changed for Alex as well. He'd cheated death once again. After spending six months in a coma, he returned to Japan where he spent two years honing his skills in unarmed combat and stealth. While mastering the use of edged weapons, Alex hoped and prayed that no harm would come to Simon. When he returned to the states, his prayers were answered. From that moment, he made Simon's destruction his priority. Nothing else mattered.

After spending some time observing Simon's operations, Alex discovered his one and only weakness; his lovely wife Tisha. Alex spent months studying her habits;

shopping, trips to the spa, gym workouts, etc. He made sure he was everywhere that Tisha was, systematically manipulating his knowledge of her until he finally seduced her, which proved to be easier than Alex had anticipated. He discovered everything she was lacking; good sex, companionship, and conversation. He gave that to her and more. The closer they got, the more of an open book Tisha proved to be. At times, she would hemorrhage information about Simon and his operations, which Alex secretly used against both of them. Much of the wealth he had acquired over the last two years was stolen directly from Simon's organization using the knowledge his own wife had provided. Before killing him, Alex vowed to cripple Simon financially, emotionally, and psychologically. He didn't care who he had to use or manipulate to do it, and even Tisha wasn't an exception.

Boston, Massachusetts

The next morning, Warren Jeffries stepped out of a rented Chevy Impala and began a long, lonely walk through the Granary Burying Ground. Though it was a windy, late spring day, he was dressed in a dark suit and dark sunglasses. The cool wind whipped around him making waves in the grass and rustling the leaves in the trees. He paused and took a deep breath while staring at the marker on the grave site. Engraved on the massive tombstone was the name, *Marcus Whitfield* and in its center was a picture of a happy preteen boy.

"You'd almost be a grown man now if we hadn't met, Marcus. You had your whole life ahead of you. You were an athlete and a pretty decent student. What on Earth were you doing in that crack house? I've spent the last few years trying to be angry at you for killing my partner," Warren said with tears falling from his eyes.

"Instead, all I've been able to do is be angry at me. Why Marcus? *WHY?*"

His pitiful cry echoed throughout the cemetery, startling birds and some people nearby. As he stood there sobbing, Warren suddenly felt a hand on his shoulder. When he turned around, he saw an elderly black woman standing behind him with a big, warm smile on her face. In her hand was a small red and white fire truck.

"In my 92 years, I ain't never heard a white man cry so pitiful for a lil' black boy," she said while wiping a tear from Warren's cheek.

"There's a reason for that ma'am."

"I know sugah, and you need to let it go. Marcus is in a much better place."

"Excuse me? Do I know you, ma'am?"

"You don't remember me, do you Officer Jeffries?" she asked while leaning down and placing the truck near the base of the headstone. "I'm Ruby Whitfield, Marcus's great-grandmother."

"I'm so sorry, Ms. Whitfield," Warren mumbled with his head lowered. "I'm usually good with faces."

"Sorry for what, honey? I've been watching you come to this cemetery for years, cursing the Lord and crying out to Marcus for forgiveness. It's not Marcus's job to forgive. That's the Lord God's job and He already forgave you. I admit it was hard for me to forgive you for taking my Lil' Marc, but I watched him growing up, and I knew it was only a matter of time before the streets claimed him. You did my baby's soul a favor. I know he's with Jesus, despite his sins."

Warren was awestruck by the compassion coming from this feeble stranger. Though she had every reason to hate him, Ruby pitied him instead. Warren's heart ached while standing there forcing smile through his tears. Like any kindly grandmother, she reached into her purse, pulled out another tissue, and began dabbing his tear soaked face.

"Come with me, Officer Jeffries. The Lord has a Word for you."

A short while later the conspicuous pair was seated at a window booth inside the local soul food cafe. It was quite an unusual sight to see a white man in this South Boston neighborhood, which was obvious by the numerous stares they were receiving. To make matters worse, he was sitting with the great-grandmother of a boy who many said was murdered by police. Judging by his clean cut appearance, dark suit, and unmarked sedan, the patrons and passersby knew he was a cop, fed, or some other form of law enforcement. Either way, Warren wasn't welcome, and he knew it. He ignored their stares and whispers, and instead, concentrated on the sweet woman across the table from him.

"Don't pay them no mind, sugah," she said while sipping her tea. "This neighborhood is a hotbed for ignorance."
"Why do you stay?"
"I've been here for over sixty years and this neighborhood is all I know. I've seen it change so much in that time. It wasn't always this bad. Kids turn to drugs 'cause there ain't no jobs around here. All they know is bling-bling and rap music. Young girls round here poppin' they fingers, poppin' they hips, and nine months later they poppin' out babies," she chuckled out loud. "They walk around all day pattin and turnin'."

"Pattin' and turnin?"

"Yep, pattin the bricks and turnin' tricks!" she chuckled again. "I made you smile," she pointed out as Warren sat across the table from her visibly more relaxed.

"You tried to make a difference and I thank God for that. You didn't become a part of the problem. Good police like you wanted to fix it. You didn't take my baby from me. Fast living did that."

"I see Marcus's face every time I close my eyes. I can't shake the feeling that if I had used better judgment...I might have been able to save his life."

"Officer Jeffries..."

"Please call me Warren," he interrupted politely.

"Warren, you keep seeing Marcus's 'cause you carrying around that guilt. Let it go, sugah. I can look into your eyes and know you didn't go to work that day to kill my Lil' Marc."

"No ma'am, I didn't."

"Your eyes tell me that. But you have to believe it in your soul. God has forgiven you for doing your job. You have to forgive yourself now."

"How do I do that?" he asked anxiously.

"Go to God, sugah. He'll show you."

Wisdom rolled off of Ms. Ruby's tongue so smoothly and without hesitation, that it was frightening. For the first time in years, Warren felt true peace. A calm feeling settled on him that he couldn't explain. He reached out, took her by the hand, and held it like a fragile flower. Though he knew he had to, Warren didn't want to let it go. Ms. Ruby had a presence unlike any he'd ever known.

"Thank you."

155

"If you really wanna thank me, pay for my lunch," she laughed when she looked at Warren and squeezed his hand.

After they finished eating, Warren drove Ms. Ruby home and accompanied her to the door. She kissed him on the cheek then watched from her window when he walked out of her building. She waved at him and smiled when he drove off, clutching Marcus's photo to her bosom the entire time. During his late afternoon flight back to Denver, Warren slept a peaceful sleep. He dreamed of the sweet old woman who'd shared so much of her soul with him. She was dressed in a white gown with a big smile on her face and glowing ivory wings. Behind her was a bright orange light that lit up everything around her. At Ruby's side dressed in white with wings of his own, was Marcus. He too had a huge smile on his face. Though he was fast asleep in his seat, Warren cracked a smile from deep in his soul.

Denver, Colorado

Alex and the team were gathered at the hangar to await the arrival of 'The Renegades.' While the rest of the team, including Doc and several technicians milled around discussing tactics, location, and available equipment, Alex was sitting at a table in the corner. Across from him was Big Mike, who was reading a copy of the King James Bible. While sitting there in silence, Alex studied the book's beautiful black and gold leather cover as well as Big Mike's reactions to what he was reading. Though he knew Big Mike was a man of incredible faith and had read the Bible numerous times, Alex still marveled at his various facial expressions. It was as if he was learning something new with the turn of each page.

"You know," Big Mike began after feeling Alex's stares, "the real message is inside these covers. All you have to do is open the book to witness the magic. You do believe in God, don't you, Alex?" Big Mike asked when he lowered the book and looked across the table.

"Of course I do," he replied before his mind flashed back to the image of his body being suspended from a crucifix at St. Stephens Cathedral. "We just haven't been on speaking terms in a while."

"Perhaps you should talk to Him. You might receive some clarity. We both know you have a lot of questions that you'd like to have answered. He's waiting for you, Alex. No invitations are necessary."

Alex stared briefly at his counterpart who'd casually returned to reading his reading and couldn't believe how smoothly he'd just him out. What was even more unbelievable was that Big Mike was right! Alex was full of questions about his life, his experiences, and his losses. There were so many questions swimming in his head that he didn't know where to begin. He just wanted to know the answers. He continued staring at Big Mike as he flipped the pages, reading and absorbing every line in his book.

"How do you think your dad would feel if he really knew where the money for his church came from?"

The covers of the book suddenly closed and a met the table top; hard. Combined looks of anger and distress crossed Big Mike's face when he gazed across the table at Alex.

"Why would you ask me that, Alex?"

"I'm not trying to upset you, Mike, but I am curious. How would your dad feel if he knew that you, the son of a preacher, were a hired gun? We both know that he wasn't happy about your stint as a Navy SEAL. And I'm not judging because I donated too."

"I'm not angry at you, Alex. I've asked myself that question and many others numerous times. I really don't know what he'd say. He might disown me."

Big Mike's usual jovial mood suddenly became very somber and, Alex knew why. His uneasiness made Alex ponder the necessity of his questions, but there were still more that he had to ask. Though he tried, Alex couldn't keep them from escaping his lips.

"Do you think God likes what we do?"

"What do you mean?" Big Mike asked curiously.

"What do I mean? Mike, we're assassins, hit-men. We travel the world killing people indiscriminately. Granted, they're the scum of the Earth and most of them deserve to die, but it's killing none-the-less. I haven't read the Bible as much as you have, but I'm pretty sure that there are rules against that."

"You're correct," Mike began while carefully choosing his words. "But the same God has declared war as well. He crushed the Egyptians in the Red Sea, He lead Joshua in the Battle of Jericho, and lead Saul into battle against the Philistines. He even allowed David to kill Goliath with a sling shot and a rock. The book of Judges is full of stories of God's generals who lead His armies into war. Remember Samson? As we both know, wars have casualties and one of the casualties of any war is death. Throughout history," Mike continued after seeing that he had Alex's undivided attention, "many wars have been fought in the name of religion, but only the wars that have been declared by God hold any meaning. And those, my inquisitive young friend are few and far between."

"So where does that leave people like you and I?"

"That depends, Alex. Do you believe in angels?"

"Of course I do. I believe in Heaven and Hell, the afterlife, and that we all have someone or something greater than us watching over us. Why?"

"What about Warrior Angels? Do you believe that angels can be dispatched into battle? Michael is such an angel."

"Is that what we are, Warrior angels?"

"I like to think so. You see, Alex, people aren't always willing to accept the presence of God, even though they pray to Him and ask Him to intervene on their behalves. I like to believe that's where we come in. We're the Warrior Angels of the Earth Realm. In our own way, we're doing God's work. We banish evil to hell where it belongs."

"Constance asked me if 'I like playing God?'"

"How did you respond?" Mike asked before laughing at the ignorance of her assumption.

"I told her what I do is balance the scales between justice and vengeance."

"Vengeance is mine, sayeth the Lord."

"Maybe I'm an instrument of His vengeance," Alex replied while seemingly embracing his dark nature again. "Maybe my whole life; my parents' murder, my time in Japan, Simone's death... maybe it's all been a setup to bring me to this point."

"And what point is that?" Big Mike asked after sensing that Alex was heading down the wrong road with his interpretations.

"The point of being cold, callous, and emotionally detached from my work," he replied very matter of fact.

"I don't think that's quite what God has in store for you, Alex. I do believe however, that the events of your life have molded, shaped, and hardened you as an instrument for His use, but I doubt He has purposely tortured you as a means of training you."

"But, Mike why me? Why any of us for that matter? Why couldn't we just be normal? I mean, I went to college, graduated at the top of my class, and I own several lucrative businesses. You and Chantelle manage several hair salons. Pretty much everyone has some sort of skill outside of this. Why make us killers too?"

"You chose to be an assassin, Alex, just like there rest of us," Mike replied with a bit-of-frost in his tone. "You could have taken another path, but you chose this one. What separates us from you is you choose to walk in, and even embrace the darkness that festers in your soul. You see your life as a punishment, but God never puts more on us than we can handle. He may test you, but He won't punish you. I've watched you deal with a lot of pain in your life. I've seen you bend but never break. It takes a strong person to walk in your shoes and God tests you because He knows you can handle it."

"But why?" Alex insisted.

"Because God wants to know who we are in Him and who He is in us. Sometimes, He strips us of all we want, so that He can give us what we need. And for some of us, our greatest need is to be needed by others. The world needs us, Alex. Once you realize that, you'll feel better about what you do."

"I made peace with what I do when I was eighteen."

"And since that day, I've seen your biggest issue become your darkness. You embrace it while continuing to ignore the light that shines inside you."

"Embracing my darkness has saved our asses more than once, Mike," Alex interrupted, slightly offended.

"Hold on, Alex. I didn't say that was totally a bad thing. What I mean is I believe that God appoints certain people to do His will in the Earth realm. That includes waging wars. In the final days, God will call upon His Warrior Angels."

"So, do you think we're Warrior Angels sent into this world by God?"

"I believe that we've been blessed with talents that we're supposed to use to advance The Kingdom."

"Even if that means murder?"

"Casualties of war, Alex," Big Mike replied attempting to reassure both Alex and himself. "Have faith, young brother. Your deeds aren't for naught. In time, you'll see that what you perceive as losses were removed to make way for blessings. The blessings you've received must be used to be a blessing to others."

"You really believe that, don't you, Mike?"

"Not only do I believe it, I live it. If you think about it, your whole life has been based on that principle. Your field of vision is just too narrow to see it. Open your eyes and your mind. You'll find something that you hadn't seen previously."

"Look alive, fellas," Gary interrupted from the hangar entrance. "Trouble is coming this way."

"Guess we're done here," Alex said when he stood up with his right hand extended.

"No, we're not," Mike answered after taking his hand and shaking it firmly, "this is only the beginning of the journey. The question is how far will you take it?"

For the second time since the conversation began, Alex was left stunned by what he'd just heard. Thus far, only Constance and Lexi were the only other people who'd been able to dissect him this effectively. Having Big Mike do it was an unwelcome, but necessary intrusion because it forced Alex to confront some of his issues.

Even though he was still in deep thought about what he'd heard, Alex joined the team at the hangar's entrance.

As they stood looking down the airport road, a constant, low rumble built off in the distance. The heat of early summer created a low-level haze just above the Earth's surface. Seconds later, a dust cloud appeared and the ground began to move. The rumble got louder as the glimmer of chrome appeared on the horizon, and within seconds, it was replaced by the roar of big-bore chopper engines. When the dust cleared and the roaring ceased, three hulking brutes stood before them dressed in black leather vests, combat boots, and jeans under their black leather chaps. Each one was standing next to a custom chopper that was decked out with flames, skulls, crossbones, and other gothic symbols. As the two groups engaged in a silent stare down, a fourth custom motorcycle roared to a stop between them, standing on its front tire before its rear slammed hard on the ground below it.

"Who's the little guy on the Ducati?" Richard whispered to Nicholas.

"Taurus the Bull, welcome to Colorado," Alex said, finally breaking the silence.

"Black Mamba, it's always a pleasure," replied the towering, bald giant with his reddish beard and a thick Russian accent.

"Where's Knock-Down?"

"He died in explosion in Malaysia. His detonator malfunctioned. He died in the fashion most familiar to him."

"How so?" Ko asked after being shocked by the news.

"How you say… he went out with bang!" Taurus replied before bursting into a fit of laughter with his two hulking comrades following suit.

"These dudes are fucked up," Gary whispered to Big Mike who was shaking his head.

"Who's the replacement?" Doc asked, motioning towards the small-statured figure who was slowly removing a helmet that matched the bright green and black racing bike.

When the long, raven hair cascaded from beneath the helmet, Doc and company were left standing with their mouths and eyes stretched wide. A whip of her head and a brush of her hair revealed a stunning Latina beauty. She dismounted her bike and walked towards Alex, unzipping her jacket along the way. The team watched as the wet, black leather that was hugging her curvaceous frame revealed a pair of stunning black lace-clad breasts.

"Think Doc will let us keep her?" Richard whispered to his awestruck twin brother.

"I want one," Gary whispered with a wide grin on his face while ogling sexy stranger.

"The infamous Black Mamba," she began while caressing his cheek. "I've heard so much about you."

"I don't believe I've had the pleasure," Alex replied while staring into her dark brown eyes and being hypnotized by her beauty and her accent.

"No you haven't, but maybe you will," she replied before winking at him. "But then again, I don't know if you're my type."

"What's your type?"

"I haven't decided yet. Do you have a sister?" she asked, smiling after observing Alex's reaction to her touch and her naughty question.

"What a waste," Ko whispered.

"Her name is Millicent Santiago. Call sign is Nine Millie."

"What are your skills?" Nick asked, attempting to flirt with the petite Latina.

"I'm a third degree black-belt in six different disciplines and I can speak seven languages fluently. I can outshoot, outdrive, and outfight any merc in the world. And, I'm pretty good with a blade," she said with a smile before pulling a butterfly knife from her pocket, flipping it open, and quickly shattering a light on the side of the hangar with it.

"How'd you come to be a member of this bunch?" Gary asked after surveying the damage.

By the scowl on his unshaven face, he was clearly unimpressed by her wanton display and her other list of credentials. Her body on the other hand, was a different story all together.

"About ten years ago, these guys broke up a human trafficking ring in Panama. I was one of many young victims. After rescuing me, Ash took me under his wing. Taurus, Knock-Down, and Machete assisted with my training. When Knock-Down died, I was activated to full time status."

"Relax, comrade. She can more than hold her own. Now on to more important things. Black Mamba, why haven't you cut your hair? Ponytail makes you look like sissy."

"There are still a few women who find it sexy," Alex replied while gazing into Nine Millie's eyes. "Besides, Ash wears a ponytail and I don't think he's been accused of being a sissy, have you big fella?"

"That's 'cause I'm a 6'9", 357lb brick-wall, brotha!" replied the burly Samoan while glaring angrily at Alex. "Calling me a sissy is a death sentence."

"Me too," Alex replied with a sinister grin etched on his face.

"I take it you all received my briefs," Doc said, interrupting the testosterone fueled standoff.

"Yes, we did. In fact, we were in the act of planning assault when we received it."

"Your team was already planning an assault?" Big Mike asked after being taken aback by Taurus' revelation. "You guys were going to take down the cartels by yourselves?"

"Precisely, Ballistic. We've had operatives stationed in Mexico for long time now. Your intel is incorrect. I have man on inside. Meeting in six days, not 2 weeks. By the way, bald head looks good on you."

"Told you," Alex growled in Doc's direction. "So you were already in Mexico, huh? Why not call us?"

"Operations like ours never get official approval to do anything. Unlike you, we don't receive orders. We receive 'recommendations.' We have been working for years inside cartels trying to find links and leaks. We have crossed paths more than once my friend; Cartagena, Sao Paulo, and Rio. You killed eight of my men, Black Mamba."

"What?"

"That is correct, my young friend. I must say I did not believe the rumors of a man capable of moving as quickly and quietly as you. Had I not seen if for myself, I would still be in disbelief."

"Are you saying you saw me kill them? When and where?"

"In Sao Paolo; the night your man froze up," Taurus replied. "You shot out the lights and proceeded to kill four of my best. Needless to say, that did not sit well with the rest of my team," he concluded before looking at Ash who looked poised to tear Alex in half. "But that is nature of the beast."

"I'm sorry. I had no idea," Alex conceded. "That does beg another question though. Why is it you know so much about our operations and we know jack about yours?"

"You'll have to refer that question to your superiors," Taurus replied before all eyes shifted to Doc.

"How many operatives do you all have in Mexico?" Doc asked while ignoring their stares.

"Trust me comrade. We have enough. We also have police and military support."

"Police and military?" Nick asked while glaring at Taurus.

"Yeah...I mean we thought they were owned by the cartels," Richard interrupted before looking at Alex who was shaking his head. "How do we know we can trust them?"

"Not all police and military are owned by the cartels," Nine Millie snapped viciously. "The media would like you to believe that all of Mexico is under cartel control, but that's not the case. Brave men and women are risking their lives to combat the greed and corruption that has overtaken my homeland. She will rise again."

"So long as they stay the hell out of our way," Gary snapped while standing with his arms folded across his massive chest. "We can't risk any clashes with the military or the police. And we sure can't have their blood on our hands."

"Gary's right. That's bad for business," Big Mike added after patting his counterpart on the shoulder.

"Hollow-point, Ballistic...relax. We're the only ones getting dirty on this one. Police and military are there for cleanup and press only."

"We do the work, they get the credit," Ko fired while running fingers through his tapered hair.

"Precisely, Tavarish."

"Okay, Tavarish," Doc began while pointing at a map of Mexico, "you have people on the inside, but what else can you offer?"

"For starters, we have the layout of compound where the meeting will be held, and manifests for weapons shipments coming from one of your military's installations."

"Shipment? What exactly are they purchasing?" Big Mike asked before narrowing his eyes on Doc.

"I take it you were not aware that your military has been supplying the cartels with weaponry for decades."

"That's not entirely true," Doc interrupted before snatching the USB-drive that Taurus was holding. "We're aware that a team of well-connected ex-Seals has been operating since the first Desert Storm. They've been secretly selling weapons on the black market that were scheduled for decommission. The Mexican cartels are their biggest customers."

"This just keeps getting better and better," Gary growled sarcastically while pacing back and forth.

"What exactly are we up against?" Alex asked, while watching his teammates' enthusiasm rapidly dwindling.

"Ruiz arranged to purchase fifty RPGs, five-hundred AR-15 Assault Rifles, fifty Kevlar body suits, similar to the ones that your team used to wear, night vision goggles, and four-armored Hummers."

"Are you fucking serious?" Alex shouted in disgust.

"I don't kid around, lil brotha," Ash replied rather matter-of-fact.

"Okay, let's backup. These cartels are very well connected and heavily armed. That being said, they know they're being watched. That's why they keep changing the dates. If we're going to put something together, it needs to be now. As it stands, Taurus has all the cards on his side of the table, which means you guys are the point on this one. We'll follow your lead."

"Alex, are you listening to yourself? You're going to let...them take the point on an operation that could get us all killed?"

"What choice do we have, Gary?" Alex asked while shrugging his shoulders.

"What exactly do you mean by 'them'?" Ash asked after stepping forward and standing toe-to-toe with Gary. "If you're getting cold feet, step aside and let the big boys handle this one."

"Let me tell you something, *big boy*," Gary snapped while being dwarfed by the massive Samoan. "While you were shaking your gigantic ass is a grass skirt, I was kicking ass and taking names. I've seen action on damn near every continent! You think you're a bad ass? Me and Big Mike over there are the baddest of the bad asses."

"What is your point, Tavarish?"

"My point, Taurus, is that your team is full of shit. This operation is too big to hand you the reigns just to wait and see what happens. No offense, but I don't trust you."

"No offense taken, comrade," Taurus began as he stepped over to where Gary and Ash were standing. "Incidentally, as I look at your team, I too see mercs, outcasts, sadists, and killers. Though your concerns are valid, I want you to keep one thing in mind. You called us. We didn't call you."

The back-and-forth bickering continued well into the night with neither camp was willing to budge, despite the fact that time was against them. Alex sat at a table in the corner wondering how Taurus had known about their operations in Brazil and why Doc had hidden it from them. *Eight men died unnecessarily,* he thought while cutting his eyes towards his mentor. Suddenly out of the corner of his eye, Alex saw Nine Millie slip out of the hangar undetected. Figuring he wouldn't be missed either, Alex decided to join her.

"Are you okay?" he asked with the warm night air whipping around them.

"When will they learn that nothing can be resolved by arguing?" she asked with tears in her eyes.

"Believe it or not, it's like this all the time. This always happens when you get this much testosterone in one place at the same time. It's kind of like a tornado meeting a hurricane."

"You seem very different from your friends, Black Mamba."

"How so?" he asked curiously.

"You have two auras; one light and one dark, and they're in constant conflict. The dark one appears to be overshadowing the light though."

"And what about you Millicent?"

"What about me?" she asked defiantly.

"I see a scared little girl whose innocence was taken a long time ago. Since then, she's been waging a war against the forces of evil; a war she doesn't believe she'll win, yet she keeps fighting anyway. Was it chance or fate that aligned you with Ash and the rest of the gang? You don't have to answer that."

"What is it that you fear most, Black Mamba?

"Failure. And you?"

"What I fear most is that if I don't keep fighting, the evil forces you speak of will win," she replied softly.

Alex watched quietly while Millicent stood in the breeze rubbing her shoulders. She'd long given up the fight against the tears streaming down her face. Though in her mind being vulnerable was a sign of weakness, her tears brought her comfort. Millicent didn't know why, but she felt safe. His words, however, cut her to her very soul. *How could he know?* she thought after quickly glancing at him. She hated Alex for exposing her, yet at the same time, she was relieved that he did.

"You wanna get outta here?" he asked after taking her by the hand.
"Yes."

Seconds later, Alex's Challenger was speeding towards Denver, and to his surprise, the phone call he expected regarding his whereabouts never came. Later that night as much of the city slept, Alex was sitting at the table next to an empty bottle of Paul Masson. Having grown stronger and cooler, the night winds whipped around them causing the flames in the torches to flicker.

"Would you like another drink?" he asked while filling his glass and looking towards the fence where Millicent was standing.

While looking out over the city's skyline and marveling at the snow capped mountains in the distance, she found a peace that had long eluded her. The pain of her past no longer existed. For the first time in her life, Millicent felt free.

"Sure."

As the wine splashed into her glass, Alex tried to imagine what kinds of horrors she was hiding. Like him, Millicent had built up so many walls around her that she was lost in the maze she'd created. He had no trouble picking up on her character traits, because they were almost identical to his own.

Millicent was so wrapped up in the peace of the city that she didn't notice Alex disappear into the penthouse until he returned with a blanket and wrapped it around her shoulders.

"Thank you, Black Mamba."
"No problem," he replied with a smile.

She had forgotten how innocent a man's touch was supposed to be. His hands on her skin, touching her in such a loving and tender way were things that Millicent Santiago longed for, yet had convinced herself didn't exist. She watched as he returned to the table and silently wished he would touch her again. He was handsome, intriguing, charming, but most of all, Alex was gentle. She couldn't help but wonder if all the stories that she'd heard were true, and found her body craving his touch.

"Black Mamba, may I ask you a question?"
"Sure. I'm an open book," he replied.
"How many people have you killed?"
"I stopped counting after the first one. It makes this madness easier to deal with."
"You don't like this, do you Black Mamba?"
"Not really," Alex replied dryly. "I've had the stench of blood on my hands for as long as I can remember. My whole life has been filled with death and carnage."
"Then why do you do it? Why don't you break the cycle?"
"Because it helps me keep the nightmares at bay," he replied in a near whisper.
"You have nightmares too?" she gasped in shock.
"When I was a little girl, my grandmother used to tell us

171

stories of the Chupacabra, the goat sucker. She said that the Chupacabra would come like a thief in the night and steal away all the children and the livestock. They suck the life out of their victims, totally draining them of blood. The only thing left is a dry, empty shell. These cartels are the new Chupacabras and this is what they are doing to my homeland of Mexico. They are sucking the blood out of her and leaving her dry and lifeless."

"This is personal for you, isn't it?" Alex asked while tracing the rim of his glass with his index finger.

"You have no idea. Everything I've been through in my life...all the pain, agony, and abuse...all of it has prepared me for this point. I've lost countless friends and family over the years to these animals. I won't rest until I do something, or die trying."

"Millie, I promise you we'll get this through together. What you saw last night was merely a difference in professional philosophies. Your friends didn't die in vain. Mexico will be free from these cartels."

"I hope so, Black Mamba, because time is running out."

"I know it is. Listen, it's late and we both need rest. You can use my sister's room. I laid out some things for you to freshen up with. In the morning, we'll head back and get the rest of the team on the same page."

"You really believe we can?" she asked while gazing into his hazel-colored eyes.

"If they don't, then you and I will go in alone. Do or die."

"Do or die," she repeated before smiling and kissing his cheek. "I knew you were different, Black Mamba."

"Not really. Good night, Millicent Santiago. Sleep well."

"Good night, Black Mamba."

A few hours later as he lay in bed, Alex was suddenly startled by the sound of his bedroom door slowly opening and closing. With his hand on the Glock 19 under his pillow, Alex watched the figure step into the blue moonlight that was shining through the window.

"I couldn't sleep," she whispered before pulling back the covers.

Alex released the trigger when she crawled in the bed next to him. He laid back down and watched her naked body curl up in a ball. In the moonlight, his eyes traced the intricate details of her tattooed back; the grim reaper holding his sickle. Alex found himself paralyzed as the tattoo suddenly came to life before his eyes. He watched in horror while the ominous character taunted him repeatedly by swinging his sickle. With a blink of eyes, the grim reaper was gone, resuming its rest on Millie's back.

"Black Mamba?"
"Yes."
"You can touch me if you want to," she whispered in a soft, shaky voice.
"Is that what you want?" he asked after taking her by the waist and pulling her towards him.

The perfume she had borrowed from Lexi's collection was intoxicating.

"Yes," she gasped when she felt his powerful arm on her side and his heart beating against her back.

Her flesh tingled with in anticipation of his entry. Millicent shuddered when Alex's hand caressed her body; first her thigh, then her back, and finally her arm. Icy shivers raced up and down her spine when his arm snaked back around her waist and pulled her body even closer to his. Her heart began racing when she felt his manhood gently nudging against the crack of her ass, a sensation that caused moisture to seep from between her quivering thighs. A muffled moan escaped her lips when she felt his hot breath on her neck.

"Good night, Millicent," he whispered after placing a soft kiss on her shoulder.
What the fuck?!!! she thought as her body teetered on the peak of a climax. "Black Mamba? Alex?" she whispered grinding her soft ass against his stiffness.

His only reply was a gentle nudge against her ass followed by a low, peaceful snore. For a few moments, Millicent lay there in dumbfounded. *Were the stories they told me lies?* As Alex slept, she silently recounted the warnings her comrades had given her about Alex's powers of persuasion. Her body was crying out for his touch while images of her legs wrapped around his waist filled her mind. In her mind, Alex, the *'Black Mamba,'* was the ultimate man and now she was in bed with him. The only indication of interest he'd given were nudges and nothing more. Millicent contemplated rolling over, waking Alex up, and making him live up to her body's expectations.

At the same time, however, she was glad he'd gone to sleep without taking advantage of her. She was feeling more vulnerable than she was comfortable with admitting. Years of sexual abuse at the hands of men and women alike had filled Millicent with doubts and insecurities about her own sexuality. In the wake of their mutual attraction and obvious connections, she was comforted by the fact that she would eventually fall asleep in Black Mamba's arms. His restraint made him that much more enticing. Throughout the night, though, she held out hope that Alex would wake up and make love to her.

Just after dawn, Millicent woke up in his bed alone. After wrapping herself in the white satin sheet, she got up and began exploring the massive penthouse. She hadn't been in a home this elaborate since being rescued from the trade. This was the lifestyle that so many like her sought, but few ever saw. She quickly realized that Alex was a pretender; a chameleon. He was nothing more than a rich man pretending to be an assassin.

After a brief search, Millicent found him on the patio dressed in gray athletic shorts and black vest. Alex's every movement; kicks, punches, leaps, rolls, spins, and even his breathing seemed fluid, precise, and direct. Not a single movement was wasted. She watched in awe as he stood in the center of four black-clad mannequins and realized that he was wearing a blindfold. Leaping into the air and spinning, he reached into the vest and pulled out several, multi pointed stars which he sent hurling into the bodies of the four mannequins. Upon landing, he grabbed a Katana from the ground, charged one the dummies and with a violent swipe, removed its head.

"He can't be doing that, not blindfolded," Millicent whispered, even though she witnessed his awesome display with her own eyes. *"He has to be able to see through that thing."* After twirling the blade in his hand, Alex parked it in a block of wood on his way to the patio door. Once inside, he closed it, removed the blindfold, and smiled at his awestruck guest.

"Good morning."

"How do you do that blindfolded? What's your secret? You have to be able to see through that thing, right?"

"When I was younger, I one of my first instructors a blind ninja master. He took a particular interest in my anger and showed me how best to use it. While our collective senses are quite extraordinary, our individual senses can be deadly. He taught me to separate them and turn each one into a weapon. That way, when one failed, I could compensate by using the others. He believed that our eyes are our greatest weakness because we're so quick to believe everything that we see. But take them away, and suddenly you become vulnerable. It's when you learn to separate your senses that you become a true master of your surroundings. Your powers of discernment are heightened to their fullest potential, because you feel with every fiber of your being instead of relying on what you think is directly in front of you."

"I don't believe you," she smiled, not wanting to accept Alex's imaginative explanation.

"No?" he quipped with a smile. "Try it on then."

After catching the blindfold and securing the sheet around her naked frame, she held it tight to her eyes.

"You've got to be kidding…its pitch black."

"I know," he replied, now squatting behind the couch with his face mere inches from hers.

"You are an intriguing man, Black Mamba."

"No more intriguing than you, Nine Millie."

"No, I'm not…if you know the right questions to ask, Alex," she replied coyly before leaning back on the couch and exposing his eyes to her bust line. "Ask me anything you like."

"Ok," he began before standing up and walking towards the dining room table, "how long are you going to keep up this charade?"

"What charade?" she asked, caught off guard by his accusation and even more disappointed that he had walked away. "I don't follow you."

"The woman that climbed into my bed last night wasn't a killer. She was afraid and lost. She's also looking for something that she thinks the death of others can provide."

"And what is it that you're looking for, Black Mamba?" she asked while gazing lustfully at his tattooed back.

"I don't know," he whispered while looking over his shoulder.

"I think I know what you are looking for, Black Mamba; closure. This morning, as you held me, you called me Simone. It doesn't take a genius to realize that she was someone important to you. My question is why would you let someone so dear to you go?"

"I didn't," he replied after a long, deep breath. "She was taken from me. She was murdered."

"I'm sorry, Black Mamba," Millicent gasped while covering her mouth. "I...I didn't know."

"It's okay. You had no way of knowing."

"Her murderer...did you kill him?" she asked after sensing his pain and thinking about her own life's losses.

"No," Alex replied softly while staring at the sky outside the door.

"Do you plan to?"

"Yes."

"After you do," she began before standing up and walking over to him, "can you make me a promise?"

"What's that?"

"Will you let go of the pain and start living again?"

"Avenging her death is all I am living for. There is nothing else."

"Then find something else," she pleaded with her head resting on his back and her arms around his waist. "I

177

did. With everything that's happened to me, I want to make damned sure it doesn't happen to anyone else. That's my purpose. That's my reason for going on. What's yours going to be?"

"Tell me about your family in Mexico," he said after a few moments of silence.

Two hours later, Alex's blacked out Ferrari 458 Italia rumbled to a stop near the hangar's entrance. When he and Millicent exited the car, they heard the two sides still engaging in their heated argument. The closer they got, the louder the shouting match became. As Alex stood in the doorway shaking his head, Millicent decided she'd had enough. She pulled a butterfly knife from her belt, flipped it open, and plunged it into the center of the table. Following suit, Alex yanked a .40 cal from the small of his back and fired two shots into the air. As quickly as the yelling ceased, Alex and Millie suddenly found themselves decorated with numerous red dots.

"Now that we have your attention," Alex began with his eyes narrowed, "let's get down to business. We have less than five days to put this op together, yet you're still fighting like a pack of wolves. Despite the millions we have invested in this outfit, the misfits, as you call them, have more connections and intelligence, which puts them farther ahead of the curve than we are. Couple that with Millie's familial ties to the military and the police, it only makes sense that we follow their lead. Now, if anyone has a problem with that, the door is behind me."

"Fine...I'm out!" Gary barked before slamming his clipboard on the table. "You wanna gamble our lives, your so-called brothers-in-arms, for a band of gun-toting psychos and a piece of ass? Go right ahead! It's your funeral, Black Mamba. I won't be there!" he growled while walking towards Alex.

"Anybody else?" Alex fired back while glaring at the angry behemoth.

"Mike, you rollin'?" Gary demanded after looking over his shoulder.

"We got a job to do, bro," Big Mike replied in his thundering voice.

"Fine. Throw your lives away if you want."

The room remained silent until Gary's black Chevy Suburban disappeared leaving behind a cloud of dust and flying rocks.

"Now that that's over, let's get to work."

Chapter 7

Later that evening in the night skies, a custom G-6 containing the remaining members of the *'The Agency'* and 'The Renegades' was cruising towards Mexico. Millicent and Alex were seated in the luxurious forward cabin while their teams were assembled behind them in a state-of-the-art passenger compartment. With her head resting on his shoulder, Alex stared out the window into the night sky. His mind was filled with thoughts of Simone, Lynn, and this mission that he was about to embark on. Though they were united in their beliefs, not a single soul wanted to be on that plane. With so much at stake, the lack of a proper plan of attack was weighing heavy on his mind. They were going in blind, and to make matters worse, their efforts were actually benefiting Simon. That alone was like rubbing salt in an open wound.

"Black Mamba," she whispered while gently squeezing his arm.
"Yes?"
"Thank you."
"For what?"
"For last night...for not taking advantage," she whispered while nestling up to him.
"No problem," he whispered before kissing her forehead.

When Alex returned to staring out of the window, various thoughts continued racing through his mind. *When did I dream about either of them?* Even though he barely knew her, Lynn's presence made his world complete. In his heart he wished this whole Mexican debacle was behind him, so that he could be in her arms.

Meanwhile Millicent, aka 'Nine Millie' continued squeezing his arm. Alex looked at her and wondered if she was the soul mate he'd heard people speak of. She seemed to be so much more in tune with him than Lynn or Simone. Her life, her mission, her pain…all seemed to mirror his own. Though he contemplated it, Alex was glad he didn't make love to her. Their bond was above and beyond anything physical. It was spiritual and not worth risking for a few moments of pleasure. He was content to let her be the one that got away.

"Alex, can I talk to you for a minute?" Doc asked when he entered the cabin.

"Have a seat," he replied before returning his attention to the window.

"I meant alone," Doc said while nodding towards Millicent.

"She can't hear anything that you're saying."

"Fine," Doc reluctantly replied before taking a seat across from them. "I like the way you handled that situation earlier. You're growing into the leader that your dad was, the leader I know you can be. I'm proud of you, son."

"Pride is a dangerous thing," Alex replied without looking at Doc. "It can make fools out of the greatest men."

"I don't follow you."

"Why didn't you tell me I killed eight of Taurus's men? And before you answer, now isn't a good time for you to lie to me."

"Ok, Alex," Doc began callously, "I didn't want you to lose your edge. I can't have my best hitter second guessing himself in the field, especially when he's paired up with a basket case."

"Basket case," Alex growled with his eyes narrowed on Doc.

"Face it, Alex. Warren is shell shocked."

"You knew that when you recruited him," Alex fired back angrily.

"Be that as it may, he's no good to himself or anybody else in his current state. The fact of the matter is, if you had hesitated to kill them, they would've certainly killed both of you. It was a mission, and like many others, signals got crossed. Your antiquated senses of honor and nobility will eventually be your undoing if you don't stop ignoring what you really are."

"And what exactly am I, old man?"

"Simply put, you're a killer. In fact, you're the greatest killer walking the planet. It's in your DNA. Your father, Ko's father, the twins' father...all killers; even that little lady snuggled up on your arm. That's right," Doc continued while Alex gazed down at Millicent, "she's no different than the three animals she rode up with. She'd slit your throat without a second thought if she got half a chance. Look at her; young, talented, beautiful, and *so* gifted. She's like a wild horse on the prairie just waiting to be broken. Face it, Alex it's in her blood too. No wonder you two are so close," Doc mused. "Is she wild in bed too?"

The seasoned gladiator and his heir apparent were locked in such a pensive stare that neither of them noticed the pearl-handled blade twirling end-over-end above their heads until Millicent sprang from her seat. When she landed on Doc's lap, Millicent grabbed him by the throat, snatched the blade from the air, and thrust it into the headrest; a quarter-of-an-inch from his left ear.

"I see why he hates you so much," she whispered into Doc's right as sweat poured from his brow.

"Alex?!!" he plead while staring at the wild eyed woman perched on his lap.

"She's right," Alex replied before standing up and walking towards the door. "One more thing," he began after Millicent slithered off Doc's lap, "you once said you sent a boy to Japan and they sent back you back a killer. That was the first time. Do you have any idea what came back the second time?"

Chills raced up and down Doc's spine while looking at the icy stares being shot at him.

What did come back? he wondered when they disappeared through the cabin door.

Meanwhile n a deserted stretch of highway west of the city, *'Loco and the Midwest's Finest'* were returning from Chicago where they'd just headlined a sold-out concert. With music blaring from the speakers and weed smoke all around him, Loco was busy trying to conduct business.

"Yeah man, (cough, cough) we're here!" he hacked into his phone while passing a blunt to a member of his entourage. "We just toe it up in Chi-town, and now we're headed back to the Nati!" he declared proudly with his index finger stuck in his ear. "This shit is gonna put us on the map. A'wight nigga! Peace! Hey listen up niggas! Castro is on the way. As soon as we make this buy, we head to the spot and break it down. We gotta get it back on the street ASAP!"

"What about Dee, Loco?" asked the light skinned brother to his right with the long braids and the half-naked groupie on his lap.

"Fuck dat bitch yo! Castro is da man now. If she wants to roll with us, she has to beat his price!"

When the money-green King Aire motor coach rolled to a stop, a pair of headlights appeared over the horizon, and within seconds, a pair of Escalades stopped several yards from the front of the tour bus. The entourage quickly gathered themselves when men began to exiting the two, dark-colored SUVs. The men in the rear of the SUV to the right each carried a titanium colored briefcase while the men in the SUV on the left began unloading large foot lockers.

"Castro, what up homie?" Loco yelled while holding up a bottle of champagne and a half-empty glass.
"You, my brother!" replied the tall, tan Caucasian in the dark suit and slicked-back hair. "Glad you stopped playing in the minors and finally stepped up to the majors."
"Yeah man, let's do this."
"Of course," Castro replied before snapping his fingers.

The men from the second SUV brought up the foot lockers and placed them at Loco's feet. His eyes widened with delight when their lids were flipped open and he saw the shiny hardware.

"Everything gangstas like yourselves need; AR-15's with suppressors, MAC 11's with laser sights, and of course the Desert Eagles. Just like you requested, right?"
"What about the dope?" Loco demanded after snapping his fingers and summoning his crew to bring up a pair of Dallas Mavericks duffle bags.
"Four keys of pure Columbian, bro. This is what you requested, right?"
"Hell yeah," replied the short, stocky brother in the Heat Jersey before taking the briefcases.

"What's with all the heat?" asked the blond-haired henchman while staring at the careless way Loco was holding one of the rifles.

"We got a lot of haters, bro."

"I see," Castro replied while puffing on his Cuban. "Show me the money. Toss it over."

"You wanna count it first?" asked the brother in the Cincinnati Reds baseball jersey after dropping the bags at Castro's feet.

"I trust you, bro," Castro replied with a smile while blowing smoke into the night air.

"That's why I fucks wit you Castro! You da mutha-fuckin' truth, baby!"

"One more thing Loco," Castro said before tossing his cigar on the ground and stomping it out.

"What's that, playa?"

"You're under arrest."

"What the fuck?"

For a split second Loco thought he was in a dream. Blinding lights appeared from every direction. Choppers with blinding, halogen lights hovered overhead while voices crackled over numerous radios. Agents dressed in dark fatigues, helmets, and vests displaying FBI and ATF in bright yellow letters appeared out of the darkness with guns their guns raised and began yelling orders at Loco and his entourage. Shock then pain shot through their bodies after being slammed to the ground and handcuffed. For the next hour, the bewildered group sat on the ground as their Miranda rights were read and the tour bus was searched. The women who had been on the bus with them were herded off in another direction before being loaded in separate vehicles.

185

Denial, fear, anxiety, and betrayal set in as their lives unraveled right before their eyes. A few hours earlier, 'The Midwest Finest' was on stage in Chicago performing before a screaming crowd. They blew up the stage and afterwards, made it rain on a pack of money-hungry groupies. Now they were sitting on the cold concrete with guns pointed at them and canines snarling in their faces. At least three of the group's members lost control of their bladders and stomachs, which was evidenced by the streams of yellow liquid and chunks of partially digested food running past their crispy new Jordans and fresh Timberlands. The group watched helplessly as their luggage was dumped onto the ground and the bus was torn apart. Over the next three hours, the rappers were taunted by agents who retrieved three pounds of marijuana and four unregistered handguns.

"I don't believe this shit!" Loco cried towards Heaven with tears streaming from his eyes and urine pooling at his feet.

That evening around dusk, on a deserted farm deep in the heart of Mexico, 'The Renegades' and members of 'The Agency' were gathered for a strategy meeting. Unlike the hangar in Colorado, this meeting was being conducted in a series of tents and a dilapidated barn. There were no custom jets, state of the art computer equipment, or technicians running about. Instead, there were numerous laptops, spotlights, and GPS based communications links being powered by old, ragged generators. The 3-D maps and overheads projections were replaced by large paper maps with push pins, and a wall plastered with pictures, and post-it notes.

Though he didn't subscribe to the numerous stereotypes that had been heaped upon 'The Renegades', Alex couldn't ignore the obvious differences between their teams. They were made up mostly of men and women who would otherwise have no reason to ever be in the same room, let alone work together. There were bikers, white supremacists, Neo Nazis, black radicals, and some who looked like urban gang members. Though they were a melting pot from various backgrounds and ethnicities, they spoke a common language; the mission. What they lacked in technology and equipment, they made up with unity and brotherhood.

In addition to Taurus, Ash, Machete, and Nine Millie, there were thirty additional Renegades present with an additional fifty on standby in an undisclosed location. There were factions of the police and military present as well. While sitting in the corner and observing the action, Alex began feeling a little discouraged. His team was supposed to be the cohesive, highly-skilled unit that stood shoulder-to-shoulder with the best in the world. Their inability to cooperate and remain focused prior to coming to Mexico had proven them to be quite the contrary. As a result of this revelation, Alex's mighty ego was dealt a crushing blow.

"Heavy is the head that wears the crown."
"What are you talking about, Ko?" Alex asked when he looked over his shoulder.
"I know that look, bro. That's your *'what the fuck are we doing here'* look. The only time you have that look is when we work with these guys or you think we're in over our heads."
"I know why I'm here, Ko. I'm just wondering why I allowed you all to follow me."
"Allowed us? You arrogant jackass! We were assigned to this mission just like you."

"I know that Ko, but none of you really wanted to be here."

"And you did?" Ko fired back. "Look, Alex. You're not some lone gun slinger or dark knight avenger. You're a man, just like the rest of us. We're here for the same reasons you are; the mission."

"I didn't mean it like that. And you're right; I don't want to be here either. But after talking to Millie, I couldn't turn my back on what's going on down here."

"What could she possibly have told you that we don't already know?"

"It wasn't so much what she said. It was how she said it."

"Are you sure all you did was talk to her?" Ko quizzed while playfully nudging his best friend.

"What would you say if I told you that she lay naked in my bed all night and the only thing I did was hold her?"

"Alex, my friend, I'd believe anything you told me; except that."

"Well, that's my story and I'm sticking to it."

As their banter continued, three men stormed into the massive tent and quickly made their way to Nine Millie and Taurus. After a brief exchange of words, she ran out of the nearest door with her hand over her mouth. Doc, who was nearby, briefly exchanged words with them before they exited the tent behind her. When Doc made his way to their quiet corner, Alex and Ko found their nerves suddenly on edge.

"What was that about?" Alex asked while watching their shadows moving near the open door.

"About two weeks ago, two men who'd successfully infiltrated the Lobo Brothers cartel went missing. What was left of their bodies was found a few days ago. Their heads and hands were found and identified a few hours ago. One of the guys was Millie's cousin, a Mexican cop.

They'd been feeding the authorities information on the cartels for the past two years. It appears their status was somehow compromised."

"FUCK!" Alex yelled before storming towards a group of armored jeeps.

"Somehow compromised my ass," Ko snapped through his gritted teeth. "You know damned well this entire op was a cluster fuck from the outset."

"I was hoping that wasn't not the case, Ko."

"Alex, where are you going?" Ko asked when he turned around.

"Black Mamba," Taurus began when he saw Alex approaching, "I take it you've heard the news."

"Level with me, Taurus. How fucked up are we?"

"I assure you no one outside this network knows the details of this mission. We have several police and military units on standby for raids against the known rogue officials. That will keep them occupied and out of our way while we assault the compound."

"How many targets are you planning to take down?"

"One hundred."

"One hundred targets and three cartels in a single night? Where did these one hundred people come from?"

"Their names came from the Mexican President," Taurus replied while handing Alex a list. "With help from your government, the Mexican President appointed an independent committee to do an investigation of his administration along with several other key officials. From findings, they compiled this list."

"If he knows who they are, why doesn't he just have them arrested?" Alex asked while studying the names.

"You are talking about men who are very deep in with the cartels, but also close enough to the President to assassinate him. Several targets are serving in his cabinet. Calling them out is very dangerous to the President and his family."

"So in addition to eliminating his cartel problem, he also wants us to get his house in order? Nice."

"I sense frustration in your voice, Black Mamba. Are you thinking of pulling your team out? I understand if you are. This operation is geared more for us than you."

"I'll be honest with you. The thought has crossed my mind, but I promised someone I'd see this through to the end."

"Promises made to be broken, Black Mamba."

"Not mine," Alex replied sharply.

"So to keep promise, you would take your men into the jaws of death? I admire you."

"I never asked them to follow me, and part of me regrets that they did. But we have an understanding. At the end of the day, we go home."

"Let's be honest with each other, Black Mamba. I never plan on everyone returning alive after mission such as this."

"That's funny, Taurus, because I do."

"Then my friend, you are very naive," he said with his eyes narrowed at Alex.

"And you my friend are very reckless."

"Okay then, as long as you are here, I would like you to see what we've been planning. This is layout of compound," Taurus began while Alex stared at a crude, 3-D replica of the target made of shoes boxes, beer cans, food containers, and anything else they could find. "As you can see, there are four buildings; main house, a garage to the east, and another structure to the west which contains the communications hub for the entire area. The fourth structure at the rear of main house is storage shed. The area is extremely remote with no cell phone towers. That hub has to be destroyed in order to keep them from alerting backup."

"Done," said Alex while studying the layout.

"The people in the garage to the east of the main house must be neutralized as well."

"Done," Alex said again before turning his attention to Taurus. "I'm gonna need a few of your best shooters. They need to be able to utilize high-powered sniper rifles with night vision scopes. Accuracy is a must which means kill shots only. Ballistic will lead them and on his cue, they'll kill anything and anyone moving. Meanwhile, a team lead by me, will assault the garage."

"Excellent. My two teams will attack from the north and south leaving no room for escape."

"What about a power source? I'm sure this place is going to be pretty well lit. Darkness is the best cover we have. Tell your people on the inside to locate it and blow it. Then get out, understand?"

"Consider it done, Black Mamba."

"Cool," Alex said before leaning on the table and studying the layout again. "By the way, I didn't get any orders to capture and detain. Did you?"

"Nor did I comrade," Taurus replied with a huge grin.

Cincinnati, Ohio

On the fourth floor of the Hamilton County Justice Center in downtown Cincinnati sits interrogation rooms A thru M. Shortly after being arrested, the members of *'The Midwest's Finest'* were processed and booked into custody, but because of the FBI's interest the case, they weren't scheduled for arraignment and their arrests were kept secret. The group's members were held separately until Agent Blackhawk and his team arrived from Denver.

Later that morning around eleven, the group's members were taken one-by-one into separate interrogation rooms. Chauncey Lucien Mitchell, aka 'Loco' was the first to be interrogated. Faced with numerous charges including narcotics and weapons trafficking, possession of deadly ordinance, intent to purchase and distribute a controlled substance, and various other charges, 'Loco' and company immediately requested their lawyers. Rather than returning them to their cells, the FBI agents on site decided to let them sit in the interrogation rooms under close supervision. While waiting for Agent Blackhawk to arrive, Cincinnati's chief of police and the Hamilton County Sheriff were at odds with Agent Gabriel Castro over which entity had jurisdiction over the case.

"Look, Sheriff Leist," Castro began while smoothing his hair with his palm, "neither you nor Chief Craigwell is going to breathe a word of this to the media. It's that simple. This is a federal investigation and we're not about to let you screw up a three-plus year sting for a few minutes of television time."
"You're way out of line, Agent Castro! The feds have no business running operations in my county without my knowledge. If there's an investigation going on, damn it I'm entitled to know about it!"
"With all due respect sheriff, we couldn't risk your department getting in our way."
"In your way?" Sheriff Leist barked while Castro checked a message on his cell phone. "You smug son of a…"
"Gentlemen, gentlemen," began the recently appointed chief of police, "I am sure that if we put our differences aside, we can come to a consensus that would work to all our benefits. Agent Castro, the sheriff makes a valid point and as the chief of police I have to agree. Any operation of this magnitude should have had full disclosure between all interested offices. If blood had been spilled, it would be this office's responsibility to

inform the public. And to be honest, standing up and admitting we had no idea what you all were doing in our own backyard would be unacceptable in the public's eyes."

"I understand your concern, Chief Craigwell and that's exactly why your offices were left out of the loop. Because of the nature of the investigation and the individuals involved, we needed experienced officers on the scene who could exercise proper judgment; not trigger happy deputies and street cops trying to get famous overnight. We've been ordered to keep a lid on this investigation until our senior officer arrives. Like I said, this case been ongoing for over three years now. For now, that is all I can provide."

"If that's all you can provide Agent Castro, then you need to find somewhere to house your thugs. My county isn't opening the doors to the feds on blind faith."

"Wait a minute sheriff," interrupted Chief Craigwell, "this may be your county, but this is my city, and even under such restrictive circumstances, the FBI has my full cooperation."

"Correct me if I am wrong sheriff, but hasn't your own office been investigated by the FBI for among other things, improper practices and procedures? And Chief Craigwell, I am sure you're aware of the issues that this city's police force has experienced. Specifically, the deaths of several unarmed black men while being taken into custody or shortly thereafter that have received global attention. No one's forgotten the riots of 2001 either."

"Wait a minute, Castro. You can't blame me for the mistakes of the previous administration."

"That's correct chief, I can't. This is your city now, but the taint of the previous chief and his administration is all over it and sadly, that won't soon be forgotten. Your

193

offices will get their day in the sun, but for now, the details of this case cannot leave this office. Any leaks to the press or any other source will be deemed an obstruction of justice and will be dealt with swiftly."

"Is that a threat, Castro?" Sheriff Leist demanded when he bolted up from his chair.

"That's a promise, sheriff," he replied with a crooked grin.

Moments later, Agents Blackhawk and Carver burst into the office and in Agent Blackhawk's hand were two letters, both emblazoned with the FBI's official logo. He handed both the chief and the sheriff a copy of the letter which they both quickly glanced over.

"Excuse me for the interruption, gentlemen. My name is Agent Blackhawk, and I'm the lead investigator on this case. This is Agent Carver, and I'm sure you've already met Agent Castro. In your hands are official letters of apology from the bureau's chief in Washington."

"Thank you very much, son," the sheriff began while studying the document. "I'm sorry, but did you just say that you're the lead investigator on this case? How old are you son; twenty-five? Thirty?"

"Yes sir, I am the lead...in the absence of Agent Burroughs that is."

"Exactly what I thought! The bureau is sending young hotshots down here to tell me how to run my county!"

"With all due respect Sheriff Leist, what does my age have to do with any of this?" Jason snapped after abandoning the calm demeanor he'd entered with.

"You're a snot-nosed kid fresh off the reservation. Now you're a G-Man trying to make a name for yourself chasing down bad guys in my backyard. I've been nailing scum like this since before you lit your first peace pipe. How dare you, and this prick storm into my county, run operations, and not tell me what's going on."

"Actually sheriff," Jason snapped viciously, "I'm an ex-Army Ranger with a Master's Degree in Criminal Justice and a minor in Forensic Psychology. I graduated in the top ten percent of my college class and again in the top one percent in sniper school. I was one of the top interrogators in my old unit. I did two successful tours in Middle East where I hunted terrorists and their financers. I joined the bureau to keep that same kind of that scum off American soil. That includes occasionally investigating and shutting down rogue law enforcers when necessary. Any yes, I came from a reservation full of proud Native Americans, many of which have fought bravely and even died for this very country that we both live in."

"That's quite a resume, son," the chief interjected, trying to ease some of the tension in the room. "The fact remains however, that we were left in the dark by your office. I understand that this is a delicate operation, but can you shed any light on it at all? I'm sure you understand the position we're in."

"Again I apologize, Chief Craigwell, but at the current time I cannot. What I can tell you is law enforcement agencies from as far away as Asia and Europe have a vested interest in this case. That's why it's imperative that we keep it under wraps. And despite my age, I can assure you that no agent here today knows more about this case than I do."

"Okay, Agent Blackhawk what do you need from us?"

"For starters, chief, I need to see Chauncey Mitchell."

A short time later, Chief Craigwell, Sheriff Leist, agents Carver, Blackhawk, and Castro were standing in a sound proof room looking at a monitor. On the screen

195

were Chauncey Lucien Mitchell and another well-dressed man. They watched as the men sat close and whispered while periodically looking up at the camera in the corner.

"Who's the suit?" Castro asked while eyeing the curly-haired fellow with a pair of thin rimmed glasses sitting on the edge of his nose.

"His name is David Gebhardt from the law office of Gebhardt, Garret, and Howell. He's the group's attorney. His associates have already met with each member individually."

"The entire group is represented by one law firm? Well, so much for the old 'divide and conquer' tactic," Jason quipped sarcastically.

"I know, right? If these guys have any balls, it's going to be difficult to turn any one member against the others."

"Have a little faith, Gabe. As 'gangsta' as they are, none of them would last five minutes in jail. We'll get the one who'll want to cut a deal the fastest."

"Deal?" Sheriff Leist yelled while staring angrily at Agent Blackhawk. "Who the hell is talking deals? These shit bags deserve to have the book thrown at them."

"Sheriff, you used to be a prosecutor, right?"

"Yeah, so what? What does that have to do with anything?"

"Then you should be able to see that these guys are mid-level operatives at best, which means they can get us to the top of the food chain; the primary supplier."

"That's why you kept us out of the loop, isn't it?" interrupted Chief Craigwell. "You don't care about arresting these local boys. Your office is trying to shut down the entire global operation, and you think these ten boys can help you do it."

"Okay hot shot, what if your plan backfires? I mean, what happens if they decide not to play ball?"

"It won't," Agent Blackhawk replied abruptly while staring the sheriff down.

"Okay, but hypothetically, what if it doesn't work? Then what will you do?"

"Then we'll feed the media a bullshit story about a joint operation between the FBI, ATF, the Cincinnati Police, and your sheriff's department which resulted in this major bust. That way, you get another notch in your belt and the chief appears to be making a difference in the city's crime rate. Would that make you happy?"

"Well actually Agent Castro…"

"Actually Sheriff Leist, you don't have to say anything because your answer is irrelevant. At the end of the day, these guys are nothing more than pawns in our end game."

"I'm going in," Jason declared before grabbing a three-inch thick folder packed with papers, photographs, and other documents.

The remaining officers and agents watched as Agent Blackhawk entered the room and laid the large folder on the table, an act that drew the attention of 'Loco' and his attorney. Seeing that he had an audience, he unbuttoned his blazer and sat at the end of the table, 90 degrees from where Loco was sitting.

"I apologize for keeping you gentlemen waiting. My name is Agent Jason Blackhawk of the FBI. Before we begin, is there anything I can get for you; cigarette, water, coffee, or a soda perhaps?"

"No, Agent Blackhawk," replied the attorney before whispering in his client's ear.

"So, Mr. Mitchell, I understand you're a rapper. What's that like?"

"Let's cut to the chase, Agent Blackhawk. My client is aware of the situation and all of the charges against him. Let's be frank, shall we?"

"Okay Mr. Gebhardt, as you wish. I'll be very frank. Mr. Mitchell, we have enough charges against you to put you away until you're a very, very old man, but it's likely you won't survive a day in prison. That being said, we all know that you're not the person we want. We want the people that you've been getting your dope from, aside from Agent Castro of course."

"My client is aware of his options at this point. At the risk of a long drawn out ordeal which will include a media circus and a lot of negative publicity for a lot of people, we are prepared to offer you a deal."

"Offer me a deal?" Agent Blackhawk asked pretending to be surprised.

Deep down inside however, Jason was licking his lips.

"Yeah man...I mean sir," Loco replied while shaking like a leaf. "Look, man we can't do no jail time."

"Why not? Aren't you *Loco; the Midwest's Finest*? Aren't you the same rappers who talk...I mean flow about drug-dealing, scream fuck the po-lice, and represent the homies in the struggle? What's a little jail time to you? I'm sure those same homies would..."

"They would try to fuck the lining out of our asses! Sir, we're not gangsters! We're a bunch of performing arts students who won a damned talent contest. This is an act; nothing more."

"I see," Agent Blackhawk replied while taking notes and trying not to laugh. "What about the album sales, the shows, and the music videos? You guys are artists. You should be rich! Why are you dealing guns and dope on the streets?"

"Don't answer that," Mr. Gebhardt interrupted.

"I got this, man. Sir, record companies get rich from selling records, not the artists. Oh sure, they show you a contract with six or seven figures on it and it looks great. What they don't tell you is that everybody around you gets a percentage. The record company, the promoters, the producers, the P.R. people, and a bunch of other people... everybody gets a damned percentage, including the artists. We're being pimped! After we pay all those percentages, we barely make the rent. My peeps got child support and student loans to cover."

"Ok...what about the cars, the condos, the clothes, and the jewelry? Surely you must..."

"The label owns all that stuff, sir. And what they don't own is rented."

"Intriguing," Jason replied. "Why sell drugs, Mr. Mitchell?"

"Don't answer that," his attorney interrupted.

"It's cool, man," Loco replied while waving Gebhardt off. "Why sell drugs you ask? Why not sell them is a better question, sir. Dope makes the world go round. In this world, you're either dealing dope or doing it. Drug culture drives rap culture. Without drugs, half of these so-called *gangsta*-rappers wouldn't have shit to rap about."

"You seem like a very intelligent man, Mr. Mitchell. How the hell did you end up dealing drugs in the first place?"

"Don't answer that," Gebhardt cautioned again. "I can't effectively represent you if you keep admitting to guilt."

"It's cool, man. I got this. Like I said, dope drives this industry, which means it drives record sales. We can't rap about what we don't know about. When they see us in the streets grinding and hustling, we get recognized. That boosts album sales and eventually the money trickles down to us. Half of these platinum artists have

199

never touched coke or done any time. They're rapping about what other people did or what they heard. Most of have never even fired a gun, but they make a living rapping about them. Ironic, ain't it?"

"Speaking of guns, I see you attempted to purchase some very heavy artillery. What did you plan to do with so much firepower?" Jason asked, more out of genuine curiosity than investigative procedure.

"Protection, man."

"Protection from what, the Taliban?" Jason asked half-laughing.

"Agent Blackhawk, when you're in this business and trying to keep it street, somebody is eventually gonna to try to test your heart; to see if you really are *gangsta*. We have families to support. We had to arm ourselves. Armed security costs a fortune and that was coming directly out of our pockets. It was cheaper this way."

"I see. You said you have a deal for me," Jason said after prepping them for the early kill. "What can you offer me?"

The room grew silent when Loco looked at the table, then at his attorney, then at Agent Blackhawk.

"I can give you Simon Felix," he said after a long, deep breath.

"Simon Felix...you can give me Simon Felix?" Jason scoffed while baiting Loco into a deeper conversation. "What could you possibly know about Simon Felix?"

"I know he's the biggest dope boy out of Jamaica and controls most of the dope that comes from there. He runs the shit out of Colorado with his wife Tisha and his sister-in-law, Dawn."

"What's your connection to them?" Jason asked, pretending to be unconvinced.

"I used to buy dope from his sister-in-law. She tried to sell us four keys, but her sister, Tisha, blocked the sale.

She said we were too flashy and were probably being watched by the feds. She was right," Loco concluded after looking around the tiny room with its plain white walls. "I can get you to the head man."

"Bingo, you son-of-a-bitch," Castro blurted out in the quiet observation room. "Keep him talking, Jason. Interrogation my ass, this is a full blown surrender, just like Pakistan."

"That's quite generous of you, Mr. Mitchell. But since it's not Christmas, I know that you'll want something in return. So, what is it?"

"Immunity," Gebhardt replied sharply.

"Immunity?" Jason scoffed sarcastically.

"Yes, immunity. By the way, that means immunity for the entire group."

"You want me to approve immunity for this entire group? Mr. Gebhardt, are you serious?"

"Yes, I am serious; very serious. My clients are prepared to go to trial and plea bargain for lesser charges. Look at it this way, Agent Blackhawk. I'm very aware of this Simon Felix and his operations and I know that this case could have major implications for your office. So, you can take this deal, arrest Mr. Felix, and become famous while quietly letting my clients go free. Your alternative is to go to trial, have them plead out and back on the streets making records in no time at all. Meanwhile, Mr. Felix continues his uncontested reign of terror in the Caribbean."

"This guy's good," Chief Craigwell whispered while watching the monitor.

"With my clients having no prior records, and a sheriff eager to make the headlines, I'm sure the prosecutors will jump at any deal. You admitted yourself that my clients are not the ones you want. You want Mr. Felix, and my client is willing to hand him over to you in exchange for his freedom. Think of your career and the bureau's image. You can cripple, if not shut down, the Jamaican drug trade. I am sure your superiors would hate to let such an opportunity slip through their fingers over some guns and dope."

Jason leaned back in his chair and briefly studied the brazen attorney. Although medium in stature, David Gephardt's presence suddenly became larger than the tiny room could contain. Everything he said was right. Jason Blackhawk, the FBI, and law enforcement agencies from around the world had stakes in this case. For Jason, it was more than putting another line item on his resume. It was an opportunity to finally bring his partner's murderer to justice. The bureau would simultaneously be able to cripple the drug trade in the Caribbean and bolster its global reputation.

"What is your answer, Agent Blackhawk?" Attorney Gebhardt asked, knowing full well that the ball was in his court now.
"I'll make a phone call," he replied before grabbing his folder and leaving the room.
"You do that," Gebhardt replied with a smile.
"Hey man, who said we were willing to go to jail?"
"I wasn't expecting that this early," Agent Blackhawk declared when he entered the observation room.
"Screw what you were expecting!" barked Sheriff Leist. "I know good-and-damned well you aren't planning on cutting an immunity deal for all of them. And what's this business about Jamaican dope dealers and trafficking in the Caribbean?"
"Look Jason," Castro began after ignoring the sheriff, "if you play this right we can nail Simon and his cartel. So what if these guys walk? As far as we're concerned, they're nobodies."

"Excuse me, but I object! Your nobodies just committed a laundry list of felonies in my jurisdiction!"

"It's gonna be hard to get this to walk across the director's desk without first going through Burroughs. With him being in Montego Bay, it's gonna be hard to get his approval. How do you wanna play it?"

"We're not going through Burroughs," Jason replied while staring at the monitor. "I'll get my approval directly from McNamara."

"Is anybody listening to me?" Sheriff Leist barked while glaring angrily at the two agents.

"Are you nuts? You do realize that you're violating the chain of command by going over Burroughs' head, don't you? If you do that, you're also jeopardizing your entire career and mine. Is one man really worth all that?"

"He is to me, Gabe. The way I see it, if we can catch Dawn in a buy, we can arrest her, offer her a deal, and force her to roll over on Simon. Between the surveillance photos, bank statements, and phone taps, we have enough to get her on conspiracy at the very least. All we need to do is show intent. If nothing else, we can certainly do that."

"Excuse me, got-dammit!" the sheriff protested again.

"Burroughs left me in charge. In his absence, I'm pulling the trigger on this. I know where this could lead. You don't have to go down this road with me."

"Are you kidding? I wouldn't miss this for the world. We owe it to Jim and the kids. But if it tanks, I'll personally kick your ass!"

"Deal," Agent Blackhawk replied before shaking Castro's hand.

"HELLO!!!"

"What is it Sheriff Leist?" Castro snapped viciously.

"Don't the chief and I have a say in this?"

"NO!" Agents Blackhawk and Castro yelled in unison.

203

"I was right," the chief concluded when the pieces finally fell into place, "your office never intended to prosecute these boys. You wanted them to participate in a buy to get them to rat out their supplier. That's why you didn't want us there in the first place. Your office has been onto these kids longer than you initially let on. You figured the attorney would throw you a bone because you both knew these boys were nothing more than young punks, didn't you Castro? You set them up figuring they'd roll over on this Simon Felix."

"You catch on quick, chief," Castro replied with a wink and a smile.

"And you, Agent Blackhawk, you lead us to believe that you had played directly into their hands when in reality, they played into yours?"

"Precisely, sir."

"Damn! Well, you'll have my office's full cooperation. What do you need from us?"

"Chief, I need you to keep these guys on ice until we can get approval for this deal. No press, no visitors, and no phone calls. Got it?"

"Absolutely."

"This is bullshit," the sheriff grumbled while watching his chance in the spotlight go up in smoke. "It seems to me like there's an awful lot of dealing going on here. Is that what the feds are into these days; making deals and letting criminals walk free?

"At this point, sheriff, your cooperation isn't optional. It's mandatory. Am I clear?"

"Crystal clear, Agent Castro."

"Oh, and sheriff?"

"What is it, Agent Blackhawk?"

"If you or anyone in your office leaks a word of this, I'll have your badge. Got it?"

Seething with anger, the sheriff stood cursing under his breath as the brash young agent eyed him and waited for a response.

"What do you need from me, Jason?"
"I need you to get McNamara on the line ASAP. Tell him we have witnesses who are willing to roll over on Simon Felix. Do whatever you have to do. Say whatever you have to say. Just get him on board. This is a make or break for us."
"On it," Castro replied while pulling his Blackberry out of his blazer. "Do you really think we can make a conspiracy charge stick against the sister-in-law?"
"Once I squeeze this clown for some additional information, we'll have everything we need. I'm going back in."
"Good luck, Agent Blackhawk."
"Thank you Chief."

Moments after taking a deep breath, Jason reentered the interrogation room. Even though he didn't have a deal in place, he was determined to bluff his way through. He knew that sending Loco and company to prison would be like putting blood in a shark tank. Though both men were dangling carrots, Gebhardt appeared to have the upper hand but seemed ready to serve his clients up, even though he knew Simon was the one whom Jason really wanted.

"Okay, Mr. Mitchell, you said you can lead us to Simon Felix's sister-in-law. What information can you give us?"
"With all due respect, Agent Blackhawk, my client isn't going to provide you with any additional information until we have a deal in writing from your bureau."

"I have a call in to Special Agent McNamara, but he's not going to entertain any deals unless the information is credible."

"Agent Blackhawk…"

"Look man," Loco interrupted, "the longer y'all argue, the longer we end up sitting in jail. I can give you locations, dates, quantities… anything you need."

"Now we're getting somewhere," Jason smiled with his pen in his hand.

"But you ain't getting shit else until we get that deal in writing!" Loco asserted, even though Jason could see through his act.

After a few moments of intense silence, Castro burst through the door waving his cell phone in the air.

"McNamara," he whispered while laying the phone in the center of the table.

"Special Agent McNamara?"

"Good afternoon, Jason. I understand that you have suspects in custody who are willing to cooperate with the Simon Felix investigation. Is that correct?"

"That is correct, sir," interrupted the eager attorney.

"And to whom am I speaking?"

"My name is Attorney David Gebhardt from the law firm of Gebhardt, Garret, and Howell."

"Mr. Gebhardt, please inform your witnesses as to the rules of immunity. This will require their full cooperation with any investigations and adjudications. This means that if, and when, they're called upon, they may be required testify in open court."

"What about protection for my clients?" asked Gebhardt while looking at his nervous client.

"If circumstances warrant it, and in this case they certainly will, your clients will be taken into the protective custody until they are needed. This means they'll be sequestered at one of our safe houses until further notice. Are there any questions?"

"When can I get that in writing, sir?" Loco asked while rubbing his quivering legs.

"I'll have a draft prepared and faxed within the hour. Understand however, if you fail to provide sufficient information or obstruct this investigation in any way, shape, or form, the deal is off. Do I make myself clear young man?"

"Yes sir."

"Carry on, Jason. Good day gentlemen."

"Now as I said before," Jason began with a smile, "let's get down to business."

Chapter 8

Montego Bay, Jamaica

Later that afternoon on the white sand shores, several tourists and native Jamaicans stood and marveled as the awesome sixty-foot Bertram 60 Convertible cruised along in the sparkling blue waters. The pale, stubby man at the helm could have easily been mistaken for a rich socialite or Hollywood celebrity since was surrounded by four buxom, dark-skinned, women in bikinis who were smiling and laughing while caressing his hairy arms and chest. Four eager young boys raced to tie the ropes of the docking vessel with 'Ivory Princess' scrolled along its sides. When it powered down, drunken laughter could be heard echoing up and down the docks. Three dreadlock-clad men emerged from a beachside villa and walked down the docks towards the 'Ivory Princess' and though the trio said nothing, their presence commanded attention; so much in fact that passersby scrambled to clear their path. A strong bay breeze revealed the imprints of holstered MAC-11s under their white linen shirts. While two sentries stood watch at the boat's side, the third climbed the steel ladder up to the deck.

"Gabriel, my friend, how are you on this lovely afternoon?"

"Babylon, neva a pleasure. Mi trust yu enjoying yu so-call vacation?" he groaned while frowning at the half-naked women milling about

"Yes I am," Burroughs replied while gathering up some fishing poles from the rear of the boat. "I love coming to the island and taking in the lovely sights."

"Somehow mi nah tink yu mean da mountains or da sea," Gabriel snapped sarcastically after Burroughs slapped the ass of a tray-carrying beauty.
"I love Mojitos. Would you like a Mojito, Gabriel?"
"Naa tanks, mon."
"What's the matter, Gabriel? You seem…perturbed."

Burroughs' arrogant smirk made the Rasta sick to his stomach because in his mind, Burroughs was nothing but a hypocrite. Here he was, a Senior FBI Agent, on vacation and piloting a boat purchased with drug money he'd received from the very dealer that he was supposed to be apprehending. During his years in the bureau, Burroughs had established quite a name for himself as a lead investigator while amassing a small fortune from bribes on the side. Judging by the icy stares and cold receptions there was no love lost between these two men who seemed poised to kill one another at the drop of a hat.

"Wa bring yu to Jamaica, Babylon?" Gabriel demanded after Burroughs downed the first drink and beckoned for another.
"Your boss; Simon. He's violated his agreement, and as a result my office has turned their sights back to him and is treating him as 'hostile.' While I'm not a fan of this, I have a job to do. I came here to see if I could foster another arrangement, if you will."
"Is dat so? Judging from da money being funneled through yu accounts and da house wi bought yu, me tink our debt been paid in full."
"It's not that simple, Gabriel. My superiors want to know why Simon hasn't been brought to justice. True, he's cooperated with us on more than one occasion and has helped us eliminate most of your competition. We

were content to let him operate, but as usual, he's making too much damned noise and inciting a war with the cartels. The State Department wants results and I need something to give them."

"Yu fat piece of shit! Which superiors yu talk bout; da judges, da lawyers, or da crooked politicians in D.C.?"

"Now look, Gabriel. I..."

"No! Coo yu, fat man! I an give yu all da information yu need to take Simon down and yet, he free. Why dat, Babylon? Wi give yu times and locations, and yu bloodclots not kill him! Why dat, Babylon? Yu promise him dead, yet him still alive!"

"It's very simple, Gabriel. Unlike you, Simon pays us and pays us well. And as long as he continues to pay us, we'll stay off your backs. Look at you. You sit here in your island paradise selling poison to the world and you want us to continue turning a blind eye to it? You enslave your own people and force them to process that shit for nickels while you make billions. Do you know how many palms have been greased so that people will look the other way when your product hits U.S. shores? I'll tell you, you dirty son-of-a bitch! Plenty of them! Now if you want your operation to continue running smoothly, you need to pay the piper. Take a good look at the piper, Gabriel!"

"I should kill yu right now!"

"Oh yeah?" Burroughs snapped before leaning back and smirking when his nemesis reached for his gun. "How about I serve your ass up to Simon personally? I mean, after all you *have* been trying to serve him up to us for years now. How much would he trust you then?"

"Yu tink Simon a shot-calla? Yu wrong, Babylon! He a puppet on yu string! I an cut dem strings now! Yu really tink yu can come down ere and talk war? Yu tink these whores take tacks for yu? Yu make da mistake of tinking Simon in charge. Nuttin further from da truut."

"Try it, Gabriel. I dare you! I've got trained killers all over this pathetic rock. You fuck with me and they'll burn your whole operation down from Chicago to Kingston! I thought you'd calm down," Burroughs smirked when Gabriel released his gun and began smoothing his linens. "Let me tell you something else, rude boy. My government is only a phone call away from an executive decision. On my order, they'll come in here and shut this dump down for good. Your government has already admitted that they can't handle this shit. You know why they haven't come in yet? Me, got-dammit, that's who! This rock is a money pit and the bullshit I feed them about your operations keeps money in your pockets and us off your asses. Instead of calling Simon a snitch, you should be calling him a savior."

"Hollow words, Babylon. In da past two years, yu deal wit Simon cost us seventeen million above and beyond da five million we agree to. Add dat to da deaths of my peeps and pussyclot arrests, and dat cost dear. How yu 'splain dat?"

"Beats the fuck out of me," Burroughs replied nonchalantly before sipping his drink. "Maybe there's a leak that neither of us knows about."

"A lie!"

"Call it what you want, Gabriel. Getting your house in order is your job; not mine. But I do have some information that may be useful to you."

"Wa dat, Babylon?"

"Payment first, Gabriel," he smiled while waving a yellow envelope in the air.

Burroughs' smile grew even bigger as stacks of one-hundred-dollar bills, totaling one-hundred-thousand dollars, were tossed onto the table in front of him.

211

Gabriel snatched the envelope from his hand freeing the greedy agent to thumb through the banded stacks.

"Ooo dis blood clot bwoy?" Gabriel asked after looking at numerous pictures an unknown man.

"I don't know. He's some Colorado entrepreneur named Alexis Stratton."

"Why yu tellin' mi?"

"This guy is fucking Simon's wife. I'm sure he'd like to know that."

"Indeed," Gabriel replied while staring at the long-haired brother with Simon's prize. "How yu come by dis?"

"Agent Jason Blackhawk, one of mine."

"Cha? Thought yu had him reassigned." Gabriel growled while glaring angrily at Burroughs.

"I tried, but the chief put him back on the case. Apparently, he convinced them that he was fit to be back in the field, even though you guys killed Lisa. The whole rape, mutilation deal...I mean killing her was enough. Did you really have to cut her tongue out too?"

"Dat's wa happen to dem dutty informas," Gabriel smiled. "Ooo a run tings while yu ere?"

"Agent Blackhawk is, of course. But don't worry about it. He won't make a move without my authorization. He trusts me totally and won't do anything unless I say so. Trust me. Despite his connection to the case, I have him under control."

"Yu better. Be a shame if he and his partner suddenly had a reunion. Catch mi meaning, Babylon?"

"Absolutely, and while we're talking, you'll also be happy to know that your little Mexican problem will be eliminated in a few days. My CIA pals tell me that an operation is being hatched as we speak. Details are sketchy, but when it's all said and done, none on the cartel heads will threaten your operations anymore.

"Yu dun good, Burroughs," Gabriel smirked with narrowed eyes from behind his Ray Bans.

"Glad you think so. Oh yes, I need one more thing, Gabriel. My anniversary is in four months and the wife wants to go to Europe for a couple of weeks. Think you can make that happen?"

"Any'ting for yu, Babylon," Gabriel replied while walking towards the deck.

"See Gabriel, even when you're in charge there's no reason we can't get along, right?"

Gabriel's silence while descending the ladder left Burroughs' nerves on edge. With a woman on his arm and a drink in his hand, Burroughs watched his three visitors disappear from sight. In the back of his mind, he wondered which option was better: turn Gabriel over to Simon or just have him killed. No matter what, it was clear to him that Simon's days on top were numbered. Burroughs didn't know where they'd stand after that. Gabriel's obvious hatred towards the FBI and Burroughs meant it would be difficult, if not impossible, to negotiate another deal. The ensuing chaos might set off a war between the Kingston cartel, the Mexican Cartels, and global law enforcement agencies. Though shutting them down would be a nice feather in the bureau's cap, the money he stood to lose was more important. Burroughs looked at the cash on the table, the four women, and his lavish surroundings. If Simon died, it would all be gone and Burroughs couldn't let that happen. Gabriel had to die.

"Excuse me, honey," he said after releasing her chocolate waist and picking up his phone. "This is Burroughs. We have a problem."

A while later while riding in the backseat of a white Range Rover Sport, Gabriel carefully studied the pictures that he had been given.

Weh mi know yu from, bwoy? he thought to himself.

Though he hated having dealingl with a snake like Burroughs, the information he provided always proved to be useful. Gabriel's hatred and mistrust of Simon was further fueled by constant betrayals from the man whom many assumed he was working for. To Gabriel, Simon was nothing more than a buffoon, a pawn at the FBI's disposal.

Meanwhile miles away, , Simon and three young recruits were cruising along the streets of Kingston in the plush backseats of a stretched Range Rover. Being a master manipulator, Simon quickly identified their eagerness and capitalized on it every chance he got. They listened to and worshipped him when he spoke; soaking up every word like sponges. The tales that he was spinning had them wishing they could be him. Not content to let his words do all the talking, Simon flashed his jewelry and made a show of passing out one-hundred-dollar bills to some children who were hanging out on a street corner. He was taking the trio on a tour of Kingston while simultaneously selling them a dream. To these young men, Simon was as close to a god as they could imagine. They craved the power and wealth he commanded. Although they'd lived in Jamaica all their lives, not one of them had ever spent this much time in the big city. The bricks and steel of the new Kingston, this bustling metropolis with high rise office buildings and million dollar condominiums, was foreign to them.

"Mi baan pon deez streets just like yu," Simon began after exhaling ganja smoke from his La Corona. "Yu naa seen dis side of Jamaica, but dis is weh yu should be. Coo pon dem people. Wa cha see?" he asked while pointing out of his smoked window. "I an see slaves. Dey do what Babylon tell dem to do. Yu tree...yu shottas! Yu call yu own shots! Dis new Kingston is yours."

Their thirsty looks betrayed them and in no time, Simon had them eating out of the palm of his hand. After a few more minutes of cruising, the limo headed back out of the city and into the country where they were from. The high rise buildings were quickly replaced by ragged shacks. Asphalt streets and sidewalks became dirt roads and dusty paths. Shops and stores became tall grass and banana trees. This is the Jamaica that they were used to, and Simon had them thirsty for change. They lusted after his fine linens and jewels, because in their minds, this was the life they deserved. They wanted to be the next kingpins of Jamaica and Simon had them ready to kill for it. He'd sold them a dream just like the one he'd been sold.

"It begins ere!" Simon declared with his arms raised as he and his three protégés stood among rows of run-down shanty homes.

Inside these shacks were scores of half-naked women wearing surgical masks, goggles, and latex gloves. Some of them even had babies strapped to their backs or nursing from their breasts. Though the pennies they were paid was nothing compared to the billions Simon was making in profits, they continued to toil for long hours in these stuff huts because to most of them, this was the only way to survive.

215

"I an start out just like yu. When mi young, mi work da banana fields. When mi older, I an work in da shanties cuttin' dope dat come off da boats. When mi teenager, mi join posse and in time, run all of Jamaica. Den da door open... America! In a few years, I an run all da posses. Either dey join, or dey get crushed! Naa matter. I an leave mi mark because I an shotta! Yu shottas too."

With a smile on his pitted face and dollar signs in his eyes, Simon had them captivated. They clung to his every word as if they came from the Bible itself. The trio silently replayed them in their heads like tape recorders. He watched while they looked around inside the shacks carefully studying the palettes of cocaine and the armed men guarding them. While looking into their eager eyes, Simon saw himself. He was no stranger to this environment and was always seeking new blood willing to take up his cause. With each carefully chosen word, he was drawing them in and seducing him with dreams of money, power, and respect. He quickly turned his sights to an adjacent hut.

"In dis hut, dis dope ready for shipping out of Kingston to our clients da world ova. Da posses will handle da sales. Mi workers collect da loot. Follow mi an' yu rich before yu know. Wa cha say, shottas?"

After quickly exchanging glances, the three looked at Simon and nodded in affirmation. They accompanied him back to the Range Rover and smiled gleefully as it drove off. A while later, after travelling through several boroughs, the limo turned off the main road and onto a tree-lined gravel path. At its end sat a large white manor house similar to the one Simon had built in Boulder. When the limo came to a stop near the entrance, an armed sentry rushed to the rear door and opened it. Simon greeted him with a fist pound when he stepped out of the back and walked up to the house. Like his home in Boulder, Jamaican flags hung prominently from the second floor balcony, blowing proudly in the salty island breeze. After years of running the U.S. wing of his cartel, Simon was happy to be back at home. He stood in the massive courtyard and took in the sights. The warm summer air, the clear blue skies, and the towering trees that surrounded the compound were like heaven.

Unlike his home in Colorado however, each side of the entrance was flanked by a huge stone lion with a Jamaican flag draped over its back. Simon stuck his chest out with in pride when he entered the massive house and walked through the two story foyer. Every surface from the marble floors to the textured ceilings was colored with shades of black and white. The foyer along with the rest of the rooms in the house was decorated with tapestries, vases, statues, and masks from as far away as Africa, Europe, Asia, and India. Some even came from parts of the Middle East. While some had been purchased during his travels, many more were gifts from his numerous, gracious clients.

When Simon entered the dining room, his eyes were immediately drawn to a group of women on the patio, all of whom were all dressed in black Karategies. He leaned on the door frame and gawked while they performed a series of synchronized punches, kicks, thrusts, and leaps. Moments later with a devilish grin on his face, he strolled slowly among the rows of women, lustfully admiring their fluid movements and curvaceous frames.

"Dat's enough!" yelled the dark-skinned, kimono-clad woman standing at the front of the group. "Dismissed!"

217

"Garcelle gal," he began as the women disappeared down a path into the nearby woods, "yu dun good, chile! Imagine a team full of beautiful assassins at mi command."

"Wrong, Simon. Dey unnu mi command."

"But Garcelle…baby girl, we a team."

When he took her in his arms and tried to kiss her, she quickly turned her head in disgust. After another failed attempt, Simon released her and stepped back. Standing with her back to him, she untied her kimono, and let it fall to her feet. Her white two piece bikini appeared to glow against her smooth, dark chocolate-colored skin. His eyes feasted on her voluptuous frame while attempting to ignore the venom she was spewing.

"You renk of yu American bitch," she growled as he stared at her tattooed back, round ass, and thick, juicy thighs.

"Wa mek yu bring dat Tisha business ere? Me tell yu more times she a mule, nuttin' more. Har time soon come. Den I come home to Jamaica…to mi true queen."

"A lie!" Garcelle barked with her arms folded across her soft, round breasts. "Yu been nuttin' but a liar, Simon Felix, an' mi tired of yu mess. I an shoulda lef yu dere in slumps weh mi found yu black ass!"

"Check yu'self befo yu skin yu teet! I an still da man and yu usband," he barked defiantly.

"Mi usband? A man?" Garcelle scoffed half-laughing. "Naa mek me laugh yu, fool. Yu poor excuse for both! Yu keep yu ass in Denver while mi run tings ere. Yu makin' deals wit Babylon while paradin' round like Jah! Den yu marry dat blood clot whore and use mi money ta support her fambly! Yu call dat usband?"

"I an tell yu befo Tisha an investment dat pay off more times. Her fambly…"

"Naa concern of mine! Tree generations of Malcolm clan have run Jamaica. Mi fadda, and his fadda before him, and his fadda before him...dey run dis island! Mi fadda, may him soul rest, left it ta me. One day mi leave ta mi own chile. But dere's a problem Simon! I an have no kids!"

"Mi tell yu..."

"Yu tell me lies!" she interrupted. "Yu mek me tink it me but it was yu all along. Yu empty, Simon. Yu naa make me no heir. Yu can't make me no babies, Simon! Yu call dat a man?"

"Keep yu talking and me..."

"Yu wa?" she interrupted before stepping up and shoving him. "Beat mi like yu beat Tisha? Yu wanna romp wit me? Try it pussy clot! Mi naa tink what mi fadda saw in yu! He love yu like his own son and convince me dat yu help me rule Jamaica, but him wrong. Gabriel challenge mi now! Him want me trone. Imagine dat, me own cousin...mi own flesh want me gone 'cause mi usband nuttin' but a empty shell. Gabriel become da King if mi can't produce no heir! Da bloodline dies and wit it, I an dun. Every'ting mi fadda built gone because of yu!"

"Yu fadda... bless him soul, was like fadda to mi. Him take care of mi fambly when mi mudda die in da shanty. Him have dream, and dat was to rule da Caribbean. He share dat dream with mi, and I an take it to America! Mi take dis operation off da island and into da heart of America. Plus mi hab connections in London and Tokyo! Yu complain bout da money me spend on Tisha but look 'round ere! Da money I an mek in America mek you live fat ere. Yu neva hafta lift a finger fa nuttin, but yu still complain. So what mi cut deal wit Babylon? Dat money keep dem off yu back!"

"Yu full-of-shit, Simon Felix! Yu naa a man, not even close. Yu ridin' me fadda coattail and pretending to be shotta, but yu not! Dis a my fambly, not yours! Yu not blood; yu raggamuffin! Mi neva should have listened to yu bullshit! Me fadda was wise man, but him also a fool! Yu nuttin, Simon Felix. Yu nuttin' before me and yu nothing wit'out me! A go yu American bitch!"

Disgusted and embarrassed, Simon turned to leave but, he was stopped in his tracks. The evil smirk on Gabriel's face had Simon frozen. Though he was way too smooth to admit it, there was no doubt he'd heard everything. Besides, Gabriel didn't have to admit it because that grin said it all. When he began walking towards them, Simon felt his manhood retreating. Simon could see an evil glare behind Gabriel's sunglasses and thought of a thousand ways to kill him. His attention however was quickly drawn to the manila envelope in Gabriel's hand.

"How yu meeting wit Burroughs went?"
"Nah well," Gabriel smiled while waving the envelope in Simon's direction.
"Wa dat?"
"Si'ting needs yu attention."
"Yu wanna be da don, yu handle it!" Simon barked before brushing past Gabriel and Garcelle. "Tell yu Africans wi link up in Denver. Deh's no place; nuttin' for me ere!"

As Simon stormed through the house, Garcelle snatched the envelope from Gabriel and ripped it open. Tears of rage filled her eyes while looking through the pictures. The thought of Simon spending money on a woman, any woman but her was bad enough but the fact that he was spending money on a whore like Tisha was the straw that broke the camel's back. While standing there fighting back tears, she began contemplating having her own husband killed, but she figured it wouldn't solve anything. Simon, despite his faults and shortcomings, was still useful. Besides, police interference was bad for business and thus far, he'd managed to keep them at bay.

"Find dem and dead dem both!" she declared before slamming pictures back into Gabriel's chest.

He watched in delight when she turned away and retreated down a path into the nearby woods.

Mexico, the middle of nowhere

After several hours of intense negotiations that were interrupted by fierce arguments, threats of violence, and multiple standoffs, the meeting to unite the three largest cartels in Mexico was finally under way. As their leaders sat on the second floor of the lavishly decorated villa, sentries from each cartel stood watch over the grounds and each other.

The tree-lined compound was lit by pole-mounted halogen lamps with additional ground lights along many of the cobblestone paths. There were four observation towers; one at each corner of the compound with a twelve-foot high chain-link, fence topped with razor wire connecting them. Though Ruiz's men were accustomed to the fence's ominous sight, the sensation of being caged in made his visitors extremely nervous. They were all Mexicans, but their individual alliances drew very distinct lines between them, and these alliances were worth dying for. Their attentions were so focused on each other that no one noticed the stirrings in the darkness around them. After several minutes of scouting the area, five black clad figures withdrew and travelled a quarter mile south to a tent in the middle of a make shift staging area.

"What news do you bring comrades?" Taurus asked the leader of the five-man recon team.

"There are at least one hundred fifty men patrolling the grounds around the manor house. There are ten more men in the communications hut and another fifteen to twenty in the garage."

"That's considerably more men than we anticipated, Taurus," Ko growled while loading a clip into his HK MP-5KA4. "We don't do firefights. We hit hard and fast then disappear. End of story."

"Relax, Diamond Back," Taurus said while puffing on his cigar. "We may have to modify our plan of attack in the field a little, but that in no way affects this mission.

"How many men are inside the villa?" Ko asked with the twins approaching in the darkness.

"My men on the inside estimate another one hundred to one hundred-fifty men."

"Great," Ko mumbled before shoving his submachine gun into its shoulder holster. "Please try to convince me that we're not walking into a cluster fuck. Can you do that comrade?"

"Their numbers will be irrelevant once we destroy the communications hut and blow the generators," Taurus argued before hoisting a belt-fed, .50 millimeter chain gun onto his right shoulder. "They won't know what hit them."

A feeling of jealousy overcame Taurus when the twins entered the tent, and he studied their black uniforms: Kevlar bodysuits stitched together with tri-weave fibers for maximum flexibility. They were also covered in strategically placed Kevlar plates which were reinforced titanium. Compared to his team's dark fatigues and police grade flak jackets, *'The Agency'* had a decisive edge in equipment and technology.

"How much do those suits cost you, comrade?"
"Now really isn't the time to discuss fashion, comrade," Ko snapped sarcastically while strapping a belt filled with small throwing knives to his thigh.
"Cottonmouth...Copperhead...where is Black Mamba?" Taurus asked after ignoring Ko's response.
"He's um...meditating," Richard replied while rubbing the back of his head.
"Meditating? Meditating?!! At this late hour, he should be ready for action!"
"Back off and give the man his space Taurus."
"He has five minutes, Diamondback. Either he's here or we go without him!"

When the group exited the barn, they saw Ash, Machete, and Nine Millie running towards them. As far as the eye could see, the area was teaming with armed men and women piling into jeeps, vans, and trucks.

Meanwhile, in the back of an APC, Alex aka *Black Mamba* was sitting in the lotus position with an ancient Ninjato laid across his lap and two chrome plated .40cals holstered to the small of his back. As he did before each mission, he was taking time to purge his mind of all distractions. The outside world and all the things in it needed to be put aside so that he could focus on the tasks at hand. This meant ignoring differences with friends and enemies alike. It also meant putting Simon on the back burner again, as well as forgetting about Lynn, who'd been at the forefront of his mind since he left Colorado. As he slowly inhaled and exhaled, the commotion outside the APC ceased to exist. The only sound left was the beating of his heart. Everything beyond his flesh became an extension of his being, even the air around him. His guns and swords were merely tools. He was the weapon. He was the *'Black Mamba'*, and like his namesake, Alex was ready to strike with lethal fury.

"Alex," boomed the voice inside his head, "what do you see?"
"The end," he replied, his voice muffled by the perforated, stainless-steel kakashi covering his nose and mouth.

After planting the blade in the floor next to him, Alex sprang to his feet and opened his eyes. He pulled his black balaclava over his head before donning a long, hooded cloak.

"Holy shit!" Ash exclaimed when APC's door opened and the ominous figure walked down the ramp.
"The 'Grim Reaper' cometh," Taurus said before throwing his cigar to the ground and stomping it out.

The air was unusually chilly for early summer. Dozens of nocturnal creatures created the soundtrack for what was an otherwise quiet and peaceful night. As sentries milled about the garage admiring names such names like Ferrari, Lamborghini, Bentley, and Rolls Royce, Alex, Ko, Richard, Nicholas, and Nine Millie were standing in the woods just beyond the rear entrance. The constant back and forth movements made it impossible them to keep count of the sentries inside.

"Be prepared when the lights go out. We go live in three minutes," whispered a voice over their headsets.

"I'll need a sixty-second head start," Alex whispered while looking over his right shoulder. "Once I'm inside, I'll take a head count and relay it back to you."

The wait for the lights to go out felt like an eternity. Tension and anxiety filled the teams as they laid-in-wait to execute their ambush. Suddenly, the entire compound went black and within seconds, orange, firefly-like flashes could be seen throughout the courtyard. Without warning, guards from all three cartels began toppling over; dead from shots to the head and chest. Meanwhile in the darkened garage, an argument over who was responsible for the sudden darkness was ensuing. In the commotion, no one noticed Alex bolt from his position and charge the garage door.

"When does his-sixty seconds begin?" Nine Millie asked when he ducked into the garage.
"Five seconds ago," Ko replied while looking at his watch.
"¿Qué carajo es que se mueve en la oscuridad?" asked a sentry as he stood by the garage door with four others attempting to light their cigarettes.
"¿Qué ?" replied another before clutching his throat and tumbling to the ground.

Four more glimmers appeared out of the darkness, each piercing the throat of an unsuspecting victim. As their blood spilled onto the ground, Alex's black tabi boots barely touched the ground while charging between them. Seconds later, blood curdling screams pierced the night air as limbs were slashed and severed in throughout the garage. Bodies flew through the air before colliding with metal, fiberglass, or whatever else was close. The explosion of the communications hut rocked the compound and temporarily filled the garage with blinding orange and white light. Standing in the midst of the carnage was a cloaked figure with blood-soaked blades in his hands.

"El Diablo!" they cried while cowering at the ominous sight.

They cringed when the blades disappeared inside his bulky sleeves. While scrambling for their lives, the sentries watched *El Diablo* quickly thrust his arms inside the cloak. When they reappeared, he released a group of shiny glimmers that pierced eight of their throats.

"Twenty and counting," Alex whispered before disappearing into the shadows.
"¡Fuego!" the remaining henchmen cried while watching rivers of blood gush beneath their feet.

As they searched the shadows for *El Diablo*, muffled gunfire and orange smoke began filling the garage.

"Damn!" Millie whispered after taking in the carnage and trying to make sense of what Alex had just done.
"Yeah...he has that affect on people," Nicholas whispered while panning the room.

Seconds later, Alex reappeared near the door at the far end of the garage and watched while several armed men charged out of the main house only to be mowed down by a hail of gunfire. The roar of customized, big-bore engines filled the compound when armored trucks and SUVs pummeled the exterior fences and towers. Out of the darkness, scores of black-clad figures charged forward firing at anything moving.

"Black Mamba, look out!" Millie yelled when a red dot appeared on the back of his cloak.

As quickly as she raised her gun, he disappeared into the darkness once again.

"Snick; Swish; Snick," was all they heard before Alex suddenly reappeared by the door.

As Millie approached him with her mind in a fog, she felt a nudge on the side of her left foot. When she looked down, she saw a severed head and pair of cold, dead eyes staring up at her.

"We have rabbits," Alex said when he saw five men abandon the burning house and bolt towards the storage shed behind it.
"Millie, wait!" Ko yelled when she darted past Alex and ran blindly towards the shed.

With reckless abandon, she dodged machine gun fire and shrapnel before ducking behind a tree and returning fire. Before they reached the shed, Millie mowed down two of the fleeing men, one of them being Juan Carlos Pedilla. After reloading her HK-5, she ran to the shed door but before she could open it, Alex grabbed her arm and looked into her rage-filled eyes. His mind immediately flashed back to St. Stephen's Cathedral.

"There's always another way," he said in a raspy voice before motioning towards an opening in the gable.

Millie stepped back and watched pull a pair of hand grenades from inside his cloak. He popped their pins with his thumbs before throwing them through the.

After grabbing her hand and ducking behind a tree, Alex wrapped Millie in his cloak and held her close while explosions ripped the shed apart hurling cash, cocaine residue, and body parts into the night sky. The pair emerged from behind their barrier and proceeded to walk through the smoldering rubble.

"The last one's for you," he said when he looked over his shoulder and motioned to the man in front of them.

He held his cloak open and exposed the handle of his Ninjato. Millie yanked it from its sheath and charged into the back half of the charred shed. With his grey suit covered in soot and blood, Pedro Ruiz lay on the floor dragging his battered and bloodied body over the mess beneath him. When he reached the door, his hand was crushed by the tread on Millie's boot. Tears filled his eyes when he looked up and saw the petite figure standing above him holding the shiny blade.

"Por favor no me maten," he begged while rolling over and bracing his torso against a crate. "Te voy a dar todo lo que quieras; dinero, coches, marcapáginas lo que quieras si solo déjame ir!"
"Lo que deseo, se puede dar. Por lo tanto, tengo que tomarlo," Millie growled while stalking him.
"¿Qué es eso?" he pled as tears rained from his eyes.
"Quiero tu alma," Millie growled before raising the blade above her head.

With both hands firmly gripping its handle, she swung it violently and severed Ruiz's head from his trembling body. Alex watched the head roll across the floor and come to a rest under his foot.

"You were right. I don't think I can keep this up much longer," she whispered when she handed him the blade.

Once Alex placed it back in its sheath, Millie removed her balaclava and fell into his arms. Holding her closely as she sobbed, he stroked the back of her head and stared up at the moon. In a hail of gunfire, smoke, and ash, two equal but opposite forces came together and prevented a catastrophe. Now, it was over.

"We lost Ash, Nitro, and Switchblade so far," they heard someone say in their earpieces.
"It's finally over," he whispered after looking around at the carnage left in their wake.
"Yes, it is," Millie replied softly before squeezing him tighter and listening to his faint heart beat under his body armor. "I was wrong about you, Alex. I told myself that you were a millionaire pretending to be a hit-man. Now I see the truth. You're a hit-man pretending to be millionaire."
"Duty calls, Millie! Let's go!" Taurus yelled from behind them.
"You heard the boss," she whispered while gazing up into the darkness of the hood.
"Take care of yourself, Nine Millie."
"I love you, Black Mamba," she said after lowering his hood and planting a kiss on his kakashi.
"Until we meet again," he replied when she walked away.

Compared to what they'd just been through, the sun rising outside his window was a welcome sight. Alex relaxed with a double shot of *Crown* in his glass, while traces of blood, soot, and dust plastering his boots and gloves. He downed half the glass before leaning his head back and staring out the window. As he held the chilled glass to his head, Alex imagined what they were saying about him in the rear cabin. His brutal actions had served a dual purpose, neither of which they could ever understand. In his mind however, Alex was glad that Millicent decided she'd had enough and prayed that she'd get out before it was too late.

His mind flashed back to the body bags that were stacked in one of 'The Renegades'' pickups. There seemed to be little or no remorse shown when they placed their fallen comrades in the bed next to their equipment like baggage.

"*Cold,*" he murmured while refilling his glass.

Alex knew he'd drown in a river of tears if one of his friends died in the field, even though it was a reality they all faced. After downing his third drink, he pulled out a sheet of paper and began doodling. For a brief moment, he envisioned his cloaked persona standing in a cemetery looking at the headstones of his fallen friends. He read each of them one-by-one; Ko Hinomura, Richard Chang, Nicholas Chang, Warren Jeffries, 'Big' Mike Wayne, Gary Anders, and finally the most disturbing; Alexandria Stratton.

"*That won't happen,*" he declared as his pencil glided across the blood-stained page.

Chapter 9

A few days after the dust in Mexico settled, a metallic-orange Chevrolet Corvette Z06 rumbled to a stop in front of Tango's shop. Alex stepped out and looked around at the tattered neighborhood which at one time was full of shops, a few delis, and a used car lot. So much had changed during their years in Denver, but Tango's shop remained the same run down building it had always been. Inside, however was one of the most exquisite tattoo parlors and custom auto shops in the country. From end to end, there were Choppers, Harleys, Ducatis, Suzukis, Yamahas, and BMWs. Behind them was a selection of exotic cars unlike any other in the region. Names like Ferrari, Porsche, Lamborghini, and Bugatti lined the room from end-to-end. Off to the side were some modern era Muscle Cars from Ford, Dodge, and Chevrolet, and behind them, were the original beasts that spawned them. At the rear of the shop were a group of tattoo chairs, tables, and three tanning beds and pinned to the walls above them were hundreds of intricate tattoo designs in various styles, shapes, and colors.

"Black Mamba, what's happening, brotha?" called out a raspy voice from the hallway.

When Alex turned around, Terrance *'Tango'* Donner greeted him. This well-tanned, leathery-skinned, ex-assassin was the closest thing Alex had to a father. Despite being well into his fifties and a heavy drinker, he was in excellent shape. His long, dirty-blonde hair was heavily-oiled and pulled back into a ponytail. His leather vest was wrapped tightly around his well-defined biceps and triceps. He was also a walking work of art. His arms, chest, and neck were covered in tattoos; each one telling its own story.

"What brings you to the slums, brotha?"
"I'm ready for a new tat," Alex replied before handing him the same blood-stained sheet of paper he'd been doodling on.
"Bout damn time. So, this is what you want, huh? Well, get up on the table and let's get started. Damn Alex, do you ever leave the gym?" Tango asked seconds later when Alex removed his shirt and climbed onto one of the tables.
"Only to put in work. You ever miss it?"
"Fuck no!"

After inserting a sterilized needle into his gun and turning on his compressor, he leaned over Alex's back and began the intricate sketch.

"Guess you heard about your boy, Gary?"
"No," Alex replied while lying with his arms folded under his head.
"He's back on the wagon. S.O.B. got all hammered to shit after y'all left and went to his old lady's house. He kicked the door in and demanded to see Claire. When Gabby's old man intervened, they tore the house to hell and back. The dude held his own pretty good 'til just before the cops arrived. Then they beat the shit out of Gary and locked him up. I tell you one thing, though, that bastard still has a lot of fight in him. He looked 'bout like he did when y'all tussled a few years back," Tango laughed while shaking his head.
"Where was Claire?"
"Luckily, she was with her granny and missed that bullshit."

"Good. How'd you find out?"

"I bailed his drunken ass out," Tango replied while admiring his work. "Dumb sum-bitch had to appear in court earlier today. I'm sure Doc is chewing his ass out as we speak. Got-damned attorneys...I bet Doc had to do plenty of ass-kissing and dig deep in his wallet to get that sum-bitch off."

"Suddenly, my week isn't so interesting after all," Alex mumbled while drifting off to sleep.

"Funny you should say that 'cause I heard it was damned interesting."

"Nope...just business as usual."

"C'mon son, don't bullshit me. I've known you all your life, and you can't tell me that there's not something very wrong with you."

"What are you talking about, Tango?" Alex asked, attempting to minimize the events of the past few days.

"What am I talking about? Are you serious? The whole dark ninja, head slicing thing in Mexico is what I'm talking about! You went fucking 'Ninja Assassin' on those Mexican bad boys. Your friends are beginning to wonder whether your wiring has gone bad. Frankly, so am I."

"I'm fine, Tango," Alex replied attempting avoid a lengthy debate. "I did it to prove a point."

"What point and to whom?"

"There was this girl...young woman there who reminded me of Lexi. I knew from the moment I laid eyes on her that she wasn't cut out for this madness, but she wouldn't just take that and let it be. I had to prove it to her. I had to make her see the dark side to this life, one that can steal your soul if you let it. She got the point."

"She did but what about you?"

"What about me?"

"Why are you still fucking with Simon's old lady instead of putting a bullet in his head and calling it a day?"

"Ask Doc. Every time I get close to him, '*The Agency*' pulls me back."

"That didn't stop you in L.A., did it, Alex?"

"L.A. was a long time ago, Tango," he replied sharply.

"Not for me it wasn't. You know," Tango began while repeatedly poking Alex's skin, "your daddy was my best friend and before he died, he made me promise him two things. The first was if he died, I would take care of you and your sister, not Doc. The second was that I'd never let either of you follow in our footsteps. I dropped the fucking ball and I'm sorry. I should never have let that bastard send you kids to Japan. I let your parents down. I let you all down."

No longer interested in sleeping, Alex opened his eyes and quietly listened his life's story unfolding. Even if Tango wanted to stop talking, Alex was finally ready to ask the questions necessary to get the truth. And if anyone would tell him, Tango would.

"You told me years ago that you would tell me what happened that night. You said you'd wait 'til I was old enough. I'm twenty eight so tell me what happened, and don't sugarcoat it. I need to know."

"I was there the night your parents were murdered," Tango said after a long silence and a healthy gulp of Jack Daniels.

It was at this moment they passed the point of no return. Even if Tango wanted to stop, like he'd done so many times in the past, he knew Alex wasn't about to let him. He needed to purge his soul of this darkness.

"I killed eight… maybe ten of those bastards before you came barreling out of those woods with Lexi in your arms. I knew Carlton and Shani had bought it as soon as I laid eyes on you. From that moment on, I promised myself I would look after you kids. Over time, though, I realized I'd bitten off more than I could chew. My old lady at the time couldn't see why I was investing so much time in you and Lexi. Meanwhile, the jobs kept coming in and I started boozing. Eventually, she hauled ass. When the booze wasn't enough, I moved on to harder shit. It was around that time that Doc convinced me that an 'international education' was what you all needed to get your minds off your parents' deaths. So he packed you up and sent you to live with Ko's uncle Yoshi in Japan. I knew what that S.O.B. was doing, but I was too cranked out to stop him."

"Do you regret letting us go?" Alex asked while staring into the mirror and watching Tango wipe tears from his eyes.

"I regretted it then, and I regret it even more now. It was clear from the start that Lexi didn't have the stomach for this madness, but you did. That anger you had inside you was untamable. You took what them monks showed you about discipline and weaponized it. When you stepped off that plane all grown up, I knew that little kid was gone. You came back a stone-cold killer."

Alex laid on the table and thought about the words he was hearing. For the first time, he was seeing his tragic life's story through Tango's eyes. He barely felt the needle repeatedly pricking his skin, removing his flesh and slowly replacing it with an image that had haunted him since that night in Miami. As the time slowly ticked away, he continued listening to Tango pour his heart out.

"Like I said, I remember L.A. like it was yesterday. Our first assignment together was to eliminate an east L.A. gang element that was moving dope up the coast from Mexico thru Baja. We had their shit hole of a hideout surrounded. Just as we cut the power and sent the flash bangs in, we got the pullback call. But it came in too late 'cause you were already inside. It was like something out of a got-damned Kung Fu nightmare. Twelve boys with AK-47s and Uzis and not one of them got off a single shot. When we hit the lights, you were standing there surrounded by sliced up bodies. You never said a word, even as you walked out. But I remember that look; that dark look you had in your eyes. That night, someone left the gates of hell open and a fucking demon walked out. From that day forward you were cold as a block of ice...no emotion at all."

Tango took a brief pause in his story to fix himself another drink and to change the ink in his gun. As Alex listened to him toiling with the tools, he couldn't help but wonder if his rage and anger lead to Tango's retirement. Though he wanted to ask, Alex didn't want to interrupt.

"Over the next few years, I watched you become the top earner in Doc's new *'Assassins for hire Agency'*."
"That's not what we are," Alex interrupted after raising his head and looking over his shoulder.
"Bullshit and you know it!" Tango barked before dumping half-a-glass of Jack Daniels on Alex's raw, needle-riddled flesh.

Though he knew it burned like hell, Alex barely flinched. He only sounds were a series of low grunts and a few deep breaths. He'd taken to his training extremely well. Alex didn't show any pain, physical or emotional.

After a few moments of quiet contemplation, Tango continued his story.

"I showed you how to use every manner of fire arm I could think of and you took to all of them. We were good, but you were head and shoulders above the rest of us. Guns, knives, swords, fists, feet... it didn't matter. You were the total package. In a very short time, I watched you become the ultimate money maker. I tried to admire you, but truth be told, I hated myself when I saw what you became."

"That's rather cryptic considering you trained me. You're the best marksman I've ever seen. Nobody was a quicker or straighter shot than you. Wind compensation, distance, weather, and even selecting the best weapon for the job...you gave me that. Now you're criticizing me for what I've done with it? That's bullshit."

"Bullshit, huh?" Tango asked while comparing Alex's sketch to what he'd drawn on his back. "I taught you how to put a bullet in a man's eye at a thousand yards from a moving train. Those monks taught you to take the whole damned head off at close range. I taught you to use weapons, but they made you into a weapon."

"Why'd you sit down, Tango? Was it because of me?"

"When you went down in Miami, I made up in my mind that I didn't wanna do this shit anymore. Here I was, an old man surrounded by nothing but blood and death. I've killed in every shit hole on this planet and felt more pain than a man can imagine. But none of that compared to the seeing you lying up on the slab with tubes and shit running out of you. My 'son' was dying. I ran out of shit to live for," he said with tears streaming down his face.

"Then why'd you abandon me?" Alex asked while staring in the mirror.

"Abandon you? Alex, have you lost your got-damned mind? Day after day, week after week, month after month I prayed for you. I sat by your bedside praying that God would forgive me for my sins and bring my son back to me. I'd swear off drugs and alcohol if He'd just hear my prayers. Then one day out of the blue you woke up. Man, I thought I heard angels singing when you opened your eyes. You came back from the jaws of death. I just wasn't prepared for who came back."

"What do you mean? Who came back?"

"I don't know, but it sure as hell wasn't the kid I knew. You woke up angry, angrier than any man ever should be. I figured when you said you wanted to go to Japan, it was to finish your healing process, get your mind together; maybe even retire. But when you stepped off that plane the second time, I knew I'd lost you forever. Darkness was all over you."

"You don't get it, Tango. I lost everything in Miami."

"We all lost something in Miami. You lost your woman but I lost my son.

Meanwhile in his private library, Doc and a badly-beaten Gary Anders were exchanging icy glares from across the desk while Doc was on the phone repeatedly apologizing for his team leader's actions. Gary listened half-heartedly to Doc's lies and while he was full of anger and had a thousand excuses for his behavior, the battered brute remained silent. Doc's voice sounded humble and remorseful on the phone, but his face said something else all together. He was seething with anger.

"Thank you, Roger. I appreciate everything you did," he concluded before hanging up the phone. "You are by far the stupidest son-of-a-bitch walking the planet! Do you have any idea how dangerous this type of exposure is to this organization? I'm not gonna beat around the bush. Your behavior disgusts me. You show up late to meetings. You abandoned us in Mexico and you violated the T.P.O. Gabby had against your stupid ass. On top of that, you not only broke into her house and vandalized it, but you assaulted her fiancé and put him in the hospital! And if that wasn't enough, you assaulted a member of the Denver P.D. while resisting arrest! They have a laundry list of charges against you including public intoxication, breaking and entering, aggravated menacing, assault, resisting arrest, and vandalism. They also have you on aggravated stalking and drug possession. Where the hell did you find twelve grams of high-grade Columbian cocaine? On second thought, don't answer that!"

Gary thumbed through his arrest report with a smirk on his face while ignoring everything Doc was saying. In his lap were his mug-shot, police and toxicology reports, and a list of his charges.

"What the hell do you have to say for yourself?" Doc demanded while glaring angrily at the black-eyed brute in front of him. "You know what? It doesn't matter. You'd better be glad the D.A. and the judge are friends of mine, and you'd better be glad we were able to convince Gabby, Marcus, and Officer Jones to drop the charges in exchange for counseling and financial restitution. Here, this is for you."
"What's this?"
"That, my stupid friend, is an itemized list of everything you owe; court costs, legal fees, damages to Gabby's house, medical bills, and damages to the police cruiser."
"That's bullshit Doc! I'm not paying that!"
"Not only are you going to pay them, Gary, I'm suspending you indefinitely!"
"You're suspending me? Why?"

"I'm suspending you because I can't have a gun toting junkie on my detail. I'm going to trust that you can kick this habit without my intervention. Until then, you'll be attending weekly counseling sessions with…"

"I'm not spending any time with your resident protégé! That's where I draw the line. I don't need her kind of help."

"I don't care what you think about her 'kind' of help. The fact of the matter is you need someone to help you corral those demons floating around in that thick ass skull of yours. When did you start using that crap again anyway?"

"Are you serious, McCallister? You've been in the field. You remember what it's like; dodging bullets, spilling blood, and trading your soul in the name of duty. I lost mine a long time ago and so did you."

"Don't dare include me in this nightmare you're living Gary."

"I got all fucked up in the head, and I needed help coping. I traded my family for all this bullshit just like you so stop pretending that you're so innocent and don't have any skeletons in your closet. Do the kiddies know what really happened to their mommies and daddies or how they ended up here in the first place?"

"Say another word here or to anyone else and you'll be dead by sundown."

"Yeah right, McCallister," he replied sarcastically. "It's Tango that's suddenly feeling the need to spill his guts to everybody, not me. You should have heard him going on about how 'The Agency' was his road to hell and how he should never have let you put Alex and Lexi on it. Can you imagine he actually feels responsible for that young, arrogant asshole? I don't think he ever recovered from his addictions either, do you?"

"Tango isn't the issue right now, Gary. You are. Furthermore, if you don't go see Constance, you can

consider yourself out of *'The Agency,'* and I think you know what that means. Do you understand me?"
"Loud and clear, old man."
"Good. Now get out of my sight, so I can finish cleaning up this mess you made."

When the library door closed, Doc bolted up from his chair and grabbed a picture off the shelf. At the bottom of its frame was an engraved brass plate that read *'The Five Serpents'*. Pictured from left to right were Alex, Alexandria, Ko, Richard, and Nicholas. The photograph was taken over twenty years ago in Japan where they were first introduced.

In the wake of their parents' deaths, Doc thought it best to isolate the children from the world and put them in a single location to maintain their safety. Ko's uncle, Yoshishiro Hinomura was a martial arts master and sword smith who gladly took them in. While under his tutelage, they were trained in numerous forms of martial arts including White Lotus Kung-Fu, Northern and Southern-Style Shoalin Kung-Fu, Muay Thai, Wushu, Jujitsu, Ninjitsu, and Ninpo. Like their parents before them, they eventually went on to work for the CIA and under Doc's guidance, became the most elite team of assassins in the world.

While they trained, Doc took his entire operation underground and formed *'The Agency'*, a network of highly-trained assassins-for-hire. Under his leadership they administered a new type of 'justice'; one that was unattainable through traditional means. There were no arrests, no trials, and no courtrooms. Through the joint cooperation of every major law enforcement agency on the planet, a database was developed for international criminals deemed too dangerous to live. Once they were added, a bounty was issued for them. When 'The Agency' received notification of an active bounty, Doc deployed a member or members of his team to eliminate the target, for which they were handsomely compensated.

Over the next twenty years, 'The Agency' grew into a self-sustaining organization, using an International Real Estate Investment Corporation as its front. It had its own weapons designers, computer technicians, medical staff, pilots, and a host of outside individuals with whom they contracted. This collaboration made it easy for the operation to function in various capacities while maintaining a clandestine status. Several operatives came through 'The Agency', before 'The Five Serpents' were activated, many of which either died in the line of duty or by their own hands. Though every candidate understood the risks involved, the lure of hundred thousand or even million dollar paydays made them eager to undertake potentially deadly assignments, while ignoring the mental anguish that came along with them.

Over a period of years and through careful elimination, Doc trimmed his core unit to just a handful of operatives; Richard and Nicholas Chang, Ko Hinomura, Warren Jeffries, 'Big' Mike Wayne, Gary Anders, Alexis and Alexandria Stratton, and Terrance Donner, who was semi-retired. As productive as they were, this group was not without its problems.

Richard and Nicholas were pranksters who lacked the ability to take much of anything seriously. Ko was distracted by his familial ties to the Yakuza, as well as secretly maintaining a relationship with Alexandria who ultimately wanted to live a 'normal life'. Although he was an active planner and participant, Mike was more interested his ministry and his wife's salon ventures than he was their missions. Warren's depression, nightmares, and panic attacks eventually made him more of a liability than as asset. Gary's repeated bouts with addiction and his taste for violence were both disruptive and destructive. In addition to swearing of active duty, Tango had endured his own battles with alcohol and drug addiction. And last but not least, was Alex who was becoming more volatile, enigmatic, and unpredictable with each passing day. His obsession with Simon Felix and his affair with Tisha were testing the limits of his sanity and creating rifts within the team. *'The Agency'* was coming apart at the seams, and there was little Doc could do to stop it. The looming specter of revelations and in-fighting weighed heavy on his mind when he picked up the phone and began to dial.

"Constance, it's Gregory. We need to talk."

Later that evening at the shop, Alex's tattoo was finally coming to life. In the process, he and Tango managed to empty two bottles of Jack Daniels, a bucket of ice, and a couple liters of Coca-Cola.

"How'd you come up with the name Black Mamba anyway? I named you 'Scorpion' when I put that tattoo on your gut."
"With all the changes in my life and a new mission, it just seemed to fit; strike out of nowhere and be long gone before anyone knew what happened."
"But it doesn't always work that way does it?"
"No...I guess it doesn't," Alex replied after a brief moment of contemplation.
"Take it from me, son. The longer you stay, the more likely it is that you're gonna fuck up. Do the job and get

out. Don't get emotionally wrapped up with your mark or anyone close to them. If you do…well you know the consequences of that."

"Don't get emotionally wrapped up, huh?" Alex mused while staring at Tango's reflection. "Does that include women?"

"After two failed marriages and a long line of pissed off exes, my track record speaks for itself," he laughed while pouring another shot. "I can tell you what I do know though. You can't expect a woman to live on the fringes of your life. If you expect her to stay, you'll have to let her in. Even if she decides to leave, you have to let her make the choice. If you don't, she'll hate you for it. You got a woman, son? And I don't mean some chick you're banging. I mean a real woman; someone you can share your pain with."

"Maybe," Alex replied without lifting his head.

"That's news to me. I didn't think you'd go down that road again, especially with the shit you got going with Tisha and…never-mind. The point is words only go so far. If she means something to you, do something nice for her; roses, hair, nails, and shit like that. And, if you love her, don't wait 'til she's walking out the door to tell her. Tell her every day, even if you don't feel like it. Trust me, she'll appreciate it."

After six days and several hours spent at Tango's shop, Alex returned to his café and took a seat at his usual table. He scanned the crowd while reading the morning paper and noticed at least six federal agents seated around him. Once again, his mind raced while their data scrolled before his sunglass-clad eyes. After a few minutes of reading, Alex gave up the search and returned to his paper. Suddenly, he heard the intrusive sounds of metal scraping the ground followed by vibrations at his table. He folded the paper's edge and looked at the two men who had taken seats across from him. After quickly surveyed his unwelcomed guests, Alex laid the paper on the table and leaned back in his chair. He was so overcome with anger that he completely ignored the tattoo on his back. Their pretending to read the menu only fueled his growing anger.

"Excuse me, but may I help you?"
"As a matter of fact you can, Alex. What do you recommend for dinner?"
"For starters, I'd recommend another table."
"That's funny, Alex," laughed the agent with the slicked back hair.
"Glad you think so. And you would be who?"
"My name is Agent Castro, and this is Agent Blackhawk."
"Now that we have that out of the way, what the fuck do you want?"
"We're glad you asked, Alex," Agent Blackhawk began before sliding a manila envelope across the table. "We have some questions for you."

After opening the envelope and looking inside, Alex shook his head in disbelief. In his hands were several pictures of him and Tisha. There were also pictures of Simon, Ko, Lexi, and three of his cars, including the Aston Martin. With flared nostrils and erratic breaths, Alex tossed the pictures back across the table at the smiling duo. Realizing that the six other agents were watching his every move, Alex took a deep breath and quickly regained his composure.

"What do you want?" he asked calmly.
"For starters, Alex, we'd like to know what the exact nature of your relationship with Simon Felix's wife is?"

245

"I don't think that's any of your fucking business, Agent Blackhawk. And going forward, refer to me as Mr. Stratton."

"Okay, Mr. Stratton," Castro began sarcastically, "as you may or may not know, Simon Felix has been on our radar for quite some time and the fact that you're sleeping with his wife presents us with an unusual problem."

"And what problem is that?" Alex asked smugly.

"We have reason to believe you're doing more than sampling Simon's goodies. We suspect you're actually working for them. After all, your company presents you with the perfect opportunity to move dope for his cartel. Private planes, unlimited travel, passports...the whole nine yards. You can fly all over the world and no one would be the wiser. Plus there's the little issue of your identity. Except for a few legal documents, you're a ghost. It's as if you don't exist, and yet here you are. How do you pay for all this anyway?" Castro asked while looking around the café.

"Put plainly Ale...I mean Mr. Stratton, we're going to take this entire operation down and you're going with it. That is of course, unless you're willing to cooperate with us."

"Cooperate with what?" Alex snapped. "Clearly you have no idea who you're fucking with, do you Agent Blackhawk? You two morons are in way over your heads. Your so-called investigation is so full of holes it's pathetic."

Their confident smirks quickly turned into concern when Alex began slowly dissecting them. It was clear that they'd underestimated him, and he knew it. It was also apparent that they knew less about him than they thought.

"Your office is pretending to be in the dark and has put you two idiots on the chopping block. In time, all their efforts and yours will be rendered virtually useless. You've been chasing ghosts while allowing body counts to rack up, and for what? Simon is still free! I know more about his operation than you two combined! Now you think you can waltz into my café and play good cop-bad cop? Think again! You have nothing. I know it and you know it. Neither of you assholes is ready to climb into the ring with me, let alone go a full twelve rounds. So take your little envelope and your cheap suits and get the hell out of my face or I'll have you erased: period! Do I make myself clear, gentlemen?"

"Okay, Mr. Stratton, have it your way," Agent Blackhawk began. "We'll leave but, here's a card for you. If you change your mind, give our office a call."

"Yeah, whatever," Alex scoffed while waving them off.

When Agents Castro and Blackhawk got up and walked away, six additional agents and four decoys stood up and followed them. When they drove away, Alex's rage returned. Moments later, his DBS was barreling towards Boulder at speeds well above the posted limits. He didn't bother to check his mirrors to see if he was being followed. At one hundred fifty-five miles per hour and climbing, nothing the feds had on the road could catch him anyway.

"Let me call you later," Doc said when he heard the sound of screeching tires outside his window.

After hanging up the phone, he watched nervously as Alex slammed the car door. Moments later after a brief but heated exchange in the foyer, Doc heard his ominous footsteps rapidly approaching.

"How long have I been under surveillance?" he barked when he burst through the library doors.

"I tried to stop him," the housekeeper began nervously, "but he insisted on seeing you immediately, Mr. McCallister."

"It's quite alright, Selina. Take the rest of the afternoon off."

"Thank you, sir," she replied before cringing when Alex glared at her.

"Do come in, Alex and please close the door," Doc quipped sarcastically.

"Fuck the door. Answer my question!"

"I really have no idea what…"

"I said how long got-dammit!" Alex yelled again before driving his right fist into the center of the desk, spider webbing the glass top around his point of impact.

"Fine, muscles, you wanna play this game? One year; the feds have had you under surveillance for one year! They got wind of your little games with Simon and have been on to you ever since."

"And you didn't bother to tell me? What the fuck were you thinking?"

"Tell you? You arrogant jackass! We've all been telling you. Hell, I've been warning you that if you continued with your madness, this would happen. Your antics have jeopardized this entire operation! You've played this sick and twisted game so long that you've lost sight of the real enemy. It's not Simon, it's you!"

"What do they have?" Alex growled with blood dripping from his clinched fist. "And if I have to repeat myself, you're gonna need a decorator when I'm done."

"For the most part, all they have are pictures," Doc replied while assessing the damaged desktop.

"What about my phones? Wiretaps? Cars? Email? My fucking house?"

"Well, Alex, you don't have a land line and our cell phones are encrypted, and therefore untraceable. Your office suite is nothing more than a shell with a phone line and a phony receptionist. Our email network is above secure so that's not an issue either. What they do have however, are pictures of you, Lexi, and Ko. They have taps on Tisha's phone, so they have transcripts of your pillow talk. They definitely have Simon's as well. They also have information on your LLC's holdings with Weltman, Reid, and Myers. Thank heaven there's nothing that could lead back to us, at least that I'm aware of. Still the fact of the matter is, we're potentially exposed now and damage control must be done to ensure no further compromises."

"Damage control?" Alex groaned. "Why don't you just call your friends at the Bureau and get them off my ass?"

"Yes, Alex, damage control and no, it's not that easy. You who created this mess and you need to fix it."

"Fix it how, old man?"

"I'll leave that up to you, Alex. Hopefully this episode of wanton disregard and callousness will make you more mindful in the future. Furthermore, I hope your blatant acts of recklessness cease as well."

"Recklessness? You've got nerve," Alex quipped sarcastically.

"Let me ask you a question, Alex. Do you even know where Simon is at this very moment?"

"No, Doc, I don't. But I guess you do, right?"

"Of course, you don't. And do you know why?"

"Enlighten me," Alex snapped.

"It's because you've completely lost your focus. Your quest for revenge has made you so narrow minded that you've driven wedges between you and the people closest to you. No one trusts you anymore. You're a ticking time bomb and no one knows when you're going to explode; not even you. And for the record, he's in Jamaica as we speak attempting to broker a deal with a trio of African Nationals."

"Fine. I'll fly out tonight and…"

"Wrong!" Doc interrupted angrily. "You won't do anything! As a matter of fact, I don't want you anywhere near Simon in the immediate future."

"What? There's no better time than now. I can fly to Jamaica, get a line on him, and take him out. Bang, end of story."

"You think it's that easy, don't you Alex?"

"I don't see what the problem is, Doc."

"You think you can appear and disappear like a thief in the night? Well this time you're wrong. The feds are all over Simon. Even if you did manage to get close to him, you'd never get a shot off without them being on to you."

"That's bullshit and you know it!" Alex declared before turning and walking towards the door.

"Where are you going?"

"I'm taking a vacation."

"A vacation?" Doc laughed while leaning forward in his chair. "You? Yeah right. And where will you be vacationing?"

"If you must know, I'll be in Cincinnati, Ohio."

"Alex, who the hell do you know in Cincinnati, Ohio?"

"Lynn lives there," he snapped angrily.

"I know, I just wanted to see if you'd lie. I had my people dig up some background information on her. She's definitely not your cup-of-tea, and by that I mean she's clean; simple. She's much too good for a man of your caliber which makes her perfect. Go to Cincinnati, do whatever you need to do with this woman, and get rid of her like the rest. When you're done, get back here and fix this mess you've created."

"It's not like that. She's different."

"She may be, but you're not. Do what you need to do and get back here. In the meantime, I'll see if I can buy you some time from the feds. I can't interfere directly without exposing us, but I can at least steer them in another direction. But if I think for one second you're anywhere near Jamaica or Simon, I'll have you arrested. And if you somehow manage to slip past me and get yourself caught up somewhere, this agency will deny any knowledge of you. Do I make myself clear?"
"Crystal," Alex declared before walking out of the library door.

Moments, later while standing beside his car, Alex took his cell phone out of his pocket, scrolled through his phone book and pressed *send*.

"Agent Tobey Shavers, please."
"Just one moment, please."
"This is Shavers," replied a voice on the phone after a few moments of awful hold music.
"Shavers, this is Stratton. I don't have much time so shut up and listen carefully. I need you to get the XP 390-R and some of my business cards and head to my penthouse. I'll meet you there soon. Don't tell anyone where you are going. Got it?"
"Got it, boss."

A short while later, Alex's V-12 engine was echoing off the walls of his underground garage. After looking around and checking his surroundings, he exited the car and walked towards a white Ford Taurus, where an animated young man was standing with his hand held up.

"Black Mamba, what's up?"

"I thought I told you not to call me that outside the office," Alex replied with an angry glare.

"What, no high five?" Shavers asked when he looked at his hand and then at the stone-faced man in front of him. "No problem, bro. I see you're in a mood."

"Did you bring it?"

"Of course, and I made sure I wasn't followed."

"Good. Get it and bring it upstairs."

Moments later, the pair was at Alex's dining room table and in front of them was a state-of-the-art laptop computer which was built into a black titanium briefcase. Beside it was a stack of business cards with 'XLS Enterprises, LLC' embossed on them in blue ink.

"This is my baby. It has twelve terabytes of memory, fifteen-hundred hertz, six gigs of back-up memory, and a lithium ion battery. Its super fast, super quiet, and with anti freeze running through these special lines, super cool! With this baby, I can hack phone lines, highjack satellites, crack encrypted codes, and hear any conversation within a hundred yards of one of those special business cards of yours. So what do you want with my baby, huh? Deep-cover work? Espionage? A little wet work?"

"I'm taking a vacation."

"Then what's wrong with your laptop?"

"I may do some surveillance as well."

"That's what I'm talking about!" Shavers shouted while bolting up from his chair. "When do we leave?"

"We're not going anywhere. I'm going to Cincinnati."

"C'mon Alex, take me with you! I can help, really. I'm a third degree black belt, I can run a mile in under six minutes, I can shoot, fight, and..."

"And you're a tech," Alex interrupted sarcastically.

"But..."

"Zip it, Shavers. It's not up for discussion. Stop trying to be something that you're not. You're a technician and a weapons designer. Leave the real work to the rest of us."

"Real work? That's cold, man," Shavers replied before slumping down in his chair.

"On second thought, I can use your help," Alex said after closing the case's lid.

"Hell, yeah! That's what I'm talking about. What do you need?"

"Book yourself a plane to Cincinnati and take this stuff with you. Check us into the Westin Hotel using my corporate account."

"Who's the target?"

"Dawn Tyler."

"What do you want?"

"Everything," Alex replied flatly.

"Got it. Then what?"

"Take notes."

"Take notes?" Shavers huffed. "C'mon man, that sounds so...so...boring."

"Trust me, everything you're doing is very vital to the Felix case."

"Done," Shavers beamed. "Do you think we can use codenames while we're in the field? I've always wanted to be called Wiretap."

"I'll think about it," Alex replied while shaking his head.

After escorting Shavers to the door, Alex entered his computer room and sat down at the massive console. He settled into the high-backed chair, placed his elbow on its arm, and rested his head on his clinched fist. After spinning around, he picked up a small remote control and aimed it at the wall. Almost instantly, the four panels on it separated and filled the room with blue fluorescent light. Behind those panels were a dozen handguns, sub-machines, and assault rifles. There were also two sniper rifles and a pair of twelve gauge shotguns. Along a shelf underneath the arsenal was a collection of small knives, throwing stars, and a pair of gauntlets containing spring loaded blades.

"Delilah."

"Yes Alex," she replied, causing the screens behind him to light up.

"Are you awake?"

"Of course, Alex; I never sleep."

"Good because I need you to do something for me. Use override code BMX39047236982 Alpha."

"Access granted. What can I do for you, Black Mamba?"

"I need you to access the FBI's crime data files and locate all the information they have on Simon Felix. Cross reference any information they may have on 'The Agency's' operatives."

"It is done," she replied seconds later.

"I need to you to copy it all onto my ghost drive."

"It is done."

"Next, I need you to extract every piece of information they have related to me and anyone else in 'The Agency.' That includes pictures, transcripts, notes, etc."

"It is done. What would you like me to do with it, Black Mamba?"

"Destroy it."

"There is a lot of information here. This may take several minutes."

"No hurry. Save a copy on my ghost drive and print one for me as well."

To pass the time, Alex closed his eyes and let his mind wander. *You could always kill him, Alex,* boomed a voice in his head.

Hours later, dark clouds filled Denver's midnight skies while the city was being blanketed by an icy downpour. In a top-floor suite of the FBI's regional HQ, Agents Castro and Blackhawk were working furiously into the night. They were so busy milling about in their office that they didn't notice the shadowy-figure moving along the rooftop across the street. He kept a watchful eye on them as they sifted through the stacks of papers on the table in front of them. Moments after assembling an Mk-11 sniper rifle, the assassin set up a perch and began lining his targets up in the crosshairs of his night-vision scope. While adjusting for distance and crosswinds, he sized up his two targets, and with his finger gently caressing the trigger, waited for the perfect shot. Like a predator stalking its prey, he patiently studied their every move.

For the next hour as driving rains pounded the rooftop, the patient sniper kept watching and waiting. At long last, his patience was rewarded. The two unsuspecting targets were standing side-by-side, within inches of each other. When Agent Castro leaned down to point at something on the table, the assassin squeezed the trigger and watched as the window shattered and his head exploded. Before Agent Blackhawk could react, the rifle recoiled twice; ejecting a pair of hollow-point projectiles which obliterated his chest. Seconds later, with wind and rain whipping through the office, Agents Blackhawk and Castro lay dead in pools of their own blood.

"Black Mamba, are you awake? The task is complete," Delilah said, startling Alex who'd been serenaded by the printer's hum.

"Good. Now I need you to pull up all the information the Bureau has on Agent Blackhawk. I want high-school transcripts, SAT and ACT scores, college transcripts, military records, birth certificate, driving records... anything you can find."

"It is done," she replied seconds later.

"Good. Print that as well."

The next afternoon, Alex exited flight 872 at the Greater Cincinnati International Airport, collected his bags, and made his way to the rental counter. After selecting his vehicle, a white Cadillac Escalade, he drove up Interstate 75 into Downtown Cincinnati, and after slowly negotiating some rush hour traffic, he valet parked at the Westin Hotel. With his bags on a shiny brass cart and an eager bellhop in tow, he made his way to the counter.

"Welcome to the Westin of Cincinnati," smiled the bubbly attendant. "How may we serve you today?"

"I have a reservation under the name of XLS Enterprises. The name is Stratton."

"Thank you, Mr. Stratton. Your other party has already arrived and took the liberty of upgrading your reservation to a pair of adjoining Executive Suites."

"Executive Suites, really? How much are those?" he asked while passing her his black card.

"They're fifteen-hundred dollars per night and include concierge service and gourmet breakfast at no extra charge. This pamphlet contains your room key and a description of our services. You are in Suite 1816 and your other party is Suite 1815. Enjoy your stay, Mr. Stratton."

"Thank you," Alex replied with a smile while imagining his hands wrapped around Shavers' throat.

The elevator ride to the eighteenth floor was quiet, except for the hum of the gears and Alex's breathing. He stood with his eyes closed, half-leaning on the mahogany wall behind him while contemplating which Jujitsu hold to punish Shavers with first.

"First time in Cincinnati, sir?" asked the bellhop trying to alleviate some of the tension in the elevator.
"No."
"Well, I hope you enjoy your stay, sir. The summertime in Cincinnati can be pretty hot, especially at night if you know what I mean," the bellhop replied with a smile and a wink.
"I'll keep that in mind. Thank you."

Seconds later they were at Suite 1816. When the door opened, Alex quickly took in exactly what fifteen-hundred dollars per night times two was paying for; a huge a king-sized platform bed, Jacuzzi tub, fireplace, mini bar with a fridge, a 50" flat screen TV, and a furnished living room.

"Is this to your liking, sir?"
"This will do fine," Alex replied while handing the bellhop a crisp fifty dollar bill.

When the bellhop exited, Alex closed his eyes and took a deep, cleansing breath. When his eyes opened, he leapt over the couch and stormed towards the white pocket doors separating the two suites. After briefly contemplating putting his fist through it, he knocked several times, but twisted the golden handle before anyone could answer.

"Whassup, boss? You look tense. You should let Meagan relax you. She has the hands of an angel,"

Shavers smiled while lying half-naked on a portable massage table.

"And how much are your angelic hands, Meagan?" Alex asked after gazing at the petite brunette.

"One hundred dollars per hour, sir. Would you like me to do you next?"

"Maybe later," Alex smiled with clinched fists and flared nostrils.

Meagan's warm smile and slow, feline-like movements did little to quell Alex's foul temper. Fearing for his safety, Shavers grabbed his robe, helped Meagan pack up her massage table, and escorted her to the door.

"Call me," he whispered while holding his thumb and pinky up to his head.

"Three thousand dollars-a-night!" Alex growled after the door closed. "Are you serious? Tell me why I shouldn't rip your heart out and feed it to you?"

"Ok, I can see you're pissed, but I thought you might wanna splurge a little bit on your much deserved vacation."

"It looks like you're the only one splurging on *my* vacation. Have you done any work since you've been here?" Alex growled while looking around the suite.

"Have I? Are you kidding?" Shavers quipped nervously while darting towards the desk. "Check this out! I have Dawn's cell phone and her land line. I've also gone through her text messages. I even have her Facebook page and emails. I have all her husband's stuff too. So far, there isn't much going on, although she does have several missed calls from some guy calling himself Loco. Why's she so important anyway?"

"Simon Felix is her brother-in-law, and he's rumored to be in Jamaica. I'm hoping she can give me some information on him; dealings, next move… anything I can use to find him."

"Why don't you just ask his wife?"

"Because that would be too easy Tobey. Besides, I need some time and space away from her. What else do you have?"

"I've also got some information on your friend, Agent Blackhawk. It appears that in addition to being an army ranger, he was attached to an elite intel gathering unit. You know what his specially was?"

"Shock me."

"In-field interrogation specialist," Shavers said with a smile. "He worked in a unit stationed in Guantanamo Bay where, among other things, water boarding was highly popular. He's also been on the Felix case about as long as you."

"I know," Alex replied before turning and walking towards the adjoining doors.

"Hey, where are you going?"

"Keep me posted on her activities. I have a date."

"So I'm supposed to sit here reading her spam while you paint the town? That's bullshit!"

"Hey Shavers, give it a rest. You begged me to come along, remember? I didn't promise you action or drama. Besides, you're a tech. This is what you do all day anyway, so why are you bitching? Look at the bright side. You get to work in these lavish surroundings at my expense."

Before Shavers could reply, Alex slammed the door and locked it behind him. After taking a quick shower and changing into jeans and a t-shirt, he returned to the front desk.

"Is everything okay, Mr. Stratton?"

"Yes, everything is fine. I was wondering if you could direct me to the nearest florist. I need a dozen pink roses."

Chapter 10

Denver, Colorado

After being called in for an emergency meeting at FBI regional headquarters, the Simon Felix investigative team found itself in an uproar. In their eyes, a man having just returned from a relaxing vacation in sunny Jamaica should be calm, but Burroughs was nothing of the sort. In fact, he seemed beside himself with anger and frustration. The nine man team, now joined by Agent Castro sat bewildered while the usually calm senior agent paced back-and-forth. It was obvious by the look on his face, the sweat on his brow, and his constant mumbling that he was flustered. He fidgeted with the overhead projector for several minutes before it finally came on. When the screen lit up, they noticed that although most of the pictures were still the same, the order had been changed and some were missing. At the top of the pyramid where Simon's picture was originally posted, was a familiar but little face.

"Thank you for coming to this emergency meeting on such short notice. As you know, I'm on the President's Advisory Board on Drug Trafficking in the Caribbean. During my recent fact-finding trip to Jamaica and with the help of Jamaican authorities, we've made some startling new discoveries. For years we believed that Simon Felix was the head of the Kingston Cartel when, in fact, it is this man, Gabriel Malcolm. Simon, as it turns out, is only the front man. This Gabriel is the actual brains behind the operation. He maintains connections throughout the world while never getting his hands dirty. He's a Jamaican Al Capone, if you will. He calls

261

the shots from the island, although he makes frequent trips to Denver. He even has a home in Boulder."

"Sir," Agent Blackhawk began after looking around the room at all the stunned faces, "you do realize that we've built a five year investigation around Simon Felix. Now you're suggesting that we reorganize our entire operation? With all due respect sir, I think we should stay the course and…"

"With all due respect, Agent Blackhawk, I was studying these cartels long before you were an agent. I've studied their operations from South America and Jamaica all the way to Europe and Asia. So when I tell you that I know something, take to as Bible. Is that clear, Agent Blackhawk?"

"Yes sir, Agent Burroughs," Jason replied, albeit reluctantly and unconvinced.

"Thank you. Now, Agent Carver?"

"Yes, Agent Burroughs."

"I want everything on this guy; cell phones, emails, bank accounts, credit cards, etc. I want to know when he eats, sleeps, and shits. Set up around the clock surveillance at his house."

"No offense, Agent Burroughs, but do we have a court order for any of this?"

"Do you have an issue following orders, Agent Castro?"

"No, sir. I just wanna make sure that when we get all we need, no judge halts our arrests. That's all, sir."

"Everything you need is in the folders in front of you so get to work. I understand that with the Mexican cartels reeling from recent assassinations and the deaths of some of their biggest customers, Simon and Gabriel are holding a meeting to set up distribution with a trio of North Africans. Get me all the information you can on that as well. What the hell are you waiting for? Get to work!"

The befuddled agents quickly filed out of the room and disappeared into several smaller offices throughout the floor. After making sure they were out of Burroughs' sight, Castro and Blackhawk ducked into an empty office, locked the door, and pulled the blinds.

"What the hell was that?" Castro demanded while slamming the folder on the table.

"It sounds like our senior agent is working an angle that he doesn't want anyone to know about. Did you notice that there's no information our on boy Stratton in any of these folders? And on the overhead, his pictures were missing too."

"You're right," Castro replied after quickly thumbing through the folder. "I wonder if Burroughs noticed it too. I mean, all his information is gone; pictures, transcripts, and everything else we had on him is not here either."

"He's nowhere in the database either," Blackhawk replied while sitting at the computer terminal and staring at the words *No information found.*

"What the fuck is going on, Jason?"

"I don't know," Agent Blackhawk replied before slumping back in the chair and massaging his temples.

Cincinnati, Ohio

On this sunny afternoon in a modest middle-class neighborhood, the summer heat was set to full-blaze. Happy children rode their bikes, played ball in the street, and gleefully chased a slow moving ice cream truck. Scantily-dressed young women lined the sidewalks, while eager young men in box Caprices, Impalas, and Crown Vics on oversized rims provided these would-be models with a soundtrack of loud music and cat calls. For a while, no one seemed to notice the ivory Escalade when it stopped in front of the yellow and white trimmed, two-story house near the corner. But like a celebrity, it suddenly became the star of attraction. Passersby gazed while the sun glistened off its chrome trim and 22" rims. Nosey neighbors gawked from their porches, attempting to see what dope dealer was behind the smoked glass windows. To say it seemed out of place was an understatement. The Caddy was sticking out like a sore thumb.

"Who the hell is that?" Chelle asked from the porch while spraying a pair of gleeful toddlers with a garden hose. "Whoever it is must be lost or looking for some shit to get into."
"I don't know, girl but it' too hot for foolishness today," Lynn replied while sipping her sweet tea and waiting for the driver's door to open.

When Alex stepped out with a bouquet of pink roses in his hand, a huge smiled crossed her cherry gloss-covered lips. After dropping her glass, she raced off the porch, leapt over the kids, and dove into his arms. Thinking it was all a dream, Lynn released him momentarily; just so she could stare into his eyes and make sure he was real. She melted when his soft lips touched hers. Feeling his hands on the small of her back left her body covered in goose bumps. For that brief moment, her world stood still. Alex on the other hand wasn't feeling so jovial. A grimace and finally a grunt replaced his otherwise hypnotic smile.

"Are you okay, baby?" she asked when she released him again and stepped back.
"I'm fine, but I got a new tat, and it's very sore."
"A tattoo?" she asked giddily. "Can I see it?"
"Sure."

"It's breathtaking," she gasped while staring at the most beautiful set of silver and ivory wings she'd ever seen. Below them was an inscription that read, *"Only God can judge me."*
.

"Lynn, who's this half-naked brotha on my sidewalk?" Chelle asked when Alex lowered his shirt.
"Chelle, I'd like you to meet Alex."

Ni'Chelle's eyes quickly narrowed after appraising him. He was gorgeous; too gorgeous. Flawless skin, long black hair, bedroom eyes, and enough charm to attract a whale. This was a bad combination for any man, much less for the woman who was attracted to him. Her nose wrinkled while taking him in, even scoffing silently at his extended hand.

"Look, Alex, you may be a fine, tall, drink of water, but this here is my lil' sister and I'll put a nigga in the ground before I see her hurt. You feel me, Alex?"
"You must be Ni'Chelle," he replied in a buttery tone before gently taking her hand in his and kissing it softly.
Damn, she thought when her knees began to tremble.
"Don't think that showing up at my house with flowers for my sister is gonna get you any booty points either."
"Of course not," he mused before taking one of the roses from Lynn's bouquet and passing it to Ni'Chelle.
"You know you givin' that back, right?" Lynn declared before rolling her eyes at her ambrosia-sniffing sibling.
"Girl, stop. Come inside and have a seat, Alex. I'm sure you must be tired from your trip.
"Actually, it was well worth it," he replied while gazing lovingly at Lynn.

Alex stood like sentry near the steps while Ni'Chelle and Lynn collected the children, dried them off, and brought them into the cool house. After a lunch of grilled cheese sandwiches and tomato soup, Ni'Chelle put them down for a nap then joined Alex and Lynn in the living room.

"Y'all making a sista feel like a third wheel."
"We don't mean to, Chelle. As a matter of fact, why don't you join us for dinner? Is tomorrow too short of a notice?"
"The three of us?" Lynn gasped, unable to disguise her apprehension.
"Hell yes, the three of us," Chelle replied. "Damn, Lynn, don't be greedy. All I want is dinner. You get the dessert."

The inference made Lynn's cheeks redden with heat, which wasn't helped by Alex's tender hold on her hand.

"You all have a lovely home. The two of you really have an eye for detail," Alex said while admiring the numerous statues, tapestries, candle holders, and ceramic figurines.
"Thank you, but it's nothing like the one we were planning on buying with our inheritance. Too bad our bitch-of-a brother stole everything we had coming, thieving mutha-fucka."
"Chelle!" Lynn yelled, totally embarrassed by her sister's outburst. "Alex didn't fly all this way to hear about our personal problems."
"It's okay, honey, really. I don't mind," he said with a reassuring smile.
"Yeah, Lynn, let's keep it one-hundred. Desmond robbed us blind. There's no need to hide it from Alex. It is what it is."
"I know that, Chelle, but we have been and will be fine, money or not."

"I know we will Lynn, but damn. It would've been nice to pay some shit off so bill collectors ain't callin' every five minutes. I wanna splurge a lil' bit. Hell, I wanted to take a damned vacation!!! I mean I was looking forward to Aaron and Ashley having separate rooms. And frankly, I'm tired of sharing a bathroom with yo' slow ass, especially in the morning."

"Beauty takes time, Chelle," Lynn replied with both confidence and pride in her tone.

"Chile, *please!* You work around smelly old folks. You're lucky if they remember who you are from day-to-day. At least the old men will, what with you having them big ass titties and all," Chelle said with a giggle which was followed by a pillow to her face. "I'm just sayin,' girl. Do any of them old men try to stick AARP cards in your bra?"

Feeling self conscious about Chelle's teasing and Alex's failed attempt to disguise his amusement, Lynn folded her arms across her breasts and began to pout.

"But seriously, Alex, Desmond wiped us out. We had at least a million dollars coming from our father and now it's gone. We were going to use that money to buy a house, and Lynn was gonna go to medical school. I was finally gonna be able to open a real beauty salon."

"I didn't know you did hair, Chelle," Alex interrupted.

"Baby, hairdressers do hair. I style the *shit* out of some hair."

"When it comes to hair and nails, Chelle is the best, Alex," Lynn chimed in with a hint of disappointment in her voice.

"I'm sorry you both took such a loss, but don't let that unfortunate event steal your joy. Never give up on your dreams. I know from experience that things can turn

267

around on a dime. Besides, I know some investors that might be interested in helping you get your shop off the ground."

"Really?" Ni'Chelle asked with her eyes stretched wide and her dreams flashing before her eyes.

"Absolutely. With my friends backing you, you'll never need another cent. A few phone calls are all it takes."

"For real?"

"No doubt," Alex replied with a smile.

"I hear what you're saying, Alex, but damn! It's hard out here for a single woman with two kids trying to make it, especially in the business world. I still need that cushion, you know? I thank God that Lynn is here, or I'd be batty as hell."

"I think it's beautiful that the two of you are so close. It really makes a difference, especially when a sibling has your back."

"Do you have any sisters or brothers, Alex?" Chelle asked after noticing a slight change in his demeanor.

"I have a younger sister and for all intents and purposes, she thinks I'm an asshole."

"I see," she replied, unsure of what else to say.

"Wow, look at the time," he said after looking at the carefully timed escape on his wrist. "I have to be going. I have a client I need to see before it gets too late."

"Already? Ok hon, if you have to go, you have to go. I'll walk you out."

Taking Alex by the hand and escorting him to the door, Lynn smiled and grinned while Ni'Chelle trailed them from a distance. After exchanging a few pleasantries, Lynn walked Alex to his car where they shared an intensely passionate kiss. After watching him drive away Lynn returned to the porch where Ni'Chelle was waiting.

"Lynn, that's a fine mutha-fucka."

Alex used the Caddy's GPS to navigate his way up
interstate 75 into the city of West Chester. Compared to
Lynn's modest neighborhood, *The Arbors of West Chester*
subdivision was in another world all together. There
were no cracked streets, loud stereos, or half-naked
women parading about. Trees and shrubs lined the
sidewalks on either side of the passing Escalade, which
seemed a bit down-scale among the Benzes, Porsches,
and Lexuses that filled the driveways. Upon turning
onto Weeping Willow Lane, Alex noticed an all too
familiar sight; a white van parked at the end of the
block. High on an adjacent utility pole was a technician
pretending to service the phone lines. After circling the
block a couple of times, Alex noticed a black Tahoe
parked a few doors from his destination. Realizing that
he had their attention, Alex pulled slowly into the
driveway and parked the Caddy next to Dawn's
Mercedes. As the Tahoe inched closer to the house, he
quickly donned a ball cap and his dark sunglasses.

"I want this guy," growled the man on the pole while
looking over his shoulder.
"It's a rental boss," replied the voice on his radio.
"When he steps out, I want you tight on him. By the
time he comes out of that house, I wanna know
everything about him."
"Yessir."

Seconds after taking a deep breath, Alex stepped out of
the car and quickly walked to the front door with his
hand purposely shielding his face.

"He knows we're on to him. Get that son of a bitch!"

"Our transmissions just went all fuzzy, sir. We can't get a clear shot of him."

"I didn't ask for excuses. I asked for his identity, goddammit!" he yelled when the front door opened.

"Alex!!! OMG!!! What are you doing in Cincinnati?"

"I'm here on business and decided to pop in. How are you doing, Dawn?"

"I'm fine, babe. Please come in and chill. Want some tea?"

"Sure," he replied before stepping inside and quickly closing the door.

"What are you looking at, Alex?" Dawn asked when he peeped out of her blinds.

"I was just admiring the view. You have a lovely home and this is a beautiful neighborhood."

"Well thank you, Alex. I mean, it's not a penthouse with a panoramic view of the city, but it works for me, Roger, and the girls."

"All that glitters isn't gold, Dawn," Alex said after another quick glance. "I'm sure you've heard that before. Some pleasures come with a price and some prices are much higher than others."

"Oh yeah?" she asked before sipping her tea. "What price is that?"

"You tell me," he said before sitting down and picking up his glass.

"Are you hungry, Alex?" Dawn asked, attempting to change the topic of this uncomfortable conversation.

"I had dinner with some friends before I arrived. I'll have another glass of tea though, if you don't mind."

"Of course," she replied before disappearing into the kitchen.

Once she was out of sight, Alex picked her cell phone up off the table, opened the back, and placed a tiny transmitter inside. After sliding its cover back in place, he returned the phone to the table. Without making a sound, he got up and walked over to the mantle above the fireplace. He gazed sadly at the array of pictures on it before placing a business card on the back of one of the frames.

"You said you were out here on business?" Dawn asked from the kitchen.
"Yes. We're looking at some investment opportunities in and around the downtown area. With land prices being so low, now is the best time for us to get on board. Besides, with the hotel and gaming industry exploding in the Midwest and a casino right downtown, we stand to make a ton of money. You might want to consider investing with us."
"I'll keep that in mind," she replied when she closed the fridge. "Yep, those are my babies," Dawn said when she entered the den and saw Alex looking at the pictures.
"How are they?"
"They're just fine and spoiled rotten," she replied gleefully.
"Dawn, I know it's not my place to get into your business, but I care. You can't keep playing in this arena without suffering some serious losses. You have a beautiful family, and I'd hate to hear that something happened to them. Take my card and keep it with you. If you need some investment help or anything else, please don't hesitate to give me a call."
"I'll do that, Alex," she replied when she took the card from his hand.

Though she hadn't told him herself, Dawn knew Alex was aware of her illegal business dealings.

A while later after more tea and lengthy conversation, Alex quickly donned his make shift disguise and walked out of the front door en route to his getaway car. As he sped out of the subdivision, he noticed the Tahoe in his rearview mirror. After getting on the interstate and negotiating some quick, but dangerous lane changes, Alex lost his pursuers in a sea of taillights. Later that evening at the hotel, Alex joined Shavers in his suite to compare notes.

"Ok super genius, what do you have for me?"

"Not much boss, transmitters are working great though, including the one they placed on the rear bumper of your truck. The minute you left she was on the phone with both Tisha and her Roger. She's also been playing phone tag with somebody from an unknown number. The weird thing is that's a federal phone number."

"What do you mean it's a federal number?"

"I mean they have it, boss. It's their number. I don't know if she's working with the feds or what, but that number is definitely being monitored."

"Interesting."

"You think she knows it's tapped, boss?"

"I think not knowing the number is making her extra cautious. Is it registered to anyone?"

"Nope, it looks to be prepaid. Whoever it is, they won't leave a message," Tobey replied.

"Did she discuss anything meaningful with anyone else?"

"Afraid not," Tobey said while reviewing some transcripts. "She told Roger about your investment offer, but that was it. Nobody gave up anything we could use."

"I see," Alex sighed while staring at a surveillance photograph.

"Based on what I can tell, Dawn calls the shots. Roger doesn't have the stomach for the dope game. But like any husband, he wants to please his wife."

"Even if means being lead to hell," Alex replied to no one in particular. "Stomach or not, he watched while his family was sold to Simon and now, none of them will ever be safe. When I told her every pleasure had a price, I was talking about them."

"Just like Adam and that apple, that's the choice he made Alex, not you."

"I guess. Good work as usual, Shavers. You're really earning your field name. Now if you'll excuse me, I'm going to bed."

"Hey boss, can I ask you a question?"

"Sure."

"Why haven't you killed Simon? I mean with all he's put you through...why not just take him out and call it a day?"

"There was a time when I wanted to, but now it's too damned easy," Alex replied after a long, deep breath. "There isn't a day that goes by that I don't think about killing him. But he deserves far worse than that. Some people deserve to suffer just like the people they've tortured. Some people deserve to hurt. Simon is one of those people and I intend to make sure he hurts; tremendously. Then when he can't take it anymore, I'll make him beg me to kill him."

"Do you ever think you won't get him? I mean last time you got close..."

"Everyone's day comes eventually, Tobey," Alex interrupted. "Have any more questions?"

"I guess not," he replied while looking away nervously.

"Good. Now, goodnight."

That night as a storm raged outside, Alex was again disturbed by haunting images. His body writhed under the covers while his mind raced furiously. He was no longer in Cincinnati. He was in Miami standing outside

St. Stephen's Cathedral. Lightning flashed in the heavens above him as he stood on the massive staircase loading his MK-5. Seconds later with the butt of the gun at his shoulder, Alex burst through the massive wooden doors. While staring down the length of the barrel and panning from side to side, Alex stalked through the sanctuary in total silence. The red laser beam bounced off the brass candle holders, life-sized marble statues, and ornate, stained-glass as he searched the darkness for signs of life. Suddenly ten rows ahead of him, a figure sprang up from the darkness and before Alex could open fire, the wind was suddenly knocked out of his body. The explosions that followed shook everything in the church. Steam rose from the singed Kevlar and dented metal plates shielding his badly bruised chest and abdomen. While struggling to his feet and gasping for air, Alex clawed for the .40 cal located at the small of his back. He fired wildly into the darkness before another blast knocked him to his kness. Within seconds, Alex was at their mercy. He tried to shield himself from the onslaught of kicks and stomps that were raining down on him, but it was no use. In a last ditch effort to save himself, Alex reached for a grenade that was attached to his hip but was knocked unconscious before he could pull the pin.

When Alex opened the one eye that wasn't swollen shut, he realized he had been unmasked and stripped to his waist. After looking down and hearing their taunting laughs, Alex realized he suspended from the giant crucifix at the front of the sanctuary. In front of him were seven men; Simon, Gabriel, and five of the remaining henchmen. Alex tried to speak, but broken ribs and a punctured lung were restricting his breathing. His jaw, both his arms, and one of his hands were broken. As his body cried out in agony, tears rained from his eyes. The men before him had taken the love of his life and there was no way he would be able to avenge her. When Gabriel pulled a gold-handled machete out of his coat, Alex lowered his head and waited for the death blow. Just as he raised his arms, the doors at the rear of the church exploded open and a hail of gunfire rang out. During the mêlée, Alex blacked out.

The icy cold at his back shocked him to consciousness. When Alex opened his eyes again, he was half-cradled in Tango's arms with salty tears raining down on his facial. Though his vision was blurred, he could still see dark figures standing around him. By their sobs, Alex knew that it was just a matter of time now. He turned his head slowly to the right and saw his parents standing off in the distance. Even in the darkness, Alex could clearly see his father restraining his frantic, crying mother.

"Mother," Alex moaned, unable to raise his limp arm.

Was this was the moment that so many people spoke of? Was this was the moment when the dead walk? But if his parents were there to usher him to the other side, why was his mother crying? Was he going to hell instead? Had his soul been lost to the enemy? His mind raced up until he took his last breath.

A flash of lightening and the boom of thunder shook his hotel room, snapping Alex out of his nightmare. After gasping for breath, Alex sat up in the bed and snatched off the covers. Daylight seared his sensitive retinas. Moments later, with steam billowing all around him, Alex stood at the vanity in the dimly-lit bathroom.

"You look like shit," he groaned after flipping on the lights and gazing at his own visage.

After a long shower, Alex wrapped himself in a towel and walked over to the nightstand. He picked up his cell phone, and after searching through its phonebook, selected a number and pressed send.

"Hello," croaked the voice on the other end.
"Wake up, David. I need you to do something for me."
"Alex, are you serious? It's not even seven o'clock," David Weltman moaned while looking at his watch and startling the naked brunette beside him.
"It's nine-forty-five in Cincinnati so get over it."
"Cincinnati? What the fuck are you doing in Cincinnati?"
"Never mind that," Alex demanded while pacing back and forth near the sofa. "I don't have much time so listen closely. Do you remember Lynn Turner?"
"You mean the beautiful woman who got screwed by her brother? Yes, I remember her. Who could forget?" David asked before receiving an elbow to his arm.
"I want you to advance her a million dollars from one of my accounts."
"You want me to what?" David shouted after sitting up in bed, further angering his guest.
"You heard me and I want you to manipulate it so that it appears to be a part of her dead father's estate. I want you to make sure it isn't taxed upon dispersal either."
"Let me get this straight, Alex. You want me to advance a million dollars of your money to complete stranger and make it look like it came from her father? Do you know how illegal that is?"
"Listen carefully, David. Part of the reason that your name is on that marquee is because you handle billions in cash and other assets for me and my associates. As such, we've turned a blind eye to the exorbitant fees

you've been charging. That being said, if performing specific tasks with my money as directed by me has become an issue, then perhaps someone else in another firm can handle our accounts. Noble and McNeely have been trying to steal us away for years. That should clear your conscious, although keeping your girlfriend in a condo and your wife in a mansion might become a little difficult with less capital at your disposal. Get my drift?"

"I didn't say I wouldn't do it, Alex. I just wanted to make sure I heard you properly. That's all. Is there anything else?"

"That's all."

"I'll get right on it," David replied, especially gleeful for such an early hour.

"Thank you, Dave."

When the call went dead, Alex placed a call to Tango, but as he figured, the voicemail picked up.

"Hey old man, it's Alex. I need some new wheels, something Italian with a rag-top. See what you can find."

Just as he was about to drop the phone on the sofa, Alex saw the message icon flashing. When he scrolled through, he noticed six missed calls and ten missed text messages.

"Alex, it's Ko. I don't know what you're doing in Cincinnati, but Doc is pissed. According to the old fart, his bureau contact reported that their database was hacked and some confidential information was compromised. Of course he thinks you had something to do with it, and as such is demanding a meeting upon your return. To be honest, he's requesting that you be

277

um…detained upon your return. I know you could care less. Also, you and I need to have a long talk about a private matter. Call me back ASAP, bro."

Alex stopped the message and tried to return Ko's call, but got his voicemail instead.

That's odd.

Meanwhile in a luxury townhome just off the campus of Florida State University, Ko was lying in bed with Lexi's head nestled on his chest. Trying not to wake her, he picked his phone up off the nightstand and quickly reviewed his missed calls.

"Was that Alex?" she asked while squeezing him and planting soft kisses near his nipple.
"Yes it was, and as usual, he didn't leave a message. He's probably wondering why I didn't answer too."
"Do you really think Alex hacked the FBI's database?"
"He's not above it. But if I know your brother, he had a damned good reason. As unpredictable as he may be, Alex never does anything without a calculated reason. From what I understand, those files may have contained information on all of us."
"So you think he did it to protect us?" Lexi asked while gazing into her lover's eyes.
"I know he did."
"Join me in the shower," she cooed when she threw back the covers and teased his eyes with her naked body.
"How can I refuse an offer like that?" he exclaimed before chasing her into the bathroom.

Later that evening in Cincinnati, Alex was primping for his dates with Lynn and Ni'Chelle. After donning a pair of white linen slacks and a matching long-sleeve shirt, he stood in the mirror smoothing his attire while Shavers fumed behind him.

"This is bullshit Black Ma...or Alex...or whatever the fuck you like to be called. I've been sitting here doing all this hard work while you go out on dates! How's that shit fair?"

"Shavers, how hard is it to sit in front of a computer and spy on people?" Alex scoffed half-laughing. "The damned computer is doing all the work."

"Oh, I get it. You don't respect me as a fellow professional. Just because I don't pull triggers, you minimize my work, even though I'm performing some highly-technical operations here. You think it's easy hacking phone company records, passwords, and running illegal wiretaps? This is serious shit."

"Okay, Agent Shavers, you've earned some down time," Alex conceded after reaching into his pocket. "Here's two grand, go splurge. Take your hundred-dollar-an-hour masseuse out to dinner or something. But tomorrow, it's back on the job."

"Thanks Black...I mean Alex," Shavers grinned while thumbing through the wad of cash.

Almost an hour later, Alex's white Escalade pulled up in front of Ni'Chelle's home and just like before, it drew curious stares from all her neighbors. He ignored them while ringing the bell, and waiting patiently for the door to open. When it did, Lynn beckoned for him to enter with her index finger. Her beauty was mesmerizing. Her perfume was intoxicating. For those brief moments in time, all his problems seemingly disappeared. There was no FBI, no breach in security, and no Simon. The air around them was still. The only sounds they could hear were the subtle pounding of their hearts. Their lips hovered mere centimeters apart when she caressed his cheek while gazing lovingly into his eyes.

Her slinky, black and white spaghetti-strapped cocktail dress hugged her curves like her own skin. The lace draped across her breasts and shoulders gave his eyes even more to feast on. Her ebony hair was up in a French role, except for a single auburn strand that spiraled down the right side of her lovely face. Her red nails were accented with ebony and ivory detailing, and at the end of her long, bronze legs was a pair of black, five inch stilettos. Alex was so captivated by Lynn's ambiance that he barely heard Ni'Chelle talking in the background.

"Lynn, who is it?"
"It's Alex," she cooed before kissing him like she hadn't seen him in ages.
"I swear I don't know how you walk in these damned things. If we weren't going to such a nice restaurant, I'd have my jeans and gym shoes back on," Ni'Chelle declared while struggling to put her foot into one of the heels.
"Oh, Chelle," Lynn exhaled with her head on Alex's chest.
"Ain't y'all a cute ass prom couple? Did you bring her a corsage too?" Ni'Chelle joked while shaking her head.
"Oh, Chelle hush! Don't you think four dozen roses are enough?"
"I'm just teasing, girl," she replied while adjusting her breasts in her red cocktail dress.

With her red and white nails decorated like candy canes, and her shapely legs perched atop a pair of fine inch stilettos, Ni'Chelle's voluptuous figure was exuding a radiance all its own.

"Beautiful doesn't begin to describe the two of you," Alex declared while gazing at the siblings.

"Thank you, Alex. For a mountain boy, you rock linen quite well. What kind of cologne is that you're wearin'?"

"Prada," he declared in a suave, baritone voice.

"Mmmmmmmmmm...," Lynn sighed while squeezing his body tightly to hers.

"We'd better go," he smiled after kissing her forehead.

"Yes...we'd...better...," she managed through labored breaths even though her thighs were quivering, and the juices between them threatening to betray her.

Chapter 11

A short while later, Agent Tobey Shavers who was armed with a pocket full of cash, found his way to a gentlemen's club known as 'The Velvet Rope'. After paying a cover charge and walking down a flight-of-stairs, he entered the showroom. The thumping bass and the soundtrack's seductive lyrics made the half-naked dancers gyrate like porno stars. Feeling the rhythm himself, Shaver's bobbed his head, mostly off beat, while making his way to the stage and taking a seat. The seductive bounce of juicy asses and soft, naked tits gave his hand a mind of its own and before he could blink, it was in and out of his pocket with a fist full of cash. The sight of his money and the liberal way he was tossing it out attracted the attention of every dancer on the stage, as well as the attention of a few jealous fellow patrons. One caramel-colored vixen with blond, shoulder-length micro braids and a voluptuous frame was particularly smitten by Tobey, and slowly made her way to where he was sitting. When she saw the look on his face, she knew she had his full, undivided attention. After dropping slowly to all fours, she began a slow and deliberate cat-crawl towards him. Her feline grace and sensuality coupled with her smooth skin and curvaceous body quickly stole the show. Even the DJ voiced his own approval with a resounding "Got-Damn!"

Tobey's mouth dropped when she reached him and stood back up. He was convinced that he was staring up at the sexiest, most beautiful woman ever created. Then suddenly, she turned around, bent over, and smiled at him from between her legs. The sight of her smiling face left him with shaking hands and a tent in his khakis. Beads of sweat formed on his brow when she dropped slowly into a split with her round tattooed ass stopping inches his face. His hand shook uncontrollably when he tried to place a crisp bill inside her silver G-string.

"It don't bite, baby. You can touch it," she said while looking back at her jiggling ass and his reddened face.
"What's your name?" he managed after three attempts to swallow the huge lump in his throat.
"You can call me Car'mel Delight. What's your name?"
"Tobey…Tobias Shavers," he replied meekly.
"Well Tobey, do you like what you see?"
"Yes," he replied while squirming in his seat.
"You wanna to go to the VIP?"
"Yes," he stuttered while staring at and being hypnotized by her bodacious ass.

Meanwhile at J. Alexander's, the ambiance was much more serene. Soft music played in the background while patrons enjoyed gourmet meals under the soft lights. Alex, Lynn, and Ni'Chelle were enjoying hearty laughs and warm conversation while sitting in a booth with half-eaten entrees and empty wine glasses on the table.

"That's right, Alex. Chelle did our hair and nails. I told you, she's the best!"
"Well I'm sold," he replied while filling their glasses.
"There's no doubt you have skills, Chelle. I'll put in a call to some of my friends in Denver. They manage a number of salons. With their backing and your talents, you'll have your own shop in no time."
"You really think so, Alex?" Lynn asked behind her sexy smile and glassy eyes.
"Absolutely."
"Sheeeiiit, my own shop? I'd love that, Alex. I can see it now. It's gonna have hardwood floors, eight hair

stations with sinks, two nail stations, flat screens, surround sound stereo…the whole nine yards! My spot will be the shit!" she declared so loudly, that it drew the attention of several patrons and most of the staff.

"Shhhhhhhhhh!!!!" Lynn demanded while leaning across the table half-laughing. "You're getting loud, boo-boo."

"I can dream, can't I?" Ni'Chelle asked before picking up her glass.

"Why just dream? Why not claim it?"

"What do mean, Alex? Where am I going to get the money? I have to find a spot, get it prepared, find stylists, and advertise in order to build up my clientele. It doesn't happen overnight, especially the money part."

"You didn't hear me, hon. After I make this phone call, you'll never have to worry about money again, except getting help to count it. Just be ready when they call and don't let this opportunity pass you by."

"Okay broth…I mean Alex," Ni'Chelle said, catching her mouth before it outpaced her brain.

"What about you, Lynn? What do you want out of life?"

"I told you, baby. I just wanna finish school, get my degree, and stop doing all this back breaking work. I wanna contribute more to the medical profession than being another ass wiper or pill pusher. I wanna work with scientists and doctors who do things that make a real difference in people's lives. And of course, I wanna get paid for it," Lynn declared before exchanging laughs and a high-five with her sister.

Alex sat back and observed while the happy sisters shared accounts of what they'd do if they suddenly came into some money. There were no signs of selfishness among them at all. They planned to share and take care of one another and the kids, no matter what. Throughout the evening, they continued to defer back to one another, constantly reminding each other to take care of their priorities, just as their father planned. Alex found himself saddened when he thought about Lexi and the rifts in their relationship.

Later that evening, Alex and Lynn were enjoying a nice stroll along Cincinnati's colorful and vibrant waterfront. While under the blue moonlight in the botanical garden, cool air whipped all around them and occasionally blowing Lynn's gown against her body creating a curvaceous silhouette. As she looked out over the river, Lynn found her hips swaying to the music playing on the Kentucky side. Her body suddenly quivered when she felt Alex's arms snaking around her waist. His closeness, the smell of his cologne, and the sensation of his dick pressed against her ass had Lynn ready to surrender to him right there.

"Alone at last," she whispered when she laid her head on his shoulder and felt his heart beating against her back.
"This view is beautiful."
"I'm sure Denver has more scenery than this, Alex."
"I wasn't talking about the river," he replied before gently nuzzling her ear.
"Oh," she replied when his grip got a little tighter.
"What do you want from me, Alex?" she asked before gently freeing herself from his grip, so she that she could turn around and face him.
"What do you mean?"
"I mean all this...meeting you in Denver, paying for my stay, and now you're offering to help Chelle get her business off the ground. Who does that? I just want to make sure that this is real and not some game that you are running to get me in bed with you."

"No offense honey, but I wouldn't fly half way across the country just to have sex with you or anyone else. I flew out here to invite you back to Denver. I'm interested in much more than your stunning body. I'm interested in getting to know the total you, no matter how long it takes."

"Are you sure that's what you want?" she asked before stepping in a little closer and looking up into his hazel eyes.

"Yes," he whispered before pressing his lips to hers.

He felt her body quivering under her gown as his hands flowed from her shoulders, down her back, and onto her ass. Misty rain kissed Lynn's face when she leaned her head back and allowed his tongue and lips to tease her neckline. His touch was paradise. His kiss was like heaven. Her walls began clinching when she felt his canines gently grazing her jugular vein. She wanted to feel Alex deep inside her, but wouldn't dare surrender to her inner most desires, at least not now. Feeling his manhood swelling against her stomach only made her fight that much harder. Lynn's breaths quickened when she felt her back meet the wall behind them. She was so lost in the moment that she didn't realize that she was moving until she stopped. Her nipples stood at full attention when his hands caressed and squeezed her swollen breasts. The dam between her thighs threatened to rupture if he didn't stop; now.

"I can't," she surrendered when she felt his hand creeping up her thigh.

"I understand," he whispered before smoothing her gown and stepping back so that she could breathe.

"We're getting wet," Alex whispered when he felt the raindrops on his face.

You have no idea, she thought when a cool breeze chilled the juices that had settled her satin panties.

Lynn held his arm and occasionally squeezed it on the drive back to the house and moments later as they stood on the porch, they shared one more passionate kiss.

"Call me later, baby," she said while standing in the open doorway.
"I will," he replied before turning and walking down the stairs.

She waited until Alex had driven out of sight before finally closing and locking the door. Just as she was about to go up the stairs, Lynn stopped, leaned against the wall, and wrapped herself in her own arms. She took a deep, cleansing breath and for a brief moment, her arms became his arms. She could smell Alex all over her, which made her wish she'd held him a little while longer.

"Look at you standing there like a love struck teenager. To be honest, I wasn't expecting you to be home until tomorrow," teased a familiar voice from the top of the stairs.
"It's not time for that, Chelle."
"Chile, please. It's obvious you're feeling him, and he's definitely feeling you. Men like that don't come along every day, but niggas *do* come along every day running game and selling dreams. And because of that, I'm glad you came home. He's charming and dare I say, fine as hell. Just watch him, sis."
"Trust me, Chelle, I got this," Lynn reassured her sister before beginning the long, lonely journey up the stairs.
"Okay then," she replied when she took Lynn in her arms.

287

Early the next morning, Alex found himself impatiently knocking on and jiggling the handles of the suites' double adjoining doors. When they finally opened, he was surprised to see Shavers standing there wrapped in a bed sheet with blood-shot eyes and messy hair. To Alex's surprise, he reeked of alcohol, cocoa butter, and baby oil.

"What the hell happened to you?" he demanded while pushing his way past Shavers and walking into the ransacked suite.
"Hey Alex, how about a little courtesy? I mean, you can't just barge up in here like gang-busters. For all you know, I could have company of something."
"You...company? Yeah, right," Alex scoffed before grinning uncontrollably.

Just then, Alex was stopped in his tracks by the thick, caramel-colored beauty lying on Shaver's bed.

What the fuck? Am I dreaming? he thought when their eyes met. With his head tilted and his mouth wide open, Alex watched as she stepped out of bed and waved before disappearing into the bathroom. The man in him couldn't help but admire her luscious, naked frame or her round, jiggling tits. The hater in him pondered why in the hell such a woman would be interested in a geek like Shavers.

"Who the hell is she?"
"Car'mel Delight," he cooed while smiling giddily at the closed door.
"Car'mel Delight huh? That sounds like a stripper's name."
"Watch your mouth!" Shavers barked while staring Alex up and down. "She's an exotic dancer."
"Uh-huh. And exactly where did you meet *'Bubbles'*?"

"Her real name is Carmen, and I met her at *'The Velvet Rope'*."

"*'The Velvet Rope*?' You mean to tell me that you took my money and went to a strip club?"

"It wasn't all your money. I had some of my own."

"How much?" Alex snapped sarcastically.

"I had about two grand."

"You dropped four grand in a strip club? Did it ever occur to you that the only reason she spent the night with you was because of the amount of money you shoved up her ass?"

"That's so typical of you, Black Mamba! Carmen is so much more than the sum of her circumstances."

"Of course she is. From the looks of it, she's a hooker too."

"Hold on, Tobias, I got this," she demanded after stepping out of the bathroom wrapped in an oversized hotel towel. "The problem with men, especially black men, is that they put every woman who dances in a box. They look at my occupation and immediately label me as a whore without taking the time to realize that I'm a person with a brain. I'm a double major in Criminal Justice and Forensic Pathology, who also maintains a 4.0 GPA. Stripping and dancing may be what I do, but they're not who I am. And as bad as men like you talk about me, y'all still enjoy shoving money up my ass."

Damn! You humbled me with your assessment of my ignorance," Alex said after lowering his head in shame. "My behavior was unacceptable and you're right. I was totally out of line for misjudging you, and ask that you accept my humblest apologies."

"Apology accepted, and please, call me Carmen," she replied with a smile.

"Thank you, Carmen. By the way, I'm..."

"I know who you are, Black Mamba, and don't worry. Your secrets are safe with me."

Tobey cowered at her side when he saw the look on Alex's face. His mind quickly rambled off all the details he'd shared with Carmen during their intimacy and realized that he'd broken enough protocols to warrant both their deaths.

"Secrets?"

"Tobias said you guys were Federal Agents here investigating some drug trafficking taking place in the area. That's right in line with my college studies. You guys are so cool," she declared while pinching Tobey's reddened cheek.

"Soooooo, Alex, you wanna hear about my night?" he asked nervously.

"In a strip club? Are you serious?" Alex asked while trying to make sense of why Tobey had been so careless and stupid.

"There you go assuming again," Shavers replied while shaking his head.

"You might wanna listen to this, Alex," Carmen added before leaning back on the bed and crossing her voluptuous legs.

"Sure, why not? This should be good. Okay, Tobias," Alex began before shifting his focus away from her thighs to the platinum Bulgari on his wrist. "You have two minutes to impress me."

"Cool. So I'm in the club near the VIP booth when I overhear a conversation between two guys; Loco and G-6. The whole time they were there, they kept saying that they needed to flip some birds to keep the alphabet boys off their backs. Are you with me so far?"

"Of course I am. Loco and G-6 are members *the Midwest Finest*, a local rap group. Birds are kilos and the alphabet

boys are the authorities; FBI, CIA, NSA, etc. So what?"
Alex asked while staring at his wrist.

"Okay then," Shavers began after being shocked by
Alex's knowledge of hip hop music and street slang,
"Loco received a call from a girl he referred to as Dee
and said he needed some birds. They agreed to meet
tomorrow after his concert."

"Where is this going, Tobey?" Alex demanded while
trying not to glance at Carmen's thighs.

"After doing a little numerical cross referencing, Dee is
actually Dawn Tyler. The number she dialed was the
same one we couldn't trace, the one the feds have the tap
on."

"Ok, Tobey, you have my interest. What else did you
hear?"

"Blackhawk."

"Jason Blackhawk?"

"The same. Apparently he nailed them some time ago on
some drugs and weapons charges."

"And you know this how?" Alex asked curiously.

"I hacked the FBI's database this morning and found
Blackhawk's files. After another carefully orchestrated
infiltration, I found a file on the entire group codenamed
Midwest Meltdown.' Our boy, no pun intended, is
spearheading an investigation into Simon Felix's cartel
and its various connections. His involvement in this case
goes back way beyond recent events."

"How far?"

"All the way back to Miami," Shaver's replied with a bit
apprehension in his tone.

"I see. What time does the concert start?"

"It starts at nine, but they won't hit the stage until
around midnight," Carmen interjected proudly. "The
concert is at Club Oasis."

"Can you take us?"

"Sorry Alex, but Friday night is my biggest night. I can clear anywhere from one to three grand if the ballers are in the house."

"I'll pay you four grand."

"What time should I be ready?"

Just before eleven o'clock, Alex, Lynn, Tobey, and Carmen were sitting at a table in a corner of Club Oasis. The dimly-lit hole-in-the-wall was teaming with half-naked women and t-shirt clad men. The charismatic DJ and the heavy-handed bartenders didn't have to work hard to keep the party going. The featured artists and the promise of "rain" had the club packed to capacity. Lynn couldn't fathom why Alex had chosen this spot for their date, but was determined to make the best of it. Tobey and Carmen, meanwhile, were having the time of their lives.

"I didn't take you for the hip-hop type," Lynn said after a couple hours of stiff drinks, wandering eyes, and watching Carmen and Tobey out on the crowded dance floor.

"I'm not," Alex replied while panning the room searching for familiar faces. "I'm a business man, and the Midwest is full of untapped talent. The featured act is supposed to be at the top of their game, and yet, they're relatively unknown and unsigned by any major labels. I have the connections that can change that."

"And what about the hoochie momma?" she asked when Carmen dropped it like it was hot in front of Tobey and the rest of the gawkers on the dance floor.

"She's a friend of Tobey's. She knows the city and is familiar with these guys. She told us about the concert."

"Well, she's getting pretty damned familiar with Tobey right now," Lynn quipped while watching Carmen grinding her ass against his pelvis.

By midnight, Alex had counted eight federal agents and at least twenty cops in the audience. At twelve-thirty, *'the Midwest Finest'* finally took the stage and put on an hour long performance that brought down the house. The drunken crowd rocked and swayed while reciting the anger-charged, *'dope-boy'* lyrics from the songs that were playing. By the end of the show, the stage was crowded with half-naked women looking to get 'chosen.' Suddenly, two hulking bodyguards with large black trash bags entered from both sides of the stage and walked to its middle.

"Time to make it rain!" Loco screamed before reaching into one bag, pulling out a pile of bills, and tossing them into the air.

Just as hoards of women began scrambling to grab the falling bills, Alex spotted Dawn standing off to the side of the stage.

"Excuse me for a moment," he said before exiting the table and making his way through the crowd.

He was mindful to keep his face shielded from the agents along the way and when he finally reached the stage, Dawn and Loco were involved in a particularly intense conversation.

"Excuse me folks, I'm so sorry to interrupt, but I have to say that this was one hell-of-a show."
"Alex, what are you doing here?"
"I'm a businessman, Dawn, and I see an opportunity that can be mutually beneficial. Loco, I have some friends in some very high places that can put a deal

293

together, and make you a lot of money. If you're interested, give me a call."

"Are you bullshitting me, man?" Loco asked after looking at Alex's business card.

"I don't bullshit about money, my friend. It's clear you've got the chops to make it big. So I asked myself, why isn't this group signed to a major label? I'm here to change that."

"In that case, I'll holla back, homeboy," Loco said with a smile while doing a quick appraisal of Alex.

"I look forward to it," Alex replied while exchanging a brotherly handshake. "I've seen enough," he declared moments later when he returned to the table.

"You're ready to go already?" Carmen asked. "It's open mike night."

"I'm sorry Carmen, but Tobey and I have a busy day ahead before we wrap up and leave. Lynn, I'd love to see you home."

"You're such a gentleman, Mr. Stratton. Although I must admit, you're very mysterious," she said before taking Alex's extended hand and standing up.

"No more than you my, Egyptian Princess," he replied with a seductive grin.

After seeing their dates to their homes, Alex and Tobey returned to the hotel where they began analyzing the recordings from that evening. Their portable printer was working overtime while rattling off page-after-page of transcripts. As they were reading, the system picked up a phone call coming from Dawn's cell phone to an unknown number in Denver. Within seconds of hearing the man's voice, they knew it was Simon she was speaking with.

"There it is, Alex. She just brokered a deal for twenty kilos."

"No, Tobey. She just brokered her own death warrant. We need to get back to Denver a sap."

"What's the hurry?"

"Blackhawk is using *the Midwest's Finest* and Dawn as pawns. The problem is his office is so corrupt they'll be dead before the ink on the indictment dries. Simon will never see a trial unless we can eliminate all the rogue assets working on this case."

"Rogue assets?" Tobey quipped. "We don't have that kind of legal firepower, boss. And besides Burroughs, we don't have any names. Do you really think it goes that deep?"

"There's no other logical explanation. Somebody behind the scenes is close to this investigation and calling the shots. They're keeping Simon one step ahead of us. And trust me, that person isn't working alone."

"Okay, boss. I'll check every agent that is or was affiliated with the Felix case."

"Good. Look for large purchases, off shore accounts, etc. Make sure you check their spouses' accounts and assets too. If need be, check their kids as well. Start with Burroughs."

"I'll get on it first thing, boss."

"I'm going to bed, Shavers. Good night."

Later that night as he lay in bed, dozens of images flashed through Alex's mind. He remembered the night that he met Simone Santiago, their first kiss, and the day he proposed. Next, his mind flashed to the day she lay dying in his arms. Ko stood by his side when Alex was forced to identify her body. His next image was of him dying as he hung from the cross being taunted by Simon and Gabriel. Now three years later, Alex was chasing them again and once again, the odds of success were in their favor. But then again, they always were.

The pre-dawn hours found Alex pacing restlessly in front of his hotel window. The pale blue moonlight kissed the tears that were running down his cheeks. He had already failed to protect Simone. How could he possibly protect Lynn from danger if he had to? After making his way to the in suite's bar, he quickly downed a couple a shots of cognac. His ears began ringing with angry taunts and sadistic laughter. When Alex turned around, Simon was standing there and as usual, he was dressed in all white and flanked by a pair of attorneys. Behind them was a legion of police officers, FBI Agents, and lawyers.

"I'll kill you all!" Alex growled with his teeth clinched and his body poised to strike.

One-by-one, they all disappeared until Alex was alone again.

Early the next morning after leaving Lynn a message, Alex and Tobey were busy comparing notes on the list of agents Tobey had compiled. Alex paced slowly behind his counterpart taking mental notes of the details that he was reading.

"Read me the information on Agent Burroughs again."
"There really isn't that much there, boss. He has a couple cars in his name and the house. His daughters are in college and the tax payers are picking up the tab. There's nothing out of the ordinary. Why do you keep coming back to him?"
"When I was undercover, I remember seeing him at Simon's house a few times. Burroughs was heading that investigation as well. Now after years of letting Simon slip through his fingers, Burroughs is still heading up the investigation as well as advisory board on trafficking

in the Caribbean. There's just too much there to be a coincidence. What about his wife?"
"Let me check."

Chapter 12

Denver, Colorado

In a quaint and cozy café, Agents Blackhawk and Castro were in a corner booth with a good view of the street. Stacks of folders and pictures were scattered across the table amidst the half-eaten plates of steaks, eggs, and potatoes. Blackhawk concluded a call on his cell phone, while Castro was busy searching through files on his laptop.

"Thank you very much. I'll be in touch. That was our boy. He just brokered a deal with Dawn for fifteen keys last night."

"We got Dawn on tape brokering a deal for twenty keys with Simon. Where are the other five keys going?" Castro asked while thumbing through the transcripts.

"Who cares, man? Once we get her to meet with Loco, she'll give us Simon, and we'll nail that bastard once and for all."

"That's a little ambitious, don't you think, Jason? She has to know the risks of rolling over on Simon. I don't think she's going to crack as easily as you think."

"That's why it's important that we apply a full-court press the moment we get her into custody. I'm not going to let her breathe until she gives him up. Once she does, I'm taking the information straight to McNamara."

"Burroughs is gonna go ape shit, partner," Castro said while shaking his head.

"I can't let him stand in the way, Gabe. I owe it to Lisa to bring Simon to justice, even if it means my career."

"Are you really sure you owe it to her, Jason? I mean, let's face it. Every piece of data we saw suggests that Lisa was dirty."

"I know what we saw and it's all bullshit. Lisa wasn't on the take. She was a good agent who was murdered in the line of duty. She was set up and when I find out who did it, we're gonna have a private meeting."
"Alright, partner. If you feel that strongly about it, then I've got your back. I just hope you're right."

Meanwhile outside the café behind the tinted windows an unmarked Dodge Charger, two men sat photographing the busy agents. While the driver was snapping pictures, his passenger was downloading the images to his laptop and talking into his Bluetooth.

"Yes, we have them in the café. I'm sending you the images as we speak. Unfortunately we can't make out what they're saying. Their backs are to us. Have you all had any luck with the phone?"
"Our guys are trying, but that's not a bureau phone," replied the voice in his ear. "We don't know who he's talking to or about. Castro has a ghost phone too."
"What about his files? Do we have a password yet?" the passenger asked with frustration in his tone.
"No sir. He recently changed it from a remote terminal, and our guys are having issues cracking the code."
"This is bullshit. Burroughs is gonna have our asses in a sling if we don't figure out what Blackhawk is up to and fast. We can't have him fucking up our money."
"What do you want us to do?"
"Whatever the fuck you have to!" the passenger barked while pushing the Bluetooth into his ear.
"Yes sir."
"Blackhawk still making asses out of your cronies?" the driver asked while trying to focus his lens.
"You're awful laid back for a man might go to prison if Jason cracks this case before we crack him."

"I ain't worried about him or Castro. I'll kill them both first."

"Whatever badass," his passenger replied sarcastically.

Cincinnati, Ohio: Later that afternoon

"Okay Alex, I think I have something. Burroughs makes about ninety five thousand per year. His wife reported fifty-five thousand from her interior decorating business after expenses. That salary range is consistent with the liabilities that he has listed except for the houses and cars."

"What about them?"

"The house in D.C. is a rental property and he drives a leased Ford Expedition. Their primary home is an eight-hundred-seventy-five-thousand-dollar ranch in Tampa. They also own an S550, an Audi Q7, a sixty-foot Bertram, and several accounts; all in her business's name."

"Got you, you fat bastard," Alex smirked while peering over his shoulder.

"Ok," Shavers began when he switched screens, "using the same filter I found fifteen senior agents with assets that fit the same profile. All their wives are entrepreneurs with an extensive list of assets in the names of their respective businesses. The question is how do we take them down without exposing ourselves and how do we know who's legit and who's not?"

"We don't take them down."

"What the fuck?" Shavers demanded. "After all this work, you're just gonna turn a blind eye to this corruption? What was the point?"

"Oh, I didn't say something wasn't going to be done. I just said we aren't going to do it. The easiest way to topple a structure this big is to implode it. It eliminates external collateral damage."

"Okay, Black Mamba," Tobey replied began sarcastically after turning around and leaning back in his chair, "exactly how do you intend to implode the largest, most powerful investigative agency in the world?"
"Simple. I'm going to plant a bomb inside it. Only my bomb won't have fuses, detonators, or toxic chemicals. My bomb will be Jason Blackhawk."
"C'mon, Alex, do you really think Blackhawk has the balls to take on the entire FBI?"
"He wants Simon as badly as I do, Tobey. I'm sure he'll want to be a part of the process that brings down the agents that have hidden him in plain sight for so long."
"They were right about you. You do spew venom," Shavers said before standing up. "Are you expecting company?"
"No," Alex replied when he heard the knocks at his door.

He walked through the adjoining doors, and locked them behind him. After quickly looking around, he grabbed his .40cal from under the couch cushion and cocked it.

"Hello gorgeous," he said after opening the door and seeing Lynn standing there.

She was a vision of beauty in her yellow sundress and matching sandals. Beautiful spirals were draped over her bronze shoulders and the gloss on her lips made them look even more succulent than he remembered. That familiar, attention-grabbing pendant Alex admired in Denver was resting comfortably between her round melons.

"May I come in?" she asked flirtatiously after seeing that his eyes were no longer on her face.

"Of course, but I wasn't expecting you so early," he replied when she strolled past him with her hips swaying underneath the shear material.

Alex was so captivated that he almost forgot to close the door or the fact that he had a gun behind his back.

"I didn't know you planned to leave today either," she said with hints of sadness when she saw his bags near the couch.

"That's one of the reasons I asked you to come here today. We've been called back to Denver on business. One of my high-profile clients is making some very large monetary transactions and I need to be there to oversee them. It was totally unexpected, but we have to be back first thing in the morning."

"I see. What was the other reason?"

"I want you to come out to Denver and stay for a while. The money isn't an issue," he said while gently taking her hand in his. "I'll fly you out first class, wait on you hand and foot, and when you're ready to return, I'll fly you back home."

"Alex, I don't know what to say. You make all this sound so easy."

"It's as easy as saying yes," he said softly while kissing her trembling fingertips.

"But Alex I..."

"Don't say no," he begged while pulling Lynn close to him.

"Okay, Alex," she gasped when those familiar chills began racing up and down her spine. "I'll fly out as soon as I wrap up some things here. What time does your flight leave tonight?"

"Eleven-fifteen. Why?"

"Good, that's more than enough time."

"For what?"

"For this," she replied seductively before tugging at the strap of her sundress.

Alex stood frozen as the right strap, and then the left slid slowly down her arms. With a gentle wiggle of her hips, the dress fell to the floor leaving her standing there in a black lace bra and matching thong. Looking deeply into his eyes, Lynn reached behind her back and unsnapped the bra, catching it before he caught a glimpse of her splendor.

"Let it go," he whispered while running his fingers across the lace, willing her to lower her arms and let the bra drop to the floor.

Alex's mouth watered as soon as he saw Lynn's voluptuous tits. Her big, chocolate-colored nipples hardened at his touch. She gasped when his soft lips met her shoulders and her tits swelled with anticipation of his mouth and tongue on them. Her knees threatened to give way when his lips and then his tongue finally touched her chocolate crowns. The sensation of his hot saliva on her shivering skin had her walls moist and pulsating. A brief moment of hesitation raced through her mind when she felt his finger tugging gently at her waist-band. Lynn willed her heart to stop pounding and stood there massaging and squeezing her tits while Alex slowly dropped to his knees, planting soft kisses on her body the whole way down. Up one thigh and down the other his lips and tongue travelled, leaving a trail of hot and cold behind them. Gently taking his head in her hands, Lynn guided him back to his feet and kissed his soft lips before a brief struggle to undress him ensued.

After losing a fight against his tank top, she ripped it off him and cast it across the room.

Alex lay between Lynn's thighs savoring her nipples while grinding his dick against her soft, warm lips. When his head parted her quivering flower, she suddenly felt another moment of hesitation. *I hope I'm not making a mistake,* she thought when he reached into the nightstand and pulled out a handful of condoms. Within seconds of dressing his manhood, Alex was sliding it deep inside her; the point of no return. Upon its entry, Lynn's walls clinched on him so tightly that it was uncomfortable for both of them. She grabbed his hips and arched her back when she felt him about to withdraw from her. Her breathing finally relaxed when she kissed his lips and seconds later, hot juices flooded the walls around his shaft.

Dayum Alex, she thought while guiding him in and out, enjoying each throbbing inch.

His first full, deep, thrust caused Lynn's back to arch and her eyes to open wide. The delight of his hard dick took her by surprise and before she knew it, moans of pleasure were escaping her lips.

"Yes, baby, yes," she moaned while grazing his tattooed back with her nails.
"Damn!" he gasped in return before lifting her legs up onto his shoulders.

Lynn found her body quickly succumbing to Alex's will. With her legs pointed to the heavens and cum pooling beneath her ass, she took stroke-after-impassioned-stroke. He was hitting her G-spot with breathtaking intensity. While her legs were still on his shoulders, Alex settled on his knees and proceeded to squeeze and knead Lynn's jiggling tits while pounding her sweet, dripping pussy.

"Oh my gawd!!!" she surrendered as wave-after-wave of orgasmic pleasure coursed through her body. "Don't stop! Don't stop!" she begged while squeezing his hands over her pillow-soft melons.
"Lynn!"
"Yes, baby, yes," she gasped.
"I'm cumming!"
"Yes Alex, yes! Give it to me. Give it all to me!" Lynn commanded while listening to the gentle *swish-swish* sounds coming from between her quivering thighs.

Their bodies exploded in ecstasy when Alex honored her request by releasing a torrent of hot, creamy pleasure deep inside her. The sensation of his lips on her neck and his body pressed to hers made Lynn feel like the room was spinning. Alex's relentless kisses on her neck and nipples while sliding in-and-out had him swelling again, and before long, his hard, throbbing dick was attacking her G-spot once again.

Where have you been all my life? her body asked out of sheer delight.

At nine-thirty, after hours of body-numbing passion, a long shower, and a series of sad goodbyes, Lynn and Alex waited patiently for the bellhops to arrive with the luggage carts. After a knock at the door, Alex invited the eager young man in, and watched sadly while his bags were loaded. When the trio entered the hall, the red-faced bellhop turned his head, leaving Alex and Lynn to watch the lustful display. With her body pressed tightly to his and his back pinned against the wall, Carmen mounted an assault on Tobey's lips while squeezing his ass and inhaling his grunts and moans.

"Wow," Lynn said, both amazed and jealous at the same time.
"Get a room," Alex groaned while shaking his head and looking at the gawkers who had gathered.
"We had one, Alex. But since, you're taking my boo-boo away from me, I'm gettin' it in while I can," Carmen sighed before proceeding to nibble on Tobey's earlobe.
"I see," he muttered, still shocked by Tobey's encounter.
"Well, we have a plane to catch, but I have no doubts we'll be back soon."
"You'd better," Lynn whispered after squeezing his hand.

Moments later, the quartet assembled outside the lobby loaded the bags into the back of the Caddy. After tipping the bellhop and kissing Lynn goodbye, Alex climbed into the driver's seat and waited while Tobey and Carmen enjoyed a repeat of their hallway antics. Frustrated by the delay and Lynn's sad reflection, Alex finally blew the horn. After a few more kisses, Tobey reluctantly climbed in.

"I miss him already," the ladies said in unison when the Caddy disappeared into traffic.
"You wanna grab a drink, girl?" Carmen asked while smoothing her short, form hugging dress around her hips and ass.
"Sure, why not?" Lynn surrendered with a sad sigh.

After returning the rental and passing through airport security, Alex and Tobey were seated in the first class cabin of flight 918. As Alex stared out of the window sipping on Absolute and cranberry juice, Tobey scrolled through the pictures he had taken of Carmen with his phone.

"So, how'd I do?" he asked after eagerly nudging Alex's shoulder.

"Tobey," Alex began after taking a deep breath, "as a technician you're without equal. As a field man, you have a lot to learn."

"What?" he snapped while staring daggers at his so-called friend.

"Lower your voice, and sit back. You broke one of the few unbreakable rules of 'The Agency'. Under no circumstances do you ever give up yours or your partner's cover. Normally, I would've had to kill both of you and abort the mission. Circumstances didn't call for that, however. Look Tobey, I know why you did it. And while I admit she's beautiful, your actions were reckless. Had she been a player, we might both be dead now. You don't get attached, and you don't lose your focus. The job and the protection of your fellow agents always come first. "

"What about Lynn?"

"What about her? I came to Cincinnati as Alexis Stratton, investor and entrepreneur and that's how I left; period."

"Do you think she'd betray you if she knew who you really are?"

"I hope I never have to find out," Alex replied before returning to his drink.

"Damn, being you sucks," Tobey huffed before settling back into his seat.

"I told you it would."

At 10AM in his home's library, Doc sat at his desk impatiently tapping his fingers on its cracked top. While standing silently around the room, Big Mike, Richard,

Nicholas, and Ko quietly shared their leader's mounting frustration. Fifteen minutes later, just when the library threatened to explode from the tension, the ferocious rumble of Alex's Camaro broke the uncomfortable silence. Within seconds, he entered the library, and quickly surveyed his friends before they moved in close and surrounded him.

"Who-the-fuck do you think you are?" Doc growled before bolting up from his chair and glaring angrily at Alex. "It's not bad enough that you've been playing this sick game with Simon Felix for the past few years. But it seems that you've really outdone yourself this time. Did you really think you could hack into the FBI's database using my software and I not know about it? Are you that arrogant, or are you just that stupid?"
"You think that's something? Give me a couple of days," Alex grinned while reaching into his satchel.
"What the hell is that?" Doc snapped.
"Let me paint a picture for you," Alex began while waving and envelope from side-to-side. "It's October, 1974. It's the final round of a championship bout between Muhammad Ali, the aging former heavyweight champion, and George Foreman, his younger, stronger Olympic gold medal-winning opponent. Throughout the entire fight, Foreman pounded Ali with one punishing blow-after-another. The whole time, except for a glancing blow here and there, 'the champ' lay on the ropes refusing to go down. Halfway through the final round, the younger, stronger gold-medalist ran out of gas and Ali went on the attack and by the end of the fight, Foreman lay on his back, while the battered and bruised veteran was being crowned the champ once again. I know you think I'm crazy. This man has beaten me emotionally, physically, and psychologically, yet I refuse to go down. The bell is about the sound for the final round and Simon Felix is out of gas. Ding."

"What's in the envelope, Alex?" Big Mike asked while approaching him from behind.

"It's proof that there are at least ten to fifteen bureau agents involved in a conspiracy to cover up Simon's dealings, and their own as well. That envelope contains financial records, lists of assets, and other incriminating evidence. Some have even included their wives, which makes them co-conspirators."

"Does any of this evidence link them directly to Simon?" Doc asked, skeptical of the of the contents' validity.

"It shows that they have income streams that are inconsistent with their tax filings. Other than that, no there isn't. However, we don't need proof as long as we can raise reasonable doubt."

"You're gonna try to use RICO, aren't you?" Nicholas asked after a few seconds of silence.

"You do realize that you're grabbing at straws now, right?"

"I know it sounds crazy Ko, but conspiracy charges at least get them into court. It works for them; why can't it work for us? Besides, once we get them into court, RICO statutes should handle the rest. The bad publicity alone will raise eyebrows. All we need is someone on the inside to load the gun and a judge with enough nuts to pull the trigger."

"What about the young agent who's currently dogging you?" Doc asked while thumbing through the papers.

"Funny you should mention Agent Blackhawk because he's the one with the bullets."

"I don't like the way that sounds at all, Alex. You're talking about waving illegally obtained documents under the very nose of the man who's trying to arrest you. Do you realize how insane your scheme is?"

"Yes, I do, Mike, and it's so insane that it can't fail. Jason Blackhawk and I have more in common than he can possibly know. All I have to do is throw the dog a bone and wait for him to bite."

"Why Agent Blackhawk, boss?"

"Well Rick, as near as I can tell, he's the only one on Simon's case we can trust."

"What if he doesn't bite, Alex?" Ko asked while remaining unconvinced.

"Then I'll take the dog out back and shoot him."

"I like the sound of that even less," Big Mike mumbled while shaking his head.

"Ok hot shot, say we can prove your conspiracy theory. Do you honestly think we can just march up to the doors of FBI headquarters and pull back the curtain? Have you forgotten that we receive our orders directly from the Whitehouse? Exposing the upper echelon of the FBI may potentially expose us as well, not to mention pissing off the President himself."

"Relax, Doc. No one in this office is going to get their hands dirty. Like I said earlier, Jason Blackhawk is the only person that we can trust, and he's the key to flushing out the bureau's criminals."

"Ok Alex, as outlandish as this whole thing sounds, I'm going to step back and let you operate, but listen closely young man. I'm going to be watching you very carefully. If you step out of line or screw the pooch in anyway, I'm going to shut you down; end of story. Do I make myself clear?"

"Crystal clear," Alex replied before turning to exit the library. "Can I get by, big fella?" Alex asked Big Mike who was looking at Doc for approval.

"He can go," Doc said, waving his hand while thumbing through the pages.

"Hear that, Mike?" Alex asked in a hushed, sarcastic tone. "He can go."

Moments later, the five men stood reading through the files until they heard the squeal of the Camaro's tires.

Moments later inside the speeding coupe, Alex placed a call to Agent Blackhawk's office phone number.

"This is Agent Blackhawk."
"This is Alexis Stratton. Look at the number on your caller ID and call me back from an unmarked phone. Don't lie. I know you have one."

Moments after hanging up, Alex's phone rang.

"You've got a lot of fucking nerves…"
"Shut up and listen because I won't repeat myself. Cheesman Park, midnight behind the playground. Come alone, and don't bother remembering this number, because in two minutes, it won't exist."

Before Agent Blackhawk could utter a word, the line went dead. He looked at his watch then around his office. Though ever fiber of his body was telling him to set a trap for Alex, he didn't have sufficient evidence to do so. Their entire investigation had shifted to Gabriel Malcolm, leaving Alex to once again be a ghost in the shadows. With his nerves on edge, Agent Blackhawk waited impatiently for midnight to arrive.

Cheesman Park,

In the darkness, it was nearly impossible for Agent Blackhawk to see whether anyone had taken aim on him. His heart sank while clutching the firearm at his side and realizing that he may have been set-up. Alex had purposely chosen this shelter because there were no lights in the vicinity.

311

"Holster your weapon. If I wanted you dead, I would have killed you already. I told you to come alone, but I figured you wouldn't. No matter. This won't take long."

"You're one bold S-O-B, Mr. Stratton," Agent Blackhawk snapped while nervously approaching the shadow behind some trees.

Without warning, a large brown envelope crashed to the ground near Blackhawk's right foot. Refusing to take his eyes off the shadowy figure in front of him, he bent down to pick it up.

"What's this?"

"You won't know unless you open it, which you can't do because your hands are full."

"There's no light out here anyway smartass!" Blackhawk snapped while looking at the envelope in his left hand and the gun in his right.

"There's a light in the envelope."

Though he feared for his life, Agent Blackhawk reluctantly placed his gun back in its holster. While still staring into the darkness, he opened the envelope and pulled out the small LED light. He turned it on and quickly pointed to the area where he thought Alex was standing. Chills raced up his spine when he discovered no one was there.

"Where the hell are you?"

"Behind you," replied a low raspy voice from over his left shoulder.

"Who-the-fuck are you, Stratton?" he shouted after spinning around and attempting to shine the light in Alex's face.

"That's irrelevant," he replied with his hand over the beam.

"Irrelevant my ass! So tell me, Stratton, how'd you do it?"

"Do what?"

"You know what, you arrogant prick. You hacked the FBI's database and erased confidential files on you and your friends. How'd you do it?"

"Don't blame your inferior firewall protection on me, Jason. Now, let's get down to business. I asked you here because I have a proposition for you."

"You have a proposition for me? This should be rich. What could you possibly have for me?"

"I knew Lisa, your former partner. Contrary to what you were told, she didn't flip on your unit nor did she blow her cover. She stopped receiving orders and shortly thereafter, her cover was intentionally blown. She was served up to Simon on a silver platter."

Alex's revelation knocked the wind right out of Agent Blackhawk's sails, reducing to standing there in the darkness, motionless and speechless. Just like that, his world had been turned upside down by a stranger, who until tonight, he assumed was a criminal. Suddenly, Jason found his mind racing and it immediately flashed back to that night in the alley; the night that changed him forever.

Flashing red and blue lights lit up the street from end-to-end while radio chatter crackled from every direction. Police detectives and EMS had the entire area sealed off. He remembered the alarming sight of the coroner's van parked at the alley's entrance and the squeak of the gurney's wheels as they ground against the pitted asphalt. By the looks on their faces, Agent Jason Blackhawk knew it was bad, but he had no idea how bad. When he got to the back of the alley, Agent

Burroughs was squatting next to a body and shaking his head.

"You shouldn't be here!" he barked when he turned around and saw Agent Blackhawk approaching.
"I wanna see."
"No, Jason, not like this."
"She was my partner got-dammit! I want to see her."

When Jason lifted the bloody sheet, he couldn't believe his eyes. Lisa's face was barely recognizable. She'd been brutally beaten and had voodoo markings carved into her naked flesh. It was clear by her gaped open mouth and the pool of blood in her throat that her tongue had been cut out. An autopsy later revealed that she'd also been brutally raped and tortured prior to her death. All the pain that Agent Blackhawk felt that night suddenly came rushing back to him. *How could Alex have known? Who was he? Why was he telling him this?* In a fit of rage, Jason grabbed Alex by his collar only to have his wrists violently twisted and his jaw almost broken by a vicious head-butt.

"Your personal grief aside, if you touch me again I'll kill you," Alex growled while standing over him.
"How'd you know Lisa?" Jason asked while rubbing his jaw.
"At the time she was working logistics for Simon, I too had infiltrated his organization. My job was to learn as much as I could before assassinating him. He took her out and tried to take me out shortly thereafter."
"Bullshit!" Agent Blackhawk proclaimed after springing to his feet.
"It's not bullshit, Jason. I was there. Your operation was doomed from the start, and your partner was an unfortunate casualty. Lisa was too green to be doing deep cover operations. She panicked when the orders

stopped coming in. Your entire unit has been on a wild goose chase ever since Simon came back up on the radar. Unfortunately, there's a good reason for that."

"Oh yeah? What's that reason, Mr. Stratton?" Jason demanded sarcastically.

"Somebody in the FBI is feeding him information. That's how he remains two steps ahead of you at all times."

"You almost had me going," Jason chuckled, though his jaw was still throbbing. "You want me to believe that the bureau is helping shield the very man we've spent thousands of hours investigating and paid hundreds-of-thousands in man hours worked? You sound like a damn fool."

"The money trail doesn't lie, and it leads to Agent Burroughs and several others just like him. Everything you need is in that envelope. The bureau has purposely kept you chasing ghosts like me to keep you from getting to the truth. While they may have spent thousands, they've been paid millions to look the other way."

"I don't believe you, Stratton."

"One more thing. Burroughs can't be trusted."

"Senior Agent Burroughs? What does he have to do with this?"

"Burroughs has been on this case since day one, the only constant. Now he's on a special investigative committee. Coincidence, I think not. Also, when I was under, I remember him paying several visits to Simon, although I was never able to hear any of their conversations. I can tell you that judging by the late hours, Burroughs wasn't there to do investigations," Alex concluded, while simultaneously dealing another blow to Agent Blackhawk's trust in his mentor and the bureau.

"Are you sure it was Agent Burroughs?"

"Short fat bastard with a balding head, liver spots, and a bad comb over ring a bell?"

"That's him," Jason replied with his tone clearly indicating defeat.

"Who killed my partner, Alex? Who killed Lisa?"

"Simon's number one; Gabriel."

"Gabriel Malcolm killed my partner? Burroughs just returned from Jamaica on a so-called fact finding mission declaring that Gabriel, not Simon was the head of the organization. He made us redouble our efforts to nail this guy."

"I don't know what that's about, but I can tell you that Gabriel never approved of Simon buying the loyalty of cops or feds."

"Why are you telling me this, Stratton? What's in it for you?"

"I want Simon dead, and so do you. I can make that happen, but I can't get to him if your agents are in my way. That being said, I trust you know what to do with that information. If you don't want to bring the real criminals to justice, drop the envelope and walk away. If you take it, you're in all the way. But be careful because you're being watched."

"Watched? How do you know?"

"Because there's another car parked a block from where yours is. Two male occupants are running surveillance on you. Who do you suppose they work for?"

"Son-of-a-bitch!" he exclaimed while shaking his head.

"You still have a choice, Jason. Choose wisely."

"No I don't. I didn't sign on to catch one set of criminals while watching another set walk free, especially if those criminals have badges. Even if it means my career, I'm going to bring an end to this bullshit once and for all."

"It might mean your life," Alex replied very matter-of-factly.

"So be it."

"Take some time to review that information. I'll be in touch but don't cross me, Jason. If you do, the next time I see you will be through the lens of a high-powered rifle scope."

Before Jason could respond, Alex was gone.

The next afternoon in Cincinnati, Ni'Chelle had just put the kids down for nap when she heard a knock at the door. After peeping through the blinds, she opened it and was greeted by a sweaty but smiling postman with a registered letter in his hand.

"Hello ma'am, I have a registered letter for Lynn or Ni'Chelle Turner."
"I'm Ni'Chelle Turner," she replied nervously.
"Please sign here by the X."

After signing the form and seeing the postman off, Ni'Chelle went into the dining room and took a seat at the table. She couldn't understand why they were being contacted by Weltman, Reid, and Myers. Desmond had already taken all their money. She laid it on the table and stared at it, unsure if she could handle another disappointment.

"Who was at the door?" Lynn asked while standing in the doorway brushing her hair. "What are you looking at?"
"It was the mailman. We got another registered letter from dad's accountant."
"Girl, just open it," Lynn said nonchalantly.
"You open it," Ni'Chelle replied while passing it to her sister.
"OH JESUS!"

"Girl what's wrong?" Ni'Chelle shouted after hearing Lynn's cry.

Before Lynn could respond, Ni'Chelle took the letter.

> Dear Ms. Turner,
>
> We are happy to inform you that due to an oversight on our behalf, we have located a second account in our system that was set up by your late father shortly after the first. Its designated beneficiaries are Lynn Turner and Ni'Chelle Turner, his daughters. Enclosed you will find a cashier's check in the amount of $1,000,000.00, less a ten percent standard processing fee. Please accept our sincerest apologies for this oversight and feel free to contact us if you have any questions or investment needs.
>
> Sincerely yours, David Weltman.

"Oh my God."
"Now you can get your shop," Lynn whispered with tears of joy streaming down her face and a lump in her throat.
"And you can go to medical school," Ni'Chelle replied while hugging her sister.

Aspen, Colorado

Later that afternoon in her office, Dr. Constance Willows found herself opposite a menacing brute that reeked of alcohol. Chills raced up and down her spine each time she looked at Gary Anders, and though she seemed relaxed and composed, her nerves were on edge. In fact, Constance was afraid for her life. His constant ogling and lust-filled grunts were disgusting enough, but seeing him undressing her with his bloodshot eyes made her skin crawl. Catching him staring at her breasts and thighs made Constance feel helpless and vulnerable to whatever was going through his twisted mind. She kept adjusting her clothing, attempting to hide anything that may be suggestive or provocative. She kept pondering why Doc had ignored her repeated requests to have Gary referred to another therapist. Though she attempted several times to proceed, his grotesque stares and wandering eyes had her at a loss for words.

"We're not going to get anywhere if you don't start talking, Mr. Anders," Constance managed after a deep breath and half-a-pitcher of water.
"Where exactly are you trying to go, Doc?" he asked half-heartedly while staring at her thighs.
"For starters, we can try to get to the root of your issues. Let's begin with your recent arrest. What do you think was the root cause?"
"Nothing you can help me with, Doc," he replied sarcastically. "You can't help me and I don't wanna to be here. I'm here because they're making me come see you just to keep my job. I wanna be home with my family, not here having you probing around in my head."
"We're finally getting somewhere," she exhaled, thinking that they were making a breakthrough.
"Are we? Have you figured out a way to get me back with my wife and kid? Can you help me deal with the laws that are keeping me from them? Because if you can't, then don't waste my time."
"Have you stopped to consider that maybe you're the one who's keeping you from being with your family? I may not be able to get you back with them, but I can

help you cope with the demons that are keeping you from them."

"Lady, you're useless," he snapped with an angry scowl.

"The door isn't locked, Mr. Anders. You're free to go at anytime."

"I don't think so, honey. I'm required to sit in this dump for an hour, and I have thirty minutes to go. How about I ask you some questions? Question number one. When are we gonna fuck?"

"Excuse me!" she gasped in disbelief.

"You heard me, Doc. I mean, you fucked the old man, and that bastard, Alex. I know Mike didn't nail you because he's too much in love. Ko is banging Alex's little sister and Warren is too spaced-out to be interested in pussy right now. That leaves yours truly, so let's have at it."

"Get the hell out of my office!" Constance demanded when she bolted up from her chair.

"I'm not going anywhere," he replied before standing up and removing his blazer.

Constance retreated in horror when the drunken monster began stalking her. She back peddled as fast as she could, but no matter where she moved, he was right on top of her. While cowering behind her desk, Constance picked up the phone only to have him rip its cord out of the wall. The crazed look in his eyes said it all. He was past the point of reasoning. He grabbed her arm when she bolted for the door, spun her around, and slammed her face-first on the desk. Fearing what was about to happen, Constance fought with everything she had left in her. She grabbed a letter opener and thrust it into his shoulder, but the combination of drugs and alcohol made him oblivious to the wound. His glazed eyes and demonic smile had her heart about to leap from her chest. His iron grip nearly crushed her trembling wrists before the impact of his backhand against her skull knocked her back down, face first onto the desk. As she lay there half-dazed, Constance felt a sudden breeze on her backside.

"Nice ass," she heard him say when he pushed her skirt up and ripped off her pantyhose.
"Please don't do this."
"Shut up!" Gary barked before grabbing and unbuckling his belt.

Preparing herself for his imminent attack, Constance closed her eyes and began to pray. Seconds later, she heard a click. He was no longer touching her, and in fact, he'd moved away. Believing that her prayer had been answered and that Gary had come to his senses, she stood up and turned around but panic set in immediately. She had no idea what was about to happen next when she saw her savior standing there with the barrel of his gun jammed behind Gary's left ear.

"Your timing sucks as usual, kid," Gary groaned while standing with his neck contorted.
"Not from where I'm standing," Alex replied before pulling the hammer back.
"Alex, don't," Constance begged with her mouth covered.
"Got the stones to pull the trigger, Alex?" Gary taunted while staring into Constance's eyes.
"If the lady wasn't here, you'd find out. But since I'm a gentleman, I'll let you live...for now."

Using the barrel as his guide, Alex spun Gary until he was standing between him and Constance.

"See you around Doc," Gary said with a wink. "Call me."

"Get the fuck out of here before I change my mind and H-VAC your ass."

"See you soon, Black Mamba."

"Count on it, Hollow-Point."

Constance was awestruck by what she'd just witnessed. Her knight had appeared out of nowhere and faced down her demon, a man whom she had feared since the first time they met. Her prayer had been answered by the very man who'd been shunned by most of the people that knew him. Even now as she stood with gratitude in her heart, Constance could see the darkness surrounding him. Her heart and mind raced while searching for words.

"Are you ok?" Alex asked with his back to her.

"Yes," she finally managed after hugging him tightly from behind. "I don't know where you came from, but thank you so much, Alex. I don't know what I would have done if…"

"I do," Alex replied when he broke her grip and turned around.

"What are you going to do to him?" Constance begged while staring into his eyes.

"I'm going to kill him."

"Alex, don't give into your demons. You saved me. Let that be enough."

"I promised you that I'd never let anyone hurt you and I meant that."

"And you kept that promise," she declared after taking him back into her arms and praying that his mind would change just this one time. "Please don't dishonor my prayer by doing something sinister to that man, no matter how disgusting he is. Will you promise me that?"

"No," Alex replied while holding her in his arms and caressing the back of her head.

Constance knew Alex was telling the truth and because of it, she felt so helpless. No matter how long she held onto him, the minute he left the office it was game on and he wasn't going to rest until Gary was dead, or something close to it. Reluctantly, she released him and looked into his eyes one last time.

"I love you Alex and I'm going to pray for you," she surrendered tearfully.
"Pray for him."
"I will."

Moments later, Constance stood in the window and watched as the DBS roared out of her driveway. She paced briefly behind her desk, rubbing her arms while trying to forget what had just happened. She couldn't remember the last time she felt so safe, and yet so afraid in his arms. Though her heart rejoiced in the fact that he had rescued her from Gary, it was saddened by the fact that she couldn't rescue Alex from himself. She knew where he was headed, not just his body; but his soul as well. Only a miracle could save them now.

A while later at an isolated airstrip east of Denver, Gary's black Chevy Suburban rumbled down the dusty gravel road leading towards a lone hanger. At a card table in its doorway were Tango, Ko, Richard, and Nicholas. With over one-hundred-thousand dollars on the table, the four of them carefully studied their cards and one another's faces. Though they all heard the rumble, none of them looked away.

323

"Deal me in," Gary demanded before slamming his bourbon bottle and ten thousand in cash on the table.

"Next hand, asshole," Tango growled before throwing another five thousand onto the pile.

"I'll raise your five thousand toss in another five," Ko replied with a grin.

"How'd your visit with the doctor go?" Tango asked while pretending ignore Ko's bet.

"It was interrupted before any real progress could be made."

"I see," Tango replied while staring at the three queens and the pair of twos in his hand.

Feeling that he had this hand in the bag, Tango ignored the buzzing on his hip.

Meanwhile at Doc's home library, his romantic tryst was interrupted by a frantic phone call. He listened to the details of Gary session, while sitting in his chair and watching helplessly as the shapely young blonde got dressed. He couldn't fathom the depths to which his team's leader had sunk or why he revealed the things that they'd discussed in 'confidentiality.' His frustration turned into concern the longer he listened to Constance's shaky pleas.

"Constance, I'm not sure where Gary is getting his information, but I assure you that I have never discussed the details of our relationship with anyone."

"That's neither here nor there, Gregory. We don't have a relationship, and we both know you're lying. My concern now is for Alex and what he's about to do. When he left here, he said he was going to kill Gary."

"Alex, kill Gary? Alex is a hothead and was just blowing off some steam. My concern is for you. I can drive out there right away and…"

"Don't bother Gregory!" she interrupted angrily. "I can't believe you're dismissing this so easily! Alex is going to kill him, and you're worrying about trying to get into my home? Alex was right. You are a no good bastard. I'll call Tango again. Goodbye, asshole!"

"It's not like that..." Doc managed before the line went dead. *No good bastard,* he thought to himself. "Delilah."

"Yes Doc?"

"Where's Gary?"

"His GPS indicates that he is currently at the airfield."

"I see. And where is Alex?"

"He is en route to the airfield and at his current rate of speed, his ETA is seven minutes."

"Oh shit."

Back at the hangar, Gary was sitting at the table impatiently gulping bourbon while waiting for the game to end. The twins had already folded leaving Tango and Ko in a battle of wits for the pot; over one hundred and twenty thousand dollars. Their testosterone fueled bluffing match was interrupted when Tango began receiving another series of text messages.

"So um... Gary, you said your session with the doctor was interrupted, right?"

"Yep."

"Are you sure nothing else happened?" Tango asked with his eyes narrowed.

"Nope. She couldn't help me. She does have a nice, round, fat ass though."

"Nice fat ass?" Ko repeated to himself before the wail of twelve wide open throttle bodies pierced the silence.

With each passing second, the wail got louder and louder until a dust cloud appeared just over the horizon followed by the glare of the sun reflecting off fiberglass.

"I'd know that sound anywhere," Tango said while gazing off in the direction of the rapidly approaching intrusion. "Are you sure there's nothing you wanna confess?"
"Nope," Gary replied before emptying the bottle and tossing is aside.
"You're lying," Tango replied calmly before the DBS screeched to a halt just outside the garage door.

Gary, the four gamblers, and four technicians watched silently when Alex stepped out of his coupe and walked towards its front. After removing his blazer and laying it on the hood, Alex pulled his .40's from their holsters. Their mouths dropped when he took aim on Gary's Suburban and fired twelve shots; one into each 22", gator-back tire, four into the engine block, and four more into the windshield. Afterwards, he laid both guns on the hood and rolled up the sleeves on his white Hugo Boss shirt.

"Last chance," Tango whispered before the sea of men parted.
"I got ten grand on Alex!" Richard blurted out when he passed between them.

Without saying a word, Alex grabbed the end of the card table and flipped it aside before stomping Gary in the center of his chest. The force of the blow combined with Gary's weight crushed the metal folding chair like a tin can. Everyone stood frozen when Alex yanked the drunken brute up off the floor and hurled him through a metal cabinet like a rag doll.

"That's it, boy!" Gary growled while struggling to his feet. "Doc ain't here to rescue your ass this time."

"Tango, what the hell happened?" Ko demanded while watching Alex pummel Gary with bone-crushing kicks and punches.

"He tried to rape the doc," Tango replied before grimacing when Alex repeatedly kneed Gary in the groin.

"Make that twenty-grand!" Richard shouted.

"We have to stop this, Tango!" Ko yelled while approaching the gladiators.

"Nobody move a muscle. This has been a long time coming. This needs to happen."

For the next fifteen minutes, the group watched helplessly while Alex took out years of frustration on his nemesis. With Gary on all fours and struggling to his feet, Alex circled him, repeatedly kicking him in his exposed ribs and head. Each blow seemed to knock the wind out of him while threatening to crush his ribcage and skull. After crawling across the floor, Gary found his empty bottle, broke it, and began swiping at Alex's feet and ankles. After several fleet-footed steps, Alex stomped on Gary's hand, crushing it and the glass he was clutching.

"Is that all you got?" Gary gasped before climbing to his feet and leaning on a tool cabinet.

He was a shivering mess. From head-to-toe, Gary Anders was covered in blood, sweat, oil, and dirt. Cuts and abrasions covered him like tattoos while blood flowed from several openings on his body, including the palm of his hand. Shreds of what was once his clothing clung to his trembling frame. Standing weary and out of breath, he beckoned for Alex to attack him again and when he felt his young adversary approaching, Gary pulled out a screwdriver and began stabbing and swinging it with all the strength he could muster. Within seconds, his arms fell limp at his sides. With his eyes nearly swollen shut, Gary searched desperately but couldn't locate Alex anywhere. Seconds after peering into the faces of his stunned teammates, he quickly realized where Alex was. Just as he was about to look over his shoulder, a metal folding chair collided with his spine and knocked the wind out his body. Gary tried numerous times to get back to his feet, but the more he struggled, the harder Alex swung. Bruises and lacerations appeared on his body after each crushing blow. Unable to withstand anymore punishment, he collapsed to the ground and waited for the final blow.

"Kill me," Gary gasped after rolling onto his back and coughing up a mouthful of blood.
"As you wish," Alex replied calmly before tossing the mangled chair to the floor and walking towards of his car.
"He's really gonna do it!" Nicholas shouted when Alex grabbed and cocked one of his chrome plated .40 cals.
"Stand down, kid!" Tango shouted with a vice-like grip on Alex's wrist. "Whether this piece of shit deserves it or not, I can't let you kill him in cold blood. You don't need the karma of that bullshit on your soul."

At that moment, a navy blue Bentley Flying Spur screeched to halt beside the Aston Martin. Doc and Big Mike quickly exited the car and appraised the carnage inside the garage. Tables were overturned and shelves were torn down. Cash, tools, and other equipment lay strewn all over the floor. The garage looked as if a tornado had gone through it and in the midst of the wreckage lay Gary, half naked and barely breathing.

"You fucking animal!" Doc barked when he looked at Alex.

Before Doc could utter another word, Alex had a grasp around his throat that dropped him to his knees. When Alex pulled him close, and Doc saw the rage in his eyes, the old man had no doubts that Alex was about to kill him too. He struggled mightily against the blood-soaked hand that was crushing his larynx, but it was no use. Alex was past reasoning.

"You knew...you knew she was afraid of him. She told you repeatedly that she didn't like being alone with him, but you kept sending him. You kept her in fear. Was that your sick way of controlling her?"
"He can't breathe Alex!" Ko yelled when he saw Doc's eyes roll up into his skull.
"You better be glad he didn't..." Alex began before stopping short and thrusting Doc to the floor.

Just when he caught his breath, Doc looked up and saw Alex standing over him with his gun in his right hand. He'd called Alex an animal out of anger, but at this moment, the word animal didn't describe what he was witnessing.

"You once said I have a God complex, that I like holding people's lives in my hands. How does it feel to have your life in my hands?" Alex asked when he cocked the gun and aimed it between Doc's eyes.
"That's enough, Alex! Go walk it off so I can clean this mess up. Go do whatever you need to do to calm down!" Tango demanded after snatching the gun and pointing towards the DBS.

329

Frozen by the carnage they'd witnessed, the remaining spectators watched as Alex and Tango stood locked in a silent stare down. Without saying a word, Alex honored his mentor's request of and walked away. After a few very intense moments and piercing stares, the Aston Martin disappeared in a cloud of dust and Pirelli tire smoke.

Chapter 13

At ten o'clock the next morning, a weary Agent Blackhawk sat in the parking lot of FBI Regional Headquarters with his car running and his windows up. He watched some of his fellow agents walking by and tried to imagine what they were thinking when they saw him. Their pointing, staring, and whispering when they entered and exited the building sent chills up and down his spine. He wondered which of them had been assigned to watch him the night he met with Alex.

Which one of you is in Burroughs' back pocket? he thought while staring into each of their faces.

Everything Alex told him played over-and-over like the lyrics to a song. *What was going on in the bureau and how was it connected to Simon Felix? Exactly how many people were involved? Did Gabriel Malcolm really order the hit on Lisa?* The biggest question however, was who was Alexis Stratton and how did he know so much?

"You okay in there, partner?" Castro asked when he tapped on the Charger's passenger side glass.

He threw his hands up and backpedaled quickly when he saw Jason grab his gun and aim it at the window. After releasing the hammer and turning off the engine, a frazzled Agent Blackhawk exited the sedan and walked around it.

"What the hell is the matter with you, Jason, and why the hell are you drawing on me? You look like you haven't slept in days. I've been trying to call you all night. What the hell is going on?"

"Gabe, I got something I need to talk to you about, but it can't be here. Can you come by my place later?"

"What the hell is wrong with you, man? What do you have to tell me?"

"Trust me, partner, I'll tell you later. I promise."

"Okay, Jason, I trust you. In the meantime, you need to go somewhere and get yourself together. I'll cover for you here."

"Thanks, Gabe," he replied before climbing back into the sedan.

Castro shook his head in disbelief while watching his partner drive off. Within seconds, another Charger with two agents inside sped past him behind Jason. Moments later, Castro entered the building and made his way up the elevator. As he walked towards his office, the hairs on the back of his neck stood up. He could tell almost instantly that he was being watched by the hushed voices and curious stares that greeted him when he rounded the corner and unlocked his office door.

"Hey Gabe, can I talk to you for a moment?" called a voice from over his shoulder.

"Certainly sir," he replied just before cold chills began racing up and down his spine.

"Have a seat, son," Agent Burroughs said with a smile before locking the door and closing the blinds.

Agent Gabriel Castro sat silently while studying his senior agent's body language and just like before, he was pacing nervously. Though he'd endured two tours-of-duty in the Middle East and various assignments at GITMO, nothing could have prepared him for the battle that was brewing right before his eyes. As an Army Ranger, Castro had hunted, captured, and interrogated some of the most notorious terrorists on the planet, but none of them was as ruthless and conniving as Agent Stanley Burroughs. Years of experience and hundreds of interrogations had taught agent Castro a lesson about body language. Whatever Burroughs had to say, it was going to be a lie.

"What's going on, sir?"
"So," Burroughs began after finally taking his seat, "how is the Felix investigation going?"
"It couldn't be better, sir. We have some credible leads that we're chasing down as we speak and hopefully, we'll be making some arrests soon."
"Credible leads, huh? How credible are they, Gabe?"
"Very credible, sir. Why do you ask?"
"Several reasons, actually. The first is that I haven't received any progress reports from your team lead in quite a while. The second is that I am beginning to wonder whether or not he's really ready to be back in the field. Jason took Lisa's death pretty hard, harder than her husband even. It made me wonder if they had something going on off the books, if you know what I mean."
"If you're asking me if Jason was sleeping with his partner, only he can answer that question for you, sir."
"That's not exactly what I meant, Gabe. I'm sure you read the final summary of our inquest into Lisa's final days leading up to her death."
"Yes sir, I did."
"Then I'm sure you're aware of that summary's findings."
"Yes, I am sir and those findings were inconclusive at best," Castro replied semi-defiantly.
"Inconclusive?"

"Yes sir, inconclusive. None of the evidence from that investigation linked Lisa to any wrong doing."

"Just because those assholes upstairs didn't find anything doesn't mean it didn't exist. Lisa was dirty, and I think her partner, your partner, is too."

"Sir, I don't think…"

"Precisely son, you don't think. You listen. I know for a fact that your partner had an off the record meeting with someone whom we believe is a member of the Kingston Cartel. I don't really care if you were there or not, but I do care that I have a rogue in my unit. Jason Blackhawk is that rogue and one way or another he's going down. Do you understand me, son?"

"Yes sir, I do."

"Good. Now that we have that out of the way, I expect a full progress report on my desk by the end of the day."

"Yes sir," Castro replied before standing up and walking towards the door.

"Oh, and Gabe?"

"Yes sir?"

"This conversation stays between us, understood?"

"Absolutely, sir."

Meanwhile back at Doc's library, Ko and Tango were seated across the desk from their mentor admiring his new padded neck brace. While whispering amongst themselves, they listened as Big Mike relayed Gary's medical condition over the speaker phone.

"According to the doctors, Gary has multiple deep tissue contusions and hairline fractures all over his body. He also has a broken collar bone, a severed artery in his hand, and um…a ruptured left testicle."

"Damn," Tango winced after crossing his legs and squinting.

"Thank you, Mike. I appreciate it. Well you heard it," Doc began after disconnecting the call, "your protégé did a number on Gary."

"He had it coming," Tango replied callously.

"Despite his personal demons, Gary was an excellent field operative who managed to keep it together when it was game time."

"He left us hanging in Mexico and almost raped Constance. How's that keeping it together?" Ko asked angrily.

"Are you questioning the way I handle this operation and its operatives, Mr. Hinomura?"

"No, Doc, I was just…"

"Good because I don't have to answer to you or anyone else under my command," Doc fired back. "Besides, I have enough to deal with, like your volatile sword-brother for example."

"What about Alex?" Ko fired back. "It's apparent to me, and everyone else in this unit, that yours and his relationship is on the brink of a terminal meltdown. All these years we were led to believe that Alex was the problem. Now it appears that maybe we were wrong."

"Gentlemen," Tango interrupted, "before this gets any further out of hand, we need to be looking at getting some new blood up in here and fast. Warren is out for the count indefinitely. Jinx is away at school where she belongs. Mike's days in the field are numbered as well. And Gary…let's just say after that ass whuppin,' he's ready for an early retirement as well."

"Well Tango, since you seem so concerned, why don't you strap up and clear out some of our backlog?"

"I'm like Magic and Jordan, Doc. I'm only come out for the exhibitions."

"Whatever."

Two days later at *'A Taste of Elegance,'* one of the dining establishments owned by *XLS Enterprises*, several of Colorado's elite were dining on international cuisine while being serenaded by live music. Scattered throughout the crowd were several members of the Broncos, Nuggets, and the Colorado Rockies, as well as other wealthy socialites and even a few politicians. Smiling servers darted back and forth delivering gourmet dishes prepared by some of the finest chefs from around the globe. A few Federal agents and some undercover police officers lined the outer rim of the restaurant and seemed to be particularly interested in a cluster of people seated at three tables in the center of the room. From his darkened corner booth, Alex looked towards them only to have his mouth drop wide open.

"Are you fucking kidding me?" he asked no one in particular.

At the head of the centermost table was Simon Felix with his wife, Tisha at his side. Gabriel, an unidentified woman, and three unidentified men were dining with them. At the two flanking tables were two groups of Simon's henchmen who Alex could see were armed. When he stood slowly and removed his glasses, Alex contemplated leaving the restaurant. Unfortunately, his ego wouldn't let him.

"Please, excuse my intrusion. My name is Alexis Stratton, and I'd like to welcome you to my restaurant. I hope everything is to your liking."
"Yes, it is, Alex," Tisha replied with a smile, gazing lustfully at him in his black Versace, suit and white, open collar shirt.
"If you all require anything, please don't hesitate to ask," he concluded with a smile before turning and walking away.

By the scowls on their faces, Alex could see that he'd successfully pissed off every man at the three tables. Tisha watched helplessly as he walked away, before returning her attention to the angry stares that awaited her. Her outburst was as much an insult as it was an embarrassment.

Moments later in the bathroom, Alex was standing at the vanity leaning on the counter trying to control his erratic breathing. He placed his .40s near the sink before unbuttoning shirt and fanning himself. Sweat poured from his brow as he stared in the mirror.

"I can kill'em all before anyone gets a shot off," he repeated to himself over-and-over again.

What should have been a peaceful evening had become a culmination of every unfortunate event in Alex's life. His teammates had lost faith in him and the feds were hunting him. He'd beaten Gary half to death just days ago, and now the man who'd all but destroyed his life was eating dinner in his restaurant. Alex closed his eyes and covered his ears, attempting to drown out the laughter that was echoing around him. It was the same taunting laughter he'd heard the night he was hung from the cross in St. Stephen's Cathedral. He repeatedly splashed his face with icy water, but it was no use. He couldn't arrest the demons. The end was so close that Alex could taste it. With fire in his eyes, he grabbed the guns off the counter and burst through the bathroom door.

Everything and everyone around him was moving in slow motion. Tisha was the first one to see him as he approached their table. She opened her mouth, but no words came out. His first two shots struck Simon in the center of his forehead. The next two hit Gabriel in the chest. A trio of head shots killed the other three men at the table before Alex opened fire on their counterparts seated nearby.

With his magazines emptied and his guns smoking, Alex back-pedaling towards the entrance leaving everyone at the tables dead, except Tisha and the unknown woman. As soon as his back hit the glass, Alex was bombarded by a hail of gunfire. The force from the shots hitting his body shattered the glass entrance. Moments later, while lying on the sidewalk with blood spilling from his mouth and nose, Alex found his peace. He'd finally gotten his revenge. A final laugh erupted from the pit of his tormented soul before he breathed his last breath.

After a desperate gasp for air, Alex snapped back to reality. He was still standing in the bathroom with the sink threatening to overflow.

"Fuck it!" he exclaimed before driving his fist into the mirror.

After cocking the hammers on his .40s, Alex exited the bathroom, and when he passed the threshold, he felt a hand clutch his wrist. He scowled at the hand before trailing slowly up its arm, across the shoulder, and finally to the beautiful face to which they were all attached. She was a stunning, dark chocolate goddess with jade green eyes and auburn streaks in her shoulder-length hair.

"Got enough bullets in those guns to kill all the cops too, cowboy?"
"Let go of my wrist, Karma."

"And then what? Watch you commit suicide because some asshole managed to slip through the cracks on you? You're smarter than this, Alex, and we both know it."

"What are you doing here?"

"The same as you, sexy; I'm watching Simon. Now, what I need you to do is holster those guns and come with me before you cause a scene."

"He doesn't deserve to live," Alex growled before reluctantly releasing the hammers and holstering his guns.

"You'll get him, baby. But for now, just come with me."

After a hasty exit, Karma found herself in the passenger seat of Alex's new Maserati GT. Thinking it better to let him blow off some steam as opposed to badgering him, she watched calmly as his fingers fanned the chrome shift paddles. As she sat quietly at his side, Karma found herself aroused by the rumble of the engine and the speed at which they were passing slower moving cars.

"I forgot you had a thing for Italians," she mused while caressing the back of Alex's head and running her fingers through his hair. "You sure know how to spoil yourself. This car has sexy written all over it. Are you listening to me, Alexis?"

"No."

"Fine, mean ass," she smirked before moving her hand down to his thigh and staring out of the tinted passenger window.

A short while later as they entered the penthouse, Alex immediately began disrobing. Hoping this was his way of diffusing, Karma trailed behind him as he stormed from room-to-room. She quietly picked up his trail of clothing until at last they were in his bedroom. The sight of his half-naked being bathed by the moonlight had Karma's mouth watering.

Tasty, she thought while unfastening her bra.

She'd forgotten how much his anger turned her on. Images of being pinned against the wall with her legs wrapped around his waist raced through Karma's mind. Her clit throbbed with anticipation of his dick thrusting deep inside her. She could feel the warmth of his breath as his tongue circled and teased her hardened nipples. She was so overcome by her lustful desires that she didn't realize her hands were inside her panties, stroking her clit the way Alex's used to. She had to have him.

Meanwhile, Alex was off in a world of his own. With his arms folded across his chest, he was staring out of the window into the sky. Part of him wished Karma had let him kill Simon right there in the restaurant.

Bastard, you would have deserved it, he thought as falling rains began pelting the window. "What now?"
"I don't know sexy, you tell me," she replied as her arms made their way around his waist.
"What?" he asked before realizing that he'd spoken out loud. "Karma...I can't do this...not tonight," Alex whispered when her round, soft breasts flattened against his back.
"Why not baby? You remember how it felt, don't you? I mean you coming in from the field, your adrenaline pumping, and your dick harder than steel. Please, Black Mamba, fuck me like you used to. Pound this pussy 'til I speak in tongues."
"No," Alex replied after gently lifting her hands off his underwear and turning around to face her.

"Look me in the eyes and tell me you don't want me, Alex, 'cause that sure as hell isn't your gun poking me in the stomach."

"I can't," he whispered again while staring into her sparkling eyes.

"Are you sure?" she asked before rising to the tips of her toes so that she could get closer to his lips, while simultaneously stroking him through his boxer-briefs.

"I'm sure," Alex replied before turning his cheek and stepping back.

"You didn't go and get married on me, did you Alex?"

"Not yet."

"She must be one hell-of-a woman because you've never turned me down before. I hope she realizes what she has in you, baby."

"Thank you."

"Look, babe," Karma began after taking Alex into her arms and squeezing his body close to hers, "I know Simon has taken everything from you. Lord only knows how you've kept from cracking up thus far. But now isn't the time to get careless and give into your demons. This game you're playing is pushing you to the edge of your sanity."

"You think I haven't heard this a thousand times before?" Alex asked while shaking his head.

"I know you have, but did you listen even once? Look, I see you're tired, and as much as I'd love to throw you on that bed and fuck your frustrations away, I'll behave…at least for now. But consider this a warning, because next time I get you alone and naked, that ass is mine. Understand?"

"Understood," Alex replied before kissing her forehead and exiting the bedroom.

At Simon's mansion, the three African nationals whom he'd dined with were drinking shots of cognac and snorting lines of coke in the parlor while across the hall behind locked doors, Simon and Gabriel were busy flipping through photographs. While puffing a heroin laced blunt, Simon waited impatiently for Gabriel to find a particular picture. When he found it, he waved it angrily in Simon's face.

"Blood clot!!! Dis de mon mi tell yu bout! Dis da mon fucking yu precious Tisha! Now, wa cha gwaan do bout it?"
"Pussyclot whore!" Simon growled before snatching the picture and crumpling it in his hand.
"I an dead dat bitch!" Gabriel declared before snatching a pearl handled Machete off the wall. "Den we get down to business."
"No, yu won't," Simon growled with smoke billowing from his nose. "Leave her. Keep da money happy. Mi soon come."

Moments later, Simon slowly entered his bedroom where Tisha was standing at the balcony door. She had just showered and was dressed in a silver, lace teddy and matching panties. Anger and jealousy filled him when he gazed at her body in the moonlight. The thought of Alex touching her body, sucking her tits, and grinding between her thighs, made him want to snap her neck. Simon, however, had something more sinister in mind. He wanted Tisha to suffer.

"Yu look lovely, Tisha gal," he whispered while grabbing her around the waist and nuzzling her ear with his nose and lips.
"Thank you, baby," she replied, shocked by but enjoying his new found sense of sensuality. "I'm sorry I stepped out of pocket earlier. I…"

"Hush chile," he interrupted. "None a dis possible wit'out yu. Follow for a drink and wi toast ta success."
"I thought you were entertaining guests," she said while grinding her soft ass against his pelvis.
"Naa worry bout it. Dis evening all about Tisha, mi supa star. Come now," he whispered before taking her by the hand and escorting her to the parlor.

Filled with senses of nostalgia and euphoria, Tisha kissed Simon's lips when he reached for the door handle. Upon entering the parlor however, her lustful feelings quickly turned to fright. There standing naked in the center of the room were their three dinner guests, and on her knees in front of them was a young woman Tisha didn't recognize. Oblivious to their entrance, she was taking turns enthusiastically sucking their dicks while they watched in delight. When she turned around and smiled, Tisha saw her face and panicked. She was the same young woman who'd been with Gabriel earlier that evening. The sound of Simon's sadistic laughter and the sight of Gabriel sitting at the desk smiling was all the revelation Tisha needed. She was about to be a part of the evening's entertainment.

"She needs yu help," Simon growled after grabbing Tisha's arm and shoving her to the center of the room.
"No Simon, please don't! I'm sorry," she pleaded.
"Naa be shy now. Yu naa shy when yu fuck dat rude bwoy, now was yu? Now, gwaan ova deh and make us proud or me kill yu weh yu stand!" he snapped angrily.

Fright coursed through every inch of Tisha's body. She cringed when their strange hands began touching and groping her flesh. Agonizing tears streamed from her eyes as strange lips touched hers, and foreign tongues

343

and lips licked and sucked on her skin. Tisha closed her eyes and prayed that it was all a nightmare and that she'd wake up soon. Sadly, it wasn't a dream. It was real and there was not end in sight. With each passing moment, she maintained hope that someone, anyone would rescue her, but they never did. For the next two-and-a-half hours, she endured the horrific degradation of being repeatedly raped by the three coked-up, African zombies. One, two, even three at a time they mounted her, painfully defiling her body while her husband and his best friend watched in delight. The smile on Simon's face was the most sinister mock she could imagine. Her husband, the man who vowed to love, honor, and protect her, the same man who despised the thought of another man even looking at her, was enjoying her humiliation. The pain in Tisha's heart was so excruciating that she blacked out, surrendering her body to be stripped of every shred of dignity she once had.

Hours later, Tisha sat in a sitz bath once again being attended to by the resident nurse. With a steady stream of tears running down her face, she silently contemplated suicide while resting her head on the cold, marble wall at her back. Though she never made a sound, her body and soul were crying out in misery and her heart was shattered into a thousand pieces. What was left of her soul was dead. Simon's 'punishment' had all but crushed her. Tisha quickly realized that she was worth less than the dogs barking outside. She was so lost in her daze that she didn't hear his footsteps on the Italian marble floor or his demand that the nurse leave the bathroom.

"Ku pon yo'self," Simon growled while sitting on the nursemaid's stool. "Yu tink mi naa find out bout yu raggamuffin? Him dead, yu hear me? Him dead! Yu hear me, Tisha gal?" he yelled.

"I hear you, Simon," she whispered in a low, emotionless tone.
"Stupid American bitch!" he declared before throwing a stack of photographs at her.

When the door slammed and she saw the pictures, reality set in. Tisha's silent cries turned into gut wrenching moans. She knew it was only a matter of time before she ended up dead. Though she wanted and needed to warn Alex, she was afraid to call or even text him. Simon had vowed to kill her lover and though she hated to abandon him, she had to get away from Denver. Tisha climbed out of the tub and went into the bedroom. After locking the door, she went into the closet and pulled a shoebox off the top shelf. She rifled through the papers until she found an envelope marked *Banque de Grand Cayman*. She read one of the statements she'd been secretly collecting from top to bottom.

Some time ago, Simon opened an account in her name and over the past few years, had deposited over ten million dollars million in it. *This is my ticket out,* she thought while reading the statements. *I'll get momma, the girls, and we'll run. We'll be fine,* she told herself over and over again. After reviewing the documents a while longer, she returned them to her stash and poured herself a glass of wine.

In the early hours of the morning while Karma lay asleep in his bed, Alex was at his console reading through files and looking at photographs. While staring blankly at the screen, his phone began to buzz.

"What's up Shavers?"

"We have a serious problem. Do you know that twenty kilos that Dawn brokered with Simon?"

"Yes. When is the delivery?"

"She's coming out to Denver to finalize the deal."

"So, we knew that. What's the issue?" Alex asked seemingly uninterested.

"I've been monitoring conversations between Dawn and her husband. From what I can tell, they aren't planning on giving Simon the money once that deal is done. They're planning on running with it; disappearing forever."

"This just keeps getting better," Alex groaned before leaning forward and massaging his temples. "I can't let her risk the lives of her entire family. I've got to stop this before it's too late."

"Stop it? Alex, are you listening to yourself? You're talking about obstructing justice. Do you have any idea how much heat that's going to bring to 'The Agency'? Between Blackhawk and your issues with Doc, you're playing this entirely too close to the chest."

"What would you have me do, Shavers?"

"Back off and let it go, Alex. It is what it is, and whatever that is, you have to let it play out. There's nothing you can do."

"Thanks, Tobey," he replied before disconnecting the phone call.

While he sat contemplating his alternatives, which included breaking his cover to save Dawn, Alex realized that Shavers was right. There was nothing he could do except sit back and pray for the best, although experience had taught him to expect the worst. As he continued looking at photographs of Tisha's family, he wondered if he'd ever see them alive again.

Later that morning after a restless sleep and a grueling workout, Alex was back in his computer room staring at newspaper articles. On the console in front of him were the files he'd obtained on Agents Blackhawk and Castro. Suddenly, he heard the door chime. Expecting to see Alexandria or Ko, Alex nonchalantly walked out to the kitchen and then into the living room. When he saw Tisha walking through the door, his mouth almost dropped. She was a walking mess. Under her white ball cap and bumble bee shades was her messy hair, blood-shot eyes, and swollen cheeks. She was dressed in pink sweats and a wife beater, which Alex learned from past experiences, was beneath her. In addition to her ragged appearance, Tisha reeked of marijuana and alcohol.

"Ummmm...hi," he managed barely disguising his shock. "How'd you get up here?"
"What do you mean, goof? You gave me the key a year ago." she replied in a drunken slur.
"That's right," Alex replied, trying not to be overcome by the smell of her breath. "Have you been drinking this early in the morning?"
"Yeah, and? I'm a grown ass woman, and I do what the fuck I wanna do. I'm sure you remember how grown I am, don't you?" she asked while stumbling towards him and caressing his cheek.
Fair enough, he thought. "So, to what do I owe this lovely surprise? Based on what I saw last night, I assumed you and Simon had patched things up once and for all."
"Yeah right," she scoffed while walking towards to the bar. "I can't take his shit anymore, Alex. I'm leaving him for good. I just thought you ought to know."
"This is rather sudden. May I ask why?"
"It doesn't matter. I've had enough. He knows about us, Alex. I don't know how, but he knows. And if I stay, he's going to kill me. He already told me that he's going to kill you. He even showed me pictures of us."

347

"Son-of-a-bitch," he scoffed silently while shaking his head.

"Alex, did you hear me?"

"Yes, I heard you, and I'm not leaving," he declared while resting on the arm of his sofa.

"Not leaving? Alex, are you insane? You don't know him like I do. Simon is a killer and once he sets his mind to something, he's a man possessed. Don't you get it? We're busted, and we need to go. Let's just pack up and leave before it's too late."

"You leave, Tisha. I'm not going anywhere. This is my home and I'm not about to let Simon or anyone else chase me away from it. If he wants to climb in the ring with me, so be it!"

"Alex, who-the-fuck do you think you are?" Tisha demanded while staring at the stranger who'd stolen her heart and was now on the verge of breaking it. "You're not some superman. You're a restaurant owner. What do you think you can do against an entire Jamaican army?"

"I'm not afraid. I'm not walking away from everything that I've built because of some pissed off half-a-man."

"I can't make it without you, Alex! What am I supposed to do? If it's the money, baby, I've got that covered. Here, look at this."

After quickly rifling through her purse, Tisha pulled out one of the bank statements she'd been hiding. After taking and studying the documents, Alex shook his head and passed it back.

"That's your plan, to rob your husband of twelve million dollars? Do you have any idea how stupid that is? Have you thought about what might happen to your family if you did manage to get your hands on his money?"

"There's enough money there for all of us to escape; you, me, momma, and the kids. Dawn and Peter can come if they want to. Alex, let's just go before it's too late. I don't want to…I can't be without you."

"Taking your family and leaving is one thing, but robbing Simon means that none of you will ever be safe. What kind of life is that for you or them?"

"A free one, got-damnit! Of all the people in the world, I thought you would understand."

"I do understand, Tisha. You're a woman who's suffered and had enough. You made the choice to be free. I get that."

"No, you don't understand, Alex. I made the choice to be with you, but you're choosing otherwise. Goodbye," she said before storming out the door.

"Alex, what the fuck have you gotten yourself into?" Karma gasped while standing in the bedroom's doorway.

Vision-blurring tears flowed from Tisha's eyes as her SL weaved recklessly in and out of traffic. Once again, her entire world crumbled before her eyes. After years of enduring Simon's abuse, she finally found the nerve to leave him. She just wasn't ready to be alone. Her husband didn't want her and her lover, whom she cherished with all her heart, had abandoned her. Though both men claimed to love her, neither of them was by her side when she needed them the most.

Not knowing what awaited her if she returned to the compound, Tisha kept driving until she ended up in Scottsdale, Arizona. She was resolved to laying low there for a few days, weeks if necessary, until she could gather her thoughts and figure out how to get her hands on Simon's money. Without Alex's business savvy to rely on, Tisha had to revert back to her hustling ways and street sense in order to survive. Credit cards and debit cards were a serious no-no at this point because they were so easy to trace, and Simon had the Feds under his thumb. Low on gas and weary from travelling, she checked into a roadside motel, a move that exhausted most of her remaining cash.

Late the next afternoon at Denver International Airport, flight 635 landed. While walking through the massive terminal, Dawn replayed the entire scenario over-and-over in her head. Going forward, everything she wanted to achieve was riding on what happened in the next 72 hours. After claiming her luggage, she proceeded to the exit where she was met by two thin, dark-skinned dreads in tailored suits. Years of working alongside Tisha taught her to keep her game face on at all times.

"Are you my ride?" she asked sarcastically after engaging them in a brief stare down.
"Follow back a mi," replied one after his partner turned and walked away.

The trip from the airport was as intense as it was quiet. Before Dawn knew it, her calm demeanor had disappeared. Panic overcame her while searching frantically through her purse for her anti-anxiety medication. After locating them, she looked up and noticed that the driver appeared to be watching her every move. Though she figured it might come back to haunt her, she downed a few pills and waited impatiently for them to take effect. Dawn hadn't been to Colorado in years, but she was fairly sure that they were headed to Simon's compound. At least, she hoped they were. She was looking forward to seeing Tisha, if only for a short while, because she had to get back home and put her plan into action. In the meantime, Roger was back in Cincinnati busy handling his end. When she got back, they would close the deal with the *'Mid-West Finest'* and disappear forever.

Game time, she thought when they pulled up to the house.

"So good ta see yu, sista," Simon declared after helping Dawn out of the Rover's backseat and kissing her a little too close to the lips.

"Always good to see you too, bro," she replied with a smile.

"When yu said yu wan twenty keys, me tink; ooo yu know can move dat kind of weight?"

"One of my familiars is looking to expand his business and needs some of Jamaica's best to do it. I told him I know the man who can get it done."

"Dat yu do chile, dat yu do," he smiled before escorting Dawn into the house.

"Skettle here. Mi a call when wi done," Gabriel said before quickly hanging up the phone.

"Gabriel, our guest ere, mon," Simon announced with a smile when they entered the parlor. "Sidung so we can talk da details."

"Gladly, but where's my sister?"

"Tisha handlin' bi'ness elsewhere, chile. She a come after yu gone."

"I see," Dawn said before her nerves quickly became unsettled again.

"Weh you find cowboy wit a half-million to buy dope? Dis more weight den yu handle at one time, gal. Yu sure dis good?"

"I checked it myself and my people are on the level," she replied while studying the scowl on Gabriel's face.

Dawn knew Gabriel wasn't fond of her presence or the fact that Simon was trusting her with so much product.

351

"Ease up uno self. Dawn say it's good, den it's good. Da product wit me bredren in Chicago. Yu leave in da morning."

"In the morning? I don't know if I should…"

"Nonsense, sista. I an home yu home now. Sleep true da night and in da morning we take yu to de airport. Naa a fly back tonight. It naa look so good," he said with a grin.

The sinister look in his eyes made her skin crawl. She'd been warned about Simon's strange sexual habits, and with Tisha out of the house, Dawn wondered how she'd make it through the night without him or someone else trying to rape her in her sleep.

Meanwhile in Denver, Agent Blackhawk and Alex were strolling through the Botanical Gardens. Though their tones were hushed and their bodies seemingly relaxed, the air between them was crackling with tension and electricity.

"You want me to what?" Agent Blackhawk scoffed while standing on a wooden bridge overlooking a clear blue stream.

"You heard me," Alex said while leaning over the rail and dropping popcorn to some rainbow carp below. "I want you to back off Dawn Tyler's family. Your gambles are going to get them killed. You and I both know that the feds can't protect them once Simon gets wind of what she's done. That's assuming of course that you can get her to deal."

"Oh, she's gonna deal, Mr. Stratton. I've got all the leverage I need to pull it off. She's here as we speak negotiating the exchange of twenty kilos. Once we catch her in a deal with our marks, we'll get them in court and shut Simon down once and for all. In the process, I plan on making sure my dirty colleagues go down with him."

"Listen to yourself. You're working an angle that amounts to a long shot at best. Simon may even kill his wife just to prove a point. And your marks, they're dead too. None of them will ever see the inside of a courtroom."

"That's where you're wrong, bub. I have assets in place who are ready to move in the moment she agrees to our terms. She'll be safe until the trial."

"And what about the rogue agents in your office? Do you really think they're gonna sit back and watch their number one cash cow go up the creek? Do you even give a damn about the lives at stake here?" Alex asked, attempting to reason with his persistent nemesis.

"Why do you even care? You've been screwing Simon's wife for years just to get close to him. Why should it matter how it's done as long as it's done?"

"I choose to risk my life, no one else's."

"That's where we're different, Stratton. At this point, I'll use anyone I can to get Simon and the son-of-a-bitch that killed Lisa. You have no idea what it's like to lose a partner and a friend."

"And a lover?" Alex interrupted. "I know you and Lisa were having an affair. She told me. And don't judge me or think I don't know what it's like to live with guilt. Simon's attempted hit on me cost me my fiancé. I watched her die in my arms. I'm not willing to gamble with another innocent life. I'll blow his brains out before I do that."

"Then you're going to have to do that, because no matter who you are or what you think you're capable of, I'm not backing off."

"Then we have nothing further to discuss, Agent Blackhawk," Alex growled before dumping the remaining popcorn into the stream.

"I guess we don't."

"Just like GITMO, huh?"

"What the fuck did you just say?" Blackhawk snapped when he turned around.

"You know Jason, GITMO; Guantanamo Bay? You were an expert with in-the-field interrogations, right? Are you gonna water-board Dawn to make her cooperate?"

"You motherfucker!" Jason barked while charging Alex with his fists clinched.

"Remember what I promised you, Jason? I don't give a fuck who you are or who you work for. Touch me again and those carp will have your ass for dinner. Understand me?"

"Burn in hell Stratton," Jason conceded before turning and walking away.

Alex watched in disgust as Agent Blackhawk disappeared into the crowd. His last ditch effort to save Dawn and her family had failed. Though Alex hated to admit it, he knew that Tobey was right. Whatever was going to happen was going to happen, and there was nothing he could do about it. Now all anyone could do was wait.

That night while tucked away in the one of a dozen bedrooms in Simon's mansion, Dawn lay in the center of a king-sized bed. Half-a-bottle of pills couldn't keep her from being restless and shaking with fright. Every noise she heard outside the door and the shadows that passed underneath it made her jump out of her skin. Her body refused to relax, fearing that if she did, Simon would appear at her bedside like a vampire. If not him, one of the henchmen who'd been ogling her as she walked through the mansion surely would. She got up several times throughout the night to make sure that the doors and windows were locked.

Meanwhile in his penthouse, Alex lay in bed staring at the ceiling. Jason's revelation that Dawn was in Denver and Tisha's sudden disappearance were weighing heavily on his mind. *Did she get away or did Simon kill her like she said he would?* His attempt to bring Jason to his side had failed, just like everyone said it would. Dawn's entire family was surely going to die and there was nothing Alex could do to prevent it. Around nine o'clock the next morning after packing a week's worth of clothing, Alex hopped in his GT and set out on a cross country road trip. He was determined to put as much distance between himself, Denver, and Agent Blackhawk as possible. With the miles ticking away rapidly, the black coupe sped east out of Colorado.

Chapter 14

FBI Regional Headquarters, Denver

After having endured another sleepless night, Agent Blackhawk sat behind his thumbing through case files. His clothes looked like he'd been sleeping in them. His bloodshot eyes had dark circles under them and his facial hair had grown out. He drank heavily caffeinated, black coffee hoping that it would give him a boost so that he could keep up with his partner.

"Are you sure?" Castro asked while scribbling notes on a yellow legal pad. "I need you to be one hundred percent sure or the deal is off."

"All fruits ripe, mon," replied the voice on the other end of the phone.

"Thanks, Kip. I'll be in touch. Hey Jason, wake up," Castro shouted after appraising his partner's disheveled state. "I just got off the phone with Kip. He says that Dawn left on a plane this morning at about eight-forty five bound for O'Hare International. It looks like she's picking the dope up from Simon's connection in Chicago and driving it Cincinnati from there. If what he says is true, we'll have this thing wrapped up in a matter of days."

"Good. Let's hop a plane to Cincinnati so that we can rendezvous with the rest of the unit. Tell them to remain on standby but do not engage. We need this to play out to the end."

"Hey Jason, there's something I need to discuss with you. But I need to know if we're cool. Are we?"

"Of course we are, Gabe," Jason replied before leaning forward in his chair.

"Yesterday when you pulled out of the lot, I had a talk with Burroughs. Long story short, he thinks you're on the take. He's convinced Lisa was too. He knows about your meeting the other night, and suspects that it was with a member of Simon's cartel, even though I know it wasn't. Jason, you're my best friend, but I need you to level with me. What the hell is going on?"

"Do you think I'm on the take, Gabe?"

"I know you wouldn't throw your career away for some bullshit. But I still need to know what's going on."

"Stratton," Jason replied flatly.

"Stratton, as in Alexis Stratton? What the hell does he have to do with this?"

"Everything," Jason replied with a heavy sigh. "I met with Stratton that night, true enough, and he gave me some very damning information. The list of suspects goes all through the bureau and Burroughs is at the top of it."

"Is it legit?"

"It all checks out, Gabe," Jason replied while reaching into his briefcase.

"Holy shit," Castro exclaimed while walking over to his partner's desk.

"Everyone on that list is directly related to the Felix investigation and has been since day one. How Stratton got this information beats the hell out of me. The fact that it exists though, means we can't trust Burroughs or anyone else for that matter."

"Jason, do you have any idea how bad this can affect our investigation?"

"I know, Gabe, and I haven't had a decent night's sleep since I met with him. Now, I got guys from the bureau watching me."

"Funny you should mention that. When you pulled out of the lot, Horowitz and Ramirez pulled out right behind you. I didn't think about it until just now."

"Stratton was right. Simon is their cash cow and they're not about to let him take a fall. Burroughs flipped you onto me to take the heat off him and his cronies. We need to get to Cincinnati to control this buy. If we don't, they're going to kill Dawn, Loco, and our entire investigation."

After a three hour delay in Wisconsin, Dawn's flight landed in Chicago just after two. Per their instructions, she milled around the rental counter after collecting her bags and at two-thirty, she was approached by two men with long dreadlocks and ragged beards.

"Which one of you is Rafael?" she asked after briefly appraising them.

"Shut your bumboclot mouth and follow."

Fear and anxiety had already overwhelmed Dawn and their scowls didn't make it any better. Her calls to Tisha had gone unanswered leaving Dawn to wonder whether or not her sister was safe. Still, she had a job to do, and was determined to make this deal happen. The prospect of her family's freedom from Simon's grip kept Dawn motivated, even though in the back of her mind the possibility of her plan backfiring loomed like a dark cloud. As they approached the parking lot, one of the dreadlock-clad men instructed her to stop while he and his partner proceeded down one of the rows. While waiting anxiously, she observed a late model Ford Taurus Limited emerge from one of the spaces and meet up with the duo. After a brief exchange, the man at the driver's side beckoned for Dawn to join them. When she got close to the car, two additional men stepped out; one from the driver's side and the other from the passenger.

"Drive da cyur, and don't stop nowhere, yu undastan?"
"Loud and clear," she responded to the original driver
before quickly climbing into the driver's seat.
"Deh's a phone in da glove box. Call wen yu deh an'
again when yu dun. Someone link up ta collect da loot."
"What number do I call?" she asked while reaching for
the phone.
"Digits in da bloodclot phone. Just press send."
"Got it," she replied before speeding off.

Attempting to look like a vacationing motorist as
opposed to a drug smuggler, Dawn donned a pair of
sunglasses and cranked up the stereo. This wasn't her
first time transporting dope. Thanks to Tisha, she'd been
doing it for years. She set the cruise control to the state
speed limit and didn't venture more than five miles per
hour above or below it. The last thing she wanted to do
was get pulled over for speeding and have the cops find
twenty kilos of cocaine stashed in the car.

While cruising along and watching her surroundings,
Dawn continued reciting the same pep talk she'd been
giving herself for years. This ritual continued until she
arrived at the Cincinnati Mills mall, several miles from
their pre-planned destination. She'd arranged to meet
Roger at approximately nine o'clock that evening, but
she managed to arrive over an hour ahead of schedule.
Thinking that she might have been followed, Dawn
drove around the mall for a few minutes and even
grabbed a bite to eat. After calling and lying about her
arrival, she drove into the garage and parked in a
darkened corner. Dawn checked her surroundings again
before crawling into the backseat, folding it forward,
and loading the bricks in her pink duffle bag.

Just like clockwork, her knight in shining armor arrived at nine on the nose. Her heart pounded uncontrollably while watching Roger cruise slowly through the garage. Though he was checking his surroundings as instructed, Dawn was anxious and couldn't relax. He'd barely stopped before she snatched the rear driver's side door open and began tossing her bags inside.

"Drive!" she demanded while laying in the backseat massaging her aching chest. "Where are the kids? Are they with Libby?"
"Yes Dawn, they're with Libby like you requested."
"Ok, great. Hurry to the house. We don't have any time to waste."

A while later, the black ML550 pulled into their garage and as soon as the door closed, Dawn sprung from the back and bolted into the house. By the time Roger entered with the rest of her luggage, Dawn was already in the kitchen breaking the bricks open and dumping the tightly pressed contents into a large metal mixing bowl. Roger watched in silence as Dawn added baking soda and other adulterants to the dope before carefully mixing it again. Once she was satisfied with the blend, she pulled a digital scale from underneath the sink.

"Are you sure we're doing the right thing?"
"We've already been through this, Roger," she snapped while carefully weighing her scoops. "I'm going to deal twenty kilos to Loco. That will give us five hundred-grand to work with. With the money we have in the bank, you, me, and the kids can run to Canada and settle. We'll still have ten kilos to float us until we can get re-established."

"What about your mother?" Roger asked while sitting on a stool watching his wife work like a woman possessed.

"Mom is fine, Roger. She has enough money in her account to take care of her rent and other expenses. Once we get established, we'll get her."

"Then what, Dawn? Do we continue running for the rest of our lives? What kind of life is that for the girls?"

"Stop with the fucking questions, alright? I'm sick of being under Simon's thumb. We've already been over this, so don't try to back out on me now. It's only a matter of time before Simon either cuts us off or kills us. He knows I've been skimming off the top. Our days are numbered."

"Baby, when that money doesn't arrive, he's going to come looking for us. Even if we do make it to Canada, your mother is still here. What do you think is going to happen?"

"Tisha ain't gonna let nothing happen to momma," Dawn replied, hoping that her sister wouldn't make her into a liar.

"Baby, you haven't spoken to Tisha. Does she even know what's going on?"

"Look got-dammit! I feel bad enough for getting us into this. Don't try to fuck up our last chance of getting out. Now man up and help me repack this shit."

"Whatever you say baby," Roger replied before walking over to the table and packing the finished bricks back into her pink bag.

Hours later in the center of the dining room table, was a pink duffle bag with twenty perfectly-formed, one kilogram bricks inside. Beside it was another black bag containing ten identical bricks. While Dawn lay passed out on the sofa, Roger cleaned the kitchen and all the utensils they'd used. He ran them through the dishwasher twice to make sure that no residue remained on them or in the water lines. He mopped the kitchen floor, scrubbed down the countertops, and wiped down the cabinets as well. Though he too was exhausted, Roger's nerves were too bad to let him rest.

After sitting on the loveseat near Dawn's dangling feet, Roger began to wonder how he'd let his family slip into this darkness. He had a beautiful young wife, two beautiful daughters, and a great job. Though their old home was nothing like this new one, it was a good one, and it was safe. Unfortunately, that wasn't enough for Dawn. She wanted more. She wanted Tisha's life. She wanted the luxurious home, fancy cars, fine jewelry, designer clothes, and all the other expensive trappings that her sister had. Roger vowed to do anything to keep Dawn happy, even if it meant following her into hell, which he ultimately did. Though he was against the idea from the start, the lure of the fast money and a plush lifestyle seduced him as quickly as it had his wife.

"It's just for a little while," she convinced him.

Now almost three years later, they'd amassed a small fortune. In addition to the house and the cars, they had almost half-a-million in cash. Roger wondered how long it would last given his wife's expensive tastes. His heart sank as he stood in front of the mantle staring at their collection of family portraits. In a few short hours, he'd have to gamble it all on the slim chance that Dawn's plan might actually work. The love they shared and the guilt she made him feel for not giving her the life that she "deserved" had clouded his judgment. By not putting his foot down from the beginning, Dawn effectively relieved Roger of his manhood and his promise to protect his wife and children went up in smoke. He ignored his family when they said "she'd be his downfall," and dismissed it as simple white-on-black prejudice. Now with tears streaming down his face, he was no longer sure they were wrong.

"God forgive me," he moaned while falling to his knees in front of the fireplace, and though he wept out loud, Dawn never budged.

Later that morning with the miles steadily ticking away, Alex's journey east continued. With his Bluetooth in his ear and his hands on the wheel, he listened half-heartedly to Tobey's and Karma's attempts to reason with him. Their words, however, fell on deaf ears. His sudden vacation, the mellow drone of the engine, and the soft music filling the cabin were meant to set the tone for relaxation. Unfortunately, this ambiance combined with their chatter only served as a reminder of his recent failures. Alex hadn't taken his own advice. He didn't do the job and walk away. Instead, he let it become personal. His quest for revenge clouded his judgment. In the wake of his madness, his cover, his life, and lives of those closest to him were in jeopardy.

His relationship with Lexi had also suffered. In his quest to protect her from the dangers of this lifestyle, Alex had alienated her from his altogether. He no longer trusted Doc and part of him wished he'd killed Gary. With so much swirling around in his head, Alex had forgotten that he not only invited Lynn into his home, but into his life as well. *Would she stay once she opened his Pandora's Box and saw what horrors were inside?*

"Alexis Stratton, are you listening to me?" Karma barked after realizing that she was once again being ignored.

"No."

"Well, you need to start because you're headed down the road to ruin, you stubborn jack-ass."

"Actually, Karma, I'm headed down Interstate ten, and do you think this is the first time I've heard that?"

"Then how about doing something different for a change? How about listening instead of being your usual stubborn, self-absorbed self?"

"Karma's right Alex," Tobey chimed in. "It's not like you can control fate or destiny. You didn't make Tisha or her family members get involved in this. They made the choice. It's sad that innocent people have to suffer, but what can we do?"

"Neither of you gets it. This is *all* my doing. I tried to put it off on Jason, and even Doc, but that's impossible. I didn't kill Simon when I should have. I hesitated and now because of me, an entire family is about to suffer. Those lives, along with all the other's I've taken will follow me to my grave. I own that."

"Everybody makes mistakes, Alex. What makes yours bigger than anyone else's?" Karma asked, sensing they were losing this battle.

"C'mon, Karma you've been around long enough to know what can happen when we hesitate to pull the trigger. The wrong people can end up dying."

"You can't keep beating yourself up like this, Alex. You have to accept the fact that some things are beyond even your control. This isn't your fault."

"She's right, boss. Everyone had a choice to make, and they made theirs."

"Exactly," Alex interrupted before Tobey could say anything else. "Everyone had a choice including me and I made the wrong one. I have to live with that."

"Alex, please listen to us," Karma plead.

"I have to go. I need some gas. I'll be in touch."

Later that night under the cloak of darkness, three masked men ransacked Agent Blackhawk's south Denver apartment. In their destructive wake, numerous file cabinets, storage bins, and closets had been rummaged through. In the middle of the dining room table were plastic bins, in which they were stuffing anything they deemed important. After several failed attempts at accessing the password on the desktop computer, one of them disconnected the tower and placed it in a plastic bin with the other stolen items.

At the same time, on a chartered jet, six agents including Blackhawk and Castro were bound for Cincinnati.

"Our ground spotters confirm that Dawn flew into Chicago, where she met up with some other Kingston Cartel members. From there, she drove to Cincinnati and dumped the car in a mall garage."
"What did they find?" Agent Blackhawk asked while receiving a stack of documents from Agent Castro.
"It was gutted. They did a decent job of packaging the dope too. So good, in fact, that the dogs barely picked up any traces. She left it clean too. She has to be working with someone, possibly her husband. His Mercedes was spotted leaving the area and seen a short time later entering their garage. The windows are tinted, so there was no way to confirm whether or not she was inside."
"She was in it," Jason replied. "She's being extra careful at this point. She might suspect we're on to her and hopes to keep us guessing long enough to complete this transaction."

"According to our boy, the drop is tomorrow night at a truck stop off I-74 near Harrison, Ohio. Our local office will have units on standby to move in if things go bad."

"What about local PD?" Jason asked even though he already knew the answer.

"Oh, you mean Sheriff Leist and Chief Craigwell? Let's just say they're sitting back, albeit reluctantly, to see how this all plays out."

"In other words, they hope I fall flat on my face."

"Precisely," Castro replied with a wink. "Hey, we both know that if he had his way, the sheriff would have ended this investigation with Loco and company arrested, tried, and convicted. We'd be nowhere near this close to Simon with them behind bars. Speaking of which, that does raise another question."

"What's that partner?"

"What are you prepared to do if she doesn't cooperate?" Castro asked after a brief moment of hesitation.

"If she doesn't cooperate, I'll feed her to the sheriff and the D.A.," Jason replied harshly. "I'll let them deal with the media circus. After all, the sheriff just wants another notch in his belt anyway and the chief needs to prove that he's actually making a difference."

"Yeah, they win but we're back to ground zero. Honestly, I don't think I can handle any more of Burroughs' snooping around. And once he gets wind that you went over his head, your career with the bureau is all but over."

"Gabe, my career ended when Stratton dropped those files in my lap. No matter how this ends, I'm turning in my badge. Before I do, though, I'm gonna make sure I close this case and clear Lisa's name. I never dreamed I'd be a part of such a corrupt organization. I don't know who to trust anymore."

"I think you're blowing this out of proportion partner," Castro added while leaning back in his seat. "We don't know if Stratton's data is credible, and as far as the bureau is concerned, a few bad apples don't spoil the bunch."

"That may be true, but they can leave a rotten taste in people's mouths. I checked those accounts and the figures don't lie. I told you Gabe, you don't have to go down this road with me."

"As much as I hate to admit it, part of me wishes I hadn't."

The following night around midnight in a secluded section of the TA truck-stop, Dawn was a nervous wreck. When her fingers weren't tapping the steering wheel, her sweaty palms were gripping its wood grain. She kept an eye on her watch and every set of headlights that passed by. She couldn't imagine what was keeping them and it was driving her crazy. She tried to focus on the plan and what lie ahead. She prayed that Roger hadn't backed out and was ready to carry his share of the load.

At one, get the kids and head towards the meeting spot.

Roger. Their last real conversation had been a fight. Dawn couldn't shake the look of concern on his face when she kissed him and the kids before leaving. Dawn promised herself that when this was all over, she'd settle down and be the wife she was before the money and dope. She promised to adhere to her vows; love, honor, cherish, and most of all obey. Each passing moment made her wish more and more that she'd always been the good wife, instead of coveting the life Tisha had. In many ways, Dawn resented her sister. Though she'd suffered unspeakable tortures, Dawn still envied her life of luxury, glamour, and riches. In her own way, Dawn had it now, but the cost associated with it was just too great. A strained marriage, life on the run, and a broken family were what awaited her on the other side of this.

"I'll make it right Lord. If you just get me through this, I'll make it right. I promise," she prayed with beads of sweat on her brow.

After another fifteen minutes of waiting and not being able to reach Tisha on the phone, Dawn decided to leave. Something had to be wrong because Loco had never been this late. She had to come up with another plan. Just as she started the engine and was about to drive off, she heard the familiar sound of pumping bass and profanity laced lyrics.

It's almost one o'clock and this asshole is bringing all kinds of attention to us, she thought when they pulled up along-side her. "Turn that shit off!"
"Relax Dee, it's all good," Loco replied when he stepped out of his black GMC Yukon.
"Relax my ass, mutha-fucka! You show up almost an hour late, and you're playing that loud, ghetto shit? Look at the attention you're bringing to us right now!"
"The only one bringing us any attention is you, Dee. Stop all the cussing and shit and let's get down to bis'ness!"
"Yeah nigga, bis'ness. You got my money?"
"Damn, Dee, chill the fuck out. I got the loot. You got the shit?"
"Yeah, nigga. Let's do this! Hurry the fuck up."

With a snap of his fingers, Loco summoned a member of his entourage from the rear of the truck. Over his shoulder was a large black duffle bag. Dawn waited impatiently while he meandered up to where they were standing. He stared her up and down for a few seconds before finally dropping the duffle bag at her feet.

"Five hun'ed G's, shawtay. Wanna count it?"
"No time," she replied while opening the rear tailgate
and grabbing the pink duffle bag.

With a flashlight in his hand, Loco opened the bag and
found twenty perfectly formed bricks. Much to Dawn's
displeasure, he took his sweet time testing the dope,
fumbling with his knife until he finally pierced the
cellophane wrapped foil pack.

"That's my shit," he said with his tongue tingling in his
mouth. "You a beast, boo."
"Whatever, nigga. Have your ass on time next trip. I'ma
be outta town for a few days, but if you need some more
stuff, you can hit me up. I got some birds on standby."
"Bet. Oh and Dee, there's one more thing."
"What nigga?" she shouted. "Can't you see I'm in a
hurry?"
"I love you, Dee."
"Huh?"
"I said I love you."

Her heart sank. Without warning, blinding lights
flooded the entire area. The sound of combat boots
pounding the pavement filled the still night air while
shouts of "FBI!" and "ATF!" came from all directions.

"Loco, you punk mutha-fucka!" Dawn shouted while
charging him.

Before Dawn could grab his throat, she was tackled and
handcuffed. For the next few moments, life as she knew
it appeared to be moving in slow motion. The bright
lights, the men in black, the big yellow letters scrolled

369

across their vests, and the barking dogs were all a blur. Dawn was in so much shock that she couldn't hear anything but the thumping of her heart. Despite the fact that she was bent over the hot hood of a black Chevy Caprice, Dawn felt like she was floating on air. Her body was so numb she could barely feel their hands patting her down or emptying her pockets.

"Do you understand these rights?" an agent shouted in Dawn's ear, but she was too far gone to answer.
"Roger...Lexus...Mercedes...I've got to get to my family..." she murmured to herself while staring off into space.

All Dawn could do was watch in silence as her life and everything in it flashed before her eyes. She reminisced about meeting Roger for the first time, her mother's joy when she gave birth to the twins, their wedding, the twins' first steps, the new house, and new the cars... everything she'd worked for was taken from her in a matter of seconds. It was all over. *I love you, Dee,* the words of betrayal boomed in her skull as she sat on the ground and watched the Mercedes being gutted before her eyes. When Simon's pitted face and gold teeth flashed before her tear-filled eyes, Dawn almost had a heart attack.

"He's going to kill us! He's going to kill us all!" she shouted while struggling to her feet, only to be gang tackled by four vest-clad officers.

While a group of agents forced Dawn into the back of a waiting car, Castro and Blackhawk walked up to another car that was idling several few feet away. Castro tapped on the rear window and nodded to Loco, who was suffering from his own sense of déjà vu. The same betrayal had happened to him just a few weeks ago.

Now his life, his freedom, and his career hinged on the cooperation of a woman whom he'd just served up to the Feds.

Across the lot behind the blacked out windows of a navy blue Tahoe, four men watched the events unfolding. As the feds darted back and forth, the driver took his cell out and began dialing.

"Im did dun di ting?" asked a raspy West Indian voice on the phone.
"No mon, Babylon ketch da blood clot whore."
"Wa? Weh da husband?"
"Rueben say him left da house," the driver replied.
"Find him and dead him! Dead dem all!"

Boulder, Colorado

Back at his compound, Simon was beside himself with rage. He flipped the desk in the parlor over, sending six ounces of cocaine and a bottle of VSOP flying across the room. Overcome by terror, his half-naked visitor bolted from the room, screaming and pleading for her life as she entered the hallway. Simon had known since day one that Dawn posed a risk to his organization, but her resources, her eagerness, and her street sense made her worth it; or so he thought. She was a go getter and a money maker. Best of all, like her sister Tisha, Dawn was easily controlled. Now she was in the hands of the Feds, and in a matter of hours, she'd be subjected to a grueling interrogation. The longer she remained alive, the more risk she posed to him and his entire operation. Dawn had done enough business with Simon over the years to know it in and out. Her testimony would be enough to shut him down and possibly send him to prison for the rest of his life; the thought of which frightened him more than anything else.

Simon had invested too much time, money, and effort to lose it all now. As the figurehead of the Kingston Cartel, he'd created a vast financial empire with a client base that spanned the globe. Cash ruled everything and everyone around him. He'd purchased the loyalty of judges, attorneys, police officers, federal agents, and political figures, all of whom were always eager to do his bidding. Despite numerous run-ins with the law, several high profile court appearances, and scores of dead witnesses, Simon became 'Mr. Untouchable'. Now in the wake of a careless mistake, his empire was in jeopardy. Worse yet, the true heir apparent, Gabriel was waiting in the wings to take it all over. The ruling council would certainly want Simon's head for this. Both Garcelle and Gabriel would align with the counsel, and though Simon controlled a powerful army, it would prove to be no match for what was surely coming his way. Dawn had to die.

"Rise, Babylon," Simon commanded into his cell phone. "We have problem to discuss."

Chapter 15

Later that morning around ten, after almost 2 days of highways, motels, and greasy restaurant food, a weary Alexis Stratton cruised through the Harmony Meadow Apartments in Tallahassee, Florida. The lot was full of cars decorated with Florida State University decals, license plates, and bumper stickers. FSU flags hung from poles, and banners draped over balconies and flapped proudly in the hot, summer breeze. Though the Maserati seemed out of place amidst the Hondas, Fords, and Chevys that lined the lot, its presence was nothing compared to the burgundy Continental GT and its Colorado plates. Alex's exhaustion quickly turned to rage while circling the coupe. He hadn't imagined it. The car was real and he knew who owned it.

"Coming," replied a woman's voice after hearing the knocks at the bright red door.
"Alex? O-M-G."
"Hello, Vickie," he replied while smiling and removing his sunglasses.

The panicked, bikini-clad brunette fought hard to swallow the lump that had formed in her throat when Alex walked past her. His eyes narrowed when he heard the loud music playing throughout the two-story townhouse. The enormous punch bowl, which was flanked by 1800 Tequila, Grand Marnier, sour mix, and cut-up limes in the middle of the marble counter made his blood boil. Meanwhile in the living room, three other bikini-clad women sat on a tan sofa with their mouths wide open.

"Is that Lexi's brother?" whispered the slender, but well-shaped blonde at the end of the couch.

"Vickie, who's at the door?" Lexi asked before entering the living room and seeing his scowl.

"Where is he?" Alex demanded in a low, raspy tone.

The rage in his bloodshot eyes made every heart in the room pound frantically. Then just as the front door opened, they stopped simultaneously.

"Hey, does anyone know who's driving the black Mazer with Colorado plates?" Ko asked when he stepped inside.

"Alex, wait! We can explain!" Alexandria shouted when Ko dropped the bags he was carrying.

"Outside Ko," Alex growled after grabbing him by his shirt and shoving him backwards out of the door.

Moments later with Alexandria screaming frantically in the background, her lover and her brother squared off like a pair of gladiators. Though Alex had long suspected them of sleeping together, he never dreamed he'd see them like this. It was clear by everyone's reaction that Ko wasn't there to see anyone except Lexi.

"After years of watching each other's backs and vowing never to betray one another, here you are fucking my little sister. You could have had any woman in the world, Ko, so why her? Why Lexi?"

"It's not like that, Alex."

"Don't lie to me, got-dammit! I'm seeing it with my own eyes. And to think, I actually believed you were going to see Uncle Li. Is Uncle Li even alive you, lying bastard?" Alex barked while assuming a Mai Thai fighting stance.

"No, Alex, he died two years ago. I'm surprised it took you this long to figure it out."

"What did you just say?"

"You don't have a clue, do you Alex? The world didn't stop just because of your accident. Our lives continued. When you were laid up in your coma, who do you think kept Lexi from going crazy? When you disappeared and ended up in Asia, who do you think urged her to stay in school instead of chasing you? And when you came back on your twisted mission, who do you think convinced Lexi that you hadn't lost your mind, even though I knew better? You think it was Doc or Tango? No, Alex, it was me. And now you're standing here, the great 'Black Mamba' ready to whup my ass? If that's how you feel, then c'mon, Alex. Let's you and me go one-on-one just like old times."

"You did all that for my sister? Why?"

"Because I love her, Alex. I've loved Lexi since we were kids. You were always too damned blind to see it. We've wanted to tell you for so long, but never could. You were so lost in your own darkness you couldn't see your sister's light. She's all grown up now, and I'm sorry brother, but you missed it. She's been trying to get you to notice her for years, but you never did. Her grades, test scores, even Tokyo was all to get you to notice her. All she wants more than anything is your love, your respect, and your approval. That's all we want from you right now. And if it means you whupping my ass or me whupping yours, so be it. But it doesn't change a thing. With or without your blessing, I intend to marry her."

"Marry her?"

"Yes Alex, marry her," Ko replied, watching carefully as Alex unclenched his fists and lowered his head.

"I can't take this shit anymore!" Alexandria declared before she broke free from her roommates and burst through the patio door. "Let me tell you something Mr.," she barked after pushing Alex back away from Ko.

"You may be my stubborn, asshole of a brother, but you're not my father! Do you see this ring?" she asked, holding her left hand inches from his nose. "Ko drove all this way to ask me to marry him because he was tired of us sneaking around. He loves me, Alex, and I love him. And now you're going to stand out here flexing your muscles trying to hurt my man? Well, you're going to have to go through both of us, you arrogant jackass!"

"See what you're getting yourself into, Ko?" Alex asked with a smile after Lexi assumed a Jujitsu fighting stance.

"Yes, I do, and I love her anyway."

"What?"

"Come here little girl," Alex said with open arms. "You've never needed my approval and it's not that I didn't want you to grow up. I'm just afraid to let you go. You're all I have left in the world. Ko is my best friend, and a damn good man. I don't have a problem with you and him dating or even getting married. It's our line of work. I don't know what I'd do if I had to tell you one day that he wasn't coming home."

"How do you think I felt when I told her what happened to you in Miami?" Ko asked.

"Touché," Alex replied in defeat. "Even though I don't like the way I found out and I'm feeling a certain way about it, I respect the fact that you two are united in this. Clearly, this is a battle that I'm not gonna win. That being said, I only have two requests. Ko, take care of my baby sister, and Alexandria, take care my brother. Can you both do that for me?"

"Yes, we can," they replied when Alex released his sister and stepped back to witness their loving embrace.

"Now, can we go inside?" Alex asked while motioning towards that house. "It's hot as hell out here."

"Of course we can bro."

Scottsdale, Arizona

After a couple of days of hiding out in a cheap motel room, Tisha decided she needed to come up with a plan. She sat in the center of her bed wrapped in a white bath towel that was nothing like the fluffed linens she'd grown accustomed to. Still, it had to do. The dark, poorly decorated room was nothing compared to the luxurious master suite she'd spent the last few years of her life sleeping in, but at least she was safe. Safety however came at a cost. Tisha was broke with nothing more than the clothes on her back. What was left of her life was spread between her legs; driver's license, a debit card and four credit cards that she didn't dare use, a compact, lip gloss, and seventeen dollars in cash. She shook her head while carefully weighing her options. She reached into the purse again and found her salvation. Though she hated the thought of parting with six carats worth of diamonds, she needed to survive until she could figure out how to get her hands on the real prize. Once she did that, she'd dump the Benz, head to Cincinnati to pack her family up, and begin her new life on the run. *I need a phone,* she thought to herself when she looked at the nightstand.

Back in Tallahassee after enjoying a long hot shower, Alex decided to join in the festivities. He calmly sipped a margarita while Lexi's roommates fawned over him, playing in his hair and stroking his ego. It was clear by the looks in their eyes that they were each silently plotting to seduce him. His regal treatment was suddenly interrupted by the angry sounds of his phone vibrating on the counter.

"This is Alex."

"Hey Stratton, this is Agent Blackhawk," boasted the happy voice on the other end. "I just thought I'd share some good news with you. I popped your girl this morning in a twenty kilo buy just outside Cincinnati. She's on ice right now, but in a short while, I'll have everything I need to nail Simon and his cronies."

"She'll never make it to trial, you smug son-of-a-bitch."

"We'll see. Have a good one, Stratton."

"FUCK!" Alex shouted when the line went dead.

"What's wrong, Alex?" Ko asked while salting the rims of some glasses.

"That was Agent Blackhawk. He popped Dawn this morning trying to unload twenty keys on some guys he'd already busted. He thinks he can get her to get her to rollover on Simon."

"She'll never make it to trial. Doesn't he know that? Where's Tisha?"

"She stormed out of my house a couple of days ago. I haven't seen or heard from her since. I've got to get to Cincinnati and try to reason with him before it's too late."

"What's going on in here?" Lexi asked when she stepped into the kitchen from the patio. "I thought you were going to fire up the grill, Alex."

"Sorry babe, but Alex and I have to fly out to Cincinnati A-S-A-P. Tisha's sister got popped by Agent Blackhawk, and he's gonna try to get her to testify against Simon."

"Is that true Alex?"

"Everything is true, except the Ko going with me part."

"What gives? We're a team, remember?"

"Yes, we are, but you belong here with your future wife. This is my mess to clean up, not yours. If you want to help me, point me to a computer so that I can book a flight out of here."

"What about the Maserati? I mean, you can't just leave it here."

"I hadn't planned to. The car's yours. Now, where's the computer?"

Cincinnati, Ohio

Meanwhile at the Hamilton County Justice Center, an exhausted Dawn Tyler sat shivering in a cold, damp interrogation room. The coarse, tan jumpsuit didn't coddle or flatter her the way Gucci, Prada, and Donna Karan did. The cold, steel shackles on her hands and ankles had bruised her tender flesh and left it numb. Sharp pains shot through her temples when she tried to adjust her eyes under the blinding light and the dust blowing in the air. Hell didn't even describe the last few hours of her life. Dawn never imagined it ending like this. Everything she had; the house, the cars, the kids, her husband, the money…were gone.

Several hours had passed since her arrest, and while she waited for the officers to return, she couldn't stop the tears from falling. If Simon didn't kill her, life away from her family would. Because she hadn't been able to make any calls, she had no way of knowing if Roger and the girls were safe. They were supposed to drive to Columbus and wait for her to arrive. If she didn't arrive there by 3AM, they were supposed to drive to Toledo and lay low for a while before going into Michigan, and eventually to Canada. It was twelve-thirty in the afternoon, and all she could do was hope and pray they were safe. In the back of her mind though, she'd already begun to anticipate the worst.

"How's she doing?" Jason asked when he and Castro entered the observation room where Chief Craigwell, Sheriff Leist, and two additional agents were waiting.

"Uncomfortable, just as you requested sir," an agent answered before passing Agent Blackhawk a file. "We've done the usual; no food or water, played with the heating and air, and even adjusted the lighting numerous times. It won't be long before she cracks."

"Is that what they teach you guys in the FBI; torture and manipulation? This isn't Afghanistan, Agent Blackhawk. It's Cincinnati, Ohio, and we have rules that we go by. We don't torture suspects."

"Of course you don't, sheriff. You shoot them in dark alleys and beat them to death in restaurant parking lots," Agent Blackhawk snapped viciously. "Besides, I'm not torturing her. I'm merely making her uncomfortable."

"How are you gonna handle this Jason?" Castro asked while watching Dawn in the monitor.

"We're on a timetable, Gabe. She's already broken. From this point on, it's no holds barred."

"Exactly what does that mean, Agent Blackhawk?" Chief Craigwell asked with heavy skepticism.

"It means that there's going to be a lot of kicking and screaming in the next few minutes. Whatever you do, don't interrupt. Understand?"

"Absolutely, Agent Blackhawk, but understand this. You're still in my city. If for any reason I feel like you're pushing the envelope or going over the edge, I will pull the plug on your entire operation. Now, do you understand me?"

Agent Blackhawk said nothing before exiting the observation room. Though he could still hear both Alex's and Chief Craigwell's warnings in his head, he was determined to do this his way. He'd already dehumanized Dawn, so her emotional state from this point on was of no consequence to him. Dawn was an evil, manipulative bitch, who profited from the sale of poison. As far as he was concerned, she was a co-

conspirator, not a victim. In his mind, she was no different than the terrorists he had interrogated at Guantanamo Bay. This was personal. Dawn Tyler was the key to ending years of frustration and anguish. Finding justice for Lisa and her family hinged on his ability to crush her emotionally and psychologically. Through her tear-filled eyes, Dawn shot Agent Blackhawk an angry glare when he entered the room. Perceiving this as a preemptive attack, he immediately went on the offensive.

"Mrs. Tyler, I'm Agent Blackhawk of the Federal Bu..."
"I don't give a fuck who you are! I want my phone call. I want my lawyer now!" she barked while pounding on the table.

Even though he knew at this point an interrogation would normally end, Agent Blackhawk proceeded with total disregard for protocol.

"Of course, you can have your phone call and your lawyer, but at this stage of the game, the only thing he can do is negotiate a plea deal. You're going to do some serious time in a prison where Simon will probably have you killed along with the rest of your family. You see, a man that powerful knows better than to leave any loose ends floating around. He's been killing witnesses and cops for years. He'll kill you to ensure your silence. To him, you're expendable. And once he's done, it'll be business as usual."
"You don't scare me, Agent Blackhawk," she replied defiantly. "I want my phone call."
"Oh, and your sister, Tisha? She hasn't been seen for days. If she's still alive, she won't be able to help you either. Besides, you were under her thumb, so it's not

like she'd care what happened to you. She's in it for the money. Didn't she recruit you?"

"I said I want my phone call!" Dawn persisted.

"Here's the bottom line, Dawn!" he continued before slamming the folder down on the desk. "You're going to prison. Your case is federal now, so you're looking at anywhere from five to ten years per key. At twenty keys, you're looking at more than 100 years. You're going to die in prison."

The fear in her eyes said it all. Agent Blackhawk had Dawn cornered. The reality of prison quickly snuffed out any fire she had burning. She broke down again, this time wailing so loud that they had to adjust the volume on the monitor in the observation room. Agent Blackhawk, however, was unmoved. In fact, he was smiling on the inside, enjoying the power he commanded over her. Sensing an imminent victory, he continued his emotional assault.

"It's over Dawn. Forget the house, the cars, and the clothes. There are no graduations in your future, and your marriage is pretty much over. Roger, if he doesn't turn on you, that is, is going to leave you."

"Roger would never turn on me."

"Really?" Jason asked after seeing another chink in her armor. "We picked him up last night at the house. He's down the hall right now with my partner about ready to turn state's witness in exchange for immunity."

"You're lying! I want to see my husband now!" she shouted before bolting up from the chair and running towards the door.

"Sit down, Dawn."

After a few frantic yanks on the handle, she returned to the table. When she sat down, Agent Blackhawk opened the folder. Inside were pictures of her family; her husband, her children, and her mother. He spread them out in front of her and watched with delight as tears rained from her swollen eyes.

"Sadly, your mother will probably suffer the most. All this excitement will probably kill her, if Simon doesn't do it first."
"Why are you doing this to me? Why won't you give me my phone call?" Dawn asked while staring helplessly through her blurry eyes.
"Why am I doing what? Why'd you do this to yourself? I didn't make you sell dope for Simon. You made the conscious decision to do so, and now you have to live with the consequences. And honestly, they're some very stiff consequences. Take a long hard look at those pictures, Dawn, because it's highly unlikely you'll ever see your family like this again; happy…smiling…together."

Strategically placed at the bottom of the stack was a picture of Simon and Tisha. They were smiling and laughing as if they didn't have a care in the world. As usual, they were elegantly dressed and flaunting their wealth in the faces of others. He made sure this photograph was at the bottom of the pile. He wanted to make sure that it was the last thing she saw. For Agent Blackhawk, this was his ace in the hole.

"Ah yes, Simon and Tisha. They really do make a cute couple, don't you agree? I mean here they are in the lap of luxury at the same time you and Roger were living in a dump out in Indiana. Do you really think they did you a favor by introducing drugs into your families' lives? They didn't give a fuck about you then, and they don't give a fuck about you now. All you and Roger were to

383

them were money makers. Simon is a killer, and without us protecting you, he'll get to you and the rest of the family. And your lovely sister isn't going to do a damned thing about it. Why would she? After all, she's only in it for the money, remember?"

"Tisha would never…"

"Never what; abandon you?" Agent Blackhawk interrupted. "Where is she now? Where was she when you gambled your family's livelihood on this deal? You've been calling her for days, and she's been ignoring you. She's probably on vacation somewhere spending the money that you've worked so hard earning for them."

His words cut like razors. Dawn's eyes rolled into the back of her head before she nearly lost consciousness. After quickly snapping back to her senses, she puked all over the floor near her feet. His revelations were too much for her to bear. Agent Blackhawk had taken all her fears and turned them against her. *Where is Tisha? Why did she use and then abandon us like this?* Dawn thought while her weakened stomach continued to rumble. Though she never said a word, she silently conceded that she'd sold her soul. Now she was about to pay the ultimate price for that sin, and in the end, it left her with nothing; no family, no husband, no kids. After another attack of nausea quickly ensued, Dawn found herself puking again.

"I'll send someone to clean this up. Then we'll get you that phone call."

"Wait, Agent Blackhawk. You said you could protect me. How?"

"Let's get you cleaned up first then we can talk," he replied, almost overcome by the stench.

"What the fuck was that?" Sheriff Leist screamed when Agent Blackhawk entered the observation room.

"It was a thing of beauty, that's what it was," Castro replied while patting his partner on the back.

"There were several times when I wanted to call off your assault, Agent Blackhawk. Were it not for my belief in your abilities, I would have."

"Thank you, Chief Craigwell."

"She's knee deep in puke. She's no good to us now! She's a nervous wreck, you arrogant jack-ass!"

"Thank you for that astute observation sheriff, but I think you missed one key point. She asked me for help. In chess, that would be considered a checkmate. Now, if you wouldn't mind, could you get a crew in there to clean that place up please?"

"You're one smug son-of-a-bitch, Agent Blackhawk."

"Thank you, sheriff," he replied with a smile.

Meanwhile back in Scottsdale, Tisha was busy putting her hustler tactics and feminine wiles to use. After a brief tour of the city, she drove to the local pawn shop where she was determined to come up on some quick cash. The clerk, who was more interested in her bust line than making a deal, wasn't willing to meet her price for the diamond and platinum necklace that Simon had given her. After the beating she'd taken, Tisha was determined to milk it for as much as she could.

"What do you mean you can only give me two grand? Honey, that's at least five grand worth of platinum and ice. I need at least thirty seven-fifty."

"I told you ma'am, the most I can go is two thousand," he replied to her tits. "I don't know where this stuff came from, or whether it's hot. Two thousand is it."

"Are you sure that's the best you can do?" she asked again after noticing his wandering eyes and leaning across the counter to give him a closer view.

"Well maybe I can go thirty five hundred," he replied with beads of sweat running down his forehead.

"I'll take it," she smiled before watching him hurry to the back of the store.

When the little man returned, he had thirty five crisp one hundred dollar bills in his hand, which he took his sweet time counting out.

"Will there be anything else ma'am?" he asked her tits while standing behind the counter.

"As a matter of fact, yes there is. I need a gun and some bullets. A girl can't be too safe around these parts, ya know," she cooed before gently jiggling her assets again for his delight.

An hour later after a trip to the local Wal-Mart, Tisha returned to her hotel room. Though she was eight thousand-fifty nine dollars lighter, she had clean clothes, a new gun, and some much needed cash. She was years removed from wearing off that rack jeans and shirts, and the thought of shopping at a department store was deplorable in her eyes. She tried hard not to think about what she'd lost when she spread out the Levis jeans, Fruit of the Loom panties, and other name brand clothing that she'd forgotten even existed. Instead, Tisha's mind remained focused on the real prize; the twelve-million dollars she was about to receive in severance pay. When she was done sorting her clothing, she turned her focus to the new gun. Simon had taught her enough to get by, but she never had to handle one until now.

You can do this girl, she thought while aiming the nickel-plated revolver at the mirror in front of her.

Cincinnati, Ohio

After making her phone call and donning a clean jumpsuit, Dawn returned to the interrogation room where Agent Blackhawk was waiting. The folder that he'd previously spread out in front of her was replaced by a yellow legal pad and a pen. When she laid eyes on them, Dawn knew immediately what the FBI's help meant. She'd have to tell them everything she knew. Though she didn't trust the police, as a rule-of-thumb, the thought of what could happen to her family had her backed into a corner. In order to guarantee their safety, she'd to gamble hers one more time.

"Please have a seat," Agent Blackhawk requested while motioning towards the chair at the end of the table. "Look Dawn, I don't want you. I want your brother-in-law. I want to bring Simon to justice. I personally don't care whether or not you do a day in jail. That's entirely up to you. You want my help? This is it. You give me names, dates, quantities, dollar amounts, and anything else I can use against him. I need something that links him directly to the drugs you sold for him."

"That's gonna be a difficult, Agent Blackhawk. Simon doesn't touch dope nor does he participate directly in any transactions. He has workers for that. All he does is collect money and facilitate deals. I've never picked up dope from Simon or in Denver. It was always somewhere else and from someone else. Either that, or it was delivered to me."

"I need that information, Dawn. I've been trying to build a case against Simon for years, but he's proven to be untouchable. I need your help."

"What do I get in return?" she asked before picking the pen up off the table.

"What is it you want, Dawn?"

"I want immunity for me and my family. I want to be sure that my husband and my children don't have to endure any of this drama. I want protection."

"If you agree to work with us, I can guarantee you all those things. But understand, immunity doesn't mean that you won't have to see Simon again. You may have to testify in open court."

"I don't know if I can do that, Agent Blackhawk. Simon has half the police on his payroll. How do you think he's managed to stay out of jail all this time?"

"Dawn, if you're in, then you're in all the way. There are no compromises."

"So, basically, you want me to risk my life and the lives of my family just to help you bring him in?"

"There is an alternative," he replied before standing up and walking towards to the door.

"For me, there is no alternative, and you know that. I'll give you all the information you want in exchange for my family's protection."

"Then let's talk."

For the next few hours, Agents Castro and Blackhawk sat in the interrogation room with Dawn taking notes and asking all the questions they could think of. To their surprise, Dawn was a wealth of information. Not only did she have times and dates, but she could also remember names and faces. With the help of some photographs and other FBI data, Agents Blackhawk and Castro were able to piece together a lengthy timeline on Simon's operation. They were also able to figure out where key players fit into the hierarchy.

Back in Arizon, Tisha had purchased a cell phone and was desperately was trying to reach Dawn and Roger. After numerous failed attempts, she began to wonder if they'd snubbed her for not allowing them to go through with their deal. Before, it was about protecting Simon's interests. Now, it was about getting to her family and getting them out of harm's way. Once she got her hands on the money, Tisha knew that Simon would come looking for her especially since the account was in her name. She was determined to be gone long before that happened though. No matter what, she wasn't going to deviate from the plan. Either they came with her, or they were on their own. At least she'd give them an option.

That evening around seven, and after several more hours of intense questioning, a weary Dawn Tyler was taken from the interrogation room to a holding cell, where she awaited transportation to a safe house. Two agents stood guard outside her cell while agents Blackhawk and Castro compared notes in the observation room.

"Were you able to get McNamara on the line, Gabe?"
"I've been trying to get him all afternoon. It's Friday, Jason, which means he's either at the golf course or the titty bar. Either way, he's not taking calls right now. And our guys still don't have a line on Roger Tyler either. We've checked known relatives and friends, but we have nothing."
"Hopefully, he got away with the kids before it was too late. Give our guys in Columbus and Toledo a call. Give them descriptions of the car, the husband, and the kids."
"Should we issue an Amber Alert?" Castro asked after picking up his phone.
"That's the last thing we want to do," Agent Blackhawk replied emphatically. "We don't want to panic him or make anyone else the wiser. At this point, we just want to secure and detain them until we can arrange a pickup."

389

"Gotcha."

Just as the small team was preparing to celebrate their victory, their entire operation crumbled before their eyes. Agent Burroughs and his team of field agents arrived in Cincinnati and after a few minutes of intense hazing, assumed control of every facet of the operation, including Dawn's transportation. For the next two hours, Agent Blackhawk watched while his team was debriefed and reassigned. He reluctantly surrendered all the information that he and his team had gathered surrounding the case and turned it over to Agent Burroughs' team. After he too was debriefed, Agent Blackhawk walked out into the hall, where he was greeted by his team and Agent Castro.

"Where are you going Jason, and why are you men just standing around?" Burroughs asked when he burst into the hallway. "Jason, I need to talk to you. The rest of you can leave. You have your orders."
"I'll catch up with you in a second, Gabe," Jason said as his team quickly disbursed. "What can I do for you, sir?"
"The bureau frowns on maverick agents who disobey the chain of command. It breaks down the integrity of this fine organization. For that, you'll have to answer at a later date. Your rogue, lone gunslinger act aside, your work on this case has been commendable, and I'll be sure to mention that at your inquest. With the evidence you all gathered and this witness's testimony, we're sure to nail this bastard."
"I was just doing my part, sir," Jason replied while fighting back the urge to deck his mentor.
"Good man, but we have another problem."
"What problem is that sir?" he asked, quickly sensing that a lie was brewing.
"Your place in Denver was broken into. Whoever it was tore through files, drawers, and closets. The place looks

like a tornado hit it. Do you have any idea who it could have been or what they may have been looking for? Do you think Stratton was involved?"

"I have no idea, sir," Jason replied in disbelief after his back met the wall.

"Are you sure, son? Now isn't the time to be withholding information. Was there anything in your place that could be pertinent to this case or any other?"

"No sir, nothing that isn't in the bureau's database."

"What about your computer? The bastards stole it too. Do you have any password indicators that might help them get past your security?"

"No sir."

"Well get back to Denver ASAP and get that mess together. I'm going to see that this witness is secured."

"With all due respect sir, I promised the witness I would..."

"You've already done enough here, Jason. Get back to Denver. That's not a request."

"Yes sir. Oh, one more thing sir, if you don't mind."

"What's that son?"

"How did you find out about the break-in at my place or that I was in Cincinnati?"

"Well," Burroughs began, "when you ignored my calls I had Carver and Jennings visit you. They discovered the wreckage and called it in. I contacted D.C., and they told me you were here."

"Sir, I've had my phone on twenty four-seven and I haven't received a call from you," Blackhawk replied suspiciously.

"Then you better get your phone checked, son."

"I will, sir," he replied before watching Burroughs exit the building and climb into an idling Tahoe.

Moments later, he watched as Dawn was escorted from her holding cell and to the SUV that Burroughs had entered. Within seconds, the Tahoe and two Suburbans sped off into the night.

"What's next?" Castro asked while approaching from behind.

"It's over, Gabe. I don't know how, but the fat son-of-a-bitch beat us again."

"Maybe we're jumping to conclusions, Jason. Maybe Burroughs is on the level and all this shit can be explained somehow."

"Yeah? Well maybe the break-in at my place can be explained too," Jason snapped before opening the door and walking out of the building.

"Where are you going?"

"We still have one chance, Gabe. Dawn's mother is in a nursing home not far from here. Maybe we can still save her life and possibly get some information on the whereabouts of the husband and the children. We'll pay her a visit first thing in the morning."

Chapter 16

An hour later in Worthington, just outside of Columbus Ohio, Dawn found herself trapped in the backseat between two burly, black-clad men. The silence was unnerving. Dawn struggled to read the signs on the interstate in hopes of seeing where she was, but it was useless. Each time she bent over to read a sign, she was nudged back by one of the angry passengers.

"Where are you taking me? Where is Agent Blackhawk?"
"We're taking you to a safe house Mrs. Tyler," Burroughs replied while looking over the seat and smiling. "Agent Blackhawk is returning to Denver to oversee additional phases of this operation."
"He promised me he'd be here," Dawn said before sinking back into her seat and beginning to wonder what other lies she'd been told.
"Don't worry ma'am. You'll see him again soon," the driver replied with a smirk.

A short while later after a series of turns, bridges, and narrow lanes, the trio of SUVs cruised off a rural two lane road and proceeded down a winding dirt path. At the end was a sprawling farmhouse, and when they stopped near its porch, panic set in. Dawn spotted a pair of white Rovers similar to the ones she'd seen in Denver. The agents on either side of her appeared as confused as she was, especially when Burroughs and the driver stepped out and left them in the rear of the truck. After a few moments of conversing with the two men on the porch, the driver returned and opened the Tahoe's rear door. One-by-one, the trio filed out, and afterwards,

393

were lead into the farmhouse's cellar where they were greeted by a horrific sight. Ten stranger sat bound to chairs with blood-soaked pillow cases covering their heads. At the end of the room was Roger Tyler who'd also been bound, gagged, and severely beaten.

"You fucking animals!" Dawn cried before rushing to his side and cradling his bloodied head in her arms. "Roger! Baby, I'm so sorry! Baby, I'm so sorry. I never meant for any of this to happen!"
"I know," he murmured against the gag in his mouth.
"Roger, where are the babies?" she whispered while looking into his swollen eyes.
"Naa worry bout it. We find dem pickney of yours and send dem to yu."

Chills raced up and down Dawn's spine when she turned around and saw the same four men she'd met at O'Hare and two more she recognized from Colorado. Simon was making good on his promise. He was going to kill Dawn and Roger for their mistakes. Meanwhile, the agents on the opposite side of the room were completely bewildered. With the exception of Burroughs and the driver, none of them seemed to know what awaited them at the house.

"Relax gentlemen," Burroughs said before breaking rank and stepping forward. "This is merely an observation exercise, nothing more. Our friends have agreed to take over from here. I need you all to remain here and make sure this exchange takes place. Afterwards, meet us back at the rendezvous point. Is that understood?"
"Yes sir," they replied in unison, though still puzzled by their senior officer's request and the sight of six armed men facing them.

"Consider this your trial by fire, gentlemen," Burroughs said before he and his driver ascended the stairs and exited the cellar.

As they approached the Tahoe, gun shots rang out behind them. When the melee ended, the six agents lay dead on the floor. The carnage and the sound of the machine gun fire rendered Dawn catatonic. She watched in horror as the one called 'Lefty' walked to the end of the row, and pulled out a large, silver handgun. One-by-one, he fired a single bullet into each pillowcase

"Please God no!" she cried when 'Lefty' walked up to Roger and aimed the canon.
"Wa yu gwan do ta save him life?" he taunted with Dawn clinging helplessly to Roger's leg.
"Anything! I'll do anything you want! Just don't hurt my husband or my babies!"
"Anyting?"
"Anything!" she cried again.
"Wi got no time for yu games, half-eediat. Kill dem and bring blood-fire!"
"Oh well, yu heard da boss," Lefty said with a smile before aiming the canon at Roger's temple.
"One second taught, wi bring special treat pon yu," said one of the dreads before picking Dawn up off the floor and tying her to a nearby post.

Kicking and screaming with a gag in her mouth, Dawn watched helplessly as they grabbed gas cans from a back room and began dousing the bodies. She fought with all her might against the ropes, while watching them douse Roger with gas. Moments later, when it seemed that every inch of the room was drenched, the six men disappeared upstairs. After freeing herself and running to her husband's side, Dawn felt a gust of wind followed by a burst of light and searing heat. Before she knew it, the room and everything in it was engulfed by flames. Dawn and Roger Tyler, a couple who'd vowed to remain together *'until death do us part'*, clung to one another as their bodies were burned alive. Simon had fulfilled his promise, and so had they.

Outside the house as flames leapt into the moonlit sky, Agent Burroughs and his driver sat in their Tahoe and waited while two of the six assassins approached them.

"Sir?" asked the driver while reaching for his gun.
"Relax, Carver. They're cool."
"Yu work done, Babylon."
"Excellent as always Rafael. Now get out of here before someone sees you. Tell your boss I'll be in touch."
"Fa sure mon," he replied before stepping back and watching them drive away.

6:30am Saturday, Cincinnati

After disregarding orders to leave Cincinnati, Agents Blackhawk and Castro checked into the Days Inn Motel. After a night of frantic pacing, Agent Blackhawk was suddenly startled by a series of knocks at his front door. Thinking it was his partner he quickly approached it, but stopped short given all he had just experienced.

"Who is it? I said who is it?"

After his second request went unanswered, Agent Blackhawk grabbed his gun, cocked it and crept up to the peep hole. Standing beside the door, he held the 'Do not disturb' sign over the peep hole and waited. When nothing happened, he moved to the window and peeped through a small opening in the blinds. When he didn't see anyone, cold chills began racing up and down Agent Blackhawk's spine. His mind raced while trying to imagine how they'd found him. He was careful to check-in using his personal credit card instead of his bureau expense account. *Had they tracked him here anyway? What was Dawn's fate? Where was Burroughs?* After another series of knocks, Agent Blackhawk took a deep breath and resolved to go down fighting. He snatched the door open and stood behind the doorframe while aiming into the courtyard.

"Are you really that paranoid?" asked a familiar voice from a blind spot near the door.
"Step out so I can see you!"
"Holster your weapon," Alex said calmly before stepping from his hiding spot at the right of the door.
"How'd you know I was here?"
"I've been watching you since yesterday," Alex replied before walking in and appraising the messy room. "I know Burroughs came in and took Dawn to God knows where. I think it's safe to write her off at this point."
"You don't know that, Stratton," Blackhawk snapped after quickly the parking lot.
"Then why haven't you slept?" Alex asked when he closed and locked the door.
"I have my reasons."
"I bet you do. At the risk of a long, time consuming conversation, I have a proposition for you. We still have a chance to save at least one life in this mess."
"I'm listening."
"Evelyn Norman lives in a retirement community a few miles from here. If Simon hasn't already gotten to her, there's a chance we can still get her out. Maybe she can tell us where Tisha is."

"How did you know Tisha was missing?" Blackhawk asked while eyeing Alex curiously.

"She stormed out of my home a few days ago. She was distraught, drunk, and claiming that she'd had enough of Simon's abuse. She also had some bank statements for an account with over ten-million dollars in it. My guess is she ran."

"I see. That makes you the prime suspect in her disappearance, doesn't it?"

"Surveillance footage shows her coming and going from my building. Nice try, though."

"Whatever, Alex. I'll call my partner and get dressed."

"You've got five minutes, Jason."

Meanwhile at Remington Manor, an exclusive retirement community north of West Chester, the residents were preparing for their usual Saturday morning of leisure, recreation and relaxation. In addition to a gourmet breakfast, residents were also treated to other amenities such as exercise classes, yoga, and massage therapy by a licensed masseuse. As Evelyn Norman prepared for her seven o'clock massage, a beautiful West Indian woman with long locks was signing in at the front desk.

"You're not Evelyn's normal massage therapist, Ms. Boudreaux," commented the thin receptionist after eyeing the athletically-built woman in the pink and blue scrubs.

"Mi a know," she replied with a smile. "Da agency tell me da regular girl took ill an' a needed I an fill in at da last minute. Dat's why yu not get a call."

"Oh that's fine. We just like to keep track of who comes and goes. Ms. Norman should be ready for you."

"Tank yu kindly," Ms. Boudreaux replied with a warm smile before receiving her visitor's pass and entering the living quarters.

Within a few a moments, she was navigating the cottages leading to Evelyn's suite.

"Come in," Evelyn said from her lounge chair after hearing the gentle knocks. "You're not my normal girl. Where's Carla?"
"Carla come down ill. Dey aks me to fill in at da last minute," Ms. Boudreaux replied with that same warm smile.
"Well, I hope you're as good as Carla, because she always makes this body of mine feel so good."
"Naa worry bout dat, chile. Wen mi dun, yu won't miss Carla none."

Moments later, Ms. Norman was undressed and lying on the massage table. She inhaled and exhaled deeply while Ms. Boudreaux's hands kneaded and relaxed her muscles, starting with her lower back and slowly working her way up to Evelyn's shoulders.

"Mmmmmmmmm…that sho' feels so good," she cooed.
"Glad yu tink so, chile."
"I love your accent. Where are you from?" Ms. Norman asked while on the verge of falling asleep.
"Mi from da beautiful island of Jamaica."
"Is that so? My son-in-law, Simon, is from Jamaica too."
"I know he is."
"Really?" Ms. Norman asked.
"Yes, chile and he sends his regards."
"Regards for what honey?"
"For yu dead dawta and da rest of your bloodclot kin," Ms. Boudreaux whispered before violently snapping Evelyn's neck.

Meanwhile at the front desk, Alex and the two agents were eagerly trying to get in to see her.

"I'm going to need to see your credentials, please."
"No problem," Agent Blackhawk replied before he and Castro flashed their badges.
"And you, sir?" she asked while gazing at Alex.
"I don't carry one," he replied sarcastically.
"I see. Well, that being the case, I can only let these gentlemen into the facility."
"That's fine ma'am. Wait here Alex."
"No problem," he replied before walking into the solarium and flopping down in a chair.

Seconds after disappearing through the security doors, they were at Evelyn's door. After their knocks went unanswered, Agent Blackhawk drew his gun, opened the door, and entered with Castro in tow.

"Hello? Ms. Norman, are you here?" he asked as they cleared the massive suite.

When they rounded the corner from the living room and into the den, they saw Evelyn lying on the massage table. Her limp arms dangled over the sides while her cold dead eyes stared back at them. Castro continued his sweep of the room while his partner ran out onto the patio. After a few seconds of looking around, Jason gave up his search and reentered the suite. Even though he knew she was dead, he tested her pulse to be sure. He fought back tears while thinking of Lisa and that night in the alley. This war had claimed so many innocent lives already, and now before them, was another senseless casualty.

"Hold the room. I'm going to front desk," Castro said after seeing that his partner's distress.

"She's dead, isn't she?" Alex asked when Agent Castro burst through the doors.

"Call 911 now!" he yelled, ignoring Alex's question. "I need to see your sign-in logs and surveillance footage for the past couple hours."

As Castro stood at the desk ignoring him, Alex stormed out of the lobby into the parking lot. With Evelyn dead, Alex had no doubts that Dawn and her family had met a similar fate. After all, they were no longer in Jason's care, as he'd boasted a few days ago. Minutes later while walking aimlessly about, Alex thought about his own parents and wondered how Tisha was going to cope. Except for a few cousins she had little to no contact with, she was somewhere on the run, or at least he hoped. For all Alex knew, she might be dead too. Within seconds, he heard the sound of sirens in the distance, while inside at the receptionist desk, Castro was reviewing the logs. Suddenly, the desk phone rang.

"Hello, Remington Manor, this is Debbie. How may I help you?" asked the hysterical receptionist.

"Good morning, this is Tisha Norman. I tried calling my mother's phone, but she's not answering. Is she in with the masseuse?"

"Ms. Norman, I'm sorry to inform you but there's been an accident."

"Accident…what kind of accident?"

"You're mother died this morning, Ms. Norman."

"Give me that phone!" Castro demanded after hearing the horrific cries on the receiver. "Ms. Norman? Tisha? This is Agent Castro of the FBI. Hello? Tisha? Hello?"

His pleas went unanswered. Tisha had gone into shock and was yelling too loudly to hear him anyway. With

401

Agent Castro still shouting her name, she lay on the bed in the fetal position bawling uncontrollably. Tisha's world had come to end. With Evelyn dead, a rift between her and Dawn, and having been shunned by Alex, she had nothing and no one left.

A short while later, police and EMS had the parking lot sealed off. Agent Blackhawk was briefing the first responders while CSI members photographed the scene and dusted for fingerprints. Castro and several detectives reviewed the surveillance footage before placing calls to the local FBI office. They mobilized units to monitor train stations, bus depots, and the airports. He was also hoping that doing so would flesh Burroughs out and lead to Dawn's whereabouts. After an hour of scrambling around the facility, Agent Blackhawk walked out into the front lot where Alex was leaning on the hood of his rental.

"Chevys are a little downscale for you, aren't they Stratton?"
"Not really, I have two of them," he replied as the gurney with a body bag loaded on it exited the facility.
"Surveillance footage shows a woman with dreadlocks, who identified herself as 'Ms. Boudreaux' entering the facility just before seven. She was later seen running through the parking lot shortly after we arrived. The police are trying to enhance the video in hopes of getting an image we can use for identification. Hopefully, we can get it into circulation before she flees the country."
"How'd she die?" Alex asked half-heartedly.
"Unofficially? Judging by the protruding vertebrae in the back of her neck, I'd say the dread snapped it. We have to wait for an autopsy to be done to be sure though."
"No, we don't," Alex replied before standing up and walking to the driver's door.

"Tisha's alive for now. Gabe tried to talk to her after the receptionist dropped the bombshell on her. She had a breakdown right there on the phone. We couldn't get two good words out of her; no location, just gut wrenching cries. I should have listened to you, Stratton. I gambled and people died."

"We both gambled, Jason."

"Where are you going now?" Agent Blackhawk asked when Alex started the engine.

"Back to Denver", he replied solemnly. "I failed so my work here is done. Dawn is dead and so is her mother. If her husband escaped, he probably won't last too long on the run. I just pray the girls are safe."

"We don't know that for sure, but I'll be here a few more days to find out. Hopefully I can get a line on them before it's too late."

"You do that. Goodbye, Jason."

Hours later after a lengthy wait at CVG, Alex was escorted to the first class cabin of American Airlines flight 8965. Moments after reaching cruising altitude, Alex helped himself to a double shot of Crown Royal. Tears streamed from behind his darkened Ray Bans as he stared out of his window. For the second time in his life, he felt the sting of failure. His first was failing to protect Simone. Now he'd failed to protect Tisha's family as well. Everything he thought he had in his grasp suddenly slipped right through his fingers. His sister was about to marry his best friend, and his closest friends doubting his sanity. His hatred for his mentor and nearly beating a teammate to death left his ability to maintain focus up to debate. His personal agendas had all but insured that Simon might never see justice, much less a trial. Though part of him wanted to stay in Cincinnati if for no other reason than to see Lynn again,

403

Alex knew his presence would only hinder the FBI's investigation and his own safety.

Now sitting in the darkened cabin, he began imagining a long funeral procession and a graveside ceremony, ending with Tisha wailing while her body lay draped across a pink satin coffin. Though in his heart he didn't love her, Alex felt sorry for her. He was convinced that if this didn't kill Tisha, Simon surely would. After gulping the drink, Alex pressed the overhead button to request another; his third.

"It's you, ain't it sugah?" asked a soft, gravelly voice.
"Excuse me?" he replied without turning around.
"I was in my seat talking to the Lord when all of a sudden I felt a soul in pain. Then, the Holy Spirit led me to you."

Alex barely acknowledged her presence until she sat down. The quick swivel of his head startled the feeble little woman, but her mission wasn't going to be deterred by his scowl.

"Jesus had a word for you sugah, and whether you believe it or not, he wants me to give it to you," she said after taking his hand in hers.

After glancing at the feeble hands holding and caressing his, Alex attempted to smile through his pain. The thoughts swirling in his head only made the tears flow harder. Without saying a word, he returned to staring out of the window.

"I learned a long time ago that no man, no matter how strong he thinks he is can carry the weight of the world on his shoulders. Even the mightiest oak has to bend to the breeze. It may not break, but it has to bend. Why you may ask? Because it's the will of the Lord, that's why. No matter how much we try to control the ways of this world, it's always the will of God that must prevail. He has it all in His hands and honestly, Ms. Ruby is happy, 'cause this ole world is sho' nuff crazy."

After a brief chuckle and a glance at Alex's tears, she continued her story.

"It's okay, baby, let it go. I can't imagine what kind of pain you must be feeling, but those dark glasses can't hide what's in your heart. It's written on your face. Whatever it is baby, let it go 'cause God has it. Just like the tears on your face, you gotta let it roll off. Let go and let God."
"You can't possibly imagine what I've been through," Alex whispered.
"That doesn't matter, sugah. The only thing that matters is that you let it go."

Alex couldn't believe what he was hearing. This feeble old woman, who couldn't possibly have known who he was or what he did, was reading him like a book. She was in Alex's soul, tugging at his heart strings while he wrestled with his pain. She was reciting the very revelations that Tango and Mike had been giving him for years.

"My God is something else, sugah. You know why? 'Cause He gives gifts; that's right gifts. Forgiveness is one of the most powerful gifts that He's given us. Not only does He forgive, but He gives us the power to forgive. The sad part is we rarely use it. Not only do we have the power to forgive others, we have the power to forgive ourselves. Life has shown me that the man in the mirror is the hardest person to forgive, sugah. We can spend a lifetime beating ourselves up over our mistakes, and all it does is give them power over us. Baby, I'm here to tell you that His grace is sufficient. We don't have to live in darkness, depression, and guilt. Those things, especially guilt are the enemies of salvation. They're just tools to keep us down, and trust me baby, it works. I left home a long time ago leaving my baby brothers and sisters behind. That was the hardest thing I ever had to do but I knew I couldn't grow up and grow old in Sumter County, Georgia. I found my way to Boston, where I settled down and started a family of my own. Though my kin was happy for me, I felt bad for leaving them. As the years rolled by, the visits turned to phone calls. Then the phone calls turned to cards, and the cards to obituaries. I ain't seen my baby sister, Agnes in over thirty years. She left Sumter County and moved to California. Now, thanks to a stranger whom I had to find it in my heart to forgive, I'm on my way to see her. She said to me, 'Ruby, you ain't neva been on no airplane. Whacha gonna do if you get up there and that thang crashes?' I said baby as long as I'm up in the sky, I'm that much closer to the Lord. Glory!" she shouted before bursting into a fit of laughter which drew the attention of some of the other passengers. "Well, baby, I'ma go back to my seat now. I hope what I said brings you some comfort. Enjoy your trip and I'ma be praying for you."

Just as she was about to stand, Ms. Ruby felt a squeeze of her hand and a gentle tug at her arm. A smile crossed her face when she looked at her hand and then Alex who was still staring out the window. Though he never said a word, she heard his request loud and clear.

"Okay baby, I'll stay."

Later that night at *'A Taste of Elegance'*, Alex was in his favorite corner booth sipping Exclusiv Berry Vodka and cranberry juice. He was searching the papers for information on what took place in Cincinnati. When that failed, he searched the web via his laptop, but again, there was nothing to be found. The three calls he'd placed to Jason Blackhawk since landing had all gone to voicemail. While he continued gazing at the paper, he noticed eight dreadlock-clad men at two tables on the other side of the restaurant. They appeared to be looking at him while whispering amongst themselves.

"Dat's da bloodclot ova deh," one of them whispered to the group after looking at the picture in the center of the table. "When him leave, him dead," he smiled with his jewel encrusted grill shining like a beacon in the dimly lit room.

For the next two hours, Alex sat at the table sizing up the men across the room and drinking heavily. He assumed that they were doing the same. Around 11:00PM, he packed up his laptop, waived to the maître de, and strolled to the valet stand. When the DBS arrived at the curb, Alex noticed the eight men approaching the exit behind him. He sped away to the next intersection and waited patiently.

"Okay mutha-fuckas, lets' play," Alex thought when he saw two pairs of headlights appear in his mirror. "Delilah."
"Yes, Black Mamba?"
"Jam the 911 network for the next sixty minutes."

Within seconds, blinding lights filled the DBS's cabin, and shortly thereafter, a pair of white Range Rovers crept up on either side of him. Alex slipped the Aston Martin in neutral and proceeded to rev the engine. He panned from side-to-side and watched as the Rover's rear windows rolled down.

"Game on bitches," he thought when AK-47 barrels appeared.

Alex dropped the coupe in reverse and sped off just as the first shots rang out. With the Range Rovers in pursuit, Alex jammed clutch and brake to the floor while whipping the DBS into a 180 degree spin. The rear 20"Pirellis painted black stripes on the pavement while leaving a cloud of thick, gray smoke in their wake. The chase was on. Within moments, the three speeding vehicles were on the interstate, and as he contemplated where he should lead them, shots were bouncing off the coupe's bulletproof body and windows. Alex knew he had to get them out of the city because unlike him, they had no regard for the innocents on the roadways.

Though he could have easily outrun them, Alex needed to keep them close, even if it meant allowing them to take uncontested shots at his most prized possession. While weaving in and out of traffic, he reached onto the parcel shelf behind him and pulled out HK-5 which was outfitted with a mini rocket launcher. While travelling at well over 100 mph, he inserted a magazine into the gun and a grenade into the launcher's chamber. After placing it on the passenger seat, Alex pulled a double barreled, sawed-off shotgun from the parcel shelf and loaded it with 'special' slugs. With both guns at his side, Alex continued sawing back-and-forth between and around the slower moving cars.

Now outside the city, Alex floored the coupe, hurling it several hundred yards ahead of the Rovers. In an attempt to close the massive gap, the drivers poured on the speed. When they returned into his rearview, Alex whipped the DBS around again and slammed it into reverse. Using the dash mounted screen as his guide, he lowered the driver's side window, stuck the HK-5 out, and took aim on the closest SUV. A hail of bullets obliterated its windshield, grill, and front tires before a blast from the rocket launcher caused the truck to somersault several times during which two bodies were ejected. When it finally came to a stop, the mangled heap burst into flames.

With the clip emptied and approaching triple digits, Alex whipped around once more. After several minutes of weaving left-to-right on a tight, winding road, the second Rover pulled up along Alex's passenger side. When the driver attempted to ram him, Alex slammed on the clutch and brake while rowing the gears and narrowly missing their bumper. After some careful maneuvering, he pulled alongside the truck and fired two slugs in the wheel well. The tire, rim, and axle exploded in fiery shower of sparks and shrapnel. The panicked driver lost control and sent the truck into a series of violent, end-over-end flips.

Alex stopped several yards from the mangled wreckage. Armed with a .40 cal and a hand grenade, he exited the coupe and stalked slowly towards the Rover as it lay on its roof spewing its fluids in all directions. In the ensuing chaos, one of the passengers was thrown from the truck and lay dying in Alex's path. Without breaking stride, he stepped over the man, putting two slugs in his forehead along the way.

"Help mi, mon!" the driver cried when Alex squatted next to his window.

At that moment, a phone which lay on the ceiling above the driver's head, started ringing.

"Gonna answer that?" Alex quipped before punching the man in his blood soaked face.
"Im did dun di ting?" asked the frantic voice on the other end of the phone.
"Not exactly."
"Wa? Ooo a dis?"
"The devil, and I'm coming for you."
"Naa kill me, mon! Naa kill me!" the driver pled before Alex laid the grenade on the cabin's roof above his head.

When Alex reached the Aston Martin, he turned and fired a single shot into the cabin which detonated the grenade. Shrapnel, orange flames, and billowing smoke filled the air as the BDS sped away from the scene.

"Delilah," Alex said when he laid the phone on his dashboard.
"Yes Black Mamba?"
"Tell me where the last call came from,"
"The call originated in Boulder, Colorado. I am triangulating the signal to get an exact location. This may take several moments."
"No hurry, Delilah. I have to change anyway."

Meanwhile in Boulder, a panic-stricken Gabriel had everyone at his mansion in an uproar. He'd grossly underestimated his ability to eliminate Alex. To make matters worse, he had no idea what type of man he was dealing with. Holding an AK-47 and pacing nervously, Gabriel shouted orders at anyone who was near him. With sweat rolling off his face, he bolted to the window and stared at the armed sentries and snarling Bull Mastiffs patrolling the grounds.

"Move yu backside!" he shouted to the men below. "Lock up! No mon come, no mon lef! Step!" he shouted to a group of women cowering in the corner.

Still not satisfied, Gabriel grabbed his cell phone and quickly dialed Simon's number only to get his voicemail.

"Yu pussyclot mutha-fucka! Dem play a card pon mi? Mi kill yu dead! Undastand?"

Denver, Colorado

In the darkened chamber below their hanger, Alex sat in the middle of the floor outside a walk-in locker. Seated in the lotus position and dressed in a red and black version of his uniform, Alex was meditating like he did before every mission. The blue lights inside the massive locker behind him casted as eerie haze on the two, fully-dressed mannequins; each wearing a differently colored rendition of his uniform. After a few moments of meditation, Alex stood up and continued dressing. He slid a pair of bladed gauntlets onto his arms, and shin guards on his legs. He slid a crimson ¾ length Kevlar vest, which contained several hidden pockets for knives and other weapons, over his head and fastened its sides. On the vest's lower back were two holsters for his .40 cal canons. Before turning out the lights, Alex donned his dark cloak and began reflecting on Ms. Ruby's words; *Forgiveness is one of the most powerful gifts that He has given us. Not only does he forgive, but He gives us the power to forgive.* With his head bowed and his eyes closed, Alex whispered a prayer.

411

"I know that you're a forgiving God, so I ask your forgiveness for what I'm about to do."

Boulder, Colorado

4:00AM arrived, and with it came misting rains and a dense fog. Except for the creatures of the night and coyotes howling in the distance, there was an eerie silence around Gabriel's home. On the second floor of the eight bedrooms, four bathrooms mansion was its frightened and agitated owner, who'd barricaded himself inside the parlor. In an attempt to stay awake and calm his nerves, Gabriel was snorting lines of cocaine and drinking shots of vodka. Unfortunately, all it did was fuel his paranoia and diminish his ability to focus. Every creak of the floor or shadow underneath the door made him jump. In the hallway, outside the parlor, two sentries had already succumbed to the effects of exhaustion. Additional sentries maintained a watch weary at the bottom of a winding staircase leading into the foyer. In the woods just beyond the patio, a lone figure lurked silently in the darkness.

"Wa dat?" yelled the dog walking sentry as one-by-one the lights at the back of the house began to explode, and darkness began surrounding them.
"Sup'm ova deh!" screamed the second sentry who was losing the battle against the snarling beast at the end of his leash.

After a brief conference, the two frightened men released the Bull Mastiffs and watched them charge off into the fog. Within seconds, the barking ended in a series of pitiful yelps and then silence; cold, still silence.

"Wa a gwaan?" yelled one of the sentries before receiving a crushing blow to his head.

While lying on the ground dazed and in pain, the wounded man heard footsteps in the dew covered grass. When he opened his eyes, he saw a severed dog's head next to his face, and when he sat up, the body of his fellow sentry fell at his feet.

"Fuckery!" he cried when he looked up and stared into the red laser beam.
"Something like that," replied a raspy voice before a single muffled shot pierced his sweat covered brow.

Under the cover of night, the dark figure executed six additional sentries, and after placing three claymore mines in the ground, scaled the rear of the house until he reached the second floor balcony. Startled by the commotion, Gabriel sprung to his feet and staggered to the French doors behind him. Pressing his face to the glass, he stared into the darkened yard below. Before his cloudy mind could register a thought, he was yanked through the glass doors and suddenly found himself staring into pitch blackness of the reaper's hood. With blood pouring from Gabriel's cuts and a crowd gathering below them, the reaper hurled him back into the parlor. He stalked towards Gabriel before stopping and pulling a detonator from inside his cloak.

"Ooo a dat?" he cried when the sky outside lit up in a fiery explosion that shook the entire house.
"I told you I was coming for you."
"Help me!" Gabriel cried while scurrying towards the door.

"Open da door, mon!" yelled the sentries on the outside of the parlor while banging and yanking on the handle.

"Help me! Shoot da pussyclot door!" Gabriel cried when the ominous figure grabbed his ankle, and once again hurled him across the room.

After dropping two grenades on the floor, the reaper darted behind the bookcase. Shotgun blasts blew the doors off the hinges and seconds later, the sentries stormed in. Two muffled shots came from the corner, and struck the grenades whose ensuing blasts ripped their bodies to shreds. Meanwhile parked outside in a surveillance van, a small group of FBI Agents was suddenly awakened by the chaos.

"What-the-fuck was that?" demanded the agent in charge when he burst through the van's rear doors and stared at the house.

"It sounds like a fucking war zone, sir! Do we go in?"

"No," he replied reluctantly. "We're supposed to be running undercover surveillance, nothing more."

"But you heard the call, Agent Davis. Gabriel thinks Simon double crossed him and now his house sounds like it's under attack."

"There's no way for us to confirm what's going on in there, Agent Fields. We're not going in until I say otherwise. In the meantime, call 911 and report the explosions."

"Sir, the 911 network is down."

"Wa yu waan, mon?" Gabriel pled while cowering on the floor and reaching for his gun.

"Your life; nothing more," the reaper replied before a stainless-steel blade appeared from his bulky sleeve.

When his fingertips grazed the gun's handle, Gabriel's head was yanked back with neck-snapping force. He watched in horror as the blade passed before his eyes, and came to a rest on his Adam's apple.

"Wa Simon pay, mi a double! Triple!"
"What makes you think Simon sent me? I'm here to finish what we started years ago. I escaped hell just so I could come back and savor this moment. You should have killed me in Miami, Gabriel," he whispered while crouching near Gabriel's ear.
"Alex!" he cried before a violent swipe severed his head from his body.

As more gunmen approached the parlor, Alex placed the head in the leather satchel beneath his cloak, and after dropping two more grenades near the door, leapt over the balcony rail. As soon as his feet hit the ground, the house erupted in another explosion.

"Fuck it! We're going in!" Agent Davis yelled when another pair of explosions lit up the sky.

Within seconds, three vans and two SUVs sped up the driveway towards the smoldering inferno. The vest-clad agents were greeted by horrific carnage when they entered the house screaming for the injured occupants to "Get down!"

Bloodied and scorched body parts were scattered as far as the eye could see. Gaping holes replaced the back wall and ceiling where the parlor used to be. A giant crater was all that remained of the patio. One team of agents sealed the first floor while the second team searched what remained of the second.

"Damn!" shrieked Agent Fields while looking at the charred remains of one of the bodies. "Jesus Christ! Where the fuck's that guy's head?"

"Burroughs is gonna shit a gold brick," Agent Davis replied while shaking his head.

Chapter 17

Miles away at Simon's compound, the still night air was suddenly interrupted by the sounds of someone revving an engine near the end of the driveway. The Ducati's angry shriek both the Rottweilers and the sentries holding them. When the group of armed men and their canines approached the intruder, he sped off leaving a cloud of smoke and a leather satchel in his wake.

"Wa a dat fuckery?" asked one of the men after he wrestled the mangled satchel from the snarling beasts.

Upon lifting the flap and holding it up to the light, one of the sentries proceeded to vomit on the ground at their feet.

"Bumboclot!"
"Deh's a head in dat deh bag!" cried the nauseated man after repeatedly gasping for air.
"Wa a gwaan deh?" Simon barked from the second floor porch.
"Yu got a package mon!"
"Bring it ere!"

A hush fell over the group as Simon stood in the foyer holding Gabriel's severed head, and looking into his cold dead eyes. Attached to the back of the head with a small knife was a note with two words scribbled on it on blood.

"You're next," mumbled one of the sentries as blood pooled at their feet.

"I an read!" Simon growled before shoving the head back into the satchel. "Clean up. Gates gwaan crawl wit Babylon."

Fifteen minutes later, while still covered in Gabriel's blood, Simon sat in the parlor contemplating his own fate. The message was loud and clear; he was next. Unfortunately, he didn't know who was coming for him. His mind raced while trying to figure out who'd murdered his nemesis and delivered his head. It couldn't be the counsel, because they wouldn't kill one of their own, especially one in the bloodline. Based on the note, Simon figured it wasn't the FBI either because he was way too valuable to them alive.

Regardless of who killed Gabriel, the blame was going to fall on Simon. The entire Malcolm clan, even his wife would be out for blood; his blood. Though he knew their wrath would be fierce, Simon's heart was still filled with joy. He was happy that his rival was dead and hoped he'd suffered in the process. Even though his union with Garcelle had produced no children, Gabriel's death would ensure her uncontested rule. Now, it was a matter of maintaining control over his wife because control over Garcelle meant control over the empire he'd helped to build. In the wake of Gabriel's death, she would be too distraught to run the day-to-day operations, and the counsel would be in disarray. Their only choice would be to leave Simon in charge which suddenly made him feel untouchable all over again.

Just before dawn, Tango was awakened by an alert from the shop below. He heard water running in the shower as he crept down the stairs while loading shells into his .12 gauge Mossberg. When he reached the shop, he chambered a shell before and peering around the corner. On his way to the shower, Tango noticed one bike that wasn't there when he went to bed. On its seat was the ominous cloak that Alex had taken to wearing and it was soaked in blood. On the floor, in front of the bike, was a trail of bloody tactical gear; gauntlets, a baklava, a kakashi, shin guards, and gloves.

When he reached the shower, Tango lowered the shotgun and shook his head. Standing there amidst the steam and water was his 'son.' His trembling hands were pressed firmly against the wall in front of him, while hanging on the wall behind him was his uniform and vest while his blood-stained tabi boots sat on the floor beneath them. Tango couldn't fathom what Alex had done or why he'd turned up at the bike shop. All he could do was thank God that Alex was safe.

"Is any of that yours?" Tango asked while watching blood circling the drain. Just as he had expected, Alex said nothing. "Wanna talk about what happened?" Tango pressed again, but the silence spoke volumes. Something was wrong, but he wasn't about to find out what it was now. "Nice talking to you," Tango surrendered after Alex turned off the shower, wrapped himself in a towel, and walked past him with his head down. "I'll clean this mess up."

Hours later, after bleaching the bathroom and the showroom floor, Tango retired to the upstairs loft. He found Alex asleep in the same room where he'd spent so many nights as a youth. Only now, he wasn't that boy anymore. He'd grown into the man that Tango promised he wouldn't let him become. While watching his 'son' sleep, Tango's eyes filled with tears. He hadn't forgiven himself for allowing Alex to descend into such a dark place. He was even more grieved that he'd participated in the process. Now like a predator on the loose, Alex was free, full of anger and pinned up rage that no one could control. Tango prayed that Alex was at peace with whatever had happened over the course of the night, but feared its outcome. The blood, the silence, and the mystery were more than his old heart could take. After a few more silent moments, Tango decided to help himself to some breakfast, which usually consisted of Jack and Coke.

"Maybe you should try some coffee today, old man," he said to himself before filling the pot with water.

Minutes later, he was on his way to the living room with a fresh cup of premium roast in his hand. Figuring nothing would be on television at ten o'clock on a Sunday morning besides televangelists, Tango decided to watch the local news.

"That's right, Bob," the reporter began while standing in the middle of the street, "eyewitnesses say that the chase began at this intersection, at the corner of Main and Fifth streets. We're told that a pair of white SUVs pulled up alongside of a dark colored coupe and opened fire. The coupe however sped away in the opposite direction."

Tango's mouth dropped when the screen switched to a CCTV feed of the high speed chase. Even though the image was distorted, he knew it was Alex's Aston Martin. He immediately recognized the precision driving, because he'd taught Alex those moves.

"Tower cams show the two SUVs which appear to be white Range Rovers pursuing the gray coupe, which some described as either a dark colored Corvette or some exotic European sports car. Unexplained equipment malfunctions kept the cameras from getting a good look at it."

Unable to believe what he'd just seen, Tango changed the channel. Unfortunately, the news only got worse. Another news reporter had picked up the story, giving even more startling revelations than the last one.

"That's right, Skip. It's believed that the chase started in downtown Denver and ended here, in the middle of this wooded area. It's here that police discovered two burned out SUVs and at least eight bodies spread out along this three mile stretch of road. One body was found on the ground not far from the second wreckage. According to police, in addition to severe burns, the victim had two gun shots wounds to the head. If you look behind me, you can still see both SUVs, or at least what's left them. All around me, on the ground, are empty shell casings and shrapnel. Investigators are on the scene now trying to piece together these tragic events."

Reeling from shock and awe, Tango changed the channel once more and found yet another news report. This time however, the scene was a quiet residential neighborhood in Boulder.

"Tim, I'm on the scene at the Whitman Estates Subdivision, where it appears that a severed head with a note attached was dropped on the lawn at around 5:00AM this morning. Witnesses say a figure in a long hooded over-coat revved a motorcycle engine repeatedly, before dropping a package and speeding off. Police and FBI are on the scene questioning the reclusive homeowner. Although it's believed that this is related to the night's events, no one has confirmed it as of yet."

"Son-of-a bitch!" Tango cried when the scalding hot liquid splashed onto his bare feet.

He had tilted the saucer so far that the mug slid right off of it.

"You should have opted for the Jack," Alex said while standing in the doorway.

The fact that Alex was so calm in the midst of all this chaos sent chills throughout Tango's body. His demeanor was sinister to the point of being demonic. Except for a slight grin, Alex showed no emotion at all. If he hadn't known better, Tango would have sworn he was in the room with the devil.

Meanwhile back at Gabriel's house, a CSI team was busy combing the grounds looking for clues and attempting to piece together the horrific events. A small group of FBI agents and police officers gathered in the library, on what was left of the first floor, to view video from the home's security system. They watched in awe as a figure whom they'd dubbed 'The Reaper' made his way through the darkened courtyard, up the back of the house, and into the parlor where he subsequently beheaded Gabriel. They watched in silence as numerous explosions ripped the house apart, flinging bodies and body parts in all directions. After watching the video, Agents Burroughs and Carver sifted through the wreckage while quietly speculating as to who was responsible.

"This is way too sophisticated for a low-life loser like Simon. This was a precision hit. These guys were taken out by a trained pro, just like the one in New York. I'll even bet it was the same guy. He shot out the lights out before scaling that back wall. Bodyguards don't do that. This was a professional assassin."

"Okay, Agent Burroughs, if we rule out Simon, who else do we have? We know he had it in for Gabriel, because he was tired of being his bitch. So he hires a pro to come in and take him and about fifteen of his goons out. Then to send a message, he cut the bastard's head off."

"I'm not ruling Simon out at all. His connections afford him the convenience of being able to hire hitters from all over the globe. The question though is why would he have Gabriel's head delivered to his own house and then call the cops? Whoever did this meant to send a message to the both of them."

"Didn't Gabriel put a hit out on that Stratton guy? What if he's responsible for all this?"

"Stratton?" Burroughs quipped sarcastically. "Alexis Stratton is nothing more than an idiot who got caught with his dick in the wrong man's punch bowl. He may be a playboy, but he's not a killer, and he sure as hell couldn't pull something like this off."

"He does drive an Aston Martin and one of the witnesses is positive he saw one being chased down the interstate by two Range Rovers. There can't be many of them registered in Denver. And what about Jason, sir?" Carver asked while watching charred body parts being loaded onto a gurney. "He's still in Ohio, and we haven't been able to crack his codes yet."

"Hell, with Gabriel, the *Midwest Finest*, and the Tylers dead, Jason's case is shot right to hell. When I'm done with him, he'll be lucky if he and Castro still have jobs. All the same though, keep an eye on him and arrange a little surprise for him whenever he returns. I wanna make sure that he doesn't have a card up his sleeve that he hasn't played yet."

"Yes sir, but what about Simon?"

"That dumb, pothead son-of-a-bitch called the police, and now, they have his place locked down tighter than a virgin's ass. I'll swing by later to so see if he can shed some light on this."

Meanwhile in Worthington Ohio, Agents Castro and Blackhawk were walking around the smoldering farmhouse where Dawn had been taken. The midday air was filled with the pungent aroma of charred flesh, gasoline, and burnt wood. As they looked on in the late summer heat, police, arson investigators, CSI personnel, and a forensics team combed through the wreckage before carefully removing bodies and loading them into the coroner's vans.

"I can't believe this, Gabe," Agent Blackhawk said while shaking his head. "He murdered all of them, even some of the guys from his own unit. What the fuck is Burroughs doing?"

"C'mon, Jason, don't go jumping to conclusions. For all we know, this could still be a huge coincidence. It'll be weeks before the coroner can positively identify any of these bodies. For all we know, they could still be out there somewhere."

"Do you hear yourself, Gabe? Evelyn Norman was murdered right under our noses. Burroughs exterminated everyone else. Then to make it look like a hit, he killed a couple of ours. He's covering his tracks. He knows we're on to him and he's getting rid of the witnesses. He probably staged that so-called break in at my place in Denver."

"Oh yeah, I forgot about that," Castro replied nervously.

"The son-of-a-bitch had the nerve to try and coax my passwords out of me. He even had the audacity to implicate Stratton in the break-in. None of this shit is a coincidence, Gabe. It's all been carefully orchestrated to keep his buddies rich and Simon out of jail."

"Damn," Castro replied in disbelief. "You don't think they found what they were looking for, do you?"

"Not on my computer. All the same, once we get wrapped up here, I've got to get back to Denver. Once I assess the damage, I need to go see McNamara."

"Why?"

"Because if Burroughs is going to end my career, I'm going to make sure I end his too. I wanna see that fat fuck in cuffs for what he's done."

"I'm with you Jason. Whatever it takes, I've got your back," Castro declared as more bodies were hauled from the charred wreckage.

Later that afternoon, Tango and Alex were in the shop discussing the events of the past few weeks. Just like he was when they were upstairs, Tango was amazed at Alex's calm demeanor. In the last twenty four hours, he'd single-handedly killed two dozen men and from the sounds of it, he wasn't done yet.

"I hope you realize once the old man gets wind of this, he's gonna go ape shit. That's probably him now," Tango said when the shop's phone began ringing. "Where's the Aston Martin?"

"It's out at the airstrip."

"What kind of condition is it in?"

"It's filthy but the body held up great against those bullets. Thanks for the modifications."

"No problem," Tango replied before taking a huge gulp of coffee. "We'll go out there later with the flatbed and get it. I'm sure that by this time tomorrow, half the cops in the state will be looking for it."

That night as Alex and Tango journeyed to the airfield, Agent Burroughs arrived at Simon's compound. Though the forensics team and police had long since departed, Simon's nerves were still on edge. The last thing he needed was more attention being brought to his operation. Now in the wake of Gabriel's murder, he was faced with the notion that Burroughs himself may have masterminded this massacre like he did in Ohio. After all, he and his associates stood to lose a lot of money if Gabriel assumed power. As they sat in the parlor, Burroughs and Simon quietly sized one another up. Neither knew what the other was thinking, but it was clear that there was tension between them. Though a cloud of marijuana smoke hovered above the desk, Burroughs was completely oblivious to it. Years of working narcotics had made him all but immune to the effects.

"Nice work handling Gabriel," Burroughs said finally, interrupting the annoying silence. "Now maybe we can get down to business."

"Nice work?" Simon asked in shock. "Mi gwaan tell yu da same ting."

"It wasn't me, Simon. My team had nothing to do with it."

"Yu 'spect mi ta believe dat, Babylon? Gabriel bout to cut yu head off. Looks like yu return da favor. Yu wan him dead ta keep yu pockets fat."

"Don't think for a second that I don't know that you stand to profit from Gabriel's sudden demise. With him out of the way, you keep control of the American operations. The way I see it, you were tired of being his bitch and called in a pro to off him. A little theatrical if you ask me though."

"Mi no mon's bitch, Babylon!"

"Yeah, right," Burroughs snapped with a smirk. "You had me fooled for a long time. I thought when I started dealing with you that I was dealing with the head man. Imagine my surprise when I found out I was dealing with a lackey instead."

"Mind yu tongue Babylon. Pussyholes have died for less."

"Whatever you say, you ugly son-of-a-bitch. The fact of the matter is Gabriel is out of the picture and all your loose ends have been tied up. That being said, it's time for a new deal. You're gonna kick up an extra ten percent effective immediately."

"Ten percent?" Simon scoffed half-laughing. "I say fuckery, Babylon. Dat cost dear! Yu too likky-likky."

"Your black ass can't afford to have my people snooping around and interfering with your operations, because as we know, it's bad for business. So like I said before you *so* rudely cut me off, you are going to kick up and extra ten percent and in return I'll make the rest of your problems go away."

"And wen I an refuse?" Simon asked with flaring nostrils and boiling blood.

"Stop trying to be a hard ass," Burroughs replied, quickly dismissing Simon's assertion. "We both know you will. Now, go about your business as usual and you'll hear from me in a few days."

"Gabriel fadda was a don in da posse. Him death gwaan spill blood."

"That's your problem, not mine."

"It become yu problem wen war bruk out ere on yu streets," Simon growled before taking a long hit from his cigar.

"I'll see what I can do," Burroughs replied after briefly contemplating the proposition.

"Irie, fat man, irie."

Later that afternoon as Alex pounded relentlessly on Tango's heavy bag, television reporters broadcasted news about the violence that had erupted in the streets in the past twenty-four hours. His whook his head in disbelief each reporter put their own individual spin on the details. The more they talked, the harder he hit. Every punch, kick, knee, and elbow would have crushed a normal man, but the canvas bag withstood it; barely. It was like Miami all over again.

"That's right, Jim," began the young reporter as he stood in front of a burned out farm house, "we have confirmed that at least sixteen bodies were pulled from what's left of this house. Sources close to the investigation say that at least one of the victims was female, though that has yet to be confirmed. FBI and local police are currently on the scene trying to figure who these people are and how they ended up here. We'll keep you updated as we get more information on this gruesome discovery."
"Thank you, John. That was John Kramer on the scene from our CBS affiliate in Columbus, Ohio. In other, possibly related news, we've received reports that eight men were found murdered in a wooded area east of Denver. According to police and eyewitness reports, a gun battle erupted in downtown Denver and spilled out onto the interstate before ending just outside the reserve east if the city. We'll bring you more information as it develops."
"One thing about the news," Tango began after tossing Alex a towel, "you can count on it to be bad."

Before he could reply, Alex's phone began to ring.

"You know anybody from a 602 area code?" he asked before tossing Alex the phone.
"Nope. This is Alex."

"Alex, it's Tisha," sobbed the voice on the other end of the phone after a lengthy pause. "My momma is dead and I know Simon killed her."

"What?" he asked loud enough to get Tango's attention. "What do you mean he killed your mother?"

"I haven't spoken to Dawn in weeks, because we had a falling out. I called my mother Saturday morning and the receptionist told me she had an accident. That was no accident, Alex. The FBI was there. Momma was murdered. I tried calling back and the receptionist kept trying to direct me to an Agent Blackhawk with the FBI. Now the news is talking about how an FBI safe house was torched and sixteen bodies were pulled out of it. I know my sister was one of them."

"Tisha…honey, I'm so sorry. I don't know what to say."

"Why, Alex? Why momma? She never did anything to anybody. She was just a sweet old woman who loved her family. Why did she have to die?"

"Tisha, where are you?" Alex asked after looking at the number again.

"I'm in a shitty motel in Scottsdale, and I'm running out of money. I'm coming back to Denver."

"Don't come back to Denver, Tisha. If Simon killed your mother, you know he's going to kill you too. Take my advice and just run away. I'll send you some money. I don't want to know where you end up. At least that way you'll be safe."

"Alex!" she cried before breaking down again. "That bastard took everything away from me and now you're pushing me away when I need you the most? What kind of man are you?"

"I'm a man who can see that wherever you are right now, you're safe. He can't touch you. We know he's figured us out, and he'll be looking for me soon. Why risk your life in the process?"

"He's already taken my life, Alex. My mother's gone. My family's gone. I have nothing left to live for."

"You have your freedom. Take that to heart and be thankful. Anywhere you want to go, I'll take care of you. Please Tisha, I'm begging you. Don't come back to Denver."

"Goodbye, Alex. Of all the people in the world, I never thought you'd turn your back on me. Dawn once said I was nothing to you but some pussy on the side. I didn't believe it. I thought you loved me. Now, I know better."

"I do love you, Tisha."

"Fuck you, Alex. You don't know the meaning of that word."

Before he could say another word, the line went dead. Tisha saying he didn't know the meaning of love rung in Alex's ears like a church bell. Though he'd denied it all this time, he realized that he really did love her. But she wanted more. She wanted him to be in love.

"You wanna know where she is?" Tango asked while sitting at the computer console across the room.

"It's better if I don't."

"It's on the screen if you change your mind. I'm gonna get back to work on your car."

"Thanks, Tango."

"No problem, kid."

Later that afternoon, Agent Blackhawk returned to Denver. With the help of the maintenance men who'd changed the locks and repaired the doorframe, he slowly, but surely, put the apartment back to the way it was, or at least close to it. He couldn't stop wondering whether or not they'd return since they hadn't found what they were looking for. His next concern was the extent to which Burroughs had gone to cover his own ass. Jason knew that the break-in along with violating the chain-of-command would provide the spin they needed to implicate him in the Ohio murders as well. Though it wouldn't point the finger at him directly, it would give Burroughs enough leverage to sabotage his career.

As night fell on the city, the weary agent showered and prepared to go to sleep. Meanwhile outside his building, four men dressed in black fatigues exited a navy blue Ford Explorer and entered his lobby. Seconds later, Alex exited his black Lamborghini Aventador and followed them in. Within moments, the four men were gathered outside apartment 10E.

"Excuse me," Alex slurred while stumbling, "would one of you fine gentlemen happen to have a light?"

Inside, Agent Blackhawk was pacing the floor with a bath towel around his waist when he heard what sounded like a scuffle in the hallway. After taking a deep breath, he grabbed his gun and opened the door. Kneeling near the four unconscious men was his nemesis turned savior.

"Are they dead?" he asked while watching Alex root through their pockets.
"Nope, but they're going to wish they were," he replied while unmasking them one-by-one. "You know these guys?"
"Fischer, Baker, Daniels, and Carver: all members of Burroughs' elite investigation squad."
"Judging by the hardware, they weren't coming to bring you flowers," Alex said when he drew a suppressor equipped 9mm from one of their jackets.

"That's great! My boss is trying to kill me too. What-the-fuck am I gonna do now?"

"Get dressed and come with me, unless of course you think you can keep these shenanigans up all night."

"I'll be ready in a few minutes."

Minutes later after stuffing two duffle bags and a briefcase, Agent Blackhawk and Alex exited the building, leaving the would be attacker bound and gagged in the janitor's closet. A short while later they arrived at Tango's shop where they cruised into the vast showroom.

"Thanks for saving my ass back there."

"Your ass is far from safe," Alex replied when he exited the coupe. "Your boss has a bulls-eye on your back. Like me, you're one step from being labeled a fugitive."

"So what are we supposed to do? I mean, are we supposed to just hide out here at Tango's while my career circles the drain and Burroughs walks away a free man?"

"No. There's been too much bloodshed already. Tomorrow morning, I'm gonna put my ego aside and do what I should have done a long time ago. I'm gonna bring an end to this madness once and for all, and you're gonna help."

"How?" Agent Blackhawk asked while slinging one of the bags over his shoulder.

"I've got some friends in some very high places. They're a little pissed off at me right now, but I'm sure they'll be anxious to hear what you have to say."

"I can't imagine anyone being pissed at you, Stratton," he replied sarcastically.

"For that, you get to sleep in the shop," Alex replied before motioning to a cot in the corner.

At 9AM the next morning, Doc, and the rest of the team were assembled in his office watching replays of the weekend's news reports while combing through CCTV video and still photographs. Though none of the images were clear, everyone was sure that it was an Aston Martin that they were looking at. And by the looks of the precision driving, they had no doubts that Alex was the culprit. None of them, except Doc, could believe that he was capable of the wanton destruction that had been reported. Delilah's satellite imaging, however, placed him at the scene of both crimes.

"I can't believe Alex could just go off like this, Doc. I mean twenty-four dead and counting? There has to be a logical explanation."
"Of course there is, Mike. Alex has gone bat-shit crazy and is started hunting Jamaican cartel members."
"I don't necessarily agree with your assessment, Doc," Ko interrupted. "There's always a method to Alex's madness."
"Ko, there's no rhyme or reason for this senseless rampage, except that he's finally lost his mind. Do you have any idea how bad this would look if someone discovered that one of mine murdered two dozen men after tearing the entire city apart?"
"So what do we do, Doc?" Warren asked while watching Gabriel's security video.
"We've got to bring him in," Doc replied flatly.
"You're welcome to try."

Awestruck and full of disbelief, the seven men stared at the ominous, black-clad figure entering the room with Tango and unknown stranger in tow. One-by-one, they swallowed hard as Alex eyed them. Doc, who was

433

seated at the far end of the table, felt a sharp pain shoot through his neck.

"Let me make something clear to all of you. Contrary to popular belief, I'm not a sociopath. Those twenty-four men you're reading about got what they deserved: justice. Gabriel Malcolm put a hit out on me which eight men attempted to execute after I left my restaurant. They failed. Gabriel tried to do the same but wasn't up to the task. Now, which one of you is ready to climb into the ring with me?" Alex growled while glaring angrily at them.
"Boss, what the hell is going on and who is that?" Ko asked.
"The man on my right is Agent Jason Blackhawk of the FBI. He has the same problem I have. People are trying to frame and kill him because he has some information that he needs to share. We have a mutual problem and it's time to fix it. Are there any questions?"
"Then let's get started," Tango snapped before anyone could speak.

For the next three hours, Agent Blackhawk broke down every detail of this case from the beginning to the present. Through his own investigations coupled with the evidence that Alex had provided, he was able to piece together a lengthy paper trail on Agent Burroughs and several other senior agents. He was also able to establish motives for the mass murder that took place in Ohio and the one that almost took place in his apartment.

Meanwhile after a lengthy grilling and subsequent reprimand of Agent Castro, Agent Burroughs was called to St. Luke's Medical Center. He arrived at that ER and was shocked to see his four agents battered, bruised, and badly beaten.

"You're telling me that one man did this to you?" Burroughs growled while standing in the triage area. "Are you serious?"

"He came out of nowhere, asked for a light...next thing we knew we're waking up in a broom closet."

"Shut up, Fisher!"

"I'm telling you sir, I've never seen anything like this," Baker groaned while rubbing his bandaged head.

"I have," Carver began, while sitting on the edge of his bed in a neck brace and an arm sling. "We all have, in both New York and Boulder. His movements were lightening fast and deliberate, just like those hitters."

"Did you a happen to see the man who whipped your asses?"

"Stratton," Carver said flatly.

"Stratton?" Agent Burroughs scoffed. "You want me to believe that Alexis Stratton, a nobody, beat four of my agents senseless. Then he disarmed you, took your badges, and left you in a broom closet? The man is club owner for chissake! He was fucking Simon's wife! What the hell was he doing there and where is Jason?"

"We don't know, sir. When we got out of the closet, we came straight here. Jason's car was there, but he wasn't home."

"You're pathetic!" Burroughs shouted in disgust. "I sent you to do a simple job and you dropped the fucking ball again. Do I have to remind you what's at stake if we're caught?"

"No, sir, you don't," Carver groaned while massaging his shoulder.

"Good. Pull yourselves together and find Jason Blackhawk. In the meantime, I'll track down Mr. Stratton and see exactly what he knows."

After reviewing Agent Blackhawk's information, Doc and the team found themselves faced with another dilemma. After last night's car chase and subsequent massacre, Alex was quickly becoming a liability to the team. They knew it wouldn't be long before the Aston Martin was traced back to him. His run in at Agent Blackhawk's apartment only added fuel to the fire. There was also the matter of getting all this new information into the hands of the FBI director before Burroughs descended upon them.

"We have to contain this before it gets out of control," Doc declared after closing the folder that Jason had provided. "We have scores of dead witnesses, rogue FBI agents hunting one of their own, and one of mine turning the city into a warzone. I can't have this."

"We can't have criminals thinking they run the city either, badges or not," Alex snapped sarcastically.

"Let's start with your Aston Martin then, Alex. Where is it?" Doc asked while massaging his temples.

"It's at Tango's garage, out of sight and out of mind."

"Out of sight and out of mind? Do you realize that in a matter of hours, every law enforcement agency in the country is going to be looking for you and your car? There can't be many Aston Martins registered in the state of Colorado," Doc growled while staring at the fizzing concoction on his desk.

"There are nine to be exact. Four of them are DBS's and only two are registered in the city of Denver. Mine is the only one that happens to be charcoal gray."

"Don't worry about the Aston Martin, Doc," Tango assured him while checking the bar's selection of beverages. "The twins and I will take care of it. We'll have it detailed and restored in no time. That bullet proof shell only has minor damage to it. It's mostly dirt and cosmetics."

"Okay, what about the plates?" Doc asked, not fully convinced that their plan would be successful.

"The car has the same cloaking technology we use in the field. Why do you think the images are so shitty? Plus, my plate covers are smoked, so no one could have made them out, especially at those speeds. Look, as far as I'm concerned, the car isn't the issue. Keeping Jason alive long enough to get to McNamara is."

"I'll take care of that. In the meantime, I want *you* out of sight and out of mind."

"Come again?"

"I can't have you roaming the streets, Alex," Doc said after his previous frustrations subsided. "You have to lay low until we can do some damage control."

"Lay low as in hide?" Alex snapped angrily.

"No, kid; lay low as in stay the fuck outta the way!" Tango barked. "Look, Jason already told us Burroughs has his team stacked with trained killers. He sent four this time. Next time it could be forty. We can't monitor Burroughs, keeps tabs on Simon, and watch your back too."

"He's right, Alex," Ko added. "The feds have your place staked out. They're near your lobby and all around your building. They're waiting for you to slip up."

"If you don't listen to Doc, at least listen to Ko and Tango," Big Mike plead, finally breaking his silence. "Nobody is asking you to run or hide, just stay out of the way for a while."

"Fine," Alex surrendered before standing up. "I'll hang out at Tango's until we can get a handle on this nightmare. What about Jason?"

"Yes sir, what about me? I can't go home, and clearly, I can't just waltz into FBI HQ without Agent Burroughs knowing about it. The minute he gets wind of what I've done, he's gone."

"Leave that to me, son. I know Director McNamara personally. We go back a long way. In fact, we've collaborated several times in the recent past. I'll arrange a private meeting between the three of us."

"You can do that, sir?" Agent Blackhawk asked.

"Son, we're capable of a lot more than you can even imagine. What you're seeing here is just a glimpse of it. As far as that goes, I need you to understand something. When you go through those doors to blow the whistle, your career is over. Are you ready for that?"

"With all due respect sir, my career was over when they murdered my partner and left her body in that alley. I took this job to fight corruption, not be a part of it."

"Enough said," Doc replied before picking up the phone. "Yes, I'd like to speak with Director McNamara. Tell him it's an urgent call from Gregory McCallister. Bob, it's Austin," Doc began after a few moments of silence, "I have an Agent Blackhawk in my office whose been collaborating with one of my operatives on a highly sensitive investigation involving some of your top brass. We need to arrange a private meeting."

"How soon can you be in Arlington?" Director McNamara asked urgently.

"We can fly out tonight."

"I'll be waiting," he replied before quickly disconnecting the call.

"Whoa," Jason replied in shock.

"This is only the beginning," Alex said before he and Tango disappeared through the door. "I'm sick of this shit," Alex snapped a while later.

"What are you talking about, kid?" Tango asked while peering into the passenger seat.

"This lifestyle, I'm sick of it. After I'm done with Simon, I'm done with *The Agency*. No more missions. No more killing. No more drama. I want a nice normal life."

"Alex, do you even know what a normal life is? I mean, let's face it. Besides your college degrees and business ventures, what do you do with your time? I'll tell you. You kill people for a living. Do you realize how dysfunctional that is? Do you have any idea how much hell you're gonna have to go through to be normal?"

"What the hell does that mean?" Alex scoffed while staring out the window.

"You gotta learn to be like just like everyone outside that window; a drone. You gotta be completely oblivious to the world around you. Forget what you know about marksmanship and martial arts. You have to ignore everything we've learned and practiced. You have to pretend that nothing exists outside your own little box. Forget conspiracies, terrorists, dope kingpins, dictators, and the other vermin we're paid to kill. You gotta to learn to get up early, work all day, come home late, kiss your kids, screw your wife once in a while, and lead a dull boring life just like them. Being normal ain't in our DNA, kid."

"Thanks for the pep talk," Alex replied, both disgusted and defeated.

"It is what it is, kid."

Chapter 18

Over the course of the next week, details continued emerging about the murders that took place in both Worthington and Denver. Under Burroughs' watchful eye, the FBI leaked enough details about the massacres to make them look like the results of an investigation that had been compromised. During a Friday morning press conference, Agent Burroughs found himself at the forefront of a media circus during which he fielded several pre-selected questions. Among them was whether or not there was conspiracy within the FBI itself.

"At this point, we're exploring all possibilities," he replied nonchalantly.

At the same time, details were also emerging about the murders that took place in Boulder. Again under Burroughs' watchful eyes, Gabriel's death was classified as an "assassination" by a contingent of the Mexican drug cartel whom he had double-crossed.

Meanwhile, Tango and the twins were busy prepping the DBS for a repaint. By Saturday afternoon, it was returned to its original pristine state. Alex however, had become very restless. Being locked away at Tango's for a week had given him too much time to think. The deaths of Tisha's family, his issues with the FBI, and the deterioration of his working relationships had taken hefty tolls on his nerves. By Saturday evening, anxiety and loneliness had all but consumed him. He missed Lynn more than he thought possible. Though short, the time they spent together had given him reason to revisit the idea of retirement. Alex wondered what type of husband and father he might be. As he sat at the shop's multi-screened console, he wondered if he could give up the one part of his life that he knew the best. Tango's description of a normal life was as unsettling as it was boring. Though he'd earned more money than he could dream of spending, Alex still wondered what he would actually do for 'work.' Before finally going to bed, he sent Lynn a text message to remind her of his invitation to visit him in Denver.

By Sunday morning, Agent Burroughs was beside himself with anger because his office had no leads on Alex's or Jason's whereabouts. He'd also become increasingly suspicious of Castro and resorted to having him followed as well.

"This isn't looking good," Agent Burroughs declared while hacking and sawing through the steak on his plate. "With both Blackhawk and Stratton M.I.A., I'm hard pressed to build a case against either of them."
"We're trying to find them sir, but they've gone off the grid. Our guys are scouring the city looking for Stratton's car. Despite the damage it should have taken, there isn't a single vendor that's ordered body or engine parts for an Aston Martin in the past two months."
"Stay on it, Baker," Burroughs commanded. "That car has to turn up somewhere. What about Jason?"
"Nothing sir," Agent Carver replied. "Our guys are watching his place, monitoring his credit and debit cards, and his expense account. He hasn't made a peep since that night Stratton jumped us."
"Two fugitives don't just disappear off the fucking planet!" Burroughs shouted before pounding the table and rattling the dishes atop it. "I want them found got-dammit! I don't care what you have to do. I don't care

where they are! I want them found tonight! Am I making myself clear?"

"Yes, sir," Agent Baker replied after noticing the attention they had drawn.

"Good, now pay this bill and get back to work," Burroughs growled before leaving the table.

By Monday afternoon, Alex had reached his limit. He'd finally destroyed Tango's heavy bag and had taken to pacing back and forth through the loft like a caged panther. He was fed up with the endless lectures, Tango's terrible cooking, and the loose women that had been parading around. He was hungry, bored, and nearly psychotic. He needed some air and some real food.

After a long hot shower, Alex got dressed and walked down into the shop where he expected to find his mentor hard at work on either a tattoo or a car. Luckily, he was nowhere to be found and though he was tempted, Alex thought twice about taking the DBS. By now, every cop and fed in the city was looking for it. Instead he took 'Eleanor', Tango's two-tone gray '67 Shelby Mustang clone. After a short tour of the city, which he hadn't seen in what felt like forever, Alex valet parked at his curbside café. Within moments of sitting down, he found himself besieged by undercover FBI agents.

Meanwhile in his office, Agent Burroughs was nervously sifting through the stacks of files on his desk. His window for throwing suspicion off himself and onto Jason or Alex was closing rapidly. In addition to that, Burroughs had another set issues brewing. He hadn't talked to Simon in days, and though he had him under surveillance twenty four-seven, Burroughs was convinced that he was up to something. His spotters inside Simon's cartel hadn't been able to provide him any concrete evidence to that effect though. Suddenly, the phone rang and just like that, manna rained from the heavens.

"This is Burroughs."
"Sir, we have Stratton."
"Where the hell is he?"
"He's at his cafe ordering lunch, sir."
"Don't let him out of your sights. I'm on the way," Burroughs yelled after bolting up from his chair and grabbing his blazer.

Everyone in the office, including Agent Castro watched while Burroughs, Carver, Baker, Fischer, and Daniels darted towards the elevators. Several minutes later, while sipping Muscatto and waiting for his food to arrive, a smile crossed Alex's face. A pair of Black Dodge Chargers screeched to a halt at the curbside, and when they did, out stepped Burroughs and company. After commandeering the two tables nearest him, four pissed off agents sat scowling at Alex while Agent Burroughs helped himself to glass of wine.

"I had no idea this café was so popular with the feds," Alex said after laying his paper on the table. "I've got to change the menu. You guys are bad for business."
"Very funny," Burroughs replied after inhaling his drink. "You're a hard man to find, Mr. Stratton."
"Really? Did you check my office?"
"What office?" Burroughs scoffed before looking at his bewildered team. "Never mind. You know, I woke up this morning contemplating whether or not miracles actually existed. Then low and behold I get a call stating

that you're right here under my nose. Do you have any idea how good that made me feel?"

"Does it look I care?" Alex asked sarcastically.

"You see these four men surrounding us, Alex? They're very upset with you for jumping them, and would like nothing more than to bring you in so they can question you with extreme prejudice. But before they do, I'd like to know something."

"What's that chubby? And please, call me Mr. Stratton."

"I want you to tell me where Agent Blackhawk is."

"You really wanna know?" Alex asked with a sinister grin etched across his face.

"Yes, Mr. Stratton, I really wanna know."

"He's at a secret meeting with Director McNamara. They're discussing some evidence we uncovered that links you and some of you cohorts to bribery, extortion, and murder schemes involving Simon's cartel. In addition to that, we have proof of evidence tampering and wire fraud. Did I also mention the attempted murder of a Federal Agent, Dawn Tyler, and several other witnesses?"

"You're bluffing," Burroughs responded defiantly while his four counterparts sat visibly shaken.

"Am I? Then why are they sweating?" Alex asked, grinning as he inspected the watery beads that were forming on Burroughs's brow.

"You almost had me, Stratton; almost. Now let's get down to business. A few nights ago, an Aston Martin DBS like the one owned by your company was involved in a shootout that began not far from here and ended out by the reserve. Know what else?"

"Do tell."

"We found the other two vehicles involved in that same shootout. They were burned to a crisp along with seven of the eight passengers. The eighth was shot in the head after his body was thrown from the wreckage."

"I see. And exactly what does the have to do with me?"

"Well for starters, my office has accounted for all the Aston Martins in Colorado except yours. We can end all of this if you tell me where it is."

"Do you have a warrant?" Alex asked while leaning back in his chair and crossing his legs.

"Do I need one, Mr. Stratton?"

"If you wanna see my car, then yes, you do. After all, why should I make your job easy? Now, are there any other ridiculous accusations you'd like to make?"

"As a matter of fact, there are. Later that same night, some dude with a fetish for cloaks and daggers strolled into a Boulder residence and murdered sixteen men, all Jamaicans like the ones from the wreckage. One of them was even beheaded. Strangely enough, that head ended up on the lawn of Simon Felix, your girlfriend's husband. Judging by the pounding you put on my men, I'd say that you could have pulled that off too. Here's the icing on the cake, though. Tisha Norman hasn't been seen in a while and was last spotted leaving your building. Do you have any idea where she would have gone?"

"At the rate her family is dying off, I'd say into hiding."

"Okay smart ass, let's do it this way. I've got twenty four stiffs, a missing house wife, and a suspect Aston Martin. It's all pointing to you, Mr. Stratton."

"And your plan is to pin two dozen homicides and a missing person on me? Good luck," Alex scoffed while reaching for his glass of water.

"I'm the FBI, asshole. I can pin this on anyone I want. It comes with the territory. Now, with the amount of blood on your hands and your unwillingness to cooperate, I have enough to get you into custody, where I'm sure these gentlemen behind us would love perform a lengthy interrogation."

445

"Well, if it's anything like the one they performed in the hallway of Agent Blackhawk's building, I'll take my chances," Alex smirked. "But since we're talking, let's flip the script for a moment, shall we? Keep in mind it's not what you know. It's what you can prove and here's what I can prove. In all the years you've been investigating Simon, you've only gotten one thing right. Yes, I am fucking his wife; quite well in fact. Sadly, that's all you have, and from that, you're trying to fabricate an elaborate scheme to cover-up your own agreement to turn your head while he deals drugs and murders witnesses."

"That's bullshit and you know it!" Burroughs snapped, drawing even more attention to himself and his entourage.

"I did some background checking on you, Agent Burroughs, and I uncovered some serious financial discrepancies. One of the biggest is the sixty foot Bertram you have docked in Tampa Bay. I'm rich, and I don't own a boat of that caliber. That had to set you back quite a bit. But that's not all. You have two homes; one in Denver and another in Tampa. You have three daughters in very good colleges, which I'm sure the taxpayers are happy to fund for you."

"I invest well, asshole. What's it to you?"

"Investment," Alex began half laughing, "is that what you're calling it now? Look, I know what you're thinking. I'm speculating at this point, right? That's where you're wrong and here's something else I can prove. Your own people are on to you and you know it. That's why you're wiping them out one-by-one. That massacre in Worthington was just your way of tying up some loose ends. Jason was another one. Sending these goons to his house to murder him was the icing on the cake."

The looks on their faces said it all. Alex had them. He'd completely dissected their entire operation. Though they were exposed, Burroughs maintained his poker face; barely. He and his benefactors had too much riding on their agreement with Simon to let it slip away. The wily veteran knew that Alex had more information than he was letting on and the fact that he'd revealed Jason's whereabouts was the tip of the iceberg. *Was Jason really talking to McNamara? If so, what exactly did he know and how much did he share?* Letting Alex off the hook this early would be disastrous, and Burroughs knew it. He had to keep pressing for information.

"Here's something else, jackass. I've been to Simon's home numerous times, even fucked his wife in his bed. At one time, I knew his operation inside-and-out. He's been running game for years but nothing like the one he's been running on you. Watching him play you like a fiddle has been very entertaining. Did you know he keeps a coded ledger in his parlor, and that inside that ledger are some very detailed entries that include names, dates, and amounts? Gabriel had one too, but it was probably blown all to hell along with him. Then again, maybe it was recovered from the debris. Whatever the case, I remember your name very vividly, which means you had the motive to kill him. Wanna know what else?"

"Enlighten me," Burroughs growled angrily.

"Simon's been feeding information about you to someone in your very own office. I guess you figured if he double crossed you, you'd simply set your dogs loose on him. It looks like he beat you to the punch, though. He's just waiting for you to try to fuck him over."

447

Alex's bluff was a thing of beauty. While Carver, Baker, Fischer, and Daniels sat quietly staring back and forth at each other, Burroughs was fending off a total meltdown. The once tough senior agent had cracked. Alex however, was as cool as a cucumber. The 'Black Mamba' had struck first and the blow was deadly. Even though he was lying, Alex had them right where he had wanted them.

"I don't believe you."

"Really?" Alex asked with a smirk. "Here's the clincher. Tisha can put you at the house too, even going so far as to point out when you were there to receive payoffs. She also has a copy of the ledger, and she knows what all the codes mean. I know because we discussed it in bed. You wanted Gabriel dead more than anyone else. In fact, you needed him dead, because he'd been trying to cancel your meal ticket for years. With him outta the game, it's business as usual for you and Simon, right? Tisha's disappearance is most likely the result of another loose end you had to tie up."

"What do you want, Stratton?"

"I want to humiliate you. I want you to suffer. I want the five of you to go home and draft letters of resignation effective immediately. None of you is fit to wear those badges in your pockets. Secondly, and this is for you Agent Burroughs. I want you to go home and think of a number, a very big number. When you do, I want you to give me a call."

"Are you out of your fucking mind?" Burroughs barked when Alex slid his card across the table. "Are you trying to blackmail me, a federal agent, for crissake? Do you realize I can have you killed with a snap of my fingers?"

"If you could, you would have already done it," Alex replied while inspecting his nails.

"You clearly don't know who you're fucking with, Stratton! I've got trained killers on my payroll. You

think you're safe because you and some whore saw some bullshit in a ledger? You think Blackhawk can drop a dime on me and get away with it? I own McNamara! I am the Federal Bureau of Investigations! I'll bury you in that piece-of-shit Aston Martin, you prick!"
"Is that your gun you're reaching for Agent Burroughs? Are you really going to shoot an unarmed man in the middle of this crowded café?"

After looking around and seeing numerous eyes fixed on them, Burroughs removed his hand from his blazer, grabbed the card, and excused himself from the café. His four man entourage quickly exited behind him followed by the six other agents who were seated throughout the café. Once they had driven out of sight, Alex removed the digital recorder from his lap and placed it on the table in front of him. With a smile on his face, he put his Bluetooth in his ear.

"Delilah."
"Yes, Black Mamba?"
"I want his phones, every last one of them."
"I'll get right on it," she replied.

Later that night after a lengthy lecture from Tango, Alex sat at the console patiently monitoring signals from the business card he'd given Agent Burroughs. At about 2:23AM, his vigilance was rewarded. Still fuming from Alex's revelations, Burroughs called Simon's phone repeatedly until he finally answered it.

"Wa yu wan, Babylon?"
"You sneaky son-of-a-bitch, you think you can set me up and get away with it? You think I'm gonna sit here and

wait while you railroad me? I made you, you banana sucking piece-a-shit!"

"Doncha' bring dat banana sheet ere mon, yu hear??!!!! Yu dead wit a snap of mi fingas!"

"You're lucky I don't send a team into your house right now and blow your ugly black ass to hell! I know all about your inside man and the ledgers and I know your whore of a wife has one too! You think you can fuck me over? I can nail your ass right now for multiple murders and make them stick! Between Gabriel, your sister-in-law, and the rappers, you're guaranteed a trip to the gas chamber. Add my six agents and the other twenty plus stiffs that keep piling up, and you're suddenly swimming in an ocean of blood. Don't think I can't pull it off, because I can, motherfucker! I have all kinds of evidence against you and what I don't have, I can sure as hell create!"

"Whacha talkin' bout, Babylon? Yu sounding real paranoid."

"Don't toy with me, Simon! My army is bigger and deadlier than yours, and they all have badges! One word from me and your whole operation is shutdown! I have all the cards, and you have nothing. You got that? I'll burn your shit to the ground!"

"Yu wan bring war? Yu wan I an dead? Try it blood clot! Yu bosses take deh last dime from dis shotta! From dis minute, yu cut off!"

Before Burroughs could utter a sound, the line went dead. His meal ticket had officially been canceled. Alex's plan had worked to perfection. He'd killed both Simon and Agent Burroughs without firing a single shot.

The next afternoon and much to Tango's dislike, Alex returned to the comfort of his penthouse. After a workout and a hot shower, he walked in the kitchen and began seasoning some chicken breasts while angel hair pasta boiled in the stove. When he placed the chicken in the oven, the phone rang.

"Hello, this is Alex."
"Mr. Stratton, this is Chet. I have a Miss Lynn Turner at the desk, sir. Should I send her up?"
"Lynn's here? Now?"
"Yes sir, she's here in the lobby."
"Sure Chet, send her up," Alex replied before disconnecting the call and looking around his place. *You've got to be kidding me,* he thought.

There couldn't have been a worse time for Lynn to show up than now. At Simon's request, Gabriel had just tried to kill him and Alex was sure more hit men would follow. Since his meeting with Burroughs, the Feds weren't about to let up. Doc and Jason were still somewhere between Virginia and Denver and to make matters worse Tisha was missing and was probably en route to Denver. Alex couldn't begin to imagine how he'd explain all of this, or even protect Lynn if someone came after him. After all, she was convinced that he was nothing more than a real estate investor. If it came down to it, the truth would be next to impossible to keep hidden. While leaning against the counter massaging his throbbing temples, Alex heard a series of ear-splitting knocks at the door. To him, each one sounded like thunder. After taking a couple of deep breaths, he removed his apron and put on his game-face.

Meanwhile on the other side of the cherry-stained, six-pocket doors, Lynn waited nervously with Chet and her bags. She had no idea what awaited her on the other side. Apprehension and curiosity had battled within her from the moment she decided to return to Denver up

451

until she arrived at Alex's door. Her heart fluttered when she heard the tumblers inside the lock. Goosebumps rose on her flesh when light began peeping around the opening door. The warmth in his smile almost made her knees buckle.

"Welcome home, baby."

His words, *'Welcome home baby,'* were like music to her ears. Lynn struggled with a massive lump in her throat when Alex took her in his arms and gently kissed her lips. His arms felt like Heaven as they nestled her close to his chest with his heart happily thumping and thudding in her ear.

"As much as I'd love to stand here with you in my arms, this hallway can get chilly, and I have to check on dinner."
"Okay," she chuckled when she let him go and watched him grab her bags.
"Follow me, sexy."

The aromas of seasoned chicken and black cherry candles filled the air. Lynn looked around but couldn't find a single item out of its place. Every room was meticulously decorated with items she'd only seen in magazines or in the homes of wealthy socialites. Priceless crystal lined the table, buffet, and china cabinet, while custom window treatments held the sun at bay. The built-in fireplace was one of the tallest she had ever seen, and were it not for the brick wall at the back of it, someone could literally walk straight through it. On the mantle above it were several photographs of people she assumed were close to her enigmatic lover. High on the wall above the mantle was a painting of a half naked woman whose face and intimate body parts were covered by the large hat she was wearing. Lynn didn't know whether it was art or one of his past lovers, but the picture was exquisite.

The view from the patio to Lynn's right was breathtaking. As the sun settled in the west, it painted a picturesque silhouette behind the buildings in front of it. The warmth on her face and body was just enough to offset to coolness of the early autumn breeze.

"Do you like it?" Alex asked when he walked up behind her and wrapped his arms around her waist.

"I love it," Lynn cooed while resting her head on his shoulder.

"Dinner will be ready in a bit. I have chicken parmesan, angel hair pasta in seasoned sauce, tossed salads, garlic bread. Sound good?"

"It sounds delicious, baby."

"Splendid," he replied before kissing her cheek. "I laid out a towel and washcloths for you. I figured you'd want to freshen up before dinner."

"You read my mind."

"I put your bags in the closet as well," Alex began moments later when they entered the massive bedroom.

Lynn fell head-over-heels in love with the massive bookcase headboard and the California king attached to it. The matching nightstands, dresser, and bureau with their black matte finish and marble tops were the cat's meow. It was the fireplace at the foot of the bed sealed the deal. If this was what heaven was like, Lynn was determined not to leave.

The octagon shaped closet reminded her of an upscale department store. The acres of fine linens, tailored suits, shirts, and high-end shoes lining the walls inside this brightly-lit showplace were nothing short of stunning. His sweaters, jeans, thermals, slacks, shirts, jackets, coats, ties, and shoes were neatly stored on shelves in several built-in compartments. It was beyond Lynn's understanding how a man whose life seemed to go at a mile-a-minute could maintain so much order. The skyscraper-shaped jewelry box mounted on a carrousel in the middle of the floor stole the show.

"I cleared some additional space to hang your things up, if you'd like."
"I can't believe my eyes! Baby, this is amazing," Lynn cooed before turning around and smiling at him.

After a lengthy, passionate kiss, Alex exited the bedroom and closed the door behind him. Moments later with hot water cascading all over her body, Lynn was surrounded by purple haze. The darkened bathroom with all its chrome and marble glistened like jewelry around her. Before Lynn knew it, she'd been totally seduced by Alex's lifestyle. He had everything she could ever want; wealth, a beautiful home, taste, charisma, and class. The thought of making love to him in his bed sent chills up and down her spine. He'd already proven that he could satisfy her physical needs, but now she saw firsthand his ability to satisfy her financial needs as well.

Just as she was about to be swept away by this fantasy whirlwind, Lynn snapped back to reality and when she did, hesitation and anxiety set in. Even though she'd made love to Alex, she still didn't know him that well. Now she was in his home, and surely if they shared his bed, he'd expect her to make love to him again. Their chance encounter in Cincinnati made her throw caution to the wind. Now while standing in his shower, the wind threw caution back at her. While she wrestled with her apprehensions, Alex was on the patio fending off a nervous breakdown.

"I don't care what you have to do, Alex. Put her on the next thing smoking and get her the fuck out there!"

"It's not that easy, Tango. After all, I did invite her."

"Then un-invite her dammit!" he growled. "Look, Alex. All bullshit aside, do you have any idea how dangerous her being here is? Let's look at the facts for a moment. The leader of a Jamaican drug gang wants you dead and recently made an attempt on your life. The feds are watching every move you make. On top of all that you're the prime suspect in at least two dozen murders. With all that going on, there's no possible way you can keep your head on swivel around the clock. C'mon Alex, something has to give."

"You're right, Tango. I'll think of something. She'll be getting out of the shower soon. We'll have dinner then I'll make up a lame excuse and put her on a plane back home. I'll be back on the job in the A.M.," Alex replied into his Bluetooth while pacing back and forth.

"That's my boy," Tango replied before disconnecting the call.

Even though he'd heard it from Alex's lips, Tango knew he was lying and Alex knew it too. He loved Lynn, and he needed her. Regardless of the costs, Alex was willing to risk everything just to have a few moments of peace. She didn't have to know his dark secrets right now, or at least that's what Alex kept telling himself.

Back in the bedroom, a totally renewed Lynn sat on the bed's edge wrapped in a fluffy black bath towel. Next to her were a white robe and a pair of fluffy slippers. Surrounded by serenity and the sultry sounds of neo-soul, she massaged cocoa butter into her soft bronze skin. Though she had no idea what was waiting for her on the other side of the bedroom door, Lynn was anticipating it with schoolgirl-like giddiness. Her time with Alex in Cincinnati had been too brief to truly enjoy, and she was determined to rectify that for both of them. After contemplating walking out and greeting him with nothing more than a smile on, she removed the towel and put the robe on.

Waiting for her at the bedroom door was her lover with a glass of chilled Bollinger, 1965 and a single red rose. She took his gifts and smiled before taking a long sip of wine. Lynn followed Alex to the table where she stopped and admired the spread before them. After helping her to her seat, Alex placed a napkin in her lap, refilled her glass, and prepared her salad. She was convinced she'd stepped out of the shower and into a dream. Alex's attentiveness was turning her on so fast that she had to clinch her thighs to catch the moisture.

"I hope you like it," he smiled after taking a seat and placing a napkin on his own lap.
"Are you sure you're not trying to spoil me, Alex? Because if you're not, you're failing miserably. Where did you learn to cook like this?"
"One of my best friends is a master chef. I met him a few years ago while I was working in Europe. His food was so good I hired him to run all my restaurants."
"Wow! It must be pretty cool to have money at your disposal like that," Lynn said, remembering the financial windfall she'd just received.
"It has its moments, but it requires me to work long hours, travel extensively, and to spend more time than I'd like away from home. To be honest, I don't see this place much."

"You're kidding," she replied while studying his décor. "It looks like you spent ages putting this place together."

"This place is the product of a baby sister with a lot of time on her hands and unlimited access to my credit cards. If she likes it, she buys it."

"Wow!" Lynn chuckled. "Just when I think I might have you figured out, I learn something new about you, Alexis Stratton."

"Is that good or bad?" he asked while gazing into her shimmering eyes.

"I don't know yet, but I think I like it. Would you bless the food so we can eat? I'm starving."

"My pleasure," he said before taking her by the hand. "Heavenly Father, we thank you for allowing us to gather before you in the spirit of sharing, and in the spirit of love. We pray that you dwell amongst us as we share this meal, this time, and all the things that you have in store, both seen and unseen. We ask these things in Jesus' name, Amen. So honey," Alex began after picking up his fork, "what finally made you decide to come back to Denver?"

"Well, I decided that I needed a break from the Cincinnati. And get this, Dave Weltman contacted us about another account my dad had for us."

"Really?"

"Yes, and it had a million dollars in it just like the first. I'm not greedy, but two million is a whole lot better than one. But I won't complain. After a ten-percent deduction for processing, Chelle got her beauty shop and I got registered to go to medical school."

That greedy son-of-a-bitch, Alex thought to himself. "That's great. I'm glad you all received that blessing."

"Me too, and Alex, you should see Chelle's shop. With your investor's help, it's gorgeous! It has hard wood floors, flat screens on the walls, and eight stylist stations with pedestal sinks and all new equipment. She also has two nail techs on sight and four massage chairs. Best of all, we put the kids in a private school and bought a new house with two full and two half baths!"

"It sounds like you've been busy," Alex said with a grin.

"I told you great things happen when you have faith."

"The best thing to happen to me lately, though, is you walking into my life. Since I met you, my whole world has opened up. You don't have to lie and say you feel the same way. I'm just expressing my feelings."

"You're right. I don't have to lie, so I won't. Meeting you has been like a weight being lifted off my chest. I can breathe again. I'm so glad you're here, and I'll do everything I can to make sure that you have the time of your life. My home is your home."

The conviction and sincerity in his voice almost brought tears to Lynn's eyes. As she gazed into his eyes, her heart began beating to the rhythm of the soft tune playing in the background. Alex was the total package; her prince charming in the flesh. After dinner, they retired to the patio, where they lit the torches and enjoyed the beautiful night sky. With Lynn on his lap and a blanket wrapped around them, they held each other close while listening to the sounds of the city below. The snow capped mountains in the distance looked simply majestic.

Later that night while sleeping peacefully at Alex's side, Lynn was suddenly awakened by a series of groans and twitches. At first she tried to dismiss it, but it got progressively worse with each passing second. Suddenly, Alex's groans turned to growls, and before long he was mumbling something in Japanese. Lynn rolled over and watched in horror as he struggled beneath the covers. It looked like he was fighting for his life. Helpless and confused, she watched while he kicked and clawed until he finally freed himself. Without looking in her direction or saying a word, Alex jumped up and bolted out of the bedroom. Now sitting alone, Lynn clutched the covers close to her heart and tried to make sense of what she'd just seen. She'd never witnessed a display that intense. Though she wanted to follow him, she decided that it was best to leave well enough alone for now.

While sitting at his computer console, Alex's tear-filled eyes were glued to the screen. In front of him was a newspaper article with a headline that read, "Model Latest Victim in Miami Drug War." His mind kept replaying that night's events over and over. Its images were etched onto his memory like graffiti. Now, years later, it was like déjà vu. Once again, he was hunting Simon and once again, blood was spilling onto the streets. He began to wonder if going against Tango's advice to send her home was a good idea since the body count was steadily mounting. Alex couldn't imagine Lynn being one of them. Despite his best efforts, he knew there was no way he could protect either of them if this war escalated. It had to end; now. Hours after she'd fallen back asleep, Lynn was awakened by the feel of Alex climbing into bed and softly kissing her partially exposed shoulder.

"Good morning, baby. Are you leaving me already?" she asked when she saw that he was fully dressed. "Where are you off to?"
"Something major came up at the office, and I have to go in for a while. I promise I won't be too long. The place is yours and everything you need is right here. Okay?"
"Okay, baby. Alex, is everything okay," she asked with his display from earlier still fresh in her mind.

"Sure babe, why do you ask?"

"Well, it's just that...never mind. You have a good meeting and hurry back home."

"I will," he replied before kissing her lips and leaving.

Chapter 19

Moments later, Alex was standing in his garage. With the feds on his trail and his vehicular choices severely limited, he was bedside himself with frustration. He figured that by now, his Caddies, his and Tango's Shelby Mustangs, his Camaro, and his M5, were all compromised. *I haven't driven you in a while,* he thought after looking at the silver 911 Cabriolet parked in the corner. Within seconds of rumbling to life, the Porsche was weaving and winding its way towards the garage's exit. After cruising to its edge and looking around, Alex was surprised to see no feds or police parked near his building. Except for regular traffic, it was totally clear. While driving through downtown, he continued searching for Feds but found none. Within minutes, he was parked in *'The Agency's* garage and headed up the elevator to the top floor.

"You know," Doc began when Alex entered the conference room, "you're like that teenage kid that parents dread leaving home alone. You're too old for a babysitter, yet you constantly prove how badly you need one. We ask you to lay low, and what do you do? You steal Tango's car, leave the garage, and go to one of the hottest places in the city; your penthouse! From there you proceed to go to your café, where you confront Agent Burroughs, and now you have some strange woman staying with you."
"You told him I stole your car?" Alex asked when he looked across the table.
"He put two and two together," Tango replied with a grin.

461

"Never mind that, dipshit. Do you have any idea what kind of heat you're bringing to us?" Doc growled angrily.

"It's about to cool off," Alex replied while reaching into his pocket and pulling out a digital recorder.

"What's this?" Agent Blackhawk asked after Alex slid it across the table to him.

"Press play."

Within seconds, the room went silent as the recording began to play. Their heads shook in amazement while listening to the exchange. Once again, Alex had proven that he was at his most dangerous when his back was against the wall.

"There's more," he announced when the recording ended and he pulled a CD case from his blazer. "This is a conversation between Burroughs and Simon hours after the café incident. I think you'll find everything you need to take him down once you listen to it."

"Making a case with illegally obtained recordings can be very difficult Alex."

"I know, Jason. That's why I'm giving them to you," he replied when he slid the jewel case across the table. "Speaking of which, how'd your meeting with Director McNamara go?"

"We're waiting for him to green light 'Operation Clean House.' On his word, we're going to execute arrest warrants against everyone one on that list you provided. He's in the process of securing subpoenas to temporarily freeze all their assets. Once that's done, we'll move in."

"And how's your partner Castro?" Alex asked after sizing Jason up.

"He's not doing too well, and he's as anxious as I am."

"Good. As much as it may pain him, we need him to stay as close to Burroughs as he can, at least for a little while longer."

"All that aside," Doc interrupted, "we still have a big problem Alex; Lynn. She can't stay."

"Excuse me?" Alex replied with a scowl.

"You heard me, she can't stay."

"With all due respect Doc, you can kiss my ass! I'm not asking or telling Lynn to leave. She just got here and besides, that would be flat out rude and inconsiderate."

"Rude and inconsiderate?" Doc fumed. "Isn't there enough blood on your hands? You've already buried one lover because of your games with Simon. What do you think is going to happen to Lynn if she stays?"

"Lynn will be fine, old man."

"Yeah, but will you?" Big Mike asked with more conviction than Alex wanted to deal with. "Look bro, you're playing this entirely too close to the chest and if you keep it up, all your problems are gonna show up right at your front door."

"Are you all done? She's staying; end of story," Alex snapped before bolting up from the table and walking towards the door.

"I guess so."

"Good. And, Tango?"

"What's up kid?"

"All my cars have been compromised. I need some new ones."

"I'll see what I can do."

"I don't know whether to admire him or hate him," Agent Blackhawk said after Alex disappeared.

"We're split on that one too," Big Mike replied with a smile and a wink.

As Alex was about to exit the garage, Tango stepped out of the stairwell and into his path. As the Porsche sat idling, he walked up to the passenger side and pulled the door handle.

"What's up?" Alex asked when Tango climbed in.

"Just drive kid."

"Where are we going?"

"Your place and take the scenic route."

"My place? Why do you wanna go to my place?"

"Because I'd like my Shelby back," Tango replied with a grin.

"Ok, will do."

"You know Alex," Tango began after a few moments of silence, "contrary to what you may believe, there isn't a guy in that room that doesn't want what's best for you. But when you go off on these tangents, you tend to make us nervous. Your confrontation with Agent Burroughs didn't help the confidence factor either."

"Running and hiding doesn't suit me, Tango. You of all people should know that."

"Yeah, I know it doesn't, but we've never had to deal with this kind of heat before."

"I knew Burroughs didn't have the balls to arrest me. And if you're about to tell me how bad you all think I fucked up, don't bother because I already know."

"I'm not about to lecture you, kid. I'm proud to see you taking ownership of this mess and rectifying it with your brain instead of your muscles. No, what I wanna talk to you about is Lynn."

"What about her?"

"Are you truly ready for this again?" Tango asked.

"I don't know, man. I had another nightmare about Miami last night. Only this time, instead of Simone dying in my arms, it was Lynn."

"That's what I've been trying to tell you, Alex. Her being here is putting you both at risk. You can't be everywhere at once. This thing is too far out of hand. Something has to give."

"I know that, Tango, and trust me, I've thought about it every moment since I met her. The last thing I want is for anything to happen to her."

"Do you love her, Alex?"

"And what if I do?"

"Then you're a damned fool," Tango replied sharply. "Ok, so you love her. The worst thing that can happen is that she loves you back. Because if she does, she's gonna wanna be inside your head to see what makes you tick. And if you love her, really love her you're going to have to let her in. Then what?"

"I don't know, Tango."

"Well, I do. Best case scenario is that she simply walks away free and clear. However if she panics and runs, you'll have to consider those consequences as well."

"Consequences?"

"The same consequences you faced when you found yourself getting in too deep with the doc, and don't trick yourself into thinking this situation is any different than you faced with her or Simone. If the shit hits that fan, either you or someone else in 'The Agency' may have to take her out. Are you ready for that?"

"I'll cross that bridge if and when I come to it. For now I'm content to be happy."

"Yes, but will she be happy? Don't get me wrong, Alex. She sounds like a special woman and I sure as hell don't want you to spend the rest of your life alone. But you have to be careful with this slippery slope you're on."

"She is special, Tango. She's special to me."

"Then why didn't you tell her where the money came from?" Tango fired back.

"Why does that matter?"

"Because if you go in lying, you'll have to keep the lies going. Then one day without warning, all those lies are gonna show up at your door."

465

"What do you suggest I do?"

"Go with your gut, not your heart, son. Don't let your ego get in the way this time. Protecting her isn't going to be easy with Simon and the cops on your ass. Think long and hard about it. I trust you to make the best decision for both of you, not just yourself."

"I can protect her, Tango," Alex declared with more conviction in his voice than Tango had heard before.

"I trust you kid. Now take me to meet my daughter."

Meanwhile at Simon's compound, Tisha's dirt-splattered coupe crawled to a stop behind the S 550 and the Rovers. To her surprise, there were only two sentries posted near the front entrance, and neither one of them budged when she opened her door. Upon entering the foyer, however, she saw twice the number of guards than were normally there. It looked like they were preparing to go to war. Each one was armed with the largest machine guns she'd ever seen.

"Jus stay deh," commanded the sentry posted at the patio doors when she entered the dining room.

Tisha took a deep breath and watched as he walked over to Simon and whispered in his ear. After looking over his shoulder, Simon nodded at the sentry who then returned to the doors and escorted her to the table.

"Gwaan inna gates," he commanded while snapping his fingers to summon one of the housemaids. "Yu look like shit."

She did. Tisha's time on the lamb had taken its toll on her beauty. She looked about ten years older than she actually was. Except for some lip gloss, her face was bare and her normally immaculate hair was gelled to her head and hidden under a ratty ball cap. Her baggie, off that rack jeans and t-shirt made her look like she did when she first met Simon, before she became his 'queen.' Everything about her look screamed exhaustion and desperation. Slung over her shoulder was a purple duffle bag which she kept her hand in while sitting across from her husband.

"I'm not going anywhere until you tell me why you killed them," Tisha growled while choking back tears.
"I an kill no one. Dey kill dem selves. I an here da whole time. Dem dutty Babylon da one yu need ta aks why dem dead."
"That's bullshit and you know it! You pull their strings. You call the shots. You know what they do and when they do it. You pulled the trigger, Simon. You killed my entire family, the only people who ever truly loved me. What did my mother ever do to you?"
"Wa yu gwan do wit dat burner in yu bag?" he asked while glaring at Tisha with his hand under the back of his shirt.

When she Tisha the nickel-plated nine in his waist band, her hand slowly retreated from her bag. Clearly, she was no match for Simon or the dozen or so guards milling about the patio. The tears that had formed in her eyes began a slow descent down her cheeks. When she stood up and tried once more to muster the courage to kill her husband, Tisha felt a gentle tap on her shoulder. The short, chubby nurse with the big smile who'd cared for her so many times took Tisha gently by the hand and lead her into the house. Once inside, she drew Tisha's bath and got rid of her ratty clothes. After bathing Tisha, the nurse washed her hair and manicured her nails. Shortly afterwards, a pair of stylists entered the bathroom and transformed Tisha's ragged mop back

467

into an immaculate crown. In no time at all, her regal elegance had been restored. Despite his demonic ways, Simon demanded that her appearance was perfect at all times. In his eyes, just looking good wasn't enough. Tisha had to look better than good, because like his clothes and jewelry, she was a reflection of his power and status.

Having had her beauty restored, Tisha decided to take a tour of the home she'd abandoned. While walking through the halls, she found herself missing this house where she had spent the last few years enjoying life in the lap of luxury. She missed the pampering she'd grown accustomed to. The soft linens caressed her skin like soft clouds. While strolling towards the parlor, Tisha detected that familiar stench of marijuana in the hallway. When she passed the door, she could hear Simon involved in a heated conversation. Though she had no idea who he was talking to, she could tell the conversation about her.

"Mi not wan tell you 'til it was hangle. Of course I an know what dis means. Yu give tanks him dead! Hell no, me not hab no parts of it! Yu crazy ooman? Dem dead, all of dem."
Who is he talking to? Tisha wondered while standing with her ear pressed to the door.
"We find dis mon and deliver him head! Den me done for good; too damn hot ere. I return to Jamaica to be wit you. Wa bout har? No, she not dead."
That must be his wife, she thought while continuing to eavesdrop.
"I an feel no way bout dat pussyclot whore. She stay here wit da rest of har fambly dat ain't dead for all mi care. Hello? Hello?"

Alex was right. Tisha's days were numbered. Any day now, Simon would be returning to Jamaica leaving her penniless, dead, or both unless she could get her hands on the money he had stashed away. She ran to the master suite, locked the door, and immediately began rifling through the closet. All the bank statements were still in the shoebox where she'd left them. She breathed a sigh of relief when she dialed the customer service line and discovered that not only was the money was still in her account, but the balance had grown by two million dollars since she last checked it. There was still the issue of moving the cash and she knew of only one person capable of pulling it off. By advising her not to return, though, Alex had basically severed ties but with her family dead, Tisha had nowhere else to turn. The pain of his rejection made her heart ache. Once she had the money, Tisha was determined to try one last time to convince him to leave with her. If he refused she was leaving him and Denver behind forever. Meanwhile at his penthouse, Alex and Tango were sitting in the dining room patiently waiting for Lynn to finish her shower.

"This building has the most amazing fitness center!" she declared when she burst into the living room.
"Is that so?" Tango quipped with a smile while admiring the statuesque goddess. "Alex has a pretty amazing fitness center just off the kitchen. He prefers working out alone and at odd hours of night, isn't that right, Alex?"
"Is that true, honey?" Lynn asked as Alex sat red-faced and staring at his old friend.
"Yes, it is, baby, but I didn't mention it, because I was so wrapped up in having you here."
"Awwwww," she said before for sitting across his lap, "you're so sweet."

"Yep, that's Alex; a real sweetie pie. By the way, I'm Terrence Donner, but everyone calls me Tango."

"Pleased to meet you, Tango," Lynn replied while offering him her hand.

"She's a real looker Alex," Tango mused.

"Thank you."

"So Lynn, in addition to looking great and working out, what other skills do you have?"

"That depends, Tango. What did you have in mind?"

"How are your bartending skills?" he asked with a wink.

"I make a mean Martini."

"I'll take an extra dirty, three olive Martini if you don't mind."

"Coming right up. Would you like anything, honey?"

"Just a bottled water please," Alex replied while gently caressing the small of her back.

"So Tango, how long have you known Alex?" Lynn asked a few moments later while handing him the hazy green concoction.

"I've known Alex all his life," Tango replied before taking a sip from his glass. "That's damned good. Anyway, I've known young Mr. Stratton all his life, and let me tell you, he's a handful."

"Is that so?" she asked after Alex pulled her chair out from the table. "Tell me all about it."

"You bet."

Later that night after dinner, hours of conversation, and several Martinis, Alex and Lynn retired to his bedroom. As he lay on his stomach with Lynn straddling his thighs, she massaged back and shoulders while admiring his tattoos.

"So honey, how'd your meeting go today?"

"Not well I'm afraid. My colleagues and I are having some philosophical differences."

"Is my being here one of those philosophical differences?" she asked.

"What? Of course not, babe. What would give you that idea?"

"Tango's nice and all, but I get the feeling that I'm not welcome. He kept alluding to the fact that you guys are dealing with a high-dollar client who's very volatile and that keeping you guys busy. I know I came here unexpectedly so it's okay if you want me to leave."

"Babe," Alex began while pushing up and forcing Lynn to dismount his back, "there's absolutely nothing that I want more than to have you here with me. Yes, we're busy but that comes with the job. The point is you're here and I want to make sure that we enjoy each and every moment possible. Okay?" he asked while caressing her soft thigh.

"Are you sure?"

"Come here."

Before Lynn could utter another word, his tongue was probing the depths of her mouth. Her pulse quickened when he untied her robe and began caressing and teasing her soft, round tits. The combination of his tongue swirling her chocolate crowns while his finger teased her clitoris caused the juices between her quivering thighs to flow like a river. Soft moans escaped Lynn's lips when he abandoned her nipples and his tongue began its decent down her abdomen, inching closer and closer to the river that his fingers were bathing in.

"Oh my gawd!" she cried as his hot, wet tongue flicked across her swollen clit.

Lynn hoped and prayed that Alex wouldn't drown in the juices that were spilling from her river. The sensation of him feasting on her glistening peach had her hips bucking uncontrollably. Her best attempts to flee his tongue were met with a grip on her hips that was powerful, yet sexy at the same time. With her thighs resting on his shoulders, Lynn found herself at Alex's mercy, like a gazelle in a tiger's clutches. Her fingers got lost in his ebony strands as he lapped up her juices and fingered her throbbing flower. She tried desperately to stop the room from spinning after Alex paused long enough undress. Moments later, he was deep inside her. His powerful thrusts combined the taste of her juices on his tongue sent Lynn over the orgasmic edge. His name escaped her lips several times as tears of ecstasy flowed down her cheeks.

"Deeper Alex, *deeper!*" she commanded each time her hips rose and fell in rhythm with his.
"I love you," he whispered, his hot breath in her ear igniting a wild fire at the base of her spine.

This moment, this time, was *oh so* perfect. Determined to make up for what they missed in Cincinnati, Alex transformed Lynn into his personal playground. Her nails digging into his shoulders combined with her soft, musical moans fueled his desire to pleasure her deeper, harder, and faster. With her legs around his waist and her hands pinned to the bed, Alex filled with a passion unlike any other. From the front, the back, on top, and below, Lynn was his to enjoy. Her every movement was mesmerizing and her grip on his shaft had Alex fighting against nature with each stroke. Seconds turned into minutes and minutes into hours, and no matter how many times he came, Alex couldn't quench his thirst for her. Just when Lynn thought she couldn't cum again, she released yet another gush of sheet-drenching cum.

Where have you been all my life? his heart asked when he stared into her flickering eyes and tenderly kissed her lips.

Throughout the night as they slept, Lynn's aura kept his demons at bay. The peace that surrounded them gave Alex calm unlike any he had experienced in years. Lynn completed him. Her nearness, her touch, and her kitten-like purr were what he missed and needed so desperately. For the first time in a long time, the pieces to his puzzle were all in place. Alex vowed to never let her go, and was willing to do whatever it took to protect her, even if it meant fighting the devil himself.

Over the next week, Alex entertained Lynn and showered her with love and affection, while trying to figure out how to clean up his mess. Her presence, though quite soothing, was hindering his ability to move freely.

At the same time, Agent Burroughs and his team were busy trying to build a case again him, but with so much key evidence missing and Jason still in hiding, they had very little to go on. They were pulling all the information they'd gathered from previous investigations, as well as new information, in hopes that it would amount to something. Burroughs had assets working day and night turning Denver up-side-down, while Agent Castro, whom he'd reassigned, kept a watchful eye on them.

"It's pretty fucked up around here, Jason," Castro whispered into his cell while peeping through his blinds. "He has two teams on Stratton and another looking for you. They're investigating every Aston Martin

473

dealership in a five-hundred-mile radius. To make matters worse, our spotter inside Simon's compound reports that Tisha came back."

"Really? That's a damned shame. I mean her family's murderer was the only person she could turn to? She's either crazy or desperate. Where has she been?"

"I don't know Jason, but wherever it was, she was completely off the grid. No cell phones, no credit or debit cards, and no paper trail. It's like she disappeared and reappeared but at the wrong damned time."

"Well there goes that murder theory he was trying to fabricate," Agent Blackhawk replied while shaking his head.

"What about Stratton? Is any of the stuff he provided legit?"

"Look around, Gabe. I don't know how he did, but he got Burroughs to implicate himself twice on tape. I sent the recordings to McNamara for review. We should have the go ahead by week's end."

"I hope so 'cause that fat son-of-a-bitch has me chained to this desk doing bullshit busy work. I know for a fact he's having me watched."

"I appreciate it, Gabe and I promise this'll be over soon."

"Just make sure I don't get burned on this one, Jason. Your career may be over, but I'm trying to salvage mine."

"I know, Gabe. For a while now, Burroughs has been feeding McNamara lines about my instability and you possibly working both sides of the fence. I got all that taken care of though, and with the help of Stratton's boss, we got the shit turned around. As soon as we get the word, I'll be in touch."

"I'll be waiting," Castro replied calmly, but still unconvinced.

Seven o'clock Thursday morning found Lynn perched atop Alex's lap. With one hand planted on his chest and the other massaging her tits, she unleashed intensity on him he never imagined possible. Shudders of electricity raced up and down his spine with each sensual rise and fall of her hips. Not content to let her do all the work, Alex grabbed two hands full of her ass and proceeded to guide Lynn up and down on his thrusting manhood. Her eyes shimmered like diamonds while looking down at his glistening chest, occasionally running her nails across it before resuming her teasing of her own throbbing nipples.

When Alex opened his eyes, Lynn made a show of playing with her bouncing tits by pinching and even licking her nipples. Her tantalizing display combined with the massage of her sugar walls had Alex releasing small, but intense, blasts of cum inside her. She sat up and arched her back when she felt his mighty hands release her ass and travel slowly up her sides before settling on her bronze melons.

"Feed me baby," he whispered while pulling her body to his and taking her nipples into his mouth.

This sensual mix of pleasure and pain had Lynn raining cum all over him. No man had ever taken control of her body the way Alex was doing now. He took her senses to places she only dreamed were possible. This bliss was the stuff of erotic novels, yet this was real and so was Alex. Feeling his shaft and head swelling against her walls added to Lynn's orgasmic delight. When her ass began bouncing faster and harder, she reached down and pinned his hands to the mattress waiting for his volcano to erupt.

"Lynn!" Alex gasped as wave-after-wave of cum erupted from his pulsating shaft.

Their hearts raced wildly as she lay atop his chest and their sweat-covered bodies glowed under the moonlight.

"I love you," he whispered while kissing her salty brow. "I love you more."

Aurora, Colorado.

While pacing nervously in his motel suite, Agent Blackhawk was watching his entire life passing slowly before his eyes. Before the FBI, he was simply Jason Blackhawk, a Native American kid who grew up on a reservation fifty miles southeast of Tempe, Arizona. When he reached school age, they moved to Tempe with his grandparents where he endured endless hazing by the other children, most of them white. He resented being forced to integrate into their world, while they ridiculed his. By the time he reached high school, Jason had grown accustomed to his classification as "special citizen." His heritage was the primary reason he received a scholarship to the University of Arkansas, where he excelled in track and field. Upon graduation, he enlisted in the Army and for a brief time endured similar ridicule.

After several successful tours in the Middle East, two medals for valor, and a stint at Guantanamo Bay, Jason sought employment with the FBI. His skills quickly made him an agency darling, and before long, he was assigned to the Felix case. That's when his life and career fell apart. Every day since had been nothing more than a growing web of lies, that were covered up with murder, mayhem, and money. He'd already lost one partner, and was on the verge of losing another. Even his boss, a man whom he'd admired and even idolized, was conspiring against him. Jason even began to doubt whether or not his friendship with Castro was a façade. The only person he could trust now was Alex, a man so mysterious that Jason had begun to fear him.   His attention was so scattered that he didn't hear the door open behind him or the footsteps that accompanied them. His nostalgic journey was abruptly interrupted by a crushing blow against the back of his skull.

Jason's head throbbed while the nauseating smell of ethanol burned his nostrils. When he finally regained consciousness, his eyes struggled to focus under the blinding light. Meanwhile black-clad men were dousing the floor and everything else around him with gasoline. When his eyes finally adjusted, one of them approached him and proceeded to pour gas into his lap.

"Now asshole, you have one chance, and one chance only. What the fuck did you tell McNamara?"
"Is that you Carver? Why should I tell you? You're just gonna kill me anyway, right?" Agent Blackhawk asked while struggling against the ropes on his wrists.
"True, we are but at least you get to live a little bit longer…if you start talking now, that is."
"Okay, what do you wanna know?" Blackhawk asked after freeing his hands and waiting for an opening.
"For starters, tell me everything you told McNamara, and I'll put a bullet in your head. That way you won't suffer too much," the masked man joked before dropping the can and striking a match.
"Ok, but that could take a while," Jason replied when two more men came into view.

"Then start talking!" a fourth man blurted while dumping gasoline on the floor.
"Talk got-dammit!"

As the flame wielder moved closer, Jason sprung up, grabbed him by his arm, and slammed him through the chair. The falling match ignited the gasoline on the floor around them. Jason leapt clear of the flames and quickly stripped out of his clothing while his first captor burned alive. After dodging a series of shots that were fired by two of the other fleeing men, Agent Blackhawk found himself trapped by a wall of flames. After searching frantically for an escape, he found a window hidden behind a massive shelf. He grabbed a brick off the ground and hurled it through the glass before scaling the shelf and leaping to safety. When he hit the ground, he narrowly escaped being rundown by a charcoal-colored Dodge Charger, similar to the one he'd been issued. Panting, panicked, and half-naked, he watched the flames that nearly sealed his fate consume the abandoned warehouse.

Hours after their passionate, early morning interlude, Lynn awoke to find Alex's side of the bed empty. Thinking that he'd slipped out to work again, she got up and showered. With hot water and steam all around her, Lynn's body was reeling from the pleasure they'd shared earlier. Her gentle stroking and caressing of her throbbing clitoris combined with the hot water against her skin made her body tingle with delight. These erotic sensations caused her dam to rupture and her juices to intermingle with the water running down her quivering thighs.

Meanwhile outside on the patio, Alex was standing near the wrought iron fence with Richard and Nicholas behind him. His grip on the rails said it all. Alex was ready to blow a gasket.

"Are you fucking kidding me? Why the hell did she come back?"

"Sorry big man," Richard began while scratching his head, "but it gets worse. Our guy on the inside said she returned over a week ago and has been in the compound since. He also said that Simon is preparing to flee the country."

"Flee the country?"

"Yeah, boss, flee the country," Nicholas replied. "Look Alex, I know you want this fucker. We all do, but the window of opportunity is closing quickly. On top of that, the feds still haven't given the go ahead to take Burroughs and the others down."

"What the fuck are they waiting on?" Alex snapped while peering out over the city. "Where the hell is Jason?"

"He's hold up in a motel room in Aurora," Richard replied.

Suddenly, Alex's phone began buzzing on the table behind them.

"This is Alex."

"Stratton, it's Jason. They just tried to kill me...again."

"Where are you?"

"I'm in the industrial district in Aurora. They tried to torch a warehouse with me in it. I'm pretty sure they tossed my motel room too. I need EVAC like now!"

"I'll send two of my guys to get you. Stay out of sight. They're on the way."

"Get to Aurora and find him before they double-back. Delilah will help you find his exact location."

"We're on it boss," Richard replied before freezing in his tracks.

"Hi, baby. I didn't know you had company."

"Ummm…yes, babe, these are my business associates, and they were just leaving."

"Wow, okay. Well, it was nice almost meeting you," she said when Alex quickly ushered them out of the door.

Though he tried, Alex couldn't hide his agitation from Lynn. His body language betrayed him. Whatever he'd been told on the patio didn't sit well with him, and his secretive behavior wasn't sitting well with her. Lynn had no idea what to say or do. He was standing silently by the front door with his hands on the frame. She couldn't see his eyes but imagined that at this moment they were full of rage.

"I'm gonna ask you this one more time, and I need an honest answer," Lynn said while wrapping her arms around his waist and pressing her body hard against his. "Is now a good time for me to be here?"

"Stop asking me that, please. Everything is fine, just a few unexpected surprises that's all. Rethinking strategy at the last minute can be nerve racking."

"I understand that babe and I don't wanna distract you," she said before resting her head on his shoulders.

"You're not babe…trust me."

A short while later, Richard, and Nicholas accompanied Jason to his ransacked suite. Just as they'd anticipated, the bed was overturned, his drawers were pulled out, and his clothes were everywhere. His laptop, the keys to his rental, and the car itself were all gone.

"Looks like they got what they came for," Richard said after surveying the mess.

"No, they didn't," Jason replied before standing up and walking into the bathroom.

After a few moments of fumbling with a ceiling tile, he reappeared with a flash drive.

"Shower, grab your shit, and let's roll," Nicholas said while looking out of the window. "If your boss is trying to kill you, nine times out of ten they're coming back again."
"I know. Give me twenty minutes."
"You've got ten minutes bub."

Chapter 20

Two hours later, after breakfast and a brief sight-seeing tour, Alex was standing in the waiting area of Chantelle's Beauty Salon and Day Spa. Though there was endless chatter and commotion behind him, his attention was focused on the black Ford Taurus that had been parked across the street since he and Lynn arrived. He figured that Burroughs had gotten desperate since Jason escaped death and resorted to having him followed again. *I guess you think I'm gonna lead you to him,* Alex thought while glaring across the street.

Their constant whispering and gawking had worn on Lynn's nerves. She tried to ignore it at first, but these women were eyeing and talking about Alex like she was invisible. They seemed completely oblivious to the fact that he and Lynn had arrived together.

"Don't pay these heffas no attention, honey," Chantelle said when she saw the look on her face. "Alex has been coming in here for years, and it's always the same. They flirt with him until he leaves."

"Coming here for years?" Lynn asked while looking up at the short, busty beautician who was rinsing her hair.

"Yes, honey," Chantelle began nervously. "Alex and my husband Mike work together. Their investments purchased this shop and four more just like it. Plus, they're in the process of building his father a church in Alabama."

"Really? Does it bother you that Mike travels so much?"

"Honey, between managing five salons and raising a pair of toddlers, I don't have time to worry about Mike's work. Now don't get me wrong, I love my man and I miss him when he's gone. But I know he's coming home and we more than make up for it when he gets back. The key is to keep your mind occupied. That's how I pass the time."

While Lynn sat contemplating Chantelle's words, a handsome and hulking brotha walked through the front doors dressed in a gray tailored suit with a matching Fedora. She quickly surmised it was Mike by Chantelle's radiant smile and the way he and Alex were whispering at the door.

"I see you brought company with you."
"I take it you're not talking about Lynn," Alex quipped with a smirk.
"Nope. Follow me to the back so we can talk."
"Hi, Alexis," whispered the slender but shapely, dark-skinned stylist with her green eyes and blonde-streaked hair.
"Hello Monique," he replied, barely making eye contact.
"Babe, we're going in the back," he said before leaning down and kissing Lynn's lips.
"Okay," she smiled before shooting a glare at the gawkers.
"Take good care of my baby, Chantelle. Whatever she wants, make sure she gets it."
"Don't worry, Alex. Lynn is in good hands. And by the way, it's nice to see you dressed down for a change. Can you talk to the good reverend back there and remind him that he looks good in jeans too?"
"I'll see what I can do. These guys are relentless," Alex said a few moments later while staring into a monitor. "They tried to torch Jason this morning in a warehouse in Aurora."
"I heard," Big Mike replied while zooming in on the driver's face. "They have him over at Tango's shop right

now. It says here that this guy is Peter Fields, a seven year G-Man."

"I need to get over there and talk to him. Think you can cover for me for a few minutes?"

"No problem. Wanna take the 300?"

"Nah, I wanna see what these pricks have under the hood."

"I hate the sound of that," Big Mike said when he sat down and watched Alex slip out of the back door.

Within seconds, the 911 was speeding down the street with the Taurus trailing behind. Alex wrestled with the idea of leading them on a wild goose chase before simply flooring it and watching them disappear from his rearview mirror. After making sure no one had followed him, Alex screeched to a halt in Tango's garage.

"I can't turn my back on you for a second, can I?"

"How about some compassion, jackass?" Jason groaned while holding a bag of ice on the back of his head. "I can't help but think that you're by far the worst thing to happen to me in my entire life."

"Does that include the two murder attempts that we rescued you from?" Alex quipped sarcastically. "From where I stand, the worst thing to happen to you is joining the FBI."

"Touché."

"How do you know it was Burroughs?" Tango asked with Alex sitting on the stool opposite the frazzled agent.

"They made sure to ask what I talked to McNamara about. Alex's little chess game with Burroughs nearly got me killed, again."

"No, Jason, asking the right questions almost got you killed. Ask yourself this. Who else knew you were in Aurora? If it's not McNamara himself, somebody in his office is in bed with Burroughs."

Suddenly, everyone was silent. *Besides Burroughs, who else stood to lose if this case went public?* The integrity of the entire United States justice system would be in jeopardy. As the head of the FBI, neither McNamara nor the powers that be could withstand the public outcry for transparency and justice. The most powerful investigative body in the world would suddenly be held up to domestic and international scrutiny. Everyone with a soapbox would have questions and demand answers for them. Decades of investigations, legal precedents, and convictions would be erased overnight. When Alex got up and walked towards the showroom, Jason realized that everything he'd uncovered this investigation made him a threat who was too dangerous to remain alive. He had nowhere else to turn.

"What am I supposed to do now?"
"You might not believe this, Jason, but the men in this room with you right now are the only people you can afford to trust. If McNamara is the man you think he is, then maybe he can be trusted too. In the meantime, kick your feet up relax. We'll take care of everything else until then."
"Alex is right, Jason," Richard said after grabbing his bag up off the floor. "Looks like you're going to be spending some time with us."
"By the way, you play poker?" Nicholas asked while shuffling a deck of cards.
"Good speech, kid," Tango said while approaching Alex. "What are you doing with those blueprints?"
"Move your ass, and I'll show you," Tango replied before unrolling them and laying them on the hood of his Shelby. "I've been working on this for years. I call it *'The Basement.'* It's a secondary staging area, and I found

the perfect location for it. I just need you to approve the purchase of a decommissioned fire house."

"Why a fire house?"

"It's not so much the old garage as what's underneath it."

"I see," Alex replied when he turned the page.

"Oh, here's a list of the latest and greatest vehicular metal. Take a look and let me know which ones you want."

"I'll take them," Alex replied after a quick glance.

"Ok, but which ones?"

"All of them. Now if you'll excuse me, I have to get back to Chantelle's. Keep Jason on ice for me."

"No problem, kid."

After a brief phone call and a short drive, Alex returned to Chantelle's salon. When he approached rear door, Big Mike opened it and quickly ushered him in.

"Come in and have a seat, Alex."

"Is everything ok, Mike?"

"Of course it is. I just need to speak with you for a few moments before you go back outside."

"Okay, what's on your mind, reverend?"

"I'm concerned about the way you're handling this situation with Simon. In particular, I'm worried about how you plan to keep Lynn safe should the FBI or his men come knocking at your door. In fact, we all are."

"In all honesty, I'm worried about that too. I had a nightmare the other night, and Lynn was in it. It was so real. I could actually feel her take her last breath."

"That being said, do you honestly think she needs be here?"

"What are you saying, Mike?"

"I think you know what I'm saying. The world doesn't revolve around you and your agendas and unless you have a plan to end this nightmare, like now, Lynn doesn't need to be here. You've been picking off Simon's buddies for a while and now they're on to you. You've spent the last two years sleeping with his wife and stealing his money. Do you have any idea how dysfunctional your life is right now? Don't let Lynn become a casualty like Simone."

"I know, Mike," Alex replied before slumping down in his chair. "I've done a lot of soul-searching lately and had to come to grips with my mistakes. The biggest was thinking that I could manage my self-made madness. I'd convinced myself I was invincible; nothing could touch me. I was wrong. Simone's death changed that. Separating from Constance left a void I couldn't ignore. Now, Lynn's here, and I don't want to lose her too. I know it's selfish, but I don't wanna be without her."

"Alex, if you really love her then, you're going to have to make some decisions. She has to know what she's up against if she stays with you. I fought it as long as I could, but I had to break down and tell Chantelle the truth. The prospect of losing her was the hardest thing I ever had to face. Thank God she stayed or otherwise I'd be a wreck. My wife and my ministry are my rocks. Without them, I don't know where I'd be."

"That's where I want to be, Mike. I want that *one*. I want that *one* who makes me want to come home every night and be glad I left this bullshit behind."

"Is Lynn that *one*, Alex?"

"Yes, she is," he replied emphatically.

"Then if she's that one, you're gonna have to let her choose. Otherwise everything you do for her will be out of your own selfishness. Eventually, you're gonna have to let her in. Take your ego out of the equation and look at the entire picture. You can't allow yourself to operate the same way you have been for so long. You do the job and you get out. Don't get attached and don't take it personal."

"What if I do and she doesn't stay? What if she hauls ass and never returns? Then what, Mike?"

"Then my friend, she wasn't that *one*."

Before Alex could reply, the ladies burst into the office all smiles. Shimmering spiral curls hung down just below Lynn's shoulders. Her lips and nails were most beautiful shade of red Alex had ever seen. Though both of them were gorgeous, Lynn's radiance seemed more captivating. Her smile melted Alex's heart and rendered him speechless at the same time.

"Is this macho man meeting over yet? What do you think, Alex? Is Lynn a fox or what?"

"She's an angel without wings," he replied with a smile while almost choking on the lump in his throat.

"Thank you, sexy," Lynn whispered before gently kissing his lips.

"Another slam dunk, sugar dumplin'," Mike said before hugging Chantelle and kissing her temple. "Why don't we all have dinner tonight?"

"That would be lovely," Alex said before stepping back and admiring Lynn once more.

Later that night after of an evening of dinner and dancing, Lynn and Alex lay snuggled in the comfort of his bed. As she lay on his chest being serenaded by the soft thump of his heart, he gently played in her curls while attempting to drown out the voices in his head. His conversations with Big Mike, Tango, and the rest of the team were playing over and over like a recording. And though Alex hated to admit it, they were all right. Playing games with Simon's life had compromised his judgment and his sanity. Later when she rolled to the opposite side of the bed, Alex crept out of the room and into his gym.

Sweat poured from his body as he pounded on the heavy bag. He'd been detached from his emotions for so long that he'd forgotten what it felt like to be alone or afraid. After Simone died, he vowed never to let anyone get that close to him again. He'd encased his heart behind a brick wall that nothing could penetrate. Then Constance came along and all that changed. Despite Alex's enigmatic behavior and sinister ways, she managed to tear down those walls and love him in spite of him. Had it not been for Doc's jealous manipulation, he might have married her. Though that chapter of his life hadn't been officially closed, Alex had resolved to remove himself for her safety. Having Lynn come into his life was like déjà vu. Once again, Alex found himself afraid to lose a woman, who in a short time, had come to mean so much to him. He was determined to hold on as long as he could despite his growing fears that Simon might kill her too.

By ten o'clock that morning, tensions around Tango's garage had reached their boiling point. Agent Blackhawk hadn't heard from McNamara or Castro, and assumed that he'd been lied to. So far, the only thing the FBI's man inside the compound had been able to confirm was that Simon was leaving the United States, although he didn't know exactly when or how. According to Castro, Burroughs hadn't been in the office for the past two days and feared that he might be trying to make a clean break as well. The longer Jason paced the floor, the more Alex's revelation made sense. Someone near, or at the top, of the bureau was purposely preventing his investigations from moving forward. With his window of opportunity closing rapidly, he began devising a way of taking Burroughs down by himself, even if it meant lying to his entire team.

At the same time, Tango and the twins were busy running around the shop fielding phone calls and researching information on their computers. Away in his library, Doc was facing his own dilemmas. He and Director McNamara were in a heated phone debate that had Doc questioning his old friend's integrity.

"This wasn't what we agreed to Robert!" he shouted while pounding on his new desk top. "We had a deal. My people would furnish you all the information you needed in exchange for taking Burroughs out of the game. Why are you dragging your feet and why hasn't your office green lighted this operation yet?"
"Because of the delicate nature of it, that's why. Even though all your information is credible, the manner in which it was obtained, as well as the fact that it involves some of the bureau's most decorated agents, presents us with a dilemma."
"That's bullshit and you know it, Robert! You're not worried about justice. You're trying to protect the integrity of your office."
"Aren't you trying to do the same, Gregory?" McNamara fired back. "If your man had done what he was supposed to do, neither of us would be in this mess. Simon should've been in either a coffin or custody years ago. The son-of-a-bitch has used the law like a shield and made millions in the process. Now, he's on the verge of walking away, and we can't get a single charge on him to stick. And yes, this operation could destroy the reputation of the FBI and undermine years of criminal convictions. The list of appeals would read like a got-damn phone book."

"I provided you with recordings that show Burroughs implicating himself as a co-conspirator in Simon's organization. What more do you need?"

"Really?" McNamara asked angrily. "Did you listen to any of the recordings? I did and so did a team of experts who concluded that Burroughs didn't confess to anything. You and I know that they're damning as hell, but a defense attorney would rip them to shreds. The very method your man used to obtain them screams entrapment. He'd have to testify under oath, not only to the nature of the recordings, but to everything disclosed on them going back for years. With him taking the stand, your entire organization is dead in the water. You and I both know that Burroughs is guilty as hell, but he knows the law, and so far he's managed to keep his hands clean. I've been watching his fat ass for years and haven't been able to tie him to anything or anyone. As good as your information is, it's just not good enough."

"Did you know that he sent a team of men to kidnap, torture, and murder Agent Blackhawk twice?"

"Can you prove that, Gregory? I thought not. Look, the last thing I want my office known for is protecting criminals, murdering witnesses, or murdering fellow agents. That being said, I'm issuing an order to bring all the men on your list in, but for questioning only. You'll have that order by noon your time. At this point, that's the best that I can do. I have rules that I have to follow whereas you don't."

"You fucked me, Robert," Doc declared angrily.

"I'm sorry you feel that way. I'll be in touch."

Less than two hours later, Agent Blackhawk along with several other regional agents, received the go ahead status for *'Operation Clean House.'* At 0800 Eastern Time the following day, teams around the country would begin executing a series of coordinated strikes against the men that Alex and Tobey had identified. Although he was happy that his bureau chief hadn't totally caved, Agent Blackhawk was disappointed that full indictments hadn't been handed down against Burroughs and his co-conspirators. He knew they needed to be tried and convicted for all their crimes, including the murder of scores of innocent people. But with their knowledge of the law, waiting for them to crack under questioning with no real threat of prosecution was almost futile.

At his penthouse, Alex was at his dining room table pecking away feverishly on his laptop. With Delilah's help, he discovered four additional accounts throughout the Caribbean in Tisha's name with cash assets totaling around fifty million dollars. After some careful manipulation, he discovered Simon's end game. On Monday morning, he was going to have all the money transferred into one account for immediate withdrawal. Alex, however, had different plans. He set the system up to bounce all the funds from Tisha's accounts through a series of his own dummy accounts before landing in one of his own. With his money gone and his protection out of the way, Simon would be forced out into the open. From there, it was only a matter of time before Alex had his revenge and this nightmare was over.

"Whacha doing baby?" Lynn asked with her arms draped over his shoulders.
"Just a little banking," he replied when her soft lips hit his earlobe.
"Come with me and let's see if you can make another large deposit," she said before licking his ear and spinning him around in his chair.
"Don't worry, there won't be any early withdrawals on this one."

"That's my kind of investment Mr. Stratton; a long term one," she replied while gazing into his eyes and untying the strings on this sweat pants.

Later that evening and after weeks of failed attempts, desperation set in forcing Agent Stanley Burroughs to bring in a convicted computer hacker to break into Agent Blackhawk's encrypted files. Within minutes, the skinny, curly-haired nerd bypassed Jason's security. In no time at all, Burroughs, Carver, Baker, and Fischer, and Daniels, went to work. They wasted little time copying the files before printing them out and combing through the data. Just as Burroughs expected, they found numerous entries on Blackhawk's investigations into the Midwest Finest, the Tyler family, and Simon Felix. There was an additional file dedicated to Tisha and Alex. As his counterparts read and compared notes, Burroughs continued his search until he came across a file with his name on it. After opening it and reading some of the entries, it became clear that Agents Blackhawk and Castro were on to him. There were scanned copies of his bank statements along with a lengthy list of assets for which his and his wife's combined salaries couldn't account for. Also in the file was a list of nineteen other names, all top level officials within the bureau and all somehow associated with the Simon Felix investigation. Panic set in when Burroughs began contemplating his fate. *Was this was the reason Agent Blackhawk had gone to see McNamara or was Alex bluffing him? Where had Blackhawk disappeared to and who was helping him? Who was Alexis Stratton and who did he work for?*

"Pack it in boys. We'll get back to it tomorrow."

The first in the series of raids against the men on Agent Blackhawk's list and were carried out beginning on the east coast. Within the first hour, half of the men were in custody and prepared for questioning, just as McNamara had promised. At 7:05AM Denver time, Agent Stanley Burroughs's peaceful slumber was interrupted by the sounds of his phone ringing. He tried several times to ignore it, but the calls kept coming one after the other.

"Burroughs," he groaned after rolling over and looking at the clock.
"They're on to you. Pack your shit, and get out now. You don't have much time."
"What? Who is this? Hello? Hello?" Burroughs demanded repeatedly, even though the line was dead.
"Janie! Janie! Wake up!"
"Not now, Stanley," she groaned while enduring his frantic nudging.
"We have to go! Get up and get dressed now!"
"Stanley, what's wrong?"
"Stop asking questions and move your ass! They're coming for me!"
"Who's coming for you?"
"Who do you think got-dammit? Move your ass before they get here!"

Minutes later, the pair was scrambling throughout the house throwing everything they could grab into bags and loading them into their cars. By 7:35AM, Janie Burroughs was standing in the foyer out of breath and shaking uncontrollably.

"I'm ready."

"Then get going!" he yelled from the library to her right. "Don't wait for me! I'll catch up to you later! Get on the interstate and don't stop driving 'til you reach your mother's."

"Okay," replied the nervous red head when she grabbed her keys and bolted out of the door.

Within seconds of hearing her A7 screech out of the driveway, Burroughs began snatching books off the bookcase, so that he could get to his safe behind them. After opening it, he quickly dumped its contents: two ledgers, a .45 caliber Beretta, and nine-hundred-fifty-thousand in cash into a black duffle bag. With the safe emptied, Burroughs zipped the bag and headed towards the door.

"Going somewhere, sir?" Agent Blackhawk asked while leaning against the doorframe between Burroughs and freedom.

Hairs stood up on Burroughs's neck when he saw those familiar cold irons he'd used dangling his young protégé's index finger. Jason's badge was in plain sight and the latch holding his side arm in place had been unlocked. It was clear that Agent Blackhawk was there for one reason: to take him in. Frozen in his tracks but unwilling to accept defeat, Burroughs dropped the bag and looked around. Though there was nowhere for him to run, the wily veteran was determined to play this out until the end.

"I was planning on it."

"Kind of sudden, isn't it sir?" Agent Blackhawk he asked after sizing up his retreating mentor.

"Yeah, well I have some time saved up and decided to use it."

"I see. Your phone is ringing, sir. Are you going to answer it?"

"It can wait. So, Jason, what brings you to my home so early in the morning?"

"You may want to answer that, sir," he replied while nodding to the phone on the desk. "It might be important."

"Hello, this is Burroughs."

"Are you out yet? They got everyone else."

"I apologize, but I'm tied up right now and can't go into that. I'll have someone from my office contact you first thing Monday."

"Trouble, sir?"

"Just a last minute change in my travel arrangement. It's nothing major."

"Speaking of travel arrangements, I've got one for you," Agent Blackhawk said before tossing the cuffs onto the desktop.

"What the fuck is this about?"

"It's the end, sir. I'll spare you the embarrassment and humiliations by letting you cuff yourself."

"You're arresting me, Jason? What the hell for?"

"Bribery, extortion, and murder: any of these sound familiar, sir?"

"Where's your proof son?" Burroughs asked with a smirk on his face.

Without saying a word, his young protégé pulled the digital recorder from his blazer pocket, laid it on the desk, and pressed play. For the next few minutes, the two men listened as Burroughs' conversation with Alex played. Meanwhile outside the house, Castro and a group of agents listened as the events unfolded inside.

"What the hell is he doing?" Castro heard over the angry footsteps approaching from behind him. "We're here to take Burroughs in for questioning, not make an arrest."

"Put a sock in it and relax. This is Jason's play. We're here to back him up, so get back on your post and wait for my signal."

"That proves nothing," Burroughs scoffed when the recording ended.

"By itself, no sir it doesn't. But the two conversations that you've had with Simon Felix since then along with the evidence I turned over to McNamara are more than enough to get you into court."

Agent Burroughs's brash anger suddenly turned into defeat when he peered through the blinds. The sight of Agent Castro standing on the lawn wearing a bullet proof vest and holding an M4 Carbine assault rifle in his hands seemed like the beginning of the end.

"Where's my wife?" he asked after flopping down in his leather office chair.

"She was taken into custody shortly after she left the house."

"So I guess this is it then, huh Jason?"

"Keep your hands where I can see them sir!" Agent Blackhawk commanded when Burroughs reached into the bottom desk drawer.

"Relax son," he mused after grabbing a bottle of aged scotch that lay next to a chrome-plated .38 Special and a pair of cocktail glasses. "Wanna a drink?"

"I'll pass."

"You sure, son?" he asked again while filling the glasses. "There's nothing like hundred year old scotch."

"I wouldn't know, sir. I can't afford that on my salary."

"I forgot," Burroughs chuckled before downing the second glass. "Tell me, son, what would you have done if you were me?"

"Keep your hands where I can see them sir!" Agent Blackhawk commanded after drawing his weapon and cocking the hammer.

"I got this pretty lady when I first hit the field," he began after pulling the revolver from the drawer. "We've seen a lot of action over the years and taken down quite a few bad guys along the way."

"I don't want to sir, but I will put you down if I have to!"

"Let me ask you a question, son. When you were out in that God forsaken desert kicking ass and taking names for this country, did you ever dream you'd be labeled a traitor? I mean look at you standing there all full of piss and vinegar. Do you really think you're like those morons outside? Well, you're not. Do you think the bureau recruited you because of your test scores? Think again. We recruited you because you get shit done. You're a killer who didn't let things like morals and ethics get in the way, especially when you were torturing terrorists. Right, Jason?"

"That was a long time ago and has nothing to do with today," he replied when a red dot appeared on Burroughs's temple.

"Stop it, Jason! It has everything to do with today. You're no different than I am. We both get the job done. So what I extorted money from dope dealers and murders!" Burroughs scoffed while filling his glasses again. "My work resulted in more arrests than anyone else in the bureau's history. It put us in bed with one of the biggest traffickers in the Caribbean, and gave us control over his entire operation. You tortured and killed terrorists for Lady Liberty, so don't judge me motherfucker! Your tactics probably saved countless lives once they finally talked, didn't they?"

"No, Stan. Your work has resulted in the murder of dozens of witnesses and fellow agents, including my partner, Lisa."

"Weaklings, all of them," Burroughs snapped before downing a glass of liquor. "I did the world a favor by letting that weak trash die. I offered Lisa a chance to be rich, but like you, she just had to play by those damned rules. Then she panicked and threatened to blow the whistle. Lisa was a liability who caved under pressure when the assignment got too rough."

"By those rules, do you mean the rules which we're sworn to uphold?"

"I had high hopes for you, Jason. With your skills and training, you could have easily been my successor. You're head and shoulders above the rest. You deserve better, and you could have had it. Money, boats, cars, women…you name it. It could have been yours."

"I have something better than all that sir; my integrity."

"Integrity? How can you talk about integrity when you were banging your ex-partner? Was she as good as she looked?" Burroughs taunted with a grin. "Did Castro fuck her too? I wish I had."

"You will not drag Lisa's name through the mud, you fat son-of-a-bitch! Lisa was a good woman and a great agent. You sold her out just like the rest of us."

"Stop talking like them Jason, because you're not one of them. Integrity is bought and sold every day, like candy. You're an entirely different animal and you know it."

"Lisa and the rest of the agents you helped murder deserved better! I should kill you for the things you've done, because a trial is more than you deserve," Jason declared while aiming at Burroughs's head.

"But you won't, will you, Jason? And do you know why you won't?" Burroughs taunted before cocking the revolver and placing it under his chin. "Like the rest of them, you're weak, too weak to do what's right. Here's the perfect chance for you to deliver 'your' justice. You can take me down here and now, yet there you are standing around and doing nothing. Where is that fire you had in Cuba? Watch me, son, and I'll show you how it's done."

"BOOM!"

"Shots fired! Shots fired!" Castro yelled as he and the other agents stormed the house and quickly secured the first floor.

When they entered the library, Agent Blackhawk was smiling by the desk with a huge grin on his face. Agent Burroughs however was slumped over the side of his chair with a gaping hole in the top of his head. His jawbone and chin had been all but obliterated. Blood and bone fragments were scattered on his clothes and the desk, while brain matter decorated the window treatments behind him.

"What the hell happened in here, Jason?" demanded the same agent who'd challenged Castro moments earlier.

"Justice," he replied callously.

At Tango's garage, Alex, the twins, Ko, and Tango were assembled in the showroom eagerly awaiting news of the raids, which they figured by now were complete. While they waited, they were also engaged in a heated debate. The team was mercilessly chastising Alex for his close involvement with Agent Blackhawk, which included saving his life, bringing him to 'The Agency' for assistance, and bringing him to the mansion unannounced. Despite his best efforts, Alex couldn't convince his friends that he was still in control.

"C'mon kid," Tango began while shaking his head, "there's no way you could have predicted this outcome.

There are entirely too many variables at play, even for you."

"He's right, Alex. You're playing this way too close to the chest. I mean, you've been to Blackhawk's house, met with him and Burroughs in public, and basically challenged them on every possible occasion. What the hell do you hope to gain by toying with these guys?" Ko asked before throwing his hands up in the air.

"A partner," Alex replied calmly.

"A partner?" the twins repeated emphatically.

"Yes, a partner."

"Kid, in the words of Ricky Ricardo, you got some 'splaining to do."

"Let's face it guys, the body count around here is getting thin. Jinx is away at school where she belongs. Warren isn't mission ready, and God only knows when or if he will be. Big Mike will be leaving to take up his ministry any day now, and Tango, you've sworn field work off altogether. Jason has the skills, the savvy, and the resources to become a valuable asset to this team. I had to test his mettle to see what he's made of."

"It's not that easy, kid. The selection process for this program is way more complicated than just drafting somebody. It takes years to make a person field ready, and years after that to make sure they don't crack up while working."

"The man has seen combat as an army ranger, he's trained sniper, and he's highly skilled in interrogation and torture. How's that for field ready?"

"First 'The Renegades' and now this...you sure know how to pick'em, kid."

Before Alex could respond, his phone started ringing. Thinking it was Lynn, he quickly answered it only to hear Jason's voice on the other end.

"He's dead, Stratton. Burroughs is dead."

"Dead? Did you kill him?" Alex asked after I'm putting him on speaker.

"Nope, he blew his brains out right in front of me. The thought of going to jail was too much for him."

"Jail? I thought you were supposed to bring him in for questioning."

"I took a page out of your playbook and bluffed him. He called my bluff by taking himself out. Oh yeah, your recording from the café probably helped him with his decision."

"You really are a ruthless bastard, Jason. What's next?"

"We wait for Simon to slip up, and hope we can nail him before he decides to leave the U.S. for good. After that, maybe I'll look into the massacre that took place at Gabrielle Malcolm's house, and the eight dead cowboys in the Rovers. Who knows? It may all be the work of Simon Felix or some master assassin. Or, I might not turn up a damned thing. Either way, those are likely to be my last investigations. I need a change of scenery."

"I'm sure you'll find what you're looking for, Jason. Thanks for the heads up."

"Anytime, Stratton," he replied calmly before disconnecting the call.

"Well, I'll be damned. The kid's got balls. I'll give him that." Tango said in disbelief.

"Burroughs being dead...that's a good thing, right?" Richard asked while leaning on the hood of his black coupe. "I mean, with him outta way and an investigation into his corruption underway, the heat's off us, right?"

"It's never that easy Rick, and I have myself to blame for that. Their focus will shift for now, but we still have a problem. Our man on the inside says Simon is preparing to flee the country, and they're no closer to stopping him than we are. Unless some strange twist of fate takes place, he's gone."

"Couple that with the fact that your mistress came back, and the fun just keeps coming."

"She's not my mistress, Tango," Alex replied flatly.

"Wait…Tisha's back?" Nicholas asked. "With everything that's happened to her family she's either desperate or nuts."

"Unfortunately, Tisha has a hidden agenda. She found a Cayman Island account that Simon set up with her name on it. She thinks she can steal the money from it before he leaves the country."

"Yep," Ko began while shaking his head, "she's both desperate and nuts."

"Let it go," Alex growled after snatching the cover off his Aston Martin.

"I wouldn't get all attached to that thing just yet, kid. The heat is still on and you know somebody is going to be looking for it. Besides, it's been sold."

"You sold my car?" Alex asked while clutching his heart and stumbling. "To who?"

"Some rap guy, 'Loose Change' or 'Double Nickel', or something like that. Anyway, he has some so-called enemies and when he heard there was a bullet proof DBS for sale, he was all over it. Besides that, I sold it for four times what you paid, so that should offset some of your new vehicular purchases. As a matter of fact, I sold most of your cars. I know you're a little distraught, so we'll give you a few moments to say your last goodbyes."

Seconds later, Tango escorted the rest of the team out of the showroom.

Hours later, detectives and CSI investigators had entered and secured Agent Burroughs's house and its perimeter, while fending off the large crowd that had gathered just beyond the yellow tape. Investigators and technicians were busy photographing the library and Burroughs' body, while others interviewed the agents on-site. Castro and Blackhawk meanwhile were standing across the street near an unmarked Dodge Charger watching in silence as investigators filed in and out of the home removing boxes marked **'Evidence.'**

"This is gonna make one hell-of-a report, partner. Almost a million in cash, passports, cases files, weapons…it's gonna be next to impossible to keep a lid on this now. You do realize you're gonna have to answer all kinds of questions on this one, right?"
"I don't care anymore, Gabe."
"What the hell are you doing, Jason?" Castro snapped when Jason laid his badge on the roof of his car.
"C'mon Gabe, my career is over, and you know it. I just uncovered one of the biggest scandals in the bureau's history. You think anyone is gonna to wanna work with me after this? Even if they did, I can't see myself going on like this anymore. I've seen too much as it is."
"Why'd you let him kill himself? Why'd you let him think you were arresting him? You knew we were here to take him in for questioning. You tricked him into committing suicide then stood by and watched. Why, Jason?"
"Like I said, Gabe; justice. McNamara wasn't gonna do anything more than question Burroughs. Despite all the evidence, he was gonna walk along with the others. Do you really think they'd want something this big to leak out? Hell no, that's why McNamara kept dragging his feet. He didn't want to deal with this humiliation on his watch. If it hadn't been for Stratton, Burroughs would be

free, Simon would still be running dope, and I'd probably be dead."
"Jason, who the fuck is Stratton?"
"You know, after all this, I still don't know."

Later that evening, after hours of answering questions and filing length a report, Agent Blackhawk was finally able to relax, albeit in the most unusual place. With a Margarita in his hand, he sat with his feet up while watching the sunset from Alex's patio. The cool autumn air and the threat of rain did little to deter their private celebration. For the first time since they'd met, the two men seemed to connect on the same accord. Animosity, jealousy, and hatred were nowhere to be found. At this moment, they were just two men having a drink and some peace.

"What's next for you, Stratton?" Jason asked while filling his glass. "With Burroughs dead, his team under investigation, and nine senior guys on the hot seat, you're sure to be forgotten in no time."
"Jason my friend, we both know you're lying. They'll be combing through his files trying to piece together the puzzle what was his life. Despite the fact that he had nothing on me, they'll come looking. I think I'll be taking a long vacation away from Denver."
"I hear you. You know what burns my ass, Stratton?"
"Do tell."
"The fact that none of these guys are going to do any serious time. Their inquest is going to be followed by an 'offer' of immediate retirement in lieu of prosecution. Under normal circumstances, the bureau would be all over another agency for fraud on this level. But when it comes to one of their own, it'll be swept under the rug quickly and quietly."

"Such is life, Jason, but hey at least the bad guy is dead."

"He's not the only one and you know it, Stratton."

"So what is it you want, Jason?" Alex asked when he sat up and faced his drunken guest.

"I want justice, dammit. I wanna see these pricks paraded around in the media like the criminals they are. I wanna see them in chains right next to the jackals that they've locked up over the years. I wanna see them suffer like Lisa's husband and daughters are suffering right now."

"So how far are you willing to go to see this? Because, justice was served as far as I'm concerned. Burroughs died by his own hand and the rest of them are out of the bureau for good."

"It's not enough!" Agent Blackhawk declared before bolting up from his chair and walking to the fence. "The citizens have a right to know the type of corruption their tax dollars are supporting. I have enough information to go to the media and pull the curtain back on this whole charade. I'll expose the entire justice system if I have to!"

"I agree the citizens do have a right to know. There are times, however, when the truth is too much for them to handle. In this instance, maybe they don't need to know. Sometimes people need to believe that everything is okay and that their heroes are incorruptible. There are times when people need to be left in the dark, and this is one of those times. That is why, as noble as your crusade is, it's bound to fail. The FBI is going to dismiss you as a disgruntled former agent suffering from PTSD. None of the major media outlets will even entertain your story."

"Somebody will listen, dammit!"

"And suppose someone does," Alex began while filling his glass, "let me paint a picture for you. Suppose you do go out and raise some eyebrows with your story, and Lord knows, I can think of one or two media outlets that will eat it up. Let's say you happen to get people to asking questions, and it begins causing ripples in the water. One day, somebody somewhere is going to receive a message and attached to it will be a name, a brief description, and a dollar amount. Shortly thereafter, you're going to have an unfortunate accident and that will be the end of that. Take my advice and let this go before it's too late."

"You think they'd send someone to take me out?" Jason asked half-laughing.

"No. Somebody *is* going to take you out. Men and women in this line of work make quite a living eliminating ripples in the water."

"Is that what you do, Stratton; eliminate ripples?" Agent Blackhawk asked, still musing from Alex's ridiculous assertion.

The lengthy silence that followed made the hairs on the back of his neck stand up. Suddenly, Jason found himself staring nervously at his host who was calmly looking out at the Denver skyline.

"All you need to know about me is that I believe in your cause, and as such, I won't pull the trigger. However, my peers might not share my sense of nobility."

Icy chills began racing up and down Jason's spine. The calm, emotionless demeanor of Alex's delivery had him paralyzed. Alex had won his trust and even saved his life, yet now, Agent Blackhawk was petrified. Here they were several stories above Denver with no witnesses anywhere. Jason had no idea what manner of treachery Alex was capable of. *Was he poisoning the drinks? Had Alex purposely gotten him drunk to make it easier to take him out? Had he been marked for death already, and Alex was toying with him like he'd been doing all along?* Jason nearly

507

fell over his chair while stumbling towards the patio door.

"Relax, Jason. I didn't let you into my home to kill you, but I do need you to listen to me carefully. You won. The bad guy is dead, and Lisa is resting peacefully now. You wanna help her and her family? Fine, I'll have my CPA set up a couple of trust accounts in the kids' names to pay college educations. I'll even start her husband off with a lump sum to get him back on his feet. How does a quarter-mill sound? Whatever, the money doesn't matter. The point is you don't need to throw your life away chasing ghosts on a quest for revenge. I've been down that road and it leads nowhere. To protect your sanity, you have to get off it at some point."

"You'd do all that for people you don't even know? Why?"

"Jason, when you make a career out of taking lives, it's nice to be able to save a few once in a while."

"In that case, make it a half-million for her husband and a quarter for each of the kids. I'll get you their names. Oh yeah, don't forget about the Tyler kids."

"Done. Anything else?" Alex asked before taking a healthy drink from his glass.

"Actually, there is. Sometime in the near future, I'm gonna need a job. Do you know anyone that can help me?"

"I'll make some calls. Now go home and get some rest. You look like shit."

"Thanks, asshole," Jason groaned while following Alex to the front door.

When they opened it, Lynn and Chet were stepping off the elevator with a brass cart filled with shopping bags.

"Drive safely, Jason," Alex said while shaking his head at the cart and smiling. "Did you leave anything at the mall, babe?"

"Just your money," she replied with a wink. "Who's this honey?"

"This is Jason, a future employee of my company. He stopped by to go over some recent acquisitions and the elimination of some of our most annoying competition."

"I'm pleased to meet you, Jason. I'm Lynn Turner."

"I'm pleased to meet you as well, Lynn. I'll talk to you later, Alex."

"All work and no play can make you a dull boy, Alexis," she said with a smile while caressing his cheek. "Hurry into the bedroom. I have a few things I want to model for you."

The story of Agent Burroughs' suicide didn't make the Saturday evening news, but it was the lead story on all the local stations the next morning. According to the reports, he committed suicide due to 'Post Traumatic Stress Disorder.' Though McNamara didn't hold a press conference, his office released a statement expressing its "sorrow over the loss of such a fine agent and offered condolences to his family." There was no mention of the investigation into his alleged corruption, nor did it mention the nine senior agents who'd been detained as a result of 'Operation Clean House.' Agent Blackhawk seethed with anger while sitting in his new apartment watching the lies unfold. Years of hard work was circling the drain right before his eyes. Just as he anticipated, everything that happened was being carefully manipulated so that it could be easily dismissed. The world would never know the true Burroughs or the operation that led to his death. Thanks to the powers that be, the media was going to portray him as a hero, a veteran crime fighter who was overcome by the stress of his workload. The public would never know that he was really a criminal who was no better than the ones he arrested. Maybe Alex was right. Maybe the people are better off not knowing.

Meanwhile at Simon's Boulder mansion, his eyes were glued to the television. With a smile etched on his face, Simon flipped back and forth between the stations listening for the confirmation. His eyes raced from left-to-right while reading the headlines scrolling across the bottom of the screen. His wish had been granted. His greedy oppressor was finally dead. The fact that Burroughs had killed himself was the icing on the cake. Years of extortion and payoffs had come to an abrupt end, but at a substantial cost to Simon's organization. With Gabriel dead and his killer unknown, Simon still thought it best to flee the U.S. and remain away indefinitely. As he strolled through his home, he regretted having to leave the one of the greatest symbols of his power, wealth, and pride. Every piece of décor from the floor to the ceiling was a reminder to others of his status and his heritage. To his peers, he was an icon; proof that a man could come to America with nothing and turn it into something. His henchmen worshipped him like a god, a symbol of the greatness to which they aspired. Now in a matter of hours, it would all be over.

Early Monday morning after quickly devouring his breakfast, Simon left Tisha at the table and rushed into the parlor. The time on his diamond encrusted Rolex read 9:59AM which meant he had one minute before he could begin verifying his wire transfers. After locking the door, Simon logged into his computer and waited patiently for his money to arrive.

With Simon out of sight, Tisha bolted to the master bedroom, locked the door, and grabbed her tablet. Like her husband, she logged into the account and waited, impatiently for the screen to load. To her surprise, the balance had increased by an additional two-million dollars since the last time she'd logged in. Just as she was about the logoff, the screen reset, and when she looked at it, the balance had increased by fifteen-million dollars. Tisha's heart pounded furiously while watching the balance increase with each passing minute. By 10:13AM, the balance was just under fifty-million dollars. Tears of joy came to her eyes when she flopped back on the bed kicking and screaming. Little did she know that a similar celebration was taking place downstairs. After verifying the amount again, Tisha hopped out of bed and began dancing around like she didn't have a care in the world.

The beatings, the infidelity, and the murders of her family no longer mattered because she was free and she was rich. Her happy dance routine quickly turned into a strip tease when she began touching her body repeatedly, before shaking her ass and dropping it like it was hot. She opened the bedroom doors and danced out into the hallway leading a couple of sentries and a maid to think she'd gone mad. Moments later, her celebration was interrupted by a series of horrific cries and the sounds of glass shattering and furniture breaking. Several sentries rushed into the parlor and found Simon on his knees. He'd ripped his clothes and the entire room to shreds.

"Wa da fuck, mon?" shouted one sentry after surveying the damage.

"Bumboclot," Simon sobbed with tears streaming from his eyes. "Di teif a teif mi tings! A fuckery dat!"

Tisha's heart dropped when she heard his revelation. She nearly fell over the second floor rail from dizziness, before one of the maids caught her. Struggling to breathe, Tisha staggered back into the master suite and flopped onto the bed. Her hands were shaking so erratically that she could barely enter her username and password. When she saw zeros flashing on the screen, she dropped the tablet onto the bed, raced into the bathroom, and proceeded to puke her guts out. Like her dreams, the contents of her stomach were circling the drain before her eyes.

Back in Denver, Alex was all smiles. After several minutes of account jumping, he finally confirmed that all $49, 896, 543.45 had reached his account in Zurich. With Lynn still asleep, Alex slipped into his console room, sat down, and stared calmly into his gun case. A war was on the horizon and it was just a matter of time before the first shots were fired.

"What's up Ko?" he asked after picking up his phone.
"Our spotter just informed me that Simon's compound is going ape-shit. He's running around, destroying his house, and screaming that he's been robbed."
"I know."
"What? How do you know?"
"I know because I just robbed him."
"You did what?" Ko gasped after nearly dropping the phone.
"Tell your spotter that now's a good time to get out of the compound. The shit's about to hit the fan, and I don't want any more innocents caught in the crossfire."
"Crossfire? What the hell are you planning to do, Alex?"

"It's already done, Ko. Since I returned from Japan, I've been on a mission to destroy Simon. I've been looking for and manipulating ways to completely separate him from his support system. It started with his trophy wife, Tisha. Her greed was only matched by her thirst for attention and passion. Seducing her was just the beginning. She needed an outlet, and I gave it to her. In return, she gave me all the insight I needed into Simon's organization, more-so than when I was undercover. Next, I attacked his distribution network; me in New York and you in Asia. Then there was Gabriel, the real head of the organization. Learning his habits was much more difficult because he stayed in the shadows. Simon's arrogance and constant brushes with the law, kept him out in the open. Finally, there was Burroughs, his protection. He's been behind the scenes for years facilitating transactions, providing security, eliminating witnesses, and even selling out his own men. It's unfortunate for Jason that Burroughs brought him into the fold, because it nearly got him killed. Jason's nobility and sense of duty however, were Burroughs' downfall. Now he and Gabriel are dead. Simon's organization is in complete disarray. One wife has turned against him, and the other is trying to rob him, but I have all his money. It's just a matter of time before he steps out into the open and when he does, I'll be waiting."

"I don't know what to say, Alex."

"Don't say anything. Just be ready."

"Ready for what?"

"War."

Later that evening after hours of driving aimlessly around Denver, Tisha walked into Alex's lobby and summoned the penthouse elevator. Within moments, she was pounding on his front door. Meanwhile inside the master suite, Alex was partaking in an erotic stress reliever. As Lynn lay face down and naked, he was straddling her thighs with his throbbing manhood nestled along the crack of her soft, round ass. His strong, firm hands kneaded and caressed her shoulders and back causing soft purrs to escape her puckered lips. The sensation of him teasing her asshole while placing soft kisses on her back and shoulders was making Lynn dizzy and Alex knew it. He felt goose-bumps rising on her skin when he began placing soft kisses on her spine. With her body under his hypnotic spell, Alex began a slow descent down her spine while caressing and massaging her ass and thighs.

"Alex," she moaned when the tip of his tongue glided gently over the crack of her ass, "is someone at the door?"
"I don't hear anything," he replied while gently parting her legs and pulling her ass towards him.
"Baby, someone is at the door."
"Alright, I'll get rid of whoever it is. Just don't move."
"Okay, sexy," Lynn replied before looking over her shoulder and wiggling her ass for his delight.

After slipping on a pair of shorts and closing the bedroom, Alex reached under the couch cushion and pulled out a nickel plated 40cal. He quickly ejected and inspected the magazine, before reloading it as he walked towards the door.

"Who is it?"
"Open the door, Alex," replied the tearful voice on the other side.
"It's gone, Alex," Tisha cried when her head fell onto his chest.
"What's gone, Tisha? What are you talking about?" he asked while hiding the gun behind his back.

"My money is gone, Alex. I watched it disappear this morning. The balance ballooned to almost fifty million, and in seconds, it was zero! Everything I worked, bled, and suffered for is gone."

Damn. "Tisha, that money was never yours. Yes, Simon may have used and tortured you to get it, but it was never yours."

"How can you say that, Alex? That money was my ticket out. That mutha-fucka killed my whole family! He let three animals rape me after he found out about us! That money was mine got-dammit! Now, it's gone, and that bastard is going back home."

"Like hell he is!" Alex growled angrily.

"They're leaving tonight. They've been running around since this morning packing up everything in sight. He had two million in cash stashed in the house. I wish I had known. I would have taken that shit and never returned."

"Fuck!" Alex exclaimed when he turned around and walked back into the house. "That mutha-fucka is not getting away from me again."

"What do you mean he's not getting away again? Where are you going? Alex, what am I gonna do? I have no money, no family, and no husband. I have nowhere to go."

"Never mind that, Tisha. Were you followed here?"

"What do you mean? I don't know. What are you doing?" she asked while approaching the darkened console room where he was standing. "Baby, didn't you hear me? I have nowhere to go."

"You can't stay here," he replied abruptly when he stepped out of the room with a black satchel over his shoulder.

"What? Alex, you can't just throw me out on the street."

"I'm not. Take this."

"What's this?" she when after he thrust the satchel into her arms.

"Its two hundred fifty thousand dollars; enough for you to disappear. Leave Denver, go somewhere and get settled until things quiet down around here."

"I just lost fifty-million, Alex! What the fuck am I gonna to do with this pocket change?"

"Contact me when you get where you're going, and I'll get you the rest. For now, you need to get as far away from me and Denver as you possibly can."

"I can't believe you're doing this to me again," she cried in disbelief as Alex ushered her to the door. "You're throwing me out into the streets like a whore. Did I ever mean anything to you?"

"Tisha, I'm trying to save your life. I know you don't understand, but you have to trust me."

"Alex?"

"Fuck," he exclaimed before Tisha looked over his shoulder and saw Lynn.

"Oh I get it, you're done with me. It's like they say, you don't pay a whore to stay. You pay her to leave. Fuck you, nigga. You ain't shit!"

"Alex," Lynn began after forgetting she was only wrapped in a bed sheet, "who is this?"

"I ain't nobody girl, just like you when this nigga is done with you. I was only worth a quarter-mill. I hope you're worth more."

"This is not happening," Alex mumbled while watching Tisha storm out of the front door.

"Alex, who-the-fuck was she?!!!!"

"Lynn, I know you're pissed off, and you have every right to be. I won't lie and say there's a valid explanation for this. I only ask that you trust me for now."

Without turning around, Alex followed Tisha out of the door, and caught up to her just as the elevator arrived. With tears in her eyes and betrayal in her heart, Lynn ran into the bedroom and grabbed her suitcase from the closet. With tears in her eyes and heart-wrenching sobs, she began stuffing everything she could grab into it. Meanwhile, Alex's phone was buzzing and rattling on the nightstand. She ignored it as long as she could before curiosity and anger got the best of her.

"Hello!"
"Lynn, this is Ko, Alex's brother-in-law. Where is he?"
"He ran out of the door behind some bitch and I'm about to..."
"Lynn, listen carefully. Alex is in danger and trust me when I say, it's not what you think. I know you're angry, but right now, I need you to help me save his life. I need you to go to the room just off the kitchen that he keeps locked. Do you know the one I'm talking about?"
"Yes," Lynn replied while bolting through the house. "I'm here and it's open."
"Okay, now listen carefully. To your right, there's a panel on the wall and next to it is a keypad. Enter the following numbers: 5698745975."

After entering the code, Lynn stepped back and in seconds, was bathed with blue light. Her eyes widened with shock when she saw the arsenal that had been hidden right under her nose.

"Ko, what that hell is going on?"
"I'll explain later. Right now, I need you to grab his gun-belt and get it to him as quickly as you can. I'm almost there."

In the lobby, after a fever pitched elevator ride that included some pushing and shoving, Alex and a rage-filled Tisha stormed towards the exit. Their exchange was so intense that neither of them noticed Simon and his entourage coming through the entrance. After shoving Alex and breaking free of his grip, Tisha bolted for the door but was frozen in her tracks. There standing between her and freedom was her husband and eight armed men.

"Yu hab s'ting belong ta me. Come now, chile. Yu daddy waiting."
"I know you didn't," he replied before calmly watching her make the journey across the lobby.
"Alex? Yu look familiar ta me, rude boy."
"I should," Alex groaned while sizing up the men who had surrounded him.
"Cash money? Ah, yu shouldn't hab," Simon grinned after snatching the satchel off Tisha's arm and peering inside. "Come now, gal. We hab tings to talk bout. Da rest of yu meet us at da house."
"I'll see you soon, Simon."
"Naa, yu won't," he replied while grinning at Alex.

With Tisha in tow, Simon exited the lobby leaving his henchmen to deal with Alex.

"Mr. Stratton?"
"Yes, Chet?"
"What should I do?" asked the doorman who was crouching behind the desk.
"Stay down, Chet. This will be over in less than-a-minute."
"Yu ere da bumboclot mon, Chet. Stay," laughed the burly dread closest to Alex while pulling an Uzi from his shoulder holster.

As the tension in the air quickly reached its peak, Alex heard an ominous 'ding' from the corridor behind him. His calm turned to panic when he turned his head and saw Lynn coming towards him with something draped over her shoulder.

"Any last words pretty boy?"
"Yeah…see you in hell," Alex smiled after glancing over his tormentor's shoulder.

When Ko burst through the door, he tossed Alex a chrome plated Desert Eagle and when he caught it, Alex fired five shots into his tormentor's chest, and two more into the face of the man at his side. While baseball-sliding across the lobby's marble floor, Ko cut down three more bewildered sentries as they scrambled for cover. When Alex disappeared down the corridor, Chet sprang up from behind the counter and opened fire with a pump action.12 gauge quickly dispatching two more intruders. With his clip empty, and two fleeing men rapidly approaching, Alex prepared himself to disarm and kill them before they could get close to him or Lynn. That plan however, was interrupted when their chests and heads explode from multiple, ear piercing gunshots. When they hit the floor, he glanced to his right and saw Lynn ejecting a clip from the smoking .40 cal in her hand.

"Wait here," Alex demanded after grabbing the other .40 cal from the holster draped across her right shoulder. "Ko…Chet…are we clear?" he asked while stepping slowly into the hallway and kicking guns from the fallen men's reaches.
"We're clear. The fuckers got the drop on me before I could call you, boss," Chet said after ejecting an empty shell from the shotgun's chamber.
"It's cool. You okay, bro?" Alex asked when he looked at Ko.

"I'm good man, but we're short on time. Our spotter says Simon is packed and ready to bolt. He's chartered a plane at a private airfield not far from his house. They have non-stop flight clearance to Kingston."

"He's not gonna make that flight. Chet, get a cleanup crew down here stat."

"I'm on it, boss."

"Alex, who are you, and what the hell is going on?" Lynn demanded when she peered around the corner at the saw the carnage.

"I could ask you the same thing," he replied while gently removing the gun from her hand.

A short while later Lynn sat on the edge of the bed watching helplessly as Alex paced back and forth inside his closet. She struggled for words and air as he stood there dressing in silence. After he put his shoulder holster on over his black t-shirt and emerged from the closet, Lynn knew he'd reached the point of no return. Alex had a lifetime of pain and rage in his eyes. She quickly ran to him and buried her face in his chest while clutching his body tightly to hers.

"Don't go," she begged. "I don't care what's going on, just don't go."

"Thank you for saving my life babe. I'm sorry I wasn't up front with you about what I really am," he said while holding her close and gazing at the suitcase he'd missed a while ago. "I can't blame you if you wanna leave. There's so much about me that you need to know, deserve to know, and if you're here when I get back, I promise I'll tell you everything. But right now, I have to stop a killer from escaping or neither of us will ever be safe."

"Do what you need to do, babe," she whispered while gazing deeply into his eyes.

"I love you, Lynn."

"I know you do. Be safe, Alex."

With trembling lips and a broken heart, she kissed him one last time before releasing him. After a brief moment of silence and several bouts of hesitation, Alex was gone. With her mind and heart racing, Lynn sat back down on the bed and tried to process everything she'd just witnessed. The man she'd fallen in love with, the man with whom she'd shared her inner most thoughts and desires, was nothing more than a chameleon; a liar. He'd convinced her that he was one thing but turned out to be another. The man she'd fallen in love with wasn't the same man who'd moments ago shot up the lobby of his own building. Then reality set in. Moments ago, she'd helped him murder two men in that same lobby. Now, he was gone and only God knew if he would return. Everything about Alex from his lifestyle to his lies, his money to his mayhem, his sex to his secrets, made him "Mr. Wrong." But even now, "Mr. Wrong" felt *so* right.

Chapter 21

"You did everything you could for her, Alex."

"Huh?"

"Tisha, Alex you did everything you could for her. You didn't fail her or her family. They failed themselves. You gave her every possible way out, but she went back anyway. She laid up with that bastard for the past few weeks plotting one last score. In the end, she never cared about you, herself, or her family. She cared about the money. The death of her family aside, Tisha made a choice. Now, you have to make one."

"A choice?" asked while staring out the speeding Bentley's window.

"Yes, Alex, you have a choice to make. You're about to storm in Simon's home and go up against an entire army. We have your back one hundred percent, but you know she's gonna be there. If you have to, can you put her down?"

"I don't know, Ko."

"Well, you'd better figure it out fast bro, because if I have to take her out to save your life or mine, I will lay that bitch down; end of story. You understand me?"

A short while later, the coupe screeched to a halt behind the hangar. When Ko and Alex entered the lower level, they were greeted by their comrades who were already dressed in their fatigues. Though no words were exchanged, it was clear by their nods that they were all there for the same thing.

"I didn't expect any of you to be here, and I sure as hell would understand if you bailed. This demon is my own creation, and I've allowed it to grow out of control. Tonight, that demon goes back to hell."

"Then stop talking, and let's get it done," Warren said while loading a clip into his nine.

"Are you sure you're up to this, Warren? No one will think less of you if aren't."

"I'm tired of running, Alex. This is who we are and this is what we do. You stood by me, and now I'm standing by you."

"Thank you, man. Mike?" Alex asked after quickly appraising the burly brother with the Cuban clinched between his teeth.

"This is my last hoorah so I'm going out with a bang," he replied.

"What about you, Tango? I thought you were done with field work."

"I'm with the big man, kid. Like all the greats, I suit up for the exhibitions only. This really is my last dance, though. Despite my personal opinions, I ain't letting you walk into the belly of the beast again without being by your side."

"Rick? Nick?" Alex asked while watching them assist the other with his gear.

"We lost a sister-in-law and a nephew in this, Alex. If that fucker walks, he's gone forever. There's no way we're riding the sideline while you tackle this bastard alone. Right, Nick?"

"Damned straight, so let's shut this dude down once and for all. Little Alex and Simone deserve it."

"Even though you're outgunned, outmanned, and outnumbered, you're all still willing to follow Alex straight to hell. I admire that," boomed a voice from the darkened doorway.

Icy chills raced up and down their spines when an eerily familiar figure stepped out of the shadows. The air in the room crackled with electricity when the man none of them expected to ever see again stepped into the center of the room.

"What the fuck are you doing here, Gary?"

"Nice to see you too, Tango. I was at Doc's when Ko's call came in. Let's face it. I'm probably the last guy any of you wants to see right now and I accept that. But you're crazy if you think you can roll up in that compound and take on an army seven deep. You're either delusional or suicidal."

"So what's your point, Gary?" Richard asked while checking the sights on his HK-5.

"My point is that despite my past transgressions, you need all the help you can get. And besides, you know I'm pretty good with a gun."

"You're kidding, right?" Tango quipped sarcastically.

"There's no way in hell were riding with you, especially after the shit you pulled," Ko barked while standing toe-to-toe with their hulking intruder.

"Look, I know I fucked up bad. Between the liquor, the drugs, and the loss of my family I was in a bad head space. My world was a mess. But that's behind me, now. Believe it or not, I'm clean, and I can appreciate that ass whuppin' Alex gave me. It put something on my mind, put things into perspective for me. If I had died on that floor, what would my life have stood for? Nothing, that's what. I need this, I need to redeem myself. I can't take back all the things I did, but I can try to make amends for them. Give me a chance. Whadya say, Mike? Let me ride with you one more time, for old time sake."

"It's not my call, big man."

"Forget it, Gary," Nick barked while standing next to Ko. "There's no way in hell your crazy ass is riding with us!"

"What about you, Black Mamba? All bad blood aside, this may be the last time I get to right my wrongs. I fucked up bad; I know I did. I don't deserve any of your trust, but please don't shut me out of this one. I need this one."

"Stand down, fellas," Alex said when he stepped between his friends and Gary. "The man makes a very compelling argument. We're up against some pretty stiff odds and every gun we can get helps. But mark my words. The shit you did is neither forgiven nor forgotten, therefore I make you one promise. If you misstep, even a little, I will honor your request, and I will kill you where you stand. Do I make myself clear?"

"I won't let you down, Alex."

"Suit up then 'cause wheels spin in ten," Alex commanded after turning around and walking back to his locker.

"Stay close to me big fella," Tango growled while staring into Gary's eyes.

Moments later, the entire team filed out of the locker room and into a garage attached to the rear of the hangar. Inside was a fleet of heavily armored and armed SUV's, pick-up trucks, and vans. Each was totally blacked out including black matte finished paint.

"Okay, Champ," Tango began after slinging a Chevy Tac Sniper Rifle over his shoulder, "whacha got in mind? I was thinking a pair of Knight X-V's would do the trick."

"I was hoping you'd say that," Alex replied with a smile when he opened the driver's door and climbed in.

Seconds later, the two behemoth SUV's rumbled out of the garage and sped towards the interstate.

Meanwhile at Simon's compound, the maids, cooks, and housekeepers had long since gone leaving his henchmen to load bags into a caravan of white Range Rovers.

Simon's brother and several other family members had flown in from Chicago to assist with the move as well as provide security until the compound was cleared. Despite the furious commotion throughout the house, Simon sat silently in his parlor with Tisha and ten bodyguards.

The once happy husband and wife looked like they'd been through hell. Blood trickled from Simon's nose and mouth as he sat behind his oak desk with his white suit covered in blood, wine, grass, and mud. His face and neck were covered in scratches from Tisha's jagged, mangled nails. Her nose was bleeding and her right eye was almost closed. Her hair was a disheveled mixture of grass, wine, and mud. Her once sexy lips were swollen and filled with cuts and abrasions. Under the long mascara streaks, her chocolate-colored cheeks were swollen with black and blue bruises. The beauty that she'd flaunted only a few days ago was all but gone, and yet Tisha smiling.

"I an give yu every'ting yu wan," Simon began while gasping for air. "Mi take yu in when yu nothing but a broke down whore in da street and make yu mi ooman. All yu had ta do was obey!"
"Fuck you, bitch!" Tisha shouted. "You treated me like shit, beat me like a dog, let your friends rape me, and anything else you could think of to make my life a living hell. Then as if that wasn't enough, you murdered my family, you fucking no-good bastard! They never did anything to you except make you rich."
"Yu blood clot family was nuttin' before me, an dey nuttin witout! Now dey in hell fire!"

The last thing anyone expected was for Tisha to attack him again. None of the guards were prepared for the speed with which she crossed the desk and knocked

Simon to the floor. In his wildest dreams, Simon never imagined that Tisha could be this malicious. Every scratch, punch, slap, and kick hurt more than the last. No matter how hard he tried, he couldn't shield himself from her vicious onslaught. The rage in her eyes and the shriek of her voice were things Simon and his crew had never seen or heard before. Years of pinned up anguish fueled every crushing blow. Four of Simon's body guards struggled to pry her hands off his throat and it took two more to hold her legs as Tisha fought with all her might to get back to him.

"You...stupid...American...bitch!" he huffed while gasping for air.
"Let me go! Let me go! Let me go!" Tisha cried while struggling to free herself from her their grips.
"Look pon, yu stupid bitch!" Simon barked again after struggling to his feet. "I an kill yu fambly, destroy yu life, and yu still crawled back. Yu nuttin witout me, and yu had nowhere else to go. Naa even yu boyfriend wan yu!"
"You think I came back because I had nowhere to go? I was free, bitch! I came back because I found out about the account you set up with my name on it. I was only here long enough to figure out how to get my money."
"Yu knew bout dat?"
"Yes bitch, I did. I've known for two years. Now I guess now neither of us gets the money."
"Wrong! Me hab da money yu boyfriend give yu. Yu should hab run away, yu pussyclot whore! I an dead him and yu! Yu ass rot in dis ere gates, yu ere?"

Outside at the end of Aspiration Lane, Ko, Alex, and Tango were observing the compound through high-powered, infra-red binoculars. Behind them, the massive

Knights sat idling with their V12 engines vibrating the ground beneath their feet.

"Satellite imaging shows ten Rovers down there, and the spotter says that there are between 40 and 60 armed men patrolling the grounds. Everyone else was dismissed, except Tisha that is."

"It sounds like Simon's core group is providing cover while he heads for the island," Alex said after lowering his binoculars. "The rest will probably remain here in the U.S. to oversee his operations until he returns."

"What's the plan, boss?" Ko asked after checking the time.

"We don't have time to be tactical therefore the plan is simple; going in blazing. Use the rocket launchers to take out the trucks in the front. That chopper in the back doesn't leave either."

"Delilah."

"Yes Tango," replied the voice in his headset.

"Did Doc shut down the 911 network?"

"Yes Tango."

"Then kill all power on the block."

Seconds later, the mighty Knights were speeding down the lane in the pitch black dark. The roar of the one thousand horsepower engines quickly attracted the attention of the sentries who'd gathered in front the mansion. With home's entrance rapidly approaching, Alex and Nicholas targeted the Rover fleet from their passenger seats, and in flash of flame and smoke, eight rockets blasted towards them. Within seconds, the front lawn erupted in a fiery shower of shrapnel and scorched limbs. The side-mounted chain guns made short work of the remaining sentries. The gigantic block-treads decimated the manicured lawn throwing mud and grass in all directions before crushing the custom fountain. After screeching to a halt just beyond the smoldering barrier, Alex, Richard, and Nicholas bailed out the first Knight followed by Ko, Warren, Big Mike, and Gary from the second. With their guns locked and loaded, the team followed, on foot, as Tango's SUV assaulted the manor house. His suppression fire destroyed the massive pillars at the entrance, followed by the floors in the foyer, and the dining room. After blasting out the back wall and firing several rockets down the hallway, he drove out onto the patio where the demolition continued. While Warren, Gary, and the twins cleared the ground floor with machine gun fire and small-impact explosives, Alex and Ko trailed Big Mike who'd stormed the stairwell with his .50 millimeter, belt-fed cannon. With the second floor hallway cleared, Alex and Ko positioned themselves on either side of the parlor door. After reaching for the handle, Alex suddenly gave them the signal to abort.

"Be ready," Simon commanded while crouching behind his desk with his AK-47 at aimed ahead.

Simon and his minions stood silently while watching the handle jiggle. Suddenly, the shadows beneath the door disappeared. Moments later as, three sentries crept slowly towards the parlor door, a massive explosion rocked the back of the house and shattered all the windows on both floors. Stunned and confused by the blast, one of the sentries snatched the doors open and released the grenades that had been affixed to the handles. In the confusion, a shadowy figure standing outside on the second floor balcony tossed two grenades through the parlor's rear. The ensuing explosions cast body parts and debris in all directions. With the room in total chaos, a cloaked figure entered the parlor and emptied his HK-5's magazine into whoever was moving.

When that clip was empty, he quickly ejected it and inserted another before scanning the room in search of survivors.

After emptying the second magazine, he dropped the gun to the floor, pulled two .40s from the small of his back and resumed scanning. In the corner, by what remained of his desk, he found Simon writhing in agony. During the explosions, a large wooden spike pierced his upper thigh.

"Did that hurt?" taunted the black-clad menace before stomping on the end of the spike and driving it through Simon's thigh bone.

"AAAAAAAAAAAAAAAHHHHH! Ooo-da-fuck are you? Wa yu wan, mon?" Simon cried while clutching his thigh.

"I told you I was coming for you," the reaper growled in a tinny, metallic voice before holstering one of his .40s and kneeling next to Simon.

"Don't kill mi! Please don't kill mi! Mi give yu any'ting yu want! Jus name it!"

"I came for your soul, Simon. That's all I want."

"Ooo-da-fuck are you?!!"

"You really don't remember me, do you?" the reaper asked while lowering his hood. "You should. After all you took everything from me before leaving me to die in that church."

"It's you! Naa can be!" Simon declared after Alex removed his black baklava and stainless-steel face mask.

"You have no idea how many nights I've dreamed of this moment; the day I'd finally be able to take everything from you, just like you did me. I took your friends, your wife, and your money. Now I'm going to take your life," Alex declared before cocking the gun and jamming it to Simon's temple.

"I can't let you do that, Alex," a woman's voice said before placing a gun barrel behind his ear.
"Dat's my shorty! Blast dat negga!"
"So, that's what this was about, huh Alex?"

Tisha's mind couldn't process what she'd seen fast enough. Mere seconds ago, she witnessed a man stalk and gun down a room full of her husband's bodyguards. Now, that same man who turned out to be her lover was here with a gun jammed to Simon's temple.

"Revenge? You fucked me and pretended to love me for revenge? Look me in the eyes and tell me you didn't love me! Look me in the eye and tell me that I never meant anything to you. Did you ever really love me, Alex? Answer me mutha-fucka!
"Peel his cap and let's go, Tisha! I got a plane waiting. Wi can escape to Jamaica."
"Really?" Alex quipped with a smile. "How's Garcelle gonna feel about that?"
"Yes, Simon, what will she say?" Tisha asked after narrowing her eyes and taking aim on him.
"Wait, Tisha! Wait!" Simon cried when he saw the tears pouring from her eyes.
"I'm sorry I lied to you," Alex said after standing up and looking down at her. "Yes, it was all about revenge, nothing more."

The honesty and conviction in his eyes hurt more than all of Simon's abuse combined. Tisha's savior, the man in whom she put all her faith, the man with whom she shared her most intimate passions, and the man who in her eyes redeemed all other men, was nothing more than an trickster, just like her husband. Every voice in her head was screaming, *Kill this nigga!* Her whole body

531

trembled as she stood there with the barrel of her gun pointed between his beautiful, light-brown eyes.

"Squeeze the trigger, don't pull it," he whispered while gently lowering the barrel of the gun to the center of his armor-plated chest.

"Kill him, Tisha! Blast dat blood clot!" Simon demanded while scooting across the floor.

"Don't listen to him, Tisha. Listen to your heart. I admit that I used you. I should have killed Simon a long time ago. If I had, your family might still be alive. Maybe mine would too. But none of that's relevant now, because no matter what you do in the next few seconds, you'll be free."

"Free? Alex, I have nothing left. I'm broke, my family is dead, and now even you don't want me. What else do I have left to live for?"

"Move six inches to the left and I'll put one through her cerebellum," Ko whispered into Alex's headset.

"Only the past is written," Alex replied while moving slowly to his right. "The future is still yours."

"What the fuck are you doing? You ruined my shot!" Ko growled while crouching by the door in the darkened hallway.

"Naa let him in your head, gal! He played wit yu mind, gal! He naa love yu, like mi. Dead his ass and wi a go."

"Your home is in hell, Simon, and one way or another, you will get there," Alex declared while looking at the tears in Tisha's swollen eyes.

"What am I going to do, Alex?"

"Whatever you think is right," he replied before stepping up to the barrel of the gun.

"Kill him you, stupid bitch!"

Without warning, Tisha turned to her left and unloaded three shots into Simon's chest. After a brief pause, she unloaded two more into his forehead. As Simon lay there with his cold dead eyes staring into space, Tisha fell to her knees and began weeping at his side.

"Let's go, Tisha," Alex said softly with his hand extended.

Without saying a word, she simply slapped it away and continued kneeling by her dead husband. Alex stood silently and watched while Tisha stared blankly into the flames and smoke beyond the balcony door. Though he hated to admit, Alex knew his friends were right about her. She'd sold her soul long ago, and now she was lost forever. Ko kept his gun trained on Tisha until Alex cleared the room. While descending the stairs, they heard one final gunshot. When Alex turned around, Ko grabbed his arm and simply shook his head before watching a tear fall from his brother's eye.

"Is everyone clear?" Ko asked when the team filed into what was left of the foyer.
"Gary and I got separated outside by the pool. The chopper boys took out the Knight with a heat seeker, but they didn't get off the ground either. I tried to find him but there are bodies and body parts scattered everywhere. I couldn't ID him in that mess if I wanted to."
"Damn," Big Mike exclaimed while shaking his head and staring angrily at the ground in front of him. "I prayed this day would never come; the day I'd have to tell Gabby that he's never coming home."
"Sorry, Big Man," Tango offered after walking up to Big Mike and patting his shoulder. "As much of a bastard as he was, he deserved better than this."
"Thanks, Tango. But like he said, he needed this. Today was his redemption."

Hours later, the team was assembled in Doc's library watching the news and enduring another grueling debriefing. As they stood silently around the room, Doc was talking on the phone and scribbling notes on his note pad.

"Thank you very much. I'll be in touch. That was Agent Blackhawk, and he says it'll be weeks, months even, before they sort that mess out. Apparently when the Knight exploded, it left a crater that scorched everything around it. He did inform the coroner that we're looking for a 'specific' person. They have all the info on him. They did recover the bodies from the parlor, though. Preliminary reports state that Tisha died of a self-inflicted gunshot wound through the chin. The official story is that she happened upon a drug-related massacre and committed suicide with a gun she found on the floor."

Suddenly, the sound of breaking wood erupted from the doorway. When they turned around, Alex was removing his fist from a hole in the bookcase behind him.

"You might wanna get that checked, Alex," Doc said after shaking his head.
"So, that's it huh, nice and neat no questions asked?"
"You know how it works, Tango," Doc replied while leaning back in his chair.
"Take me home, Ko," Alex whispered after grabbing a black overcoat off the rack.

The ride to the penthouse seemed especially long with the miles passing slowly and the sun rising over the mountains. Though he wanted to say something to his wounded brother, Ko remained silent instead. He resolved that Alex had been through enough, and this silence was necessary. A short while later as the Bentley idled at the curbside, Ko watched Alex disappear into the fully-renovated lobby. The lonely elevator ride to the penthouse brought Alex little solace. His mind replayed his and Tisha's last conversation leading up to him standing at the business-end of her trembling gun. Their final words rang in his ears like a bell. In a hail of bullets, she cheated him of his chance to send Simon to hell. *She needed that release more than me,* Alex concluded while counting those haunting shots. *You'd still be alive if I'd just admitted that I loved you.*

Moments later, he entered his penthouse and dropped the trench coat on the floor. As he stood at the bar twisting the top off a bottle of Vodka, the lights above his head abruptly lit up the room. Instinctively, he drew a gun from the small of his back, and aimed at the doorway. In his wildest dreams, Alex never imagined that Lynn would still be there when he returned. He lowered his gun and stood motionless as she circled him. He wondered what must be going through her mind as she ran her fingers across his armor plates and stared at his uniform. She seemed almost mesmerized when she saw the collection of knives strapped to his thighs and the guns holstered to his shoulders and back.

"I want you to tell me everything, and please don't sugarcoat it. Don't protect me, Alex. Tell me what I need to know...what I deserve to know. Give me the option to decide for myself. Can you do that for me please?"
"Ok," he replied with tears in his eyes.

In the aftermath of the massacres in Denver and Boulder, life slowly was slowly getting back to normal. Though the investigations were still "ongoing", many of the official conclusions had already been made and any remaining details were being swept under the rug. Both Simon and Gabriel were murdered by remaining factions of the Mexican cartels whom they'd double crossed. Agent Burroughs was laid to rest while letters of resignation were accepted from eleven of his nineteen co-conspirators. Agents Blackhawk and Castro were given temporary assignments. *'The Agency's* members faded back into the shadows while Doc cleaned up the messes left in their wake.

Six months later in Tokyo, a secret meeting was convened at the urging of a mysterious host. Contingents from the Kingston Cartel and the Yakuza were in attendance. Seated at opposite ends of a mahogany conference table were Garcelle Malcolm and Ryugi Hiamatsu, the new head of Nakamura's Yakuza Clan. Tensions mounted as the two groups squared off, each quietly sizing up the other up in anticipation of aggression. For Ryugi, being in the presence of a woman, who was considered "his equal," was an insult to both himself and his entourage. Garcelle's relaxed, but callous demeanor did nothing to quell the foul mood in the air.

"What the fuck is taking so long?" Ryugi scoffed while glaring angrily at the phone on the table between them.

Suddenly, the phone began ringing and threatened to send the volatile tensions in the room through the roof.

"Hello!"
"Glad you could make it Ryugi, though judging by your demeanor you're not happy to be here," replied the electronically altered voice on the other end of the phone.
"And who are you, sir?"

"Who I am Ms. Malcolm is not as important as what I am."

"Then what are you?" she demanded sarcastically.

"I'm a facilitator. I'm the man who can who can deliver to you that which you want the most. Ms. Malcolm, the man who killed your late husband and cousin, and stole millions of dollars from your organization is the same man who killed Boss Peter Nakamura. The question now becomes how badly do you want him dead?"

"What do you want in return?" Garcelle snapped viciously.

"Two things; the first is the sum of $2.5 million from each of you wired to the account in the folders in front of you. Upon verification of the funds, I will give you the identity of the killer. The second is a chance to kill him once you fail."

"You seem confident we'll fail," Ryugi said after looking in the folder.

"I know you will."

"Then why don't you kill him yourself? Clearly this man has wronged you in some way."

"You're right Ryugi, he has. But I don't work for free. So what will it be?"

To be continued…

Tune in for the next installment: *Operation Cover-up Presents: Crimson Storm*

www.ingramcontent.com/pod-product-compliance
Lightning Source LLC
Chambersburg PA
CBHW020456020726
47493CB00001B/59